INDEFENSIBLE

JAMES WOOLF

BLOODHOUND
— BOOKS —

Copyright © 2024 James Woolf

The right of James Woolf to be identified as the Author of the Work
has been asserted by him in accordance with the Copyright, Designs
and Patents Act 1988.

First published in 2024 by Bloodhound Books.

Apart from any use permitted under UK copyright law, this
publication may only be reproduced, stored, or transmitted, in any
form, or by any means, with prior permission in writing of the
publisher or, in the case of reprographic production, in accordance
with the terms of licences issued by the Copyright Licensing Agency.
All characters in this publication are fictitious and any resemblance to
real persons, living or dead, is purely coincidental.

www.bloodhoundbooks.com

Print ISBN: 978-1-916978-14-0

For Philippa

Chapter One

The three girls were still lolling over the front desk. Would they ever leave?

"We don't do lifts home," Barbara said, for what must have been the fourth time.

"But the police are meant to help," the one with a topknot complained.

"Here, I expect you need this." The new officer placed a coffee cup next to the mug with the pens.

Barbara turned round. "Thanks. They get plastered, then expect me to sort the taxi. Honestly, it's been non-stop nonsense tonight."

He shook his head, smiling, and headed back to another room.

And now, a dishevelled woman was making her way purposefully towards the desk. Perhaps in her early fifties, her straggly hair fell like a fox's tail alongside her neck on one side, but on the other it was scooped into a bunch, leaving her face and left ear exposed. The unmistakable impression was that she hadn't been looking after herself.

"Ooh, what's that stink?" The tallest teenager looked outraged.

She had a point. Barbara had every sympathy for anyone living on the street, of course she did. But there were showers in the homeless hostels, weren't there?

"What can I do for you?" Barbara said to the new arrival.

"Last Sunday – I think it was Sunday," the woman's tongue pressed into the side of her cheek as she attempted to concentrate, "I was on the bridge."

"How we gonna get home?" the girl with glasses called out from in front of a missing person poster.

"Go on," Barbara said to the woman. She wasn't likely to say anything significant. She'd probably got into an argument, been groped, or kicked by a passer-by. There would be no details. These cases were dead in the water before you so much as breathed on them.

"It don't matter what day it was," the woman continued. "Probably Sunday. But I saw something. And I've been meaning to tell. Cos it wasn't…" She stopped, one eye squinting slightly. "It wasn't right."

"And what did you see?" Barbara had the book open, ready to make a note.

"I was on the bridge when I saw it."

"Which bridge would this have been? And what time of day?"

"Tower bridge. It was late. And I saw a man with a carrier bag. I was just kipping down, you know how it is. But he looked suspicious."

The way she said this last word, it would have rhymed with fishes. And her eyes briefly went from one side to the other, a recognition perhaps that she hadn't quite nailed the pronunciation.

"What happened next?"

"Well, he takes this head out the bag and throws it off the bridge."

"What do you mean, *he takes this head out of the bag?*"

"I mean, a head. It had long hair… this golden colour…" – she said this wistfully, as if it would be nice to have golden hair. "And he threw it." She mimed throwing the head with two hands, like a footballer taking a throw-in.

"He threw a head off the bridge?" Barbara couldn't wait to tell her new colleague about this one.

"It's not funny, young lady," the woman said.

"All right, shall we start from the beginning? With your name and date of birth?"

"Jackie Levine. Twenty-fourth November, nineteen forty-eight."

They went through the whole story again with Barbara taking notes as best she could, pressing the woman for clarity. She didn't get a good look at the man, she said. But on the other hand, she would definitely recognise him again. "Without a shadow of doubt." She said this twice, sounding pleased with the phrase.

"And is there any reason why you didn't report this earlier?" Barbara asked.

"I just didn't get round to it."

"Well, thank you for getting round to it now."

The comment was meant to be ironic, but the woman smiled, exposing two missing teeth at the front. "No problem, love. Now I don't suppose you have one of them nice cells free this evening?"

"You know I can't help with that."

The woman nodded, picked up her belongings and made her way out. Barbara reviewed the notes and at the bottom of the page added, *Recommendation: No Further Action.*

At some point the teenage girls must have gone too. Barbara realised she had Jackie Levine to thank for that. The girls probably left because of the smell.

Chapter Two

D aniel rushed to the phone in the hall, wondering who would be ringing so early.

"Daniel? – it's Paul." Paul was a leading barrister in his chambers. "I didn't wake you, did I?"

"No, it's fine." Daniel shivered in the T-shirt he'd slept in.

"Listen, mate, I'm in Bristol," Paul said, and Daniel remembered the high-profile trial there. "I'm having *une affaire de coeur*. And she writes these delightful letters."

"You're having an affair? Is that what you just said?"

"Yes, she used to teach my daughter horse-riding. That's how it started. Anyway, these letters – she seals them in pink envelopes and sends them to chambers."

"Okay…" Daniel wasn't sure what was more shocking. The fact that Paul was having an affair, or how blasé he was about it.

"Look, I know you're a stickler for doing the right thing," Paul continued, as if he'd read Daniel's mind. "I just need a small favour."

"Hold on a moment, Paul." He put the phone down

and went over to the coat stand, returning with his Burberry leather sheepskin on. He still had bare legs, but this would do for now. "What do you want exactly?"

"I want you to check my pigeonhole. For her letters."

Daniel couldn't help thinking about Paul's wife, Judy. He'd met her several times. "And what if there are some?"

"Just let me know. At least this way I'll be prepared if she hasn't sent anything."

"But what difference does it make? You'll know when you return to London. They're not going to go anywhere, are they?"

"I'm in love with her, Daniel! And I can't just call her, because she's married too."

"It gets better by the minute. Aren't you a bit old for this sort of thing?"

"Look, I know what you're thinking. But Judy's not interested in me these days. She's away at her genealogy conferences two weekends in four. What normal man wouldn't look elsewhere?"

"I'm sorry but your wife having an interest in genealogy doesn't give you licence to have an affair."

"Perhaps not," Paul admitted. "Are you going to help me or not?"

Daniel paused. His legs were cold, and it felt like he was being set a moral test. "Look, I don't feel good about this."

"You won't even check my pigeonhole?"

"No, because that would be colluding with you. I know Judy. It wouldn't be right."

"Oh, for crying out loud."

"I'm sorry."

"It's okay. I asked the wrong person. How's your love life by the way? Still shaking hands with Dr Winky?"

Daniel took a deep breath. There was something he wouldn't mind discussing, but certainly not with Paul. "I'm not looking for anyone new right now."

"Anyone new? You're not thinking of a *rapprochement* with Sally? That boat's sailed, mate. It left the harbour and was last seen halfway down the Menai Strait."

Minutes later, eating Cheerios in his small kitchen, Daniel cursed his old friend. In fairness, Paul had been supportive when Daniel and Sally first separated. He'd taken Daniel's side when he learned Sally had said it was never a proper marriage; that the real marriage was between Daniel and his job. More recently, Daniel's conversations with Sally had become warmer. The last time he went over to see the kids, she was almost flirty. Two days ago, his daughter Imogen had mentioned her mother had an awful cold. Daniel now thought about heading over to see Sally. He could take some Beechams Powders. He'd do it before work. He just wanted to say hello, and, who knows, perhaps Sally would invite him in for a quick coffee. He'd show Paul whether that boat had sailed or not – whether a *'rapprochement'* was pie in the sky. It wasn't as if attempting to get back together with your own wife was controversial, not compared to what Paul was up to.

On the short drive to Barnsbury, he prepared a few lines in his head. *As soon as you're feeling better, we must have lunch together. On me, of course. It's high time we had a natter. Let's pop something in the diary for next weekend.* The suggested date wasn't even phrased as a question – he was quite pleased with that.

Daniel parked his Golf GTI at the top of the street and looked at himself in the mirror. His blue eyes set slightly too far apart, his broad forehead hardly lined. He smoothed back the short brown hair which was still thick and showing no hint of grey. Not bad for a guy now officially in middle age. It would just be a quick conversation with Sally, for goodness' sake. He needn't feel so nervous about it.

He approached the house and wondered what he'd be interrupting – the children scrabbling around to find things for school, or chaotically finishing homework. But he wouldn't be distracted. Today he had his own agenda. Today he had fresh hope.

He pressed the bell and waited. A minute passed so he rang again and eventually the door was opened. By a man with short sandy hair and a moustache. Ridiculously, he was wearing Sally's silk dressing gown. Daniel felt himself shrinking on the doorstep. It was as if he'd had the air sucked out of him by a powerful extractor fan.

"Oh," the man said. "Hello."

Why else would he be wearing Sally's dressing gown if he hadn't been naked in her room in the first place? Daniel might even have interrupted something intimate. Attempting to sound normal, he said, "I'm Daniel."

"Hello, Daniel. I'm Stuart."

Although he seemed amiable enough, Daniel found himself disliking this man intensely.

"Sally's in bed, dozing," Stuart continued, in his Geordie accent.

Daniel nodded, hoping at least this was true. "I brought her this." He produced the Beechams Powders he'd just picked up in the newsagent. He'd also bought a box of Maltesers, but he wasn't about to hand that over too.

Annoyingly, Stuart let out a high-pitched cackle. "We've a tonne of that stuff." He took the medicine anyway, carelessly dropping it on the hall table behind him, the table that Daniel and Sally chose from a craft shop in Stoke Newington.

"And are they for Sally too?" Stuart had spotted the Maltesers Daniel was holding in his other hand.

"Yes, if she'd like them."

"I'm certain she'd like them!"

Daniel handed over the box. "And the children, how are they?" He tried to maintain the pretence of being unconcerned by Stuart's existence.

"Oh, they stopped over at her sister's place. We had planned to collect them, but they started watching a film and... you know how it is."

Yes, he knew exactly how it was. Sally would have been only too happy to offload the kids on her sister for the night, especially if she was feeling under par. She would have viewed it as an opportunity to spend some more time alone with this new man, this moustached interloper with a penchant for silk dressing gowns.

"Oh, you've..." Daniel couldn't quite believe it. Stuart had punctured the Maltesers box and was stuffing a handful into his mouth.

"Sorry, mate, I've not had breakfast yet. I'll make sure she gets some, honestly," he added, with a conspiratorial wink.

"I should be going," Daniel said. And then, pointedly, "I've got a busy day."

"Yes, I'll bet. Sal tells me you're a barrister."

Daniel grimaced at this shortening of her name. "Tell her I said hello," he called, as he retreated towards the car.

"I will. Nice to meet you, mate. And thanks for the Maltesers."

Daniel considered responding but thought better of it.

Inside the safety of his car, he checked himself in the mirror again, looking particularly for signs of inner collapse. Despite having just met the man Sally had chosen to replace him with, he looked relatively okay. But why hadn't he heard about Stuart before? One thing was certain. Stuart would be the one sharing her bed tonight, while Daniel would be alone in his flat – the former council property in an Islington tower block which he'd bought, almost on a whim, when they separated.

He felt like retreating to the flat now, climbing under the duvet, hoping it would all go away. But he was due in court in less than two hours. One way or another, he would have to get through the day.

Chapter Three

Trying to put the upsetting encounter with Stuart out of his head, particularly the image of him scoffing Maltesers in Sally's dressing gown, Daniel turned the key in the ignition. Traffic was light and it took only eighteen minutes to drive to his chambers, where he went into the clerks' room. All four clerks were already at their desks. The younger three were presumably busying themselves with late briefs that had come in from solicitors. Bill, a stocky dark-haired man in his early forties, was eating an apple and reading his newspaper. Daniel first went to the pigeonholes. He couldn't resist looking in Paul Summerfield's, where he found four pink envelopes, each neatly addressed in tiny handwriting. Daniel picked one up. It felt like it contained a card. He caught a light scent of perfume and felt another wave of sadness sluicing through him. Having no moral scruples clearly hadn't held Paul back. Much as Daniel disapproved of his behaviour, it also needled him that Paul was managing to enjoy the love of two women in his life, whereas he had no one. Moving on to his own pigeonhole, Daniel removed some papers, untied the pink ribbon, and scanned them quickly. An Actual Bodily Harm case. The kind of thing he used to get soon after he qualified. Things were going from bad to worse.

He tapped Bill on the back. "Do you have a minute? In private?"

Bill looked up at Daniel, raising his eyebrows. He stood and made his way out of the room, dropping his apple core into a bin en route. As ever he was wearing an immaculate dark-blue suit. In reception, Bill patted Daniel affectionately on the shoulder and placed his copy of the *Daily Mail* on a table in front of them.

"Good weekend, Daniel?"

"Not too bad, thanks. But I'd appreciate a chat."

Bill nodded. "Is there a problem?"

Daniel winced as he read the paper's headline:

SEVERED HEAD FOUND IN THAMES

"Nasty business," Bill said, noticing his reaction. "Apparently, it floated past a pleasure boat. Some poor woman's twenty-fifth birthday party."

They walked into the square where they went directly to the fountain. Two trees were inclined at a vicious angle over the small circle of water, their branches entangling in the middle, like fighters propping each other up as they traded punches.

The two men moved past the wooden bench and headed south towards Middle Temple Gardens and the river.

"Are you sure you're okay?" Bill asked.

"I'm fine, Bill. I wanted to ask whether you've heard

any more from that solicitor? The murder case you mentioned?"

"I'm afraid he wanted George in the end."

"Fuck!" Daniel didn't usually swear. "I thought he couldn't afford George."

Bill turned to look at him kindly. "I'm sorry. I did my best for you. Anyway, I see you've found that case for next week."

"But I'm a QC now. And I'd always been given to understand that meant getting the cream of the crop? The armed robberies, the kidnappings... Not Actual Bodily Harm cases!"

"And you've got the sentencing coming up, and those bail hearings too."

"Frankly, I'd have been disappointed with this stuff ten years ago."

"I know what you're saying, Daniel. But things often slow down when you take silk. The solicitors aren't used to the new fees you command. But they'll get over that."

"The problem is, this isn't sustainable. My flat was a cash purchase. It practically cleared me out."

"Oh yes, the flat." Bill lowered his tone. "Listen, you're one of the youngest QCs in the country. We have big things in mind for you."

"When you turn forty, you suddenly don't feel so young anymore." Daniel looked at his watch. "I know you're doing your best. And I'm not complaining."

There was a slight pause before they both added the word: "Much!"

"Anyway," Bill said. "Shouldn't you be getting off to St Albans? You don't want to keep Justice Pickering waiting."

Chapter Four

I t was about eight o'clock and James was sitting alone in a pub on Upper Street. He ran a hand through his bleached blond hair and took a mouthful of Belgian beer, allowing the bitter liquid to fizz on his tongue. The proliferation of European lagers in London was something he'd only noticed recently, although he approved. The pub was a way of killing time as he was early for his arrangement. But he was happy to watch the world go by, which it was doing very satisfactorily. Especially now that a striking young man had come into the pub and made eye contact with him. He was tanned with black hair; there was something appealing about him. The barwoman clearly knew the young man and said, "Pint of your usual?"

"Yes, thank you." He paid for his drink and sat at the table next to the one James was occupying.

"Not too shabby, the weather, for December," James said.

The young man smiled, although not in a way that suggested he understood.

"I mean it's warm, for this time of year."

"It is always cold for me. But I am from Athens. And I miss my home very much."

James nodded sympathetically. "I'm guessing you're a student."

"And you are guessing right."

"I'm James."

"I'm Nikos." They shook hands.

"And what are you studying, Nikos?"

"So, I'm studying business studies."

James nodded as if to confirm the wisdom of his choice.

"I am in England for just a year. But soon I will go back home for my holidays."

They sat for a moment, sipping their drinks, looking around the bar in that way people do to fill a gap in the conversation.

"Funnily enough, I'll be doing some travelling in Europe soon," James said. "All business and very little pleasure though, unfortunately."

Nikos looked him up and down for a moment. "And what is your business?"

"Property. I own a company. I started it eight years ago. And it was recently valued at over ten million pounds."

Nikos was clearly impressed. "So, you are very successful…"

"I suppose. But success brings its own set of problems."

Nikos nodded. He was probably wondering what sort of problems they might be.

"Like finding time to go to the gym," James continued. "I turn fifty next year, so I like to keep up my regime."

"You don't look anywhere near fifty."

"You're very kind. And it's been nice to chat. Unfortunately, I have to be off. I'm meeting somebody. He's a bit of an arsehole actually, and I'd far rather be spending the evening with you." He glanced up at the barwoman as he said this. She was clearly listening and looked away guiltily. James raised his eyes to the ceiling.

"I'm going too," Nikos said.

"Already?"

"Yes, I will find another pub. This one is not so interesting to me."

The two men finished their drinks and made their way towards the exit. Catching sight of himself in a mirror by the door, James wondered if the young man had any idea that his hair was dyed.

Chapter Five

"Has the hair changed colour, do you think?" DCI Ruth Hobart was studying the photographs of the head, arranged in a block on her otherwise pristine desk.

"No," Derek said.

"The water wouldn't have…?"

"Not significantly." He removed a tissue from a box on his lap and blew his nose loudly. "This is all I needed. My wife gave it to me."

Ruth nodded. Derek was the Crime Scene Manager, and they had worked together many times.

"It's not in very good shape," she said.

"Well, there's been fairly heavy loss of flesh tissue, of course. Decomposition."

"Yes, but I meant that it's actually quite damaged."

"The trauma injury is significant," he agreed, then sniffed loudly.

"Would that be from before death do you think?"

"I doubt it. It's been swimming around for some time by the looks of things. So, it'll have been battered about by river craft, maybe bridge construction work. Not to mention river predators having a good nibble. Fish."

"Understood."

"So, our forensic strategy. Apart from the head, we have no information, do we? No witnesses, no intelligence, nothing from any other sources. And it's not as if the post-mortem is going to tell us much."

"What might it tell us?"

Derek removed the packaging from a throat sweet and popped it into his mouth. "I suppose we might learn what type of tool was used to sever the head. If it has been severed."

"Could it have been separated from the torso whilst in the river?" Ruth asked.

"Possibly. I'll get a take on that from the pathologist. As well as the length of submersion."

"Of course. It will be rather difficult to make an identification if we've no idea how long it's been–"

She was interrupted by Derek having a coughing fit.

"You should be at home, shouldn't you?" she said.

"I wish I could, but I don't have the luxury. Where were we?"

"The post-mortem. Not yours, I hope."

"Oh yes." He acknowledged the joke with a smile. "I'm going to require the services of a forensic scientist. We're assuming the victim is male, but we can't be certain about anything. We can try to identify him by dental records of course, but he could be a foreign national. That might be evident from the type of work on his teeth."

"And if we can't make an identification from dental records, what then?"

"Well, I wouldn't bother with an artist's impression in the media. And facial reconstruction's rather hit and miss

18

too. It just gives an indication of what the victim looked like, at best."

Ruth sighed loudly. "Do you ever get the feeling you've been set up? I honestly think this case has been dumped on me deliberately."

"The classic poisoned chalice." Derek chuckled, rising from his seat.

"Exactly. Anyway, can we arrange the post-mortem as soon as possible? I'll want to be there, and I want our photographer present too."

Chapter Six

Justice Pickering was well into his summing up, setting everything out in a conversational tone. The jury had warmed to him, which was more than could be said for Daniel's client, Harry Dougan, whose bad-tempered display in the witness box had won him no friends at all. There seemed little doubt that Dougan would be found guilty on all four charges of rape, and two of indecency with a child.

"Mr O'Neil's cross-examination of Mr Simmons is, I'm sure, still fresh in your minds. You'll recall that Mr Simmons was a fellow teacher of Mr Dougan, who was also there on the school trip to the Brecon Beacons in the Easter holiday of 1986. Mr Simmons was working in the library when he saw Mr Dougan carrying a sleeping child through to the next room. He had a clear enough view of the boy's face to identify him as Hugo Higham. When Mr Simmons mentioned the incident to Mr Dougan the next day, Mr Dougan was evasive, talking about the perils of the boys helping themselves to cider from the kitchen. It is the Crown's case, of course, that

Hugo Higham had been given a sufficient dose of a prescription sleeping pill to have induced this deeply unconscious state."

Daniel didn't at any point look at the jury to see how they were receiving the judge's summary of the trial. It made a barrister appear unsure of their case if they kept turning to check the jury's reaction. He knew the evidence of his client's method of accumulating Zolpidem had been damning. It was just one example of the thorough preparation Dougan undertook in advance of accompanying the boys on their school trips.

"Members of the jury, I am as ever indebted to you for your close attention throughout this trial. I appreciate that the evidence you have heard has at times been both graphic and distressing. We are almost through with the summing up, and as I have come to a convenient stopping point, we will break slightly early. It seems like an excellent opportunity for you to enjoy your lunch in the sun."

Stepping out into the street, Daniel winced as he recalled his encounter with Stuart earlier that day. What an idiot he must have looked, desperately producing his small carton of Beechams Powders. He was about to head towards his usual café when he was stopped by one of the reporters covering the trial. She had piled her brown hair on top of her head, in a slightly haphazard way, and Daniel imagined her waking late and getting ready for court in a dizzying rush.

"Can I ask you a quick question?" she said, fumbling in her bag – a bold harlequin design with blacks, reds and creams.

"You do realise that I'm the defence barrister in the case?"

"Of course. That silly wig isn't as effective a disguise

as you think." She withdrew a packet of Silk Cut from the bag. "I know!" she said, as he watched her closely. "It helps me concentrate when I'm writing."

Daniel hadn't realised he made his distaste for smoking so obvious. "The point is, I'm not allowed to make any comments to the media."

"You can answer one teensy-weensy question, surely?" She lit the cigarette, inhaled, then blew smoke over her left shoulder.

"No, because my profession has ethics. Unlike others I can think of."

She laughed. "I wanted to know how you feel when you're acting for clients like this. And whether you worry you'll get 'typecast' representing paedophiles and rapists. It's really a question about you, rather than the case."

He looked at her large brown eyes for a moment longer than he normally would. "Yes, but you could twist what I say so it sounds like it's about the case. I'm sorry, I'm not having a good day and need some lunch."

"And you're sure you can't answer my question?"

"Yes! I really don't know how I can make this any clearer for you."

He felt bad straight away, but he was bored with this conversation. "How can you represent a person like that?" was something he got asked most weeks. He was forever explaining to friends, acquaintances – to everyone he met, it seemed – how barristers had no choice but to accept each case offered. It didn't matter what the defendant was charged with. "It's called the cab-rank rule," he would say, "and it's crucial to our justice system."

The café was quiet. He ordered a toasted cheese and tomato sandwich and a cup of extra strong tea and sat in a corner facing the entrance. With any luck, the judge would finish summing up this afternoon and the jury would be sent out. He didn't imagine their deliberations taking long and he couldn't see any reasonable grounds for an appeal, although no doubt he'd have to consider this carefully.

He spotted a paper on another table and crossed the café to collect it. *The Sun*. He was once told by an older advocate that he should regularly read the red tops in order to understand how "The man on the Clapham omnibus" thinks. Unsurprisingly, it also led with the head found floating in the Thames.

Daniel's food and drink was plonked without ceremony in front of him and he murmured his thanks. Part of the café's appeal was the short shrift they gave to customers; it was reminiscent of *Fawlty Towers*, a programme he fondly recalled watching with Sally when they first went out together. He took a bite of the toastie and scanned the news story. The paper was speculating that the head had belonged to a man in his mid to late forties. And that most likely it had been in the river for three months. A police spokesperson told a press conference that, as yet, the deceased person had not been identified, although a murder inquiry had been launched.

He looked up from his table as the same reporter from earlier entered the café. He shouldn't have spoken to her like that, however persistent she was. Even if she hadn't taken umbrage, it was ungracious of him – unprofessional too. He watched her, in profile, ordering from the counter. She was quite tall, perhaps five feet ten, not much shorter than him, and attractive in her own messed-up kind of style. But almost certainly single. Journalism was hardly a career for a family woman. She was in her late twenties he would have guessed, probably been working on the local paper since university.

Her bag was slung over her shoulder as she made her way towards the door. In one hand she carried her sandwich wrapped in greaseproof paper, in the other some crisps and her purse. She saw him and opened her eyes wide. "It's all right, I won't disturb your lunch."

"It's fine. I'm sorry I was rude earlier."

She stopped walking and looked at him for a couple of seconds. "I was impressed actually. I didn't know barristers were so ethical."

"We do our best."

"And my question was pretty silly."

Behind her, a man with a dog sitting at his feet was following their conversation.

Speaking more quietly, Daniel said, "Look, why don't you eat your sandwich here?"

"You mean with you?"

"Yes." He shrugged, intimating that the idea wasn't so outrageous. "I'd like that. And it's fine as long as we don't talk about the case."

"All right then." She pulled back the plastic chair opposite him and flopped into it. "God, I'm tired. How I'm even going to get through the start of the week I've no idea."

"I know the feeling," Daniel said, pleased to have company.

She was busying herself putting her purse into her bag. She wedged it in alongside a bulky novel and a bottle of eye drops.

"Do you always look inside women's handbags?" She didn't sound cross, but the question was challenging, nonetheless.

"I'm not in a great place today, I apologise."

"Yes, you said earlier." She was unwrapping her sandwich. "I expect you've been up late preparing your next case."

"No, it isn't that. I dropped in on my ex-wife today, and the door was opened by her new partner."

"Oh dear." She giggled.

"I hadn't even realised he existed. The worst thing was that he was wearing her dressing gown. He looked absolutely ridiculous."

"I can imagine." She nodded, suddenly serious, sympathetic even. She prised her sandwich open to peek inside – chicken and salad by the look of things – then took a bite.

"Until this morning, I hadn't completely given up on the idea…" He stopped, shook his head. "I don't know why I'm even telling you this."

"Well, you're talking to the queen of fucked-up relationships."

He liked the fact that she was so open, so easily herself in his company. It meant that he too could relax a little.

"Talking of fucked-up relationships, that's a pretty scary example." She nodded at the newspaper lying facing up.

"They don't even know who the guy is yet."

"But it's bound to be a relationship thing, isn't it?"

"You don't mean the wife, surely?" Daniel said.

"Could be. Who knows?"

She opened her bag of crisps, peeling back the plastic so that the contents were exposed in a neat pile in the middle. "There's something medieval about it: the severed head, don't you think? Help yourself by the way."

"Thanks."

He was struck by the delicious thought that he could just ask this woman out, this total stranger. He could ask her right now, to see a film with him this week if he wanted to. There was nothing holding him back, not now Sally had so clearly moved on.

"I'm Daniel," he said.

"Michaela."

The name itself sent a short pulse of electricity down his spine. It was the name of a confident and challenging woman.

They shook hands over the table, smiling as they did so.

"I knew that already, of course," she said. "I've mentioned you. In my reports."

"Oh, yes. Which paper is it again?"

"*The Herts Advertiser*. Do you even read these things?"

"My clerk keeps an eye out."

"That's a very nice way of saying, 'Of course I don't read that crap'."

Daniel laughed out loud. Quite suddenly the dark clouds of the day had parted to allow a hint of sunlight through.

"So, will we get a verdict today?"

"I thought we weren't speaking about the trial, you bad person. But no. They haven't even been sent out yet. I'm guessing tomorrow morning, or Wednesday at the latest."

"Okay, thanks."

"I'm going to ask you a question now," Daniel said. "Does it bother you, hearing about the worst side of life, day in day out? Having to write about it for the papers. It must dampen your view of humanity?"

She frowned as she thought about it. "Well, occasionally something might get to me. But then I'll just meet up with a friend or eat a bar of chocolate. I find either works equally well."

"And do you have a busy week this week?"

"No, not particularly. Why do you ask?"

"We could do something. See a film, have a meal."

"Blimey, you don't hang about."

"I'm not like that, honestly. I haven't asked a woman out in…" – he calculated – "…fifteen years. That was Sally, my ex-wife. And she said no. It was the day James Callaghan lost a motion of confidence, forcing an election. You remember these things."

"I expect you understood how he felt."

He laughed again. "You're actually very funny. Anyway, I can't have been too disheartened. The third time I asked she agreed to come out with me."

"I like a man with determination."

They ate their sandwiches for a moment. Did he now have to follow up on his original question, or even ask it again?

"A film sounds good," she said. "I'd like that."

"Great. How about tomorrow night?"

"Tomorrow night it is."

They looked at the table, somewhat embarrassed by the exchange that had just taken place. She took out her packet of cigarettes, then remembering what happened earlier, put them away again. At one point they caught each other's eyes and she laughed – a loud honking laugh that caught him by surprise. Then they talked about mundane things – an *Inspector Morse* rerun they'd both seen on TV at the weekend, the book she was reading, she even told him about her university dissertation – before they made their way back to the court.

Chapter Seven

Daniel stood in a neat woollen blazer in front of Books Etc, feeling the soft cuffs of wind on his face as it swirled down Charing Cross Road. Behind him, the entire shop window was a blaze of orange and green, a promotional splash for the latest book by Irvine Welsh. *Trainspotting* was one of the few novels that Daniel had read recently, and he was tempted to buy this new one, just for something to look at while he was waiting. Michaela was eleven minutes late and counting.

It had rained heavily earlier, but that at least had cleared up. When Daniel called Michaela last night to make the arrangement, she asked whether they might see a play instead of a film. The writer was a friend of a friend and she'd promised to see the show which had been doing the rounds and was now at the Arts Theatre.

He'd been feeling nervous all day. Culture and rituals around relationships had shifted, even in the time since he was last a player in the game. He would very much take his lead from Michaela.

He didn't want to read too much into her lateness,

but the play did start in less than fifteen minutes. He wondered if she were limiting the time they'd have to talk before they bundled themselves into the theatre. That might indicate that she was already having second thoughts about the whole enterprise.

It was odd seeing her earlier today. They held each other's gaze for a few moments, and he nodded twice – a wave across the crowded courtroom would not have been appropriate. He expected a smile in return, but her look was almost blank, so he turned away. The case finished well before lunchtime which removed any possibility of a repeat trip to the café. Not that he'd have suggested it, for fear of jeopardising their evening arrangement. After the verdict, she left the court promptly while he stayed behind chatting to the prosecuting counsel.

"I'm so sorry, Daniel."

She had appeared in front of him and gave him a shy peck on the cheek. Dressed in high-waisted turquoise check trousers offset by bold red shoes and a simple cotton jacket, the effect was transporting.

"That's fine," he said, feeling an instant wave of relief. "I knew you'd be on your way."

"The misery line lived up to its name tonight. It would have been quicker walking."

"I thought you lived in Tufnell Park."

"Not literally quicker. This is my favourite bookshop by the way."

He looked behind him.

"They've got a manager who can find any book, no matter how obscure. I always arrange to meet friends here."

"Well, the theatre will be busy, I guess."

"Yes, Stephen's done well with this play."

As far as Daniel was concerned, *Anorak of Fire – The Life and Times of Gus Gascoigne* – was an odd choice for a first date. It was about a real trainspotter, very different from any character in the Irvine Welsh novel. He was not sure what he was meant to feel towards the obsessively cheerful protagonist, equipped with his flask of tea made by his mother, his lunchbox and logbook. For some reason Michaela and the rest of the audience were finding it hilarious.

Coming into contact with many vulnerable individuals as he did, Daniel doubted the morality of the piece. Was it right for a comfortable cluster of young professionals to be chuckling at Gus' bizarre obsessions before heading over to Leicester Square for some Häagen-Dazs?

But then he worried that his discomfort said more about him. He'd led a pretty strange existence since Sally walked away from their marriage. Like Gus he was something of an outsider – arriving at his appointed designations, his head full of peculiar information, his attire setting him apart from the general public. He even took a thermos of tea to court sometimes, although he wouldn't be doing that again.

Daniel attempted to push these thoughts aside and enjoy the piece as pure entertainment. It was too easy to overthink art. The play wasn't trying to say anything profound about the human condition or about trainspotters for that matter. He didn't imagine the writer had even met a trainspotter when researching the play.

"So, what did you make of it?" Michaela said as they took their seats in Gaby's after the show.

"As a piece of entertainment? Or something more meaningful?"

She looked up from the plastic menu she was holding. "Shall we start with entertainment value? We can move on to the heavy stuff later."

"Well, it was *okay*," he said, stressing both syllables. "Though I'm probably not their target audience."

"Do you go to the theatre much?"

He shook his head. "Hardly ever, if that doesn't sound too awful."

"You probably get enough drama in your day-to-day life."

"Visiting my ex-wife, you mean?"

"I meant in court."

"You find that dramatic? You should get out more."

"That's where you come into it," she laughed, "assuming this isn't a one-off." He took this remark as a very good sign.

"I hope it isn't a one-off," he said.

The waiter arrived and they ordered two glasses of the house red which were delivered almost immediately. Daniel suggested having a mezze for two. Being seen to be able to share was never a bad thing in these situations.

"What made you become a barrister anyway?" Michaela asked, taking a large gulp of wine.

"Did you ever come across a TV drama called *Crown Court*?"

She shook her head.

"It was on at lunchtimes. I'd always watch it if I was off school. It was a different case every three days. I remember not wanting to recover so I could stay at home and watch the verdict the next day. And the jury were actual members of the public. So there was this thrilling moment when the foreman stood up as no one knew what he was about to say."

"Unlike this morning," Michaela said.

"Unlike this morning, indeed. And like many others, it gave me the taste for what a future career as an advocate might be like. Are you sure you never saw it?"

"Positive."

"You must have been watching something that inspired you to be a news reporter instead."

The food arrived and she ordered another glass of wine.

"Look at this," Daniel said, excited by the spread on the table.

"You never get a bad meal in Gaby's. It's an institution. Been around since the sixties."

He loaded some falafels and hummus onto his plate. "I can't wait."

"Their salt beef is amazing too."

"Maybe we should order some?"

She looked at him with sudden seriousness and he wondered what was coming next. "Do you mind if we don't talk for a while? I need to eat before I pass out."

Five minutes later, they'd made a healthy impression on the dishes.

"Is it safe to speak?" he asked.

"If you must."

"So, your turn, why did you become a reporter?"

"Well… I could do English at school. So they told me I should be an advertising copywriter. Or a news reporter. As I had no idea what a copywriter was, I went for reporting."

"My God, that's an even worse story than mine."

"I know. It shows how compliant I am."

"You could have asked."

"Asked what?"

"About copywriting," he said. "This was your careers adviser, presumably?"

"Yes, but you feel stupid. If they recommend something and you don't know what the hell they're talking about."

"I guess."

"I might be about to start working on the Gloucester case by the way. You know, the Fred and Rose West thing?"

"Oh," Daniel said, adjusting to the leap in conversation. "Yes, I understand she's complaining about having a trial by media."

"What do you expect if your husband's accused of all these murders?"

"Fair point."

She exhaled loudly and rubbed her hands down her face. "I'm not looking forward to it. I hate this kind of thing, not that I let on yesterday. That nonsense I told you about friends and chocolate? It actually scares the crap out of me."

"Well, it's a nasty case." He was happy that she was opening up to him again. "So you didn't ask to work on it?"

"It's a new job actually. I'm joining the *Sunday Mirror* as a crime reporter, doing some legwork for the main reporter on the case."

"That's great. A big step up from working on a local."

She nodded. "They've been leading on this story."

"I've got to say, I wouldn't mind representing Fred in his trial."

"Have you done murders before?" she asked. "Let

me rephrase that. Have you represented murderers before?"

"A couple. But that trial would be a significant coup. I could do with a case like that right now."

They'd finished eating and she got her cigarette pack from her bag, the same bag she had yesterday.

"Oh fuck, I forgot." She put the box away again.

"Look, I never said anything about you smoking."

"You didn't have to. Sorry about swearing by the way. I do that a lot."

"It's fine. Really. One of the reasons I like you is because you're so different to me."

"Okay." She appeared satisfied by that explanation. "Are we going back to your place by the way?"

"You mean now?" He was amazed by the casual nature of the enquiry. He really had been out of the game a long time.

"Why not?"

"You might be a bit shocked by where I live. Or at the very least surprised."

"Surprise me," she said, lightly touching his arm.

Encouraged by the conversation they'd just had, he took her hand as they walked to the bus stop. She acknowledged the gesture by squeezing his fingers.

"It's only fifteen minutes," he said, wondering if she would stay the night. Perhaps she'd even come armed with a toothbrush. That afternoon he'd stocked up on condoms, just in case. "We'll pick up the No. 38. It's a historic bus."

"Yes, Harold Pinter wrote about it."

"How on earth do you know that?"

"I remember the oddest of facts."

"We may be more alike than I thought."

The bus came and she wanted to go up to the top

deck. They sat together, looking down on the activity below.

"I work pretty close to here," he said, as they went down Theobalds Road.

She nodded and nestled into his shoulder. He took the opportunity to put his arm around her.

"Tired?" he asked.

"Just nicely relaxed. That was good wine, wasn't it?"

"Well, it was… wine."

She laughed. "You're a snob."

He laughed too. Maybe now would be a good moment for their first kiss. He looked at her intently and was starting to move slowly closer when she stopped him with a fingertip on his chin.

"Daniel, we can do all that at your place. I'm really too old to be snogging on buses."

———————

She took back the snob comment as soon as they'd set foot inside the block.

"My God, Daniel – this is rather on the radical side, isn't it?"

They went up in the lift which was noisy and had Kentucky Fried Chicken boxes piled in one corner.

"The communal areas can be a bit…" The lift doors opened, and he didn't complete the sentence.

He got out the keys and they went into his flat.

"Fuck, look at this," Michaela said.

"Do you want a cup of coffee?"

"Sure. Are you actually…" – she turned towards him as he filled the kettle – "some sort of secret communist?"

"Not exactly."

"Can I have a quick tour while we're waiting for that to boil?"

"Okay. So, this is the reception room."

"Jesus, it's spacious."

"Probably because it's almost empty."

"It's very cool. I love the wooden floors."

"I pretty much ripped everything out and started again. And if you come out here…"

"That view. I've never been up a tower block before. Bollocks!"

"The balcony's my favourite part."

"Gives me the heebie-jeebies, just leaning over."

"You get used to it."

"No, I love it. I bet you're out here all the time enjoying a cheeky glass of wine."

"On a clear day you see right across the city. Let's go back inside."

The kettle, a retro model, was whistling. She nodded approvingly as he turned off the gas.

"So, this is my bedroom obviously."

"Nice… You play the guitar?"

"That's not a real guitar. I picked it up while I was travelling before university. And the second bedroom."

"Christ, it's tidy, Daniel. Do you spend every evening on your hands and knees with a dustpan and brush?"

"I don't actually."

"Not your style? I'm guessing you have cleaners. An army of them. Poor exploited fuckers."

"Are you drunk?"

"How dare you?"

"It's okay, I don't mind. Do you take sugar?"

"Two please."

They went back into the reception room and she sat on the black leather sofa. He placed their coffees on square mats on the coffee table and stood looking down at her.

"Aren't you going to sit down too?"

"Of course." He sat next to her and sipped his drink, leaning forward and cradling the mug between both hands.

"So how does it even work?" she asked. "You own this place, right? So, what happens if something goes wrong? In the block, I mean."

He was still feeling anxious and this might be why he got stuck delivering a long-winded explanation about Islington Council's decentralised services. How each neighbourhood had an office where local residents could see their social worker, or their housing benefit officer, or their estate manager, or get put on the waiting list for a council property. There were twenty-four neighbourhood offices, he said, or at least there used to be.

"Yes, but what happens when something goes wrong?" she repeated.

"So, if there's a problem that isn't my responsibility to sort out – say there's a cockroach infestation on the stairwell – I have to report that to environmental health at the neighbourhood office."

"A cockroach infestation on the stairwell?"

"It does happen, believe me. The point is, every one of those neighbourhood offices has these small teams of people. They all have environmental health officers. All twenty-four offices. It's a pretty daft idea, when you think about it. And a fantastic waste of money."

"Well, I think it's a very good idea."

"I went down to the office to pay this old lady's rent once. It was just incredible. The drama, the raw passion. I was only in there for twenty minutes and I saw an argument about blocked rubbish chutes, a lady reporting a suspected rotting corpse in the flat opposite and a young man threatening to beat up the lettings officer. It doesn't work. It's a disaster."

"Are you sure you're not using the problems of Islington's decentralised services to avoid going to bed with me?"

Daniel put a palm on his forehead and laughed. "I'm so sorry. You must think I'm a complete idiot the way I've been prattling on."

"It's okay," she said, resting her hand on the inside leg of his jeans.

Chapter Eight

Daniel glanced at himself in the mirror and smoothed his hair. Much as he would have loved to contact Michaela again, that was now impossible. They might have been in a wine bar at this very moment, had he not ruined everything on their first date. Instead, he was heading out into the night with no particular plan, except perhaps to deliver Max's present. All this to avoid spending another Saturday night entirely alone in his flat.

Whatever could Michaela have made of him crassly fumbling at her clothes as soon as they got into the bedroom? Embarrassingly, she had told him to slow down, that they had all the time in the world. And then there were his schoolboy-like attempts at foreplay and the fact that he climaxed seconds after he was inside her. But none of that was anywhere near as bad as the episode afterwards, which started so innocently as they lay naked together, looking up at the ceiling, Michaela's leg overlapping his, her right hand exploring the hairs on his chest.

"I told you I met my wife's new partner, didn't I?" he'd said.

"I think you mentioned it." She giggled.

"What a jerk, honestly. I can't believe it's him who gets to see my kids every day at breakfast and not me."

"How many children do you have?"

"Three. Two girls and a boy."

"Nice."

"It's just that I hardly see them. It's ridiculous how complicated it becomes making the simplest arrangements. I have a birthday present for my son, and we still haven't found a suitable time for me to hand it over. I can't tell you how frustrating it is – how angry I get."

As he locked the door of his flat, Daniel wondered why on earth he'd shared these details with Michaela. He noticed the chilliness of the corridor, somehow made worse by the smell of roasting pork coming from a neighbouring flat. He headed for the staircase.

Even that conversation with Michaela would have been bad enough, but whatever had possessed him to then fetch the wallet of photos from their last family holiday and subject her to a commentary of when and where they were all taken? Before continuing his rant about Stuart until he actually started crying. Did he really break down in front of her? Daniel physically shuddered as he trotted down the twenty-flight staircase. Somewhere near ground level he approached two figures on the stairwell. The nearest had his hand under a skirt: he was quite blatantly making out with a girl who Daniel now saw had dyed purple hair. Her eyes were raised, half open and he registered heavy breathing as he went past.

He tried without success to banish the image of Michaela lying beside him, the beautiful curve of her stomach, her pale muscular thighs. Even her shoulder blades had seemed incredible to him as she reached for the bottle of water on the bedside table.

Heading down Skinner Street, he passed Exmouth Market, where, a few years ago, he used to go to a café with his younger sister. He crossed Rosebery Avenue. Earlier that week, he'd stopped at this exact spot on a bus with Michaela – how different the world seemed then.

Michaela had no doubt filed Tuesday's fiasco in her "experiences not to be repeated" folder. Most likely she was seeing another play this evening with another prospective partner. Someone who didn't come across as a complete emotional wreck. She couldn't be short of offers with her looks and personality.

He went into Amwell Street where a group of beery teenagers were talking aggressively over each other as they headed towards the Angel. The words "I'll beat the living daylights out the fucker if I see him," floated above the cigarette smoke. Would their Saturday night on the town become Monday morning's business in the magistrates' court?

Standing opposite his old house in Barnsbury Road, he heard the clattering of a bin behind him. He anxiously turned around and recognised the retired schoolteacher, standing under a lamp-post.

"Oh. It's you, Mr O'Neil."

"Mrs Marshall!" He was genuinely pleased to see her. They used to get on well. Something of a blue stocking, she used to boast that she was friends with a barrister in the same chambers as George Carman. She had told him as much.

"What brings you to these parts?" she asked.

"I'm delivering a present for my son. It's his birthday on Thursday but I don't have an arrangement to see him." He raised his hands as if to convey his bemusement at his own situation.

Mrs Marshall nodded. "I'm sorry you had to move away," she replied after a pause.

"I am too. I expect you see more of my children than I do."

"Well, I doubt that. I catch them heading off to school some mornings after I've bought my newspaper."

"And Sally? Do you see her?"

"Occasionally. We always stop for a chat when we do."

Daniel hesitated, unsure how to phrase his next question. "And, umm, I expect you've met her latest friend?"

"Stuart? Yes, once or twice. He forgot his keys, so he borrowed the set I keep."

Daniel swallowed. "I'm glad they're still coming in useful."

She reached out and touched his shoulder. "It must be hard for you."

He nodded, worried that the swirl of emotions inside him might make him start crying again. "Anyway, I'm just going to give this to Max. Then I'll head off. It's been lovely seeing you again, Mrs Marshall."

He crossed the road and rang the bell. Who would answer this time? The door opened with a widening prism of light and a young woman peered tentatively out. A teenage girl, more like. He was sure he ought to know her.

Chapter Nine

"r O'Neil?"

"Yes…"

"It's Talia."

"Of course! Talia – you've grown up so much." The daughter of the accountant from a few doors down. The last time he saw her she was a wisp of a thing.

"I'm babysitting."

"Okay. I've got a present for Max."

"I can give it to him if you want."

"Is he awake?"

"Yes, they're all watching television."

"Do you mind if I hand it to him in person?" How weird to be asking this teenage girl whether he could say hello to his own kids. But she'd been put in charge, so he had to observe the rules.

"If you like."

He followed her inside. Of course he liked. They were his children. Why wouldn't he want to see them?

All three looked up from the sofa as he stepped into

the lounge. And Audrey and Max, already in pyjamas, shouted, "Daddy!"

"What are you doing here?" Imogen asked. The eldest at ten, going on fourteen, she had become increasingly distant. He occasionally speculated that Sally was turning her against him.

"I've got a birthday present for somebody!" He tried mustering an impossibly cheerful tone.

Max leapt off the sofa and pulled the package away from Daniel.

"Don't snatch," Imogen said.

"He's all right," Daniel said, as Max tore the wrapping paper open.

Music was playing. An Elton John concert on the television. Max now had the box set on his lap and was looking at one of the books, slightly puzzled.

"I used to read those when I was a boy," Daniel said.

"Wow," Audrey said. "They're old!"

"They had steam trains when Daddy was little," Imogen said.

"You joke, but they did actually. They were just being phased out." He turned towards the television. Elton John, sitting at the piano in what looked like a bright pink cagoule and matching baseball cap, was singing 'Don't Let the Sun Go Down on Me'. "I didn't know you even liked Elton John."

"We don't," Audrey laughed. "There's nothing else on."

Daniel had missed the bustle of Saturday nights: the arguments over which video to watch, the warm shiny bodies coming out of baths, Sally running between bedrooms to read stories, cups of hot milk spilt on clean sheets, a tantrum to deal with. But now there was a new male figure amidst Daniel's personal pageant. He'd been usurped. And he had no idea how Stuart acted with Sally. Or with Imogen, Audrey and Max. Or what the children thought about this new person in their lives. Did they give him a wide berth, making whispered comments behind his back? Or had they accepted him without reservation? An image surfaced of Max hanging on to Stuart's waist as he walked down the hallway.

"I'll read one of those to you in a minute," Daniel said to Max.

"All right." He didn't sound overly excited about the prospect.

"So, are they going to be late?" Daniel asked.

"No," Talia said. "They've just gone to The Albion."

"They're having a romantic meal for two," Imogen added.

"Audrey and Max, you should be going to bed now," Talia said. "It's gone nine o'clock."

"But this finishes soon. Can't we just see the end?" Audrey pleaded.

"It finishes at twenty-five past." Imogen had a newspaper open on her lap.

Daniel suddenly realised that their desire to stay up late was very likely connected to him being there. Devastating as this was, at least it showed they still cared.

"Are you going to read to me, Daddy?" Max asked.

"Of course, I'll be up in five minutes."

"One minute! I'm in my pyjamas."

He ended up reading *James the Red Engine* to both Audrey and Max, who were seven and five years old. They took a little convincing, but soon Max was declaring *Thomas the Tank Engine* to be the best ever. Daniel took some pleasure in the thought that Sally would now have to read the books to them at bedtime for the foreseeable future.

He kissed Max and turned off his light, and after promising Audrey that he'd be back very soon, he said his goodbyes and left the house. The last half an hour had been distinctly strange. But he hadn't strayed to the wrong side of the line. All he'd done was drop off a present for his son.

He considered popping into The Albion for a meal, and accidentally running into Sally and Stuart, but realised that was a terrible idea. He was hungry but would have to settle for a pizza instead.

His answerphone was flashing when he got home. It indicated a single message. Standing over the machine, he pressed the button.

"Daniel? It's Michaela. I was just ringing to say hi really. That's all. Nothing too much happened this week, quite a bit of work I suppose. Anyway, I expect you're busy, but give me a call some time. When you have a moment. Bye for now. Bye."

He decided to order his pizza. He was still too embarrassed about what he'd done to speak to Michaela. And he didn't want to look overeager in any case, calling on a Saturday night.

He settled on the sofa and watched *Rear Window* which he'd recorded, eating his pizza in front of the television when it arrived.

The telephone rang at eleven. It couldn't be Michaela again, surely?

"Hello?" he said, picking up.

"It's Sally. I've told you this before, Daniel, you can't just barge in here. This isn't your house anymore. Everything has to be arranged in advance."

"Technically, well over half of it is my house. And it will be until you sell it. I could do with the money, by the way."

"Will you stop avoiding the issue? You know exactly what I'm talking about."

"I briefly stopped off and gave Max his birthday present. I'm his father."

"Yes, and you watched television with them and read them stories. Imogen told me everything."

"She would have done."

"It's not your home anymore, Daniel."

"When are you going to sell it? You're saving tonnes every month on a mortgage, all because of the money I put in when we bought it."

"You didn't want to go to lawyers, Daniel."

"I've done absolutely nothing wrong. And now, if you'll excuse me, I'd like to go to bed."

Without waiting for her answer, he put down the phone. He'd had quite enough for one evening.

Chapter Ten

I t was eight in the morning and Tricia knew that she shouldn't, but she couldn't stop herself. James, her boss, was a bully and a narcissist. He'd been disrespectful to her most days since she joined his property company. So this was her one act of defiance.

She carried the envelope through to the kitchen and filled the kettle. She had to be careful to ensure that no one would see her.

The Brook Street Bureau had warned her that James was difficult. But they said – as a regular user of their services, and always punctual with his payments – they needed to keep him happy. And since she'd started the job in May, he'd told the agency that he was "satisfied" with her work. "Satisfied" was the best they ever got from him.

It was a trick she'd learned from her mother. Tricia had watched her doing it with letters she'd been given: a confidential communication from her GP, say, which needed passing on to a specialist. Today it worked beautifully. She steamed it open without causing any damage to the envelope. She waited until she was back at her desk before removing the card.

> *Jim*
>
> *Very weird seeing you the other day. You're SUCH a cunt. Still.*
>
> *So many memories, eh?*
>
> *Not sure why I'm even making this offer...*
> *But I'll tie you up and suck your cock till you beg for mercy.*
>
> *If you want...*
> *R*
> *0171 254 6858*

She let out a little scream as she looked; the bit about the sex act made her hot and embarrassed. Some of the confidential letters she'd opened had been bizarre – she'd seen requests for money, a couple of threats of litigation, even an attempt at blackmail – but there had never been anything quite like this. And so much spicier coming from somebody who obviously knew him. No one in the office used the name Jim. And whatever had happened between the two of them must have been fairly dramatic for the writer to use the C word. It was true of course.

Replacing the card in its original envelope, she resealed it. She opened the rest of his post, marking on a Post-it for each what she recommended should happen next. As she did so, she thought about the person who'd written the card. She couldn't know for sure that it was a man. This was frustrating but, even going by the handwriting, she was fairly certain. Never mind the offer to tie James up; what kind of woman would write that? And she'd already decided that James was gay. He wasn't married, he never talked about girlfriends, and showed no interest in any of the women in the company.

At nine fifty he swept into the office, his dyed blond hair still wet from the gym, complaining about some shit who'd cut him up on a roundabout. When she took the post into him, she was hoping he'd start reading it straight away. He did this sometimes. And if he was in a good mood, they might make small talk.

"Good morning!" she said in her most breezy and efficient voice, depositing the bundle in his in-tray. He barely glanced up from his newspaper. She left the room, ensuring his door was slightly open so she could keep an eye on him from her desk. She'd placed the card fifth from the top. She needed to see his reaction. She cursed herself for not photocopying the note when she opened it.

He spent twenty minutes reading his paper. Then he had two meetings behind closed doors. When the second finished, his door was again left open. Around eleven forty-five he finally started looking at the post. She watched through the gap, her excitement mounting as he glanced at the first few letters. If he agreed with her suggestions, he placed them in his out-tray, as happened with the first three. The next letter, the one before the envelope marked private and confidential, was a reference for the successful candidate in the marketing job. She'd neatly written on the Post-it: *Send contract to candidate, all references now received.*

He looked up and called through the open door. "Tricia, come in here."

Taking a deep breath, she got up and went through to his office.

"I'm slightly concerned about this phrase. *In the main.* Did you notice that?" He read it out loud, adopting a stuffy voice as he did so. "*In the main, I was very satisfied with his work.*"

"I didn't spot it. Sorry." Honesty was the best policy in this situation.

"It's okay, Tricia, it's easily missed. But could you give him a ring? Just say we weren't sure what he meant." He reached his hand out and she took the letter from him.

"Of course. I'll do it right now," she said, looking at the sealed envelope on top of the pile.

He nodded, a hint of a smile. But clearly expecting her to go.

"You don't want to speak with the referee yourself?" she said.

"I don't think it's necessary. If you get the impression it's more complicated, just let me know. Is that okay?"

"Of course."

He had now picked up the envelope, flipped it over, and then turned it back again. Surely he couldn't tell that it had already been opened. Maybe he recognised the writing. He started to use his thumb to manoeuvre a space beneath the envelope flap and card, but then stopped. "That will be all, thanks."

She quickly returned to her desk, sat down and immediately looked up towards his room. He was still pulling the card from the envelope, and glanced at her. So she began typing on her computer. The next thing she knew he was striding past her, the card in his hand.

"I'm getting a coffee. A decent coffee." There was a new place just down the road which he liked.

Now, after all that, she wouldn't get to see him read it. But she could at least keep an eye on him when he returned, which he did minutes later. After he'd sat down again, he removed the card from his jacket pocket, scanning it with an expressionless face. He pulled a tiny notebook from the desk. An address book, she imagined. He copied something into the book – the phone number on the bottom, surely – then, standing up, he tore the card in half three times and disappeared from her sightline. She'd check the bin later. After he'd left for the night and before the cleaner got to it, she would retrieve the pieces and stick them back together. Her boyfriend would love it when she showed him.

Around five thirty, James was in his raincoat with his attaché case, surely about to leave.

"So… did you speak with that referee?"

"Oh yes, I forgot to say."

Normally he would roll his eyes. Tonight he just said, "Was it anything significant?"

"No, he couldn't remember writing the words: *In the main*. He was sorry to have caused confusion."

"Well, that's okay then."

He stood silently for a moment, then looking down at her as she tidied her desk he said, "Aren't you going to go yourself?"

"I'm almost done," she said.

"Well, thanks for everything today. And don't stay too late." For James Liddell, bastard boss extraordinaire, he was being remarkably kind.

He moved towards the stairs then stopped. Taking the small book from his pocket he walked back into his office and closed the door. Very quietly, she got up from her desk and fetched her raincoat from the stand. She put it on right outside his room, straining to hear what was happening inside. There was silence before she heard him talking quietly but audibly.

"Rod, you arsehole, it's James. I got your pathetic card." There was a long pause before he said, "Okay then, so what are we going to do about it?"

Chapter Eleven

In order to demonstrate that the case was being treated with the seriousness it deserved, DCI Ruth Hobart held the press conference at Scotland Yard. A twenty-minute drive from Bishopsgate police station, it necessitated her crossing the Thames twice to get there, but the venue sent out all the right messages. And as the reporters piled out, Ruth felt a sense of relief that it was over and done with. She'd experienced some nerves beforehand, but it was part and parcel of the job and, more importantly, a vital tool in keeping the media onside. An impatient press screaming for results caused all manner of problems.

Using short and simple sentences, she'd told the packed room what a forensic examination of the evidence had confirmed. The head found floating in the Thames sixteen days ago had belonged to James Liddell. Liddell, a millionaire property businessman, had been missing since early December. Thanking everyone for their time and reminding them that this remained an active murder investigation, Ruth said that the real work could now begin in earnest. There were a handful of questions, but she made it clear that she couldn't divulge further information. She twice used the phrase "for operational reasons" which worked a treat.

Prior to the press conference, there had been some rumblings about lack of progress in the inquiry. Ruth was aware of the implied criticism of her as a woman in charge of only her second murder investigation. But her plan was now a pleasingly simple one. It involved interviewing anyone who'd known or had recent contact with Liddell.

As a baby, Liddell had entered the care system, and was formally adopted aged five. His adoptive parents were dead and there were no other known relatives the police could speak to. This partly explained Liddell not being linked to the murder inquiry earlier, the other main reason being that the board of his property company had tried to keep his disappearance as quiet as possible. Liddell's name had not in fact been passed to Hobart's team until last week.

Towards the end of the afternoon, DCI Hobart was taken to see a young PC in an interview room.

"You don't have to look quite so terrified," Ruth said kindly.

The young officer nodded but still looked concerned.

"There's less difference between us than you'd think. Twenty-five years, and that's about it. There's nothing you can say that I won't understand."

"Thank you, Detective Inspector. It's just that I made an error. Somebody reported something, and I didn't realise it would be useful to the James Liddell murder inquiry. I've only just got back from holiday, so I didn't hear about the head in the Thames until today. I should have known better though when the lady came in. I didn't handle it well."

"Which lady? And when was this report made?"

"December seventh. A woman came in when I was on the front desk."

"And which station is this?"

"Tolpuddle Street. Islington."

"And you say December seventh. That was before there even was a murder inquiry. What was reported, love?"

Barbara told her exactly what happened. She showed her a photocopy of her notes covering the homeless woman's visit to the station including her recommendation and she apologised again. DCI Hobart had warmed to this young officer. It was true that she'd shown a lack of judgement, but she was still young.

"I'm impressed by your ability to own up to your mistake," Ruth told her. "There aren't many people round here who'd be capable of that."

Chapter Twelve

The sun was setting as they stood by the small fountain. A nerve on the left side of Bill's face was twitching. He had initiated the conversation and was clearly not happy about something.

"I'll get straight to the point, Daniel. I had a telephone call from your ex-wife. It was yesterday evening. Sally."

"I know what she's called. And she's not my ex-wife. Yet."

"Please don't turn this into a joke. I'm trying to help you. Because this is potentially serious."

Daniel involuntarily shivered, something he couldn't attribute entirely to the coolness of the evening. "So what did she want?"

"What do you think, Daniel? Is there any reason why she might have called me?"

"As we don't do matrimony, I can't think of one." Daniel was attempting to keep it light-hearted, but Bill was having none of it.

"Apparently you've been barging into their family

home without permission. She said it's happened several times recently and she really isn't happy about it."

Daniel looked down at the shoes he'd bought in Church's on Chancery Lane. He remembered showing them off to Sally and the children when he got home; they were the first pair he'd ever owned from the prestigious shop and they reflected his growing income and status at the Bar. Now, even in this light, they were looking scuffed and worn down.

"You were also abusive on the phone last week," Bill continued. "Sally said you sounded drunk."

"I wasn't drunk, exactly."

"She doesn't want you going into her house and watching television with the kids, without her knowing that you're there. You even read them a bedtime story for goodness' sake!"

"They're my children too."

"Quite frankly, Daniel, had that been my ex-wife turning up while I was out of the house, reading to my children, I'd think that was pretty strange behaviour."

"I can explain everything, Bill."

"I don't need an explanation, because I've seen this happen before. You remember Jeffrey Levack QC? The restraining order which he breached? The punch-up at the school barbecue? Chris Carter defended him at Blackfriars Crown Court – it was all over the papers, is that what you want?"

"Of course not."

"The judge was lenient, but it still ended his career."

"I remember."

"And you know Jeffrey. He's as mild as the proverbial dove. But it was a slippery slope. It started in much the same way, with silly arguments over the kids. It can happen to the best of us, Daniel. We're all human, but you've got to pull yourself together."

"I'm sorry, Bill. I've not been myself. It won't happen again."

"It might help if you moved on to someone else. Aren't there any other young ladies on the horizon? You're still young, you're not too bad-looking."

"There was someone recently, Michaela, but I fucked that up too."

"What do you mean you fucked it up?" Bill was now sounding worried.

"I made an idiot of myself. It's nothing for you to be concerned about. She came back to my place, it was all going perfectly well, and then – you don't need to know."

"Nothing you could be arrested for?"

"No – don't be ridiculous! She was the one that seduced me, if you must know."

"So, it sounds like she likes you?"

"She seemed to that night."

"And you like her?"

"Yes, it's just–"

"It's not just anything. Phone her, say hello. How long is it since you saw her?"

"A couple of weeks. She left a message on my answerphone, but I didn't think she'd want to see me again."

"Of course she does. She's all over you like a rash. Give her a call, she sounds lovely. Because if you don't call her, I will on your behalf."

"Oh, for God's sake, Bill."

"And don't forget, we've got great things in mind for you. You're a rising star in chambers. So please don't 'fuck it up', as you say."

"I'm not intending to."

"This whole thing with Sally and the kids is out of character, I realise that. But just remember what happens when people lose their heads."

"They're found floating in the Thames."

"Exactly, Daniel."

Chapter Thirteen

It was a ten- to fifteen-minute drive from Michaela's flat in Tufnell Park Road to Finsbury Park where she'd arranged to meet her old friend Anika. They hugged outside the train station and Michaela kissed Anika on the cheek.

"Really great to see you," Michaela said.

"I see you've gone for the denim look," Anika replied. Michaela wasn't sure how to take this. Her long skirt with its two front pockets was brand new. She'd been pleased with the purchase made in Camden market last weekend when she was feeling at a low ebb. The stallholder had assured her it was "genuine American". And her stonewashed shirt was a favourite.

"Don't you like the skirt?" she asked, hating her need for her friend's approval. Anika was understated as usual in black jeans and a navy crewneck jumper.

"No, you look great," Anika said.

They started in the World's End pub where Michaela drank bitter and Anika white wine.

"How's work?" Michaela was expecting a bog-standard answer. But instead, Anika told a complex story about a younger woman who'd recently joined her department, had already been promoted and was now technically more senior than her.

"You know these people who come in with all the right buzz words. And their face just fits. But really, there's nothing there at all, they're empty."

Michaela nodded and sipped her drink, then wiped some froth from her top lip.

"Anyway," Anika continued, "tell me about your new job. How's it been, selling your soul to the devil?"

"Pretty rich coming from someone whose livelihood is earned persuading third world continents that they should be drinking hard spirits."

Anika laughed.

"Well, what I didn't know is that the Mirror Group is in serious trouble," Michaela said. "Both papers have lost a lot of readers and there are rumours that the editor is on the way out."

"The perfect time to join."

"Precisely."

"I don't think they help themselves though, do they?" Anika said, her eyes following a thickset man as he made his way slowly across the bar.

"How do you mean?"

"It was the *Mirror* that published those photos of Diana in the gym, wasn't it?"

"Yes. And she's suing us for that."

"I don't blame her. You're not about to defend that story, are you?"

"No. Although people lap up Diana nonsense, you know that."

"Doesn't make it right to keep trailing the poor woman like a pack of bloodhounds."

"That was something Daniel kept going on about. The whole morality thing. He called it probity, I think."

Anika raised her eyebrows. "Daniel?"

"The barrister."

"Oh. The barrister. Well, he would call it probity."

"He thinks journalists have no scruples at all."

"Have you asked him what he thinks of the House of Horrors stories? Like the one that practically accused them of cannibalism. They're saying that because of the coverage, Fred West may never get a fair trial. The judge might throw it out. Ask your barrister friend what he thinks about that."

"I'm not sure I'll get the opportunity. He's stopped phoning me."

"That didn't last long." Anika almost chuckled.

"I'm actually really upset about it."

"I'm sorry. So what happened?"

"We had a date, it was perfectly okay, we had sex and he hasn't phoned me since."

"Have you phoned him?"

"I've left a couple of messages. We haven't spoken though."

"Well, it sounds like he got what he wanted."

"I don't think it was like that. He seemed to really like me."

"You're so sweet!"

"What are you talking about?"

"He gets up every day, goes to court and argues that black is white, or possibly grey, or sepia. His job is to basically misrepresent things."

"Yes, very good, but something slightly weird happened after we did it. When we were lying in bed."

"What was he like by the way? I've always fancied shagging a barrister. Did he keep his wig on?"

"Do you want to hear about what happened afterwards or not?"

"Yes. I'm dying to know what went wrong."

"It was just he started showing me pictures of his children, he was complaining he didn't see them enough – and then he kind of burst into tears. You know, properly crying – snot and everything. It was a bit embarrassing to be honest."

"It sounds like a fun evening. What happened next?"

"Well the whole photo thing seemed to go on for a while, but I thought at least he's got something out of his system, cos we kissed goodnight and fell asleep together which was really nice. And the next morning he seemed okay, a little subdued but basically fine."

"Did you do it again?"

"There wasn't time. We had breakfast, and he dropped me off at Angel Station, and he said he'd call. And that was over three weeks ago. So, what do you think?"

"I don't know," Anika said after a pause. "He sounds a bit fucked up."

"He sounds a bit fucked up?"

"Yes. He does. Sorry. Who bursts into tears looking at pictures of their kids?"

"What would you know about it? You haven't got children."

"I'm just giving you the benefit of my wisdom. He's probably still in love with his wife too."

"I don't think so."

"Well, he hasn't phoned you. I'd forget the whole thing if I were you."

"Yes, I realise I can try to forget the whole thing – I'm not fucking stupid."

"So what do you want from me?"

"I was kind of hoping for some advice."

"I suppose you could give it one last go yourself. Call him again. See if you can actually speak. Pretend you thought his answerphone wasn't working."

"I could, I just don't know. The really annoying thing is that I've given up smoking for him. And he doesn't even know. How pathetic is that?"

Chapter Fourteen

Daniel had picked up a Chinese takeaway on his way back from chambers. He had eaten it rather too quickly in the kitchen of his flat and was feeling the tightening within his temples he associated with MSG. There were some additional documents disclosed by the Crown Prosecution Service that needed wading through in advance of a conference the following morning. However, he was in no mood to start on these straight away.

Instead, he sat in his reception room and turned on a news report concerning further developments in the Fred and Rose West case. In front of the barrier which separated the journalists and curious members of the public from the work being undertaken by the police, a reporter in a tweed jacket was talking about the ground-penetrating radar which had been used. He pointed to the blue-and-white tent in the field behind him. As if passing a secret to a friend, he said that it was under this very tent that ten members of a specialist police team had been digging a trench three to four feet deep. And that yesterday, their digging had yielded human remains. This discovery had prompted the home office pathologist to travel today to the borders of Gloucestershire and Herefordshire. It was too early to say whether the human material found had been from a man or a woman.

And then, on the far right of the picture, Daniel saw a female figure talking to a man in a long overcoat. She was diminutive at this distance, but judging by her piled-up hair, her unpolished style and the way she gesticulated with her hands, he was sure it was Michaela. He remembered her saying that the West case was the last she would have chosen to work on. But there she was, playing her part, earnestly in conversation as she gathered information for a report. He felt for her. And in that moment, he missed her so much that the sensation in his stomach was physical.

The reporter was now saying there was reason to believe that the remains discovered were from Fred West's first wife Catherine Costello. They'd lived together in Much Marcle, and she'd disappeared twenty-two years ago. One or two people were speculating that the dig may have found Mr West's daughter Charmaine. She'd also vanished without trace and had never been found despite massive publicity.

The news item had been filmed in daylight. It was possible that Michaela had travelled back to London that evening after covering the day's developments. But much more likely, surely, that she would be staying in Gloucestershire. Why would the paper keep forking out on train fares when they could put her up in some cheap accommodation close to the action?

On the basis that there was almost no chance she would answer her phone, Daniel dialled Michaela's number. She picked up straight away. "Hello?" Her voice sounded distant. Slightly wary even.

"Michaela?"

"Who is this?"

"It's Daniel."

"Oh, Daniel. I thought you'd disappeared in a puff of smoke."

"Yes, sorry about that. I just saw you on the television."

"You did?"

"Yes, you were on the news report. In the background – well, at the side of the screen anyway."

"I get the idea."

He laughed. "The truth is, I've been missing you."

"So why didn't you call?"

"Frankly, I was embarrassed. You know, by my behaviour."

"I thought I must have done something wrong."

"No, you did nothing wrong at all. I just didn't think you'd ever want to see me again." There was a pause. "Would you want to see me again?"

"I'm not sure. I'm quite busy at the moment."

"Can I come round now? Give me your address and I'll drive over."

"What's the tearing urgency all of a sudden?"

He had to think about that. But all he could say was, "I want to see you. I know I've been an arsehole."

"Quite honestly, Daniel, my flat is a tip. And I'm shattered. I was just getting ready for bed."

"Of course, you've been in Much Marcle. It looks like they're making progress."

"You know, the farmers who own Letterbox Field were charging journalists fifty pounds a day to park there. Fifty pounds! Luckily my colleague paid. It's blatant racketeering, isn't it?"

"Not in the legal sense of the term, no."

"Christ, I knew I shouldn't have asked that. And they'd set up this mobile snack van – charging two fifty for a hot dog. And guess what they called their van. 'The Dig Inn'!"

"That's pretty bad," Daniel conceded. "Anyway, can I see you tomorrow? We could go to an art gallery. I've got nothing on in the afternoon."

"I'm meant to be working."

"Can't you take some time off?"

"I suppose I have been putting in ridiculous hours recently. I'll think of something."

"I'd love it if we could meet. What time would suit you? – two thirty works for me."

"All right then." She didn't sound keen.

"Great. Let's meet outside the Royal Academy of Arts. There's this statue of a man conducting a symphony. And he's also holding a plate for some reason."

———

The next day, after his client had left chambers following their conference, Daniel went to his room to collect a few things. Chris Carter looked up from his desk as he came in.

"Oh, you are here. Someone said you were."

"Yes, but not for long."

"Do you have a minute?"

"About one minute, yes." Much as Daniel enjoyed sharing a room with Chris, he didn't have time for a lengthy chat.

"Okay, I get the message. Where are you off to anyway?"

"Just a personal thing." He and Chris never discussed anything outside the law or life within chambers. It was an unspoken rule that worked well for both. Even when Daniel's marriage broke down and he spent weeks looking dreadful, Chris never asked whether he was okay or what was going on. Daniel really appreciated this lack of scrutiny. "What was it anyway?" he said to Chris.

"It's this bloody client. We're on about his fourth set of instructions. I mean how long do I have to keep putting up with this crap before I throw in the towel?"

"Is this the accountancy fraud?"

"Yeah, that's it."

"That's rather complicated, I seem to remember. Why not phone the Bar Council? They'll probably put you on to a silk on their committee."

"I thought I might cut out the middleman and speak to a silk here."

Daniel laughed and patted Chris's shoulder. "You've got the ethics helpline number, yes? Give them a call."

"All right, I might do that."

Daniel was about to go, then thought of something. "Quick question, Chris. What d'you think about the idea of Bill contacting Leo Goatley. I just want to see if he's considered it."

"Who on earth is Leo Goatley?"

"Yes, sorry – he's Rose West's solicitor. Possibly Fred's too."

"Surely not both for the trial."

"True. So what do you think?"

Chris screwed up his face. "Bill doesn't appreciate that kind of intervention. He likes to be trusted that he's doing the right thing by us."

"Fair point, thanks." Daniel closed the door as he left. Walking down the corridor, he heard a noise from one of the rooms. At first, he thought it was somebody in the throes of passion, but then realised it was the sound of crying. He stopped walking. The sobbing continued. It was a woman, surely. He should probably have knocked on the door and checked everything was all right, but frankly what was there to say? It would just be embarrassing. The room was used by a colleague in her fifties, a fierce and respected advocate. Usually she was the model of professionalism and decorum, so what on earth was the problem? He hovered outside the door, his arm outstretched, then remembered his arrangement with Michaela. Knocking on the door might lead to a knotty situation that took out the best part of his afternoon. He winced and continued walking, and the sound of her distress receded.

He was just leaving the building when a voice called, "Excuse me?" He turned to see a woman he didn't recognise. Smartly dressed in linen trousers, jacket, and a delicate orange scarf – he assumed she was a solicitor.

"Can I help at all?" Daniel asked.

"I'm looking for Bill Conner. I've been wandering around the building for a good ten minutes," she said, almost as if this was Daniel's fault.

Cursing inwardly, Daniel stretched his lips into a smile. "I'm in a bit of a rush but I'll show you to the clerks' room."

"You're a darling! I'm going to manage a big party in your chambers, so I'll make sure your glass is permanently brimming over."

He didn't answer as Bill had come over to meet them in reception.

"So, you must be Veronica." He shook the woman's

hand. "This young lady's going to be organising our summer party."

"Yes, I've just been hearing. Bill, can I have a word in your ear?"

A flash of irritation passed across Bill's face like a shadow. "If it's quick, we're about to have a meeting."

"I'm in a hurry too," Daniel said.

They moved to a corner of the clerks' room where Daniel told Bill that he'd heard crying from his colleague's room. Bill nodded. "Look, I know all about this. You don't need to get involved."

"Okay. One other thing, have you ever been instructed by Leo Goatley? Rose West's solicitor."

"Never. I hadn't heard of him until yesterday. But then he called me."

"He did?"

"Yes. He said that much as he rates the ability of the criminal Bar on the western circuit, he's looking for someone with a track record in major cases in London's courts."

Bill was smiling and Daniel felt hope soaring within him.

"He asked for George, of course," Bill continued.

"Of course."

"I had to tell him that much as George would love to take on the case, there's no way he's going to get to HMP Bronzefield to meet Rose until August."

"What was his response?"

"He said that wasn't acceptable. Rose needs to know now who'll be representing her." He looked over Daniel's shoulder. "Look, I don't want to keep my guest waiting—"

"Did you not suggest anybody else?" Daniel felt the edge in his voice.

"He couldn't get off the phone fast enough. He

obviously had his wish list. And from this chambers it was George Carman QC or no one I'm afraid."

"Thanks for trying," Daniel said, though he was far from convinced that Bill had tried. They went back into reception, and Daniel shook the hand of the visitor before making his exit.

Chapter Fifteen

The Goatley thing was annoying, but what could he do? It was the perennial problem of not being in control of your own destiny. He was in the hands of the Gods, or at least the instructing solicitors. And sometimes even his own clerk failed to make a grab for the low-hanging fruit. But at least he'd done the right thing by mentioning the crying. It was a relief that Bill had the problem in hand.

He found his car in the Inn car park and headed towards Charing Cross Road. Parking in a side street, he made his way into Books Etc. He'd considered buying the new Irvine Welsh but now had a better idea. He looked around the shop which stretched back way further than he'd imagined. Reaching the end, he found a member of staff sitting behind a desk.

"I need to speak to the manager," Daniel said.

"Is it anything that I can help with?" The young man seemed to be bracing himself for disappointment.

"No, I think I do need the manager for this one."

The young man picked up a telephone, held down a button and his voice tannoyed around the shop.

"Thank you," Daniel said.

They waited for a minute and no one appeared.

"Look, why don't you try me?" the young man said. "Just while we're waiting."

"All right," Daniel agreed. "I'm looking for a book called *The Firm* by John Grisham." He was pretty sure the staff member smirked.

"Of course, follow me." He led the way to a table of fiction paperbacks and withdrew *The Firm* from a large pile.

"Ah, thank you!" Daniel said, as if he'd never have found the novel in such an obscure location. "I have read it before, but I wanted it for a friend."

"I've heard it's gripping. We can gift wrap it at no extra charge."

From the bookshop, Daniel headed down towards Leicester Square and left on to Cranbourn Street. The Royal Academy was just over ten minutes away and despite the earlier hold-ups, he was pleased to arrive exactly on time. He saw Michaela standing in a long purple coat by the statue, just as they'd arranged.

"This is for not being in touch," he said, approaching her.

She took the present with a smile. "That's sweet, but really you didn't need to."

She unwrapped it straight away.

"It's about a lawyer who joins a firm and is immediately in trouble. His wife is in danger too, come to think of it."

"Are you trying to tell me something, Daniel?"

"You can take the plot with a pinch of salt."

They kissed on the lips and held hands as they walked into the exhibition together.

"*Truth and Fantasy*," Michaela said, reading a sign above their heads. "What made you pick this one?"

"It seemed an important subject."

They were standing in front of a painting depicting the rocky coast of a tempestuous sea, with a pitiful collection of people washed up around a rock from a shipwreck. In the centre, a woman in a yellow dress, her breasts exposed, reached up to the sky. The forlorn figures around her were also in various states of undress. They looked exhausted and almost without hope.

"Is this how you see humanity?" Michaela asked. "Has it reached this pretty pass?"

"I just think it's relevant," he said.

"That's how it should be with art," she agreed. "If it has nothing to say to us, why should we bother looking?"

———

Later, when they were having a coffee in the café, he told her that Sally used to criticise the way he went around art galleries. "She'd hate it if I took photos of the pictures rather than really looking at them."

"Do you think she was right?"

"Probably. But I'd tell her I'd have a good look at the photos when I got them developed."

"You're not taking any photos today though."

"Well, no – because I want to rewrite all my rules. I've decided with us, things are going to be different. That's if you want there to be an us."

She stopped and searched his eyes with hers. But then said nothing.

"What is it?" he asked.

"This isn't going to work, Daniel," she said, and his heart plummeted like a pebble in an underground cave. "If you're not ready for another relationship – emotionally," she continued. "I think you're still pretty cut up about your children, aren't you? And angry about that. With your wife particularly."

"No, I'm not. Really, I'm not," he said, looking back at her directly.

"That's not how it came across when we last saw each other, Daniel. You have to understand that."

"I shouldn't have gone on like that. And I was wrong to bad-mouth Stuart too."

"So, you're not thinking about her and this new man the whole time? Because I know that must be difficult."

"Not at all. I'm thinking about you."

"All right," she said, her tone difficult to decipher. "Shall we get back to the exhibition?"

After they'd finished looking at the art, Michaela asked Daniel if he'd like to come back to Tufnell Park. She promised to make a simple supper. He accepted on the understanding that if he started talking about anything inappropriate, she should either stop him immediately or throw him out the front door. They walked to his car and as he drove north on Hampstead Road, they made a list of all the things they weren't going to discuss for the rest of the day, or possibly ever. This included ex-wives, child access arrangements, disastrous relationships, decentralised council services, Fred and Rose West, cockroach infestations, professional ethics, heads found floating in rivers, trainspotters, journalists, and of course, barristers. When they arrived at her flat, they agreed they actually had nothing left to talk about at all.

"In that case, I've thought of something we can do instead," Michaela said, pushing Daniel backwards towards her bedroom. This time it was her who was in a rush. She had removed his shirt by the time they were in her room.

"What's the tearing urgency, to quote someone I heard recently?" Daniel asked.

"You are," she replied, allowing her skirt to drop to the floor.

"I thought you were going to make my dinner."

"Fuck your dinner," she said, pushing him onto the mattress and unbuckling his trousers. Within seconds, she too was on the bed, kneeling astride him, leaning forwards and letting her hair fall freely around his face while she kissed him softly and repeatedly on the lips.

"Hey, it's like we're in our own private screening." He parted her hair as if peeking through curtains at the outside world.

"But what film are we showing?" She reached back to grab hold of his crotch.

"Nothing that you should be allowed to watch, that's for sure."

She laughed uproariously and then removed her knickers. He reached behind her and pulled her towards him so that she was crouched just above his face.

"Fucking hell, Daniel." She lowered herself directly onto his mouth, grinding herself into him. Daniel had never experienced anything quite like this before.

She soon built to a loud climax, and then worked her way down his body with her lips, circling her tongue around his belly button before finally taking him in her mouth. He couldn't hold back.

"Sorry," he said, "that always seems to happen."

"It's fine," she said. "We can fuck later if you've got the energy. I'm getting quite hungry, though I can't be bothered to cook. Shall I order a curry?"

"I could eat a curry." He loved how she flipped so freely from talking about sex to what they'd be having for dinner.

"Get dressed then, man. What are you waiting for?"

They ate it in the living room, sitting side by side on the sofa watching a terrible film she had on video.

"This is my second takeaway in two days," Daniel said.

"Aren't you the lucky one? Which was better?"

"Last night I was alone, and tonight I'm with you. So I can't really compare."

"That should make it easy to compare, shouldn't it?"

He took a deep breath. "I want this to work."

"Why wouldn't you? I do too, by the way."

When the film finished, they left their plates in the living room and went straight up to bed. They didn't find the energy for more lovemaking, but they did agree that this was now a thing. Perhaps, following a shaky start, their relationship was about to take off after all.

Chapter Sixteen

D CI Hobart opened the door to the interview room and went in with a young detective on her team. A male PC stood next to a small table where a young man was seated. The young man was wearing what looked like a brand-new suit. He was clearly nervous.

"All right, ma'am?" the PC said.

"Thank you, yes," Ruth replied. The PC turned on the tape and left the room.

DCI Hobart sat at the table with the detective and smiled at the young man in a formal way, acknowledging that this wasn't easy for any of them.

"Good morning. This interview is being taped. I am DCI Ruth Hobart, and this is Detective Luke Crossley; we're both based at Bishopsgate police station. What's your full name?"

"Nikolaos Kalogeropoulos." There was a pause. "People call me Nikos."

"That's helpful, thank you. And can you confirm your date of birth?"

"November the sixteenth, nineteen seventy-two."

"So that makes you twenty-two years old."

"Yes."

"And today's date is May the eleventh, nineteen ninety-four. And the time according to my watch is ten thirty-five in the morning."

Nikos nodded. He had pulled a packet of cigarettes from his pocket and was peeling away the cellophane.

"Just to confirm, Nikos, you've decided not to have anyone with you this morning. And that means a friend who could act as an observer, or make sure the interview is being conducted fairly, or even advise you, if you wanted that."

"I don't need anyone." He was flicking his lighter, but it wouldn't produce a flame. Ruth removed some matches from her bag and struck one, holding it out. Nikos leaned forward, cigarette in mouth, and together they lit it. "Thank you," he said and exhaled.

"Not at all. And it's important to make clear this is an out of custody interview. You aren't under arrest, Nikos. You are free to leave at any time."

Nikos nodded. "I understand."

"And you are entitled to free and independent legal advice."

"I'm all right. I haven't done anything wrong."

"Okay, very good. But if you change your mind, just let us know and we'll stop the interview to arrange it."

Nikos pulled inexpertly at his cigarette. Ruth suspected he just wanted something to do with his hands, which were shaking.

"So now I'm going to read the caution to you. You are being interviewed in connection with the murder of James Liddell. You do not have to say anything but anything you do say may be taken down and used in evidence against you."

Nikos nodded. "I understand."

"That is to say, you don't have to answer any question I ask you today, if you don't want to."

"I do not mind answering, really."

"So, the reason for this interview is that I am in charge of the investigation into Mr Liddell's murder. We received a report that you were seen with Mr Liddell. This would have been on the night of the fourth of December in the Hope and Anchor pub on Upper Street. I should add that Mr Liddell was not seen alive after this date. He very probably met his death that evening."

"I know about this. The barwoman told me."

"Yes, indeed. That would be Davina Smith. So, can you confirm whether or not you remember meeting Mr Liddell at the pub that evening?"

Nikos swallowed. "I do remember it."

Ruth was scrutinising the interviewee with every answer, looking for signs of discomfort. So far, she'd seen nothing unusual, apart from his nerves – and they were understandable.

"What time did you go to the pub that evening?"

"I would say, maybe eight thirty."

"Had you been anywhere first?"

"No. I came from my home."

"And were you intending to go anywhere afterwards?"

"No."

"So, what was the purpose of your visit to the pub, Nikos? Were you meeting someone?"

"No, I went there alone. I was keen to find a new girlfriend. I was told pubs were the best place for this."

Ruth allowed herself a small chuckle. "Who told you that?"

"My friend. He is called Stavros."

"Could you tell me about your meeting with Mr Liddell? How did it happen?"

"I came into the pub and I was served by Davina. I sat down and he started talking to me straight away."

"What did he say, Nikos?"

"I cannot remember. We talked about the weather."

"Anything else?"

"Yes, it was about his work. He was a businessman."

"What did he say about his work?"

"He talked about his company. He said it was worth a lot of money. Over ten million pounds."

"And were you impressed by this?"

"Of course. I am a business studies student, so I understand these things."

"And do you remember anything else about the conversation?"

"Not much."

"Did he tell you that he was going to meet somebody?"

Nikos stubbed his cigarette out in the ashtray and looked at them both. "Yes. He did tell me that."

"What exactly did he say?"

"I don't think he was looking forward to it."

"Did he say who he was meeting? Or anything about them?"

"No, nothing."

"Did he say that he'd rather not be meeting the person at all?"

There was a pause. Nikos was now looking distinctly uncomfortable. "He might have done, I don't remember."

"Are you sure, Nikos? Because Davina Smith heard Mr Liddell saying that his friend was, and this is a direct quote, 'A bit of an arsehole'. And that he'd rather spend the evening with you."

"I do not remember this. My English is not always so good, and the pub was noisy."

"Did Mr Liddell spend the rest of his evening with you, Nikos?"

"No, that is not what happened."

"Would you like to tell us what did happen?"

"We finished our conversation and he went to meet his friend."

"And what did you do?"

"I was feeling tired, so I went home."

"But did you stay in the pub after Mr Liddell left? Or did you leave at the same time as he did?"

"We left at the same time."

"What happened when you left the pub?"

"I walked towards the Tube. And he went in the other direction."

"And before you parted, did he suggest meeting with you again. Or take your phone number? Anything like that?"

"No, there was nothing like that."

"Which Tube station did you walk towards?"

"Highbury. To get to Seven Sisters."

"And how long would you say the conversation you had with Mr Liddell lasted in total?"

"A few minutes."

"How many minutes?"

"Ten. Or maybe fifteen."

"So perhaps you can explain one thing for me, Nikos. Why is it that you went from your flat in Seven Sisters to a pub on Upper Street to spend an evening out, perhaps trying to find a new girlfriend. And you stayed only ten to fifteen minutes before beginning your journey home? Why was that?"

"I was not feeling happy that evening."

"It was a bit of a change of plan, wasn't it?"

"I decided to leave when he left."

"And you're quite sure you didn't go anywhere else with Mr Liddell?"

"I'm quite sure."

"Because we have a lot of cameras in London, and we could make a check for that night." She looked at Detective Crossley, who nodded.

"Really, I'm sure. We said goodnight as soon as we left the pub."

"And just going back to your conversation in the pub for a moment. When you were speaking with Mr Liddell, did he tell you that he was gay?"

"No. I would have remembered that."

"Are you gay, Nikos?"

"Definitely not."

"Are you bisexual perhaps?"

"No, I am from Athens."

DCI Hobart's eyes briefly met those of the young detective.

"Okay, so let me ask you about your background in Greece. What do your parents do for a living?"

"They own... I think the best word for it is a farm."

"I can help you here because we've looked into this. I believe the best word is an abattoir. We also call it a slaughterhouse."

"Yes. I didn't know the correct name."

"Is your parents' abattoir still running, Nikos?"

"Running?"

"Is it still operating as a business?"

"Not anymore."

"And do you know why that is?"

"It has been closed down. A lot have been."

"Yes, because of extreme cruelty to the animals. There are films of fully conscious pigs having their throats cut."

"Yes, I heard that too."

"And did you ever work in your parents' abattoir, Nikos?"

"Only very occasionally. In my holidays from school."

"And when you worked there, did you have to kill the animals yourself?"

"No. I only ever did paperwork. There is lots of paperwork."

Towards the end of the interview, DCI Hobart asked Nikos whether he would consent to his flat being searched. She made clear that this would be in connection with the murder. They would be looking directly for any evidence related to the crime. He understood that he did not have to give his permission, and that anything seized could be used in evidence. When she added that if he refused permission at this stage, she would apply for a search warrant, Nikos gave his consent in writing for them to proceed. He said that he did not have anything to hide.

DCI Hobart thanked him and said that they would begin that day. If necessary, Nikos could be put up in a hotel while it continued. Nikos agreed not to return home while the search was being carried out. He said he would telephone his girlfriend, but then changed his mind and said Stavros would be happy if he stayed with him. The interview was completed, and the tape was switched off.

Chapter Seventeen

The tyre shop on Lower Clapton Road was a busy one. Vasim Syed's first customer that day was driving a Diamond White Ford Fiesta. Vasim prided himself on his encyclopaedic knowledge of the colours for different models. He even used to keep a notebook where he would record the most popular and rarest colours that passed through the garage.

The driver got out of his car and told Vasim that he wanted all four tyres changed. As Vasim got to work he noticed that the tyres coming off were in surprisingly good condition, but he didn't say anything to the tall gentleman with glasses. He didn't seem like the type you would make small talk with. Vasim had a pretty good sense of which customers he could pass the time of day with and this man definitely didn't fall into that category.

Later, when the man came to collect his car, he noticed Vasim writing the registration number into his book.

"Is that a legal thing?" the man asked.

Vasim narrowed one of his eyes, not fully understanding the question.

"Does the law require you to record all registration numbers?" the man said. "Just curious."

"We do it in case the tax man starts snooping around. Good records and all that."

The customer nodded, transferring his weight from one foot to the other for a moment.

"Very good," he said. "You can't be too careful, eh?"

It was an unusual thing for a customer to ask and perhaps made the transaction stand out in Vasim's mind more than others.

Chapter Eighteen

New Court Chambers was unusually proactive in having a management meeting each month. They were held in George Carman's spacious room on the ground floor, overlooking the square and fountain, and were typically attended by five or six barristers. Bill Conner would also sit in on the meetings, except when he was told: "This item doesn't concern you, Bill," at which point he'd leave the room, knowing that they were about to discuss the way the clerks were paid or something similar.

It was already six, but so far only Daniel had arrived along with Paul Summerfield QC and senior junior Terence Corbett.

"While we're waiting, I believe congratulations are in order, Daniel." Paul was barely able to suppress a smirk, so Daniel knew he was about to be ribbed.

"I'm not sure what I've done, but I'm always happy to be toasted," he replied.

"Daniel's decree nisi just came through," Paul said to Terence, who was looking confused.

"Oh that!" Daniel said. "I thought for a moment it was something exciting."

"It is exciting," Paul said. "As a brand-new divorcee, you're joining a small but elite group within chambers. Out of our twenty-six members, a mere twenty-three are divorced."

"Yes, and some are responsible for other divorces too," Daniel added, thinking about the horse-riding teacher Paul was now living with.

"You know that new Hugh Grant film," Terence said. "That could actually be about this chambers?"

"*Four Weddings and a Funeral?*" Daniel said.

"That's the one."

"Yes, that certainly describes several members of the Bar," Paul agreed, "some of whom do maintain a modest practice after their funerals."

After a while, Bill arrived with George. Bill was talking in a low voice as he entered his room.

"And how does Laurie manage to keep decreasing his income year on year? You'd think he'd have plateaued by now."

"To be fair," Bill said in low tones, "Laurie's had all manner of health issues over the past eighteen months. And his twin sister died in a car crash."

"All right, Bill," George said. "I don't think we should be discussing this here."

"Of course," Bill said, smiling as he caught Daniel's eye.

"I'm surprised Marcus isn't earning more though," George muttered. "It's scandalous really, the man has a double first from Oxford." He turned to the others. "Good evening, gentlemen. What are we talking about first?"

The first item on the agenda was the number of milk

bottles being purchased each day for chambers. This proved to be a contentious item, as quite often entire pints had gone off in the fridge. On the other hand, there was nothing worse than working late in chambers and finding you couldn't make yourself a hot drink, particularly in the arctic temperatures the chambers reached most winters. It was an intractable problem and they talked about it for over forty minutes with feelings running high. The time taken on this subject combined with the late start meant that there was no time for the main item on the agenda, the plan to relocate chambers. They'd recently taken a decision to do so, as the building they were occupying was inadequate, having no conference rooms or library facilities. However, discussions on this important subject would have to be carried over until June.

Chapter Nineteen

"Before we turn the tape recorder on and go through this in detail, can I ask one thing?" DCI Hobart said to Tricia Armitage. "How come you didn't bring this in before? It's potentially very significant."

Tricia looked at the card held together with adhesive tape lying on the table in front of them. "Yes, I'm sorry, miss. It was at Nigel's place. My ex."

"Would that be your ex-boyfriend or ex-husband?"

"Ex-boyfriend. It's a little bit complicated. You see, I was seeing him when I worked with Mr Liddell. And the day the card arrived, I took it over to Nigel's flat to show him, because I knew he'd find it funny." The two women looked each other in the eye. "He loves kinky things – he finds them hilarious."

"Carry on."

"But me and Nigel broke up soon afterwards. I forgot about the card for a while. The split was a bit nasty to be honest, he's got a temper, Nigel has – I'm sure you don't need all the details."

DCI Hobart shook her head and lit a cigarette. "So, when did you remember about the card?"

"It must have been April. I called Nigel and said we should be handing it to the police, but he said he'd no idea where it was. I told him he should look for it, but I didn't like to keep reminding him."

"I see. So how did you get hold of the card in the end?"

"He dropped it off at my flat last night. Said I could take it to the police – as long as he's not involved." DCI Hobart looked at her curiously. "He's a bit paranoid."

"Okay, well he doesn't need to be involved. I'm going to ask you to go through all the details again in a formal interview. How it arrived in the office, what you did with it, what you saw and heard later that day. And I'll be stopping to ask you questions." She looked at her watch. "It's coming up to eight o'clock. Is it okay to do this now?"

"Yes, of course," Tricia nodded. "And there's something else I remembered too."

"Okay. What's that?"

"A couple of weeks before Mr Liddell disappeared, he went to a school reunion. I replied to the invitation for him. I think this card might have something to do with that."

Straight after the interview, DCI Hobart went to the incident room. When it was buzzing, there might be forty people crammed in there. At this time, there were just half a dozen.

"Okay, boys, have a gander at this. It was sent to Liddell at his work at the end of November."

She was immediately surrounded.

"Fuckin' hell – excuse the language."

"Blimey."

"That's a belter, ma'am – no pun intended."

"Luke, I'm going to need you to trace who this telephone number belongs to. But I don't want us phoning him yet. Also, Liddell attended a school reunion a week or two before. Sam and Colin, we need to find everyone who attended, start interviewing them."

Between the fifteenth and twenty-fourth of June, the police traced and interviewed all thirty-eight men who had attended the school reunion, which had been held in a pub near Tottenham Court Road station. The last of the men they spoke to lived in a maisonette in Hackney. For the week before, DCI Hobart's team had been covertly watching this individual, as his was the telephone number written on the bottom of the card.

It was early Friday evening when two detectives rang the doorbell. A tall, serious-looking man with glasses answered the door, his greying hair rising away from his forehead.

"Can I help you at all, gentlemen?"

"Good evening, sir. Would you be Rod Bannister by any chance?"

"Yes, that's me. How can I help?"

"I'm DC Crossley, and this is DC Harris. We are carrying out an investigation into the death of James Liddell. You may have read about it in the newspaper."

"Of course, it's very shocking."

"Could we come in for a few minutes? We have some questions."

Mr Bannister led them upstairs to his living room.

"Does this mean that I'm a suspect?" he asked.

The two detectives looked at each other. "What it is, sir," DC Crossley said, "is that we're just carrying out routine enquiries. We're trying to trace the men who attended a school reunion. Mr Liddell was also there."

The two men then gently probed Mr Bannister about his memories of attending that event. They'd been given strict instructions not to mention the card that was later sent to Liddell.

"It wasn't a very memorable evening I'm afraid, chaps. I'm not a fan of reunions. I won't be attending the next one."

"Did you speak with James Liddell that evening?"

"I did have a brief conversation with him, but for the life of me I can't remember the details. I was pretty far gone by that point."

"So you don't remember anything significant about Mr Liddell that night?" DC Harris asked.

"Not really. Sorry not to be more helpful."

"Nothing that struck you as slightly odd, or different in some way? A conversation he had with somebody, or something about his manner?"

"Nothing at all, I'm afraid."

"And what was your relationship like with him at school?"

"Oh my gosh, we're going back over thirty years here. It was fine, I think, but I don't remember having much to do with him."

Later on, Ruth Hobart quizzed the two detectives about the conversation. She was particularly interested in whether he'd dropped any hints about having got in touch with Mr Liddell after the reunion, but they assured her there'd been nothing at all. But then they agreed, why would he mention anything, when as far as he was concerned, they didn't know about the card he'd sent to Liddell?

On the twenty-seventh of June, following a tip-off from a local farmer that he'd noticed some suspicious activity and disturbance of the land, police began digging in a field in Derbyshire. Two days later, DCI Hobart took an urgent call. A headless torso buried some seven feet below the surface had just been found. She thought about driving straight up to Derbyshire herself to see the location but decided she couldn't spare the time. She would have to make do with photographs for the time being.

Chapter Twenty

Michaela was amongst a throng of journalists assembled to witness Fred and Rose West's joint appearance at Gloucester Magistrates Court. The couple were to be told that they were being jointly charged with nine murders – all of the women found buried at Cromwell Street since the police had successfully applied for a search warrant there. In addition, Fred was being charged with the murder of his first wife, Rena, and Rena's daughter Charmaine.

Michaela watched as Fred was led into Court Number Two. He squinted curiously at the eighty or so people packed inside – his mouth hanging open slightly, as if he was wondering how a simple lad from Much Marcle could possibly have attracted so much attention from the wider world.

Soon afterwards, Rose was led into the courtroom and both she and Fred had to share the tiny space in the dock together. The couple had not seen each other since February. It was hardly a joyous reunion and obvious where the power in the relationship now lay. Michaela explained as much to Daniel when she called him from her room in the hotel where she'd been staying for the previous three nights.

"It was very weird because he twice reached out to her. The first time she visibly flinched, and the second time one of the court officers pulled his arm away."

Daniel's analysis was instantaneous. "She'll have been advised to keep her distance, possibly to appear hostile. It'll be her best chance of getting off right now."

"I suppose," Michaela said. "I almost felt sorry for him. He looked bereft."

"You felt sorry for Fred West?" He sounded so surprised that she couldn't help laughing.

"I did say 'almost'. And it quickly passed." There was a loud noise at the other end of the phone. "What's going on?"

"Just having some peanuts."

"It sounds like soldiers marching on gravel." She was pleased to hear him laughing at her image.

"Sorry, I haven't eaten. My telephone's in the hallway but I can stretch the cable into the kitchen. Luckily there was a packet just within reach."

"Why haven't you eaten?" She suddenly felt concerned.

"No real reason. I just haven't."

"But you're in the middle of a trial. You need to keep your strength up."

"I don't always get around to it. How's your hotel?"

She looked at her room. She'd emptied her entire case onto the bed that morning in a mad rush to find something, and underwear and other items had spilled onto the floor. The cleaner, if there was one, had given her room a wide berth, it seemed to be exactly as she'd left it.

"It's okay. I'd rather you were here with me." She paused. "Police think there could be another thirty or so bodies buried round here."

"Not in your hotel, surely."

"I'm serious. Thirty bodies in the Gloucester area."

"Some of these press stories might be a little over-hyped."

"Daniel, this is based on what Fred is telling the police. I'm here and I'm interviewing these people, so please don't doubt what I'm telling you."

"Sorry, I wasn't meaning to doubt you."

"He's helping them with the search for bodies. Up to a point. If he doesn't tell them exactly where to look, they're completely stuck."

"Yes, I can see that. And you feel sorry for him?"

"You really are a typical barrister, aren't you? I make one little slip and you won't let it go."

"I was joking!"

"Yes, me too, Daniel."

There was a moment's silence. She hadn't spoken to him for about five nights. And it was so easy for these little miscommunications to happen over the phone.

"The point I think I was making is that it's not easy being separated from your partner," she said.

"Are you talking about Fred West right now, or you?"

After a pause, she said, "I was talking about him actually. But it applies to me too."

"I'm really missing you too! And I worry about you sometimes."

"That's so weird. Because I've been having these terrible thoughts that you'll be attacked by a mad client or stabbed in the courtroom."

"That sort of thing only happens in America."

"Stay safe, Daniel – promise me."

"I will. And you. When are you coming back by the way?"

"Hopefully tomorrow."

"We'll do something nice together, yes?"

"You bet."

They said their goodbyes and she cleared a space on her bed so she could sit down. She thought about turning on the television but couldn't bear to see anything more about the House of Horrors case.

Chapter Twenty-One

"And they're still searching his flat?"

"Yes, that's ongoing, ma'am."

DCI Hobart and DC Crossley were in the incident room, in front of the photos: several of Liddell; a close-up of him on a boat; shots of his workplace; mugshots of Nikos, Rod too; a panel dedicated to the severed head and the post-mortem.

"And when you interviewed him this morning, it was a simple no comment?" Ruth continued.

"Well, he had his solicitor."

"Uh-huh."

"So yes, it was no comment all the way."

"And he was quite chatty when you visited his flat."

"Reasonably, yes." DC Crossley smiled. "Although there's something distant about him. You'll see."

Just behind them a conversation was getting louder by the minute.

"You were actually looking in homeless shelters? You kept that pretty quiet." DC Harris was now talking at the top of his voice.

A small group had gathered around him.

"Fucking brilliant," DC Harris said. "I bet you are, girl, have a good one." He put the phone down.

Ruth looked at him expectantly.

"That was DC Barker on the phone, ma'am. She just found Jackie Levine in a homeless shelter."

Ruth formed an O shape with her lips and loudly blew air. "She did?"

"Yes, and Levine is confident she can identify the man from Tower Bridge."

Ruth clenched both fists in triumph.

"We're making headway, ma'am," DC Crossley said, close to Ruth's ear.

"There was one thing though," DC Harris said. "Levine asked whether it was likely she'd be murdered herself."

"I don't understand," Ruth said.

"You know, ma'am, if she picked him out in a line-up."

"I see," Ruth said. "Well, I'll reassure her. And I want that line-up happening this week. I don't care how long it normally takes. We can't have her disappearing again."

Chapter Twenty-Two

WEDNESDAY 6 JULY 1994

R uth Hobart and Luke Crossley sat side by side in a soundproof room with a large glass screen directly in front of them. They watched as the men assembled. Mostly middle-aged, casually dressed on the whole, two or three wearing a shirt and tie. Several were police officers, while others had been plucked from the street and paid to attend. Some appeared nervous, but mostly they were disengaged, keen to get on with the rest of the day. Ruth looked around but couldn't immediately see their suspect.

The men were told to form a single line. And there he was. Rod Bannister. Tall, extremely tall – six feet four in fact – serious, confident apparently, in his dark-framed glasses. He moved unhurriedly, his expression and body language were a puzzle to her. He took his place on the right-hand side, briefly inspected his fingernails, then brushed a fleck of something from his navy cotton jacket. Who could have known that this man might be the perpetrator of a crime that had galvanised the capital for months? He might have been a university lecturer, or the father of a schoolgirl the others all thought was dishy. His face was a perfect blank canvas.

The men were now in a line several yards from the screen, their hands behind their backs. An officer placed a blue number in front of each. They were waiting for Jackie Levine. Ruth had taken no chances, sending a car to collect her from the hostel. But she'd requested hot chocolate on her arrival at the station and was refusing to budge until she'd finished it. It seemed she was an awkward bugger.

Finally, Jackie appeared. She was escorted into the room by DC Barker. Jackie was wearing a green parka with fake white fur around the hood. Clearly dressed up for the occasion, she must have been boiling.

Jackie stood in front of the ten men, looking carefully at each. DC Barker now instructed them to take three paces forward when their number was called, turn to either side, then pick up a bag from the floor as if they were about to toss it. She placed a carrier bag containing a jacket from lost property centrally in front of the men.

One by one, the men followed the instructions. A man with thinning hair grinned as he picked it up. Another in black jeans actually threw the bag and it thumped into the screen, much to the amusement of the others. Barbara watched as Rod, eighth in the line, stepped forward. Turning to his left, then to his right, he picked up the bag and motioned to throw it, exactly as instructed. The final two men followed suit.

After they'd finished, the men stood waiting. But Jackie Levine barely hesitated before pointing her finger emphatically. "Number eight," she said. "It's number eight."

Chapter Twenty-Three

Jenny Montague was shopping for ingredients for a special meal for her husband when she ran into Rod. They worked in the same housing benefits team, but Jenny had recently been promoted to team leader. She worried that the new power dynamic might be having a negative impact on their friendship. Rod had been more reserved with her these last few weeks.

He was coming out of The Old Red Lion when she saw him. In itself this was slightly odd so early in the evening, and she watched him for a moment, looking this way and that as if unsure what to do next. She remembered how, soon after they'd met in 1989, she persuaded herself that she might be falling in love with this handsome new team member. She'd even fantasised about having an affair with him, telling herself that she wouldn't hold back if the opportunity arose. This was long before he let on to his colleagues that he was gay, much to her surprise. His arrival in their team coincided with one of those sociable periods when practically every night a core group would go out after work.

"It's a bad habit, you know, hanging outside pubs at this time," she said, approaching him with her bags.

He blinked a few times, pulling his scarf tighter around his neck, keeping out the cold, or her, she wasn't sure which.

"Having a good weekend?" she asked.

He shrugged. "Okay."

He certainly wasn't his normal self. He was morose. Edgy. She tried changing the subject. "So what are you up to tonight?" He looked down at her with an almost haunted look on his face. "I'm thinking you've got a date lined up. Who's the lucky man?"

"Come on, Jenny. I'm not in the mood. I might see a film if you must know."

"All right for some. I'm cooking for Joshua. It's his birthday."

Rod nodded.

"What's on at the Screen on the Green?" she asked.

"I've no idea," he said.

"If it's *The Fugitive*, you have to see it, honestly. It's about a guy who's sent to prison for killing his wife, but he didn't do it. So he escapes and then has to clear his name."

"People keep making the same mistakes," Rod said. "Have you noticed that, all through their lives they do it?"

She wasn't sure if he was responding to what she'd just said, but he was already walking away in the direction of the cinema. She couldn't remember him ever being in such a strange mood.

Chapter Twenty-Four

Sally and Stuart were attending a wedding in Holland, and the children were staying with Daniel for a few days. He'd taken time off work and that day they went to Highbury Fields for a game of rounders and a picnic. The rounders had not been a success. As Imogen pointed out, it was almost impossible to play with only four people.

"Is that what you used to do with your father?" she asked, after they'd all sat on the blanket and Daniel had handed round the egg and cress sandwiches and the plastic cups of orange squash. "Playing rounders in the park with your sisters."

"When we lived in Hertfordshire?" Daniel asked.

"I don't know where you lived, Dad," Imogen said. "I was just trying to make conversation."

"I don't have that many memories of him from when I was your age," Daniel admitted. "I remember being introduced to one or two of his colleagues in the sound department."

"The sound department?" Audrey said. "What's a sound department?"

"He worked in Elstree Studios, making sound effects for the films, like rain pattering on a window, or explosions, that kind of thing."

"Explosions!" Max said. "Your daddy made explosions."

"He wasn't a terrorist," Daniel laughed. "He might have created the sound, if they needed it."

"That's so much more interesting than what you do," Imogen said.

He'd talked to Michaela about this. Stay strong she'd told him. Sometimes it has to get worse before it gets better.

"I agree," Daniel replied. "When we had this school trip to the studios, my friends were so impressed. They couldn't believe he'd worked on *The Avengers* and *Lolita*. That was quite soon before my father left home."

"What happened, Daddy?" Audrey asked.

"Well, one morning, myself and Auntie Carol and Auntie Chloe heard tense voices. We thought it was just an argument, so we went downstairs and made ourselves breakfast. And because we didn't want to interrupt them, we all left the house together. To go to our different schools. When I got home later, I found both your aunties watching television, but the kitchen was just as we'd left it. A mess, basically."

"You didn't clear your own things up?" Audrey asked.

"Obviously not," Imogen said.

"No, I'm afraid we didn't. And I found my mother – who was normally so cheerful – in her bed. She hadn't been to her work. She hadn't stepped out of her room."

"Did she have tummy ache?" Max asked.

"Good guess, but no. I had to piece together what had happened, because she wasn't talking very clearly. My father had left home. He'd fallen in love with a woman from his work. 'But don't worry', my mother said, 'you'll see him very soon'. She repeated this phrase often, and the more she said it the more I doubted it would happen."

"That's terrible, Daddy," Audrey said.

"After three months, we were told by his work that the other woman was from Melbourne and that neither she nor my father had been seen for eight weeks."

"Did you ever hear from him again?" Imogen asked.

"Not until I was eighteen, when I received a birthday card with an Australian stamp. It was full of apologies from him for not being around during my childhood. But there was no address on it."

"That's sad, Daddy," Audrey said.

Even Imogen looked sympathetic.

"Did you bring crisps?" Max asked.

Daniel withdrew a catering-sized packet of Chipsticks from his bag and opened it. Everybody helped themselves.

"I wonder if Mummy and Stuart are having fun in Holland," Daniel said.

"Do you have a girlfriend?" Imogen asked.

"I have met somebody, actually. She's away at the moment, but I promise you I'll introduce you."

"Cool," Max said.

"What's she called?" Imogen asked.

"Michaela. She's a journalist."

"I love that name," Audrey said. "How old is she?"

"She's ten years younger than me."

"Ten years! That's ridiculous," Imogen said.

"It doesn't matter so much when you get to my age."

"Have you got any photos of her?"

"Not on me."

"Are you going to get married?" Max asked.

"Well, we might do. I haven't really thought about it to be honest. I've been rather busy recently."

"Busy being a barrister?" Audrey said.

"Yes, that's right. Now come on, guys. Eat up. I thought we might go to the cinema this afternoon."

Chapter Twenty-Five

Daniel didn't recall receiving too much in the way of guidance from his father. The one piece of advice that stuck in his mind was on the unlikely subject of bath water. "Every so often," his father once said, "stay in the bath after you've pulled out the plug. And just lie there as the water disappears. You won't find a better reminder of how quickly time is running away from you. You can feel it happening – literally."

Occasionally, like this Saturday morning, Daniel still performed the ritual. Lying naked and feeling increasingly cold, he wondered if it was his way of retaining a link with the father he hadn't seen since he was ten years old. Eventually, he rose from the bath with goose bumps on his legs and arms, his body hairs standing like a copse of distant trees.

He began drying himself roughly with a towel. He hoped he'd been a better father than his father had been to him. At the end of the day, he and Sally just hadn't been compatible. But with Michaela everything felt right. It was true that he'd known her only a matter of months, but what was the point in stringing things out, delaying the inevitable?

Daniel had never eaten in Thai Pepper before, but both Paul Summerfield and Chris Carter had sung its praises. Chris said that not only was the food excellent, you could actually have a conversation as they didn't play music.

It had rained earlier that day, but now it was clear and fresh. They met outside Swiss Cottage Tube, Daniel feeling the small box in his pocket as they kissed firmly on the lips. Michaela immediately reprimanded him for making her miss the national lottery show.

"Oh, that," Daniel said. "I didn't realise it had even started."

"For fuck's sake, Daniel, you've got to move with the times. I mean, it could have been you!"

"It very definitely would not have been me."

"Well, I'm going to win five million pounds. But now I have to wait until tomorrow to find out."

"I should probably advise you that you're more likely to be Fred West's next wife than win the national lottery."

"Either would be lovely, I'm sure."

The restaurant was a minute's walk from the Tube. As they were shown to their table, Daniel wondered how long he should wait before making his proposal. But the question became academic, at least for the time being, as someone was gesticulating from the table next to the one where they were being seated. Such was the confusion of the moment that it took several seconds for Daniel to recognise his sister's boyfriend, Howard, and then opposite him Chloe herself.

Chloe got up to kiss him, and motioned towards another couple, who also rose from their seats. "This is Dennis and Monica. We went to Croatia with them last summer."

Daniel found himself smiling inanely, remarking what a coincidence it was, and shaking hands with two people he had little interest in meeting.

Seeing the familiarity with which the new arrivals had been greeted, the waiters offered to join the two tables together. It wasn't even an option to protest, so Daniel and Michaela took their seats and were plunged into a detailed conversation about the menu.

"The chicken in green curry is excellent. I don't know how they cook it, but it tastes incredible," Howard said.

"And I'm really enjoying the beef with Thai basil," Monica added.

"I'm actually finding the beef a little tough," Dennis said.

"And make sure you order the tom yum soup for a starter," Howard said.

"It's all great basically." Chloe had probably identified a lack of interest from Daniel.

"Yes, except the portions are on the small side," Dennis persisted.

"God yes," Howard said. "This dish is never going to fill my enormous stomach."

Daniel caught Michaela's eye and tried to convey a subtle apology. A look which said, *They're trying to be welcoming, but I realise this is a disaster.*

Michaela seemed less put out than he was. He heard her honking with laughter at some unfunny joke Howard made, then she asked about their holiday in Croatia. Daniel paid only partial attention to the overlapping responses. They'd been on a day trip to Trieste via Slovenia – where they'd been in some amazing caves – and had been given a parking ticket in Italy, which they had no intention of paying as they were in a Croatian rental car, because surely the authorities would never catch up with them.

Daniel's plan to propose was now in tatters, unless of course he waited for his sister and friends to leave. They were nearing the end of their main course, so if he and Michaela ordered starters, he should have plenty of time after they'd gone. He deliberately dithered over his choices, sending the waiter away twice with the excuse he needed more time. The second time, Michaela whispered loudly, "I'm starving."

The holiday conversation had moved on to a Croatian nudist beach which all four had visited together.

"It was fine," Monica said. "You soon got over the embarrassment and I didn't notice the men looking too obviously at the other women."

"That's because we weren't looking at the other women," Dennis said tetchily.

"Speak for yourself. I was just incredibly subtle," Howard said.

"I'm not against nudist beaches," Michaela said. "But if Daniel and me were on holiday with another couple, I'd prefer if we went on separate days."

"What, you and Daniel?" Howard laughed.

"No, us and the other couple!"

There was laughter and expressions of relief.

"The best thing about going as two couples, is that the women get to compare the size of their men's bits and bobs," Chloe said.

Howard turned to Daniel and Michaela. "I

explained that mine is altogether different in the resting position." Daniel could never imagine talking so publicly about his penis size. Was that a good thing or was he hopelessly reserved?

"Could we change the subject?" Monica asked. "I'm sure Daniel and Michaela aren't interested in this one."

"Yes, Daniel's a barrister," Howard said. "He operates on a higher plane."

"What sort of barrister?" Dennis asked.

"I do criminal work."

"Let me ask you something. Because I've always wanted to ask a barrister this." Daniel braced himself for the inevitable. "How can you defend a client if you know in your own heart that he's guilty? Isn't that immoral?"

"Well, that's a very interesting question," Daniel said, hating his sister's friends, hating their conversation, and willing this part of the evening to be over.

———

Within minutes of Chloe, Howard, Monica and Dennis leaving the restaurant, Daniel placed the china spoon in his empty bowl with a clatter. He looked Michaela in the eye and said, "And now I have a question for you."

He pulled the box from his jacket pocket and placed it on the table between them. Michaela blinked rapidly, waiting for him to proceed. Daniel had an impression of wariness for what might be coming next, but it was too late to change course now.

"Will you marry me, Michaela Simpson? I feel sure that's what we should be doing. Because I love you. I can go down on one knee if you like."

"Daniel, I had no idea this was coming."

"Nor me until today. But I realised this morning that

it makes sense and I've worked it all out. I know who's doing the catering and everything."

Her look across the table, he thought, combined genuine affection with utter disbelief.

"So who is doing the catering?"

"Veronica something. She did our chambers party in the summer. She was charm itself and served all the drinks and food even though the clerks usually do that. She didn't charge a penny extra and I just thought it was a lovely gesture."

"It's called marketing, Daniel."

"Well you would call it marketing. Whereas I would call it…"

"Promotion?" she suggested.

"Yes, promotion – that's it," he laughed. He thought back to the café in St Albans when he first asked her out, and the question got lost in the tendrils of the resulting conversation. "Aren't you going to have a look at the ring?"

"Of course. But if it's disgusting, I'm definitely not marrying you."

"I respect that."

She opened the box and her eyes welled as she looked at the elegant diamond flanked by two sapphires on a simple silver mount.

"It's beautiful, Daniel. Really stunning."

"The man in the shop said it was distinctive and classy. I told him you were too."

She took it out of the box and slipped it onto her finger. "It fits perfectly."

"I had a look in your jewellery box when you were in the shower once. I took one of your rings, placed it on a piece of paper then drew a circle on the inside and outside. I'd heard a good jeweller can usually figure out the diameter from this."

"You cunning devil." She reached over and took both of his hands in hers.

"Is that a 'yes' then?"

She nodded.

"So let's order a bottle of something special."

Chapter Twenty-Six

The long-awaited introduction of his children to Michaela was happening that weekend, with a sleepover at Daniel's flat. In the event, Sally dropped off only Imogen and Max, pointedly explaining that Audrey had preferred a last-minute invitation to stay with a friend. She didn't feel she could force her to stay with her father.

Apart from that hiccup, everything seemed to be going well. Michaela and Imogen, in particular, were hitting it off, which was precisely what Michaela had told Daniel would not happen. They'd just finished baking a chocolate cake, which was in the oven and already smelling great.

"Next time we'll have a proper baking tray and a few more ingredients," Michaela laughed, looking at Daniel.

"It will be easier," Daniel said. "We'll have a bigger kitchen."

"I'm surprised you haven't bought a house already," Imogen said.

Daniel and Michaela looked at each other.

"It's not quite the right time," Daniel said.

"How do you mean?" Imogen asked.

"Can I lick the inside of the bowl?" Max asked. "Mummy lets me do that."

"Use this spoon," Michaela suggested.

Max began carefully collecting the remnants of the cake mix onto the spoon and licked it. "Delicious!"

"What do you mean, not the right time?" Imogen repeated.

"He means financially," Michaela said.

"Cash flow," Daniel explained.

"Does that mean you haven't got any money?" Imogen asked.

"Not exactly. It's just not the best time for me to buy a house."

"We need to wait before we do that," Michaela said.

"I thought barristers earned a fortune," Imogen said.

"Some do," Daniel laughed. "In fact, quite a few of us get by very nicely."

"What about you though?"

"Imogen, I'm sure you can't expect your daddy to tell you exactly what he earns," Michaela said.

"I suppose not," Imogen conceded.

"It's complicated," Daniel said. "It takes a while for a barrister's earnings to build up after he becomes Queen's Counsel. But it's starting to happen, definitely."

"That was delicious," Max said. "I love chocolate."

"When will the cake be ready?" Imogen asked.

"We'll take it out the oven in twenty minutes," Michaela said. "But we'll have to let it cool down."

"Otherwise you get tummy ache," Max said.

"That's right," Michaela commended him.

"Mummy told me."

Later that evening they played Risk, which Daniel

had bought specially for the occasion. Not even Max seemed to share Daniel's enthusiasm for attacking his neighbours, but they all played to humour him.

"You enjoyed that, didn't you, Dan?" Michaela said. "I think your father is preparing to take over the world."

"That would certainly be nice," Daniel said.

After that, Michaela read Max a story in his room while Daniel watched television with Imogen. During an advert break she told him that she was really looking forward to his wedding with Michaela.

Chapter Twenty-Seven

B ill always thought that it was lovely how the women made such an effort each year for the chambers Christmas party. There were only five female members, but they were joined by at least a dozen wives and girlfriends. And they brought with them more than a splash of colour in their dark maroons, mustard yellows, shimmering turquoises and avocado greens, and a taste of the exotic in their figure-hugging leopard-print dresses or red satin gowns. The men on the other hand – barring the odd velvet jacket – stuck mainly to dark suits.

He placed two bottles of white wine, two red, and half a dozen fresh glasses on the tray. He hadn't seen Daniel yet to tell him the news. Perhaps he'd been delayed. Bill's chat with Stan in the Devereux last night had involved numerous pints and had gone on much later than anticipated. It took Bill longer to recover these days, so to be serving and drinking more alcohol mid-afternoon was not ideal. But it had to be done.

Coming out of the clerks' room and into reception, Bill stopped in front of the low leather sofa where two of his chancery barristers were sitting, their long legs stretched lazily in front of them.

"Of course it's not the first time. *The Sunday Times* reported something very similar – only this summer."

"I don't recall."

"Can I top up your drinks, gentlemen?" Bill asked, looking down at the top of their heads. Neither of the barristers answered his question.

"Yes, it was also two Tory MPs. They accepted cheques for agreeing to table a parliamentary question."

"So why the hoo-ha this time if it happened so recently?"

"Enough is enough, I suppose."

They were both holding their glasses, and Bill didn't feel it appropriate to just lean over them and top them up. He might end up pouring wine over their jackets.

"And now John Major's set up the Nolan Committee."

"The standards in public life thing? I'd say we need it. The other one's admitted taking the money, but Neil Hamilton's not going to do that, is he? Have you met him?"

"Any more wine, chaps?" Bill tried again.

"Wasn't Hamilton a barrister?"

"Yes, tax law. I ran into him recently and he told me he'd never go back to our 'constipated profession'."

"Charming. It looks like he might have to though."

"Exactly!" They both laughed loudly.

Bill gave up and turned towards the other door.

"I think we're okay, Bill."

"Yes, no more wine right now."

"Very good, gentlemen." Bill continued into the corridor where he was overtaken by his most senior clerk carrying a tray of beef fillet with beetroot canapés. It was much better having the clerks doing the serving. They could talk shop with the guests, even paving the way for new instructions. And there was no way he was letting that insufferable Veronica near another chambers' party.

He turned into George's room where at least twenty people were standing in separate groups. Immediately to his left was his old friend David Goddard, the senior clerk from another set, chatting with two other clerks. David slapped Bill on the back and the glasses lurched and rattled on his tray.

"Be careful, David!"

"I was just saying, the last time I came to one of your Christmas dos I spent the whole time talking to some poor guy who didn't know anyone. The husband of one of your latest recruits – we're going back a few years now."

"I know what's coming," Bill said.

David nodded, smiling broadly. "Well now he's got a thirty-nine-point lead in the opinion polls and it looks like he's going to be our next prime minister."

"Cherie did her pupillage here and we took her on," Bill explained to the other clerks.

"She was here for donkey's years," David added.

"I lose track," Bill said. "But at least ten."

"And Tony Blair was perfectly pleasant, I must say."

Standing in front of the window looking out onto the square and fountain were two of Bill's junior tenants with a woman he didn't recognise.

"Can I top up your drinks?" They held out their glasses obligingly.

"This is my wife Lindsay," one of the barristers said.

"Nice to meet you, Lindsay. I won't reach out my hand for obvious reasons." This prompted a snigger from the other barrister. "You haven't seen Daniel, have you?" Bill asked.

The men shook their heads.

"I understand he's bringing his fiancée, so make her feel welcome." Bill was pretty sure Michaela was the woman Daniel had mentioned when they spoke about his ex-wife. It looked like that conversation had done the trick and Bill was now curious to meet her. He also wanted to tell Daniel how hard he'd battled on his behalf last night.

In the corner of a room George Carman stood with a group of QCs, some other barristers, a couple of solicitors, and a judge who'd previously been in chambers. George indicated to Bill that he could top up their glasses and Bill went around the circle as they talked. He was pleased to recognise that they were talking about the recent change to the Right to Silence laws that George had explained to him.

"Bill knows all about this," George said. "I bored him to death one afternoon with it."

"It was a Sunday afternoon, to be precise," Bill said, to appreciative laughter. Bill thought he had better things to be doing at weekends but that never stopped George calling.

The party seemed to be going with a bit of a swing, although in the next room, one of his juniors was clearly in the midst of a marital argument, so Bill proceeded directly into the room annexed to that one. This turned out to be an even worse choice as his clinical negligence specialist, who was married with teenage daughters, had his arms locked around somebody who looked a lot like their new client care and marketing officer – he was stroking her posterior through her skirt quite vigorously with both hands. Bill quickly retreated from this room too, and keeping his eyes fixed in front of him walked past the arguing couple and back into the corridor.

In the corner room, a group of female tenants were deep in discussion.

"Any views on what's happening in the conveyancing market?" one of the women asked him.

"Not that I can express publicly," Bill said, refilling the last of their glasses.

He started retracing his steps and stopped off in George's room once again. He was about to top up more glasses when he saw Daniel standing with a woman on the opposite side of the room. She had her hair piled on top of her head, Audrey Hepburn-style, and was wearing a blue cocktail dress with full-length sleeves. The word "showstopper" came instantly to his mind, and as he made his way towards them, he saw sequins and beads sparkling on the dress.

"Bill – can I introduce you to my fiancée Michaela?"

She smiled disarmingly and held out her hand for Bill to shake.

"Hello, Michaela. I'm pleased to meet you after all this time."

"Me too. Daniel told me that you're the most trusted man in the building. He said the place would fall apart without you."

"I don't know about that," Bill said.

"And I understand you keep Daniel on the straight and narrow, so I feel indebted to you about that."

"Not just Daniel, actually," Bill laughed nervously. "All of the barristers. And when will the happy day be?"

"Well, Daniel was all for marrying immediately. But I managed to delay him until May."

"A stay of execution," Bill joked.

"Something like that." She giggled.

"You know me, Bill. Patience was never my forte," Daniel said.

"Daniel, would you mind if we go into another room for a moment?" Bill said. "I'm sorry about this," he added to Michaela. "But it's rather important."

"Oh God, what have I done now?" Daniel asked. "I won't be a minute, darling."

"It's fine, honestly. Take your time."

They went through to reception for some privacy and Bill put his tray down on the desk.

"What is it that couldn't wait till Monday?" Daniel asked, slightly tetchily.

"I think you'll be interested in this," Bill said. "I was at the Devereux with Stan Lever last night. He was looking for a silk for the floating-head trial which is listed for April in the Bailey."

"Don't tell me, he wanted George."

"Of course he wanted George. That's why he was buying me drinks all evening. But George can't possibly do it, and I got him to take a chance on my most talented young silk instead."

"You did?"

"The case is yours! I stuck my neck out for you, Daniel. Stan's a difficult sod at the best of times. 'He'd better be bloody good'!" He imitated the solicitor's booming voice.

Daniel laughed. "Who's the junior?"

"I've no idea. Not one of ours."

"This is brilliant news, Bill. Thank you so much."

"Think of it as an early wedding present. Careers can be made or broken with cases such as this, Daniel."

"I won't let you down."

The two men went to shake hands but ended up

giving each other a hug instead. Bill clapped Daniel on the back as they did so.

"Thanks again, Bill."

Bill watched Daniel through the open door as he returned to Michaela in the other room. He whispered into her ear and she nodded, smiling that incredible smile at him. Then she leaned over and kissed him on the cheek. He was a lucky man in more ways than one.

Chapter Twenty-Eight

Daniel was all for walking the half mile from Acton station, but Stan said he was buggered if he was doing that, so they took a taxi. He was a tall stooping beast of a man who constantly fiddled with his pens and papers, or worse still, scratched right inside his nose with his thumb. Daniel could see why he'd become a solicitor. He would have made a terrible advocate as no one in court would have been able to concentrate on a word he was saying.

On arrival at Wormwood Scrubs, they were whisked through security and minutes later were led into a conference room. A tall man with glasses looked up from the small table. He had grey hair and there was something distinguished about him. Daniel might have used the words "gentle-looking", but as they made eye contact, he detected something steely too. Was this the man who had severed the head of James Liddell in a bathtub before walking with it to the nearest bridge over the River Thames from his flat in Hackney?

"Rod – I'd like to introduce Daniel O'Neil, your

QC," Stan shouted, as if he were addressing a deaf person.

Daniel shook his new client's hand, conscious of the piercing gaze that coolly appraised him.

"So, you're the man with all of the answers," Rod said.

Daniel sat opposite him. "Not quite. I'd say I'm the man with all of the questions."

"He comes highly recommended," Stan said, as he took the final seat at the table. "He'll fight fearlessly for your best interests in court, regardless of his own."

Not that he would have dreamt of saying as much to either, but Daniel had some concerns about the standard of Stan's instructions. They seemed to have been prepared in something of a hurry, and the lack of detail made it hard to take a view on Rod's story. But today wasn't the day to get into the nitty-gritty. The first meeting with his client was about creating trust and setting up expectations for their future relationship.

"This isn't the nicest place to have spent your new year, I'm sure," Daniel said to Rod.

"Exactly," Rod agreed. "I'd never been inside a prison before, so it's been something of a shock."

"Well – this one has that reputation," Daniel said. "Wouldn't you say, Stan?"

"Absolutely. That's why our job is to keep our clients out of prison where we possibly can."

Rod raised his hand to his mouth and coughed. "On that subject, I've spent the last few weeks devouring the prison's library books on criminal procedure. I could go on *Mastermind*."

"I'm sure you could," Stan said.

"The odd thing about our adversarial system," Daniel said, "is that it's not really about reaching the truth of what happened. The trial process is all about testing the evidence. And where possible, trying to control the manner in which that evidence emerges. So it's 'The test' and not 'The truth' that's important."

Rod nodded, weighing up what he'd just heard.

"So what we're saying is that the barristers are the lynchpins," Stan added. "If Daniel is better than his opponent, that could make all the difference."

Daniel wasn't sure he'd have said this explicitly to a client at their first conference. He decided to change the subject.

"I noticed that you work in Islington, for the local authority."

"In housing benefits, yes," Rod said. "Don't ask me how. I always wanted to produce films."

Daniel smiled. "The reason I mentioned it is that I live in Islington myself."

"Not in the kind of property I deal with," Rod said.

"You'd be surprised. I'm in one of Clerkenwell's tower blocks."

"Really? Which one?"

"Have you heard of Michael Cliffe House?"

"Of course. It's the borough's equivalent of Wormwood Scrubs. You just made me feel so much better about my temporary accommodation here."

This broke the ice and they all laughed loudly, particularly Stan, who raked his fingers through his hair as he did so, releasing small flecks of dandruff into the air.

"Glad to have been of service," Daniel said, as the laughter died down.

"What on earth made you move in there?" Rod asked.

"I had to buy something after the collapse of my

marriage. My wife couldn't wait to get rid of me, so I didn't have much time."

"Oh dear," Rod laughed.

Stan laughed again too, but at the same time Daniel was aware that his solicitor was giving him a slightly odd look.

Later, travelling back to Central London together, Stan asked why on earth Daniel had disclosed so much personal information. "I mean this is a guy who quite possibly murdered somebody in cold blood."

"I don't imagine he's about to do that to me," Daniel replied.

Chapter Twenty-Nine

B efore leaving chambers, Daniel spoke to Michaela, asking if she wanted chicken drumsticks as he was going to stop off at KFC. She said she'd already eaten. She sounded distant and he wondered if she was annoyed about something. She'd had an intense few days following Fred West's suicide, working pretty much round the clock, so when Daniel returned with his food, his plan was to keep the conversation light. But she joined him in the kitchen and began speaking straight away about a phone call she'd taken the night before.

"It was quite late and completely out of the blue. I was about to call you when he rang. Thomas, an old flame. He's been the victim of a violent crime, just a few days ago. And he was reaching out to me."

Daniel, still in his suit, was stripping a chicken drumstick at the table, following her every word. "We spent almost an hour on the phone," she continued. "By the end of the call I felt wrung out."

"I'm sorry to hear that," Daniel said, wiping his

fingers and face with a paper napkin. "So this is Arizona Thomas, right?"

"Yes. I told you about him, didn't I? – I remember now."

"Yeah, when we first started seeing each other."

"So he was calling from London. And I'm not sure what I should do."

"Do you want a beer by the way? This sounds like quite an involved story."

"Yes, sure."

He took two bottles from the fridge, pouring the first into two glasses, tilting them so the head remained small. He returned to his seat and she sat down with him. They both drank from their beers.

"So, what did he tell you about the actual crime?"

"It was in the family home in Phoenix. On Christmas Day. There were several men and they broke in around midday. Thomas is a lecturer in London now, and was only back in the States for the vacation."

"Okay. So what happened?"

"They were armed. And it was just this horrible, horrible ordeal, which lasted for hours. Obviously, they stole his valuables, but he was tied up and humiliated, and pistol-whipped – I don't even know what that means."

"Poor guy. It sounds awful."

"And they killed the family dog. Not because they had to as they'd shut it in another room. They just found it really funny to shoot the dog in the head."

"That's sick."

"And Thomas suffers from depression. Always did. He had a lot of treatment at one time. This won't have helped."

"For sure," Daniel said. "So is he looking to you for

emotional support?"

"He definitely wants to be in touch again. Particularly as he's living in London."

"And did you mention that you're engaged?"

"Yes, of course. I was very open about that, Dan. And he was pleased for me."

"And just so I'm clear," Daniel had flicked open the second beer and was topping up their glasses, "Arizona Thomas was your partner for how long?"

Michaela rubbed her forehead with her palm in two upward movements. "Just about a year. A little less actually. While he was doing his masters. It was fairly intense."

"And what was he like? Were you two good as a couple?"

"Pretty much, I'd say. But he was always going to return to America to be an academic."

"Did you ever visit him in the States?"

"We talked about it, but we lost touch."

"I see. But the fact is," Daniel said, "it's been a very long time. And you have to do what's right for everyone."

"It would be right to help him, wouldn't it? This was a terrible experience. He said – and this was something I didn't want to believe – that they stuck a gun up his butt. His word. They rammed it up. A loaded gun. I mean, why do people do these things, Dan?"

Daniel shook his head. "Fucking psychopaths."

"This is gut-wrenching for me," Michaela said. "It's churning me up inside. It's bad enough reporting on this kind of stuff without it coming right into your own life."

"I know, honey. I understand."

"But I did tell him about us. I said you were a criminal barrister. I said you were once the runner-up in the pro bono lawyer of the year award."

"I bet he was really interested in that."

Michaela laughed suddenly, a laugh so sharp and hard that she could barely breathe. Daniel was laughing too, nodding as his eyes filled with tears.

"But you know, there is a right thing to do and a wrong thing," he said. "We just have to work that out."

She agreed. It wasn't just about Thomas. They had their challenges too. "My sister is barely over cancer," she said.

"Exactly," Daniel said. "We mustn't underestimate the importance of our staying strong for her."

"Yes, and we have our own wedding to arrange which will be no small feat," Michaela continued, "and you have this massive case coming up."

"My work is no more of a priority than yours," Daniel said. "Although, you're right, this trial will be a monster. But thank God for that I say, because I need it right now."

"Life is a constant struggle for me, if I'm honest, Dan. I know you're more robust."

He assured her that this wasn't the case. She sat ruffling her hair as she considered what to say next.

"I just don't want everything we've built so painstakingly to be put at risk," she finally said. "People with these sorts of problems can become unpredictable themselves, can't they, Dan?"

"There are a lot of unknowns."

"But then again, we have obligations towards each other, as people. Don't we? I mean he's reaching out to me, so I should help him."

Daniel narrowed his eyes slightly. "An obligation as an old friend? Or as a former partner?"

"As a former partner, that's what I meant."

"Okay, I get you. And this is where it gets interesting,

really interesting." Daniel closed his eyes for a second, the way he did before saying something brilliant. "I'm going to try something out here. I'm going to say the words as they come into my head, so bear with me. Now, as a barrister, we have what we call the lawyer-client relationship. And that means I have a duty to promote the best interests of my client. In other words, I have to do whatever I can to help them achieve the best outcome in their case. I have to move man and mountain, providing it's in my client's interests and I'm not breaking some other important rule."

"I'm not sure that being a lawyer and an ex-lover are comparable."

"I don't know, I really don't. Indulge me for a minute. The professional relationship with a client involves total trust. My client has to feel that they can tell me everything. And as long as that professional relationship continues, I must put their interests first, even above my own. And I obviously can't break their confidences."

"Where are you going with this, Dan?"

"I'm just thinking this through, that's all. Because, professional ethics is a system with right and wrong at its heart. And what better parallel could you have? A person's obligations to their partner and a lawyer's to his client! Never passing on secrets, always putting their interests above your own, never being swayed from that purpose, whatever they tell you. But all of this stops when the lawyer-client relationship finishes. That's the key thing. Apart from a duty of confidentiality, everything finishes at that point."

"So, by that token, I don't need to do anything for Thomas? That's what you're saying, isn't it?"

"I don't know what I'm saying. I'm just tossing ideas

around. But what I do know is, as things stand, that special relationship you had with Thomas is over. Many years over. You have no relationship with him now."

"I kind of know what you're saying with your lawyer-client analysis. It just seems so… clinical."

"I know." He smiled. "And it's almost certainly not appropriate. It's just my training, I guess."

"No, it's useful. I need time to mull it over."

"Sure. How did he get your telephone number by the way? Cos you haven't been in Tufnell Park that long, have you?"

"I asked him that. He called my parents and they gave it to him."

"Aha. Your parents. And you haven't given him anything personal, have you? Like your Tufnell Park address? Or my address?"

"No, of course not. Nothing like that, Dan."

"So he just has your telephone number?"

"I think so, yes."

Daniel looked at his watch. "I guess we should be turning in soon, it's getting late."

"I agree," Michaela said, standing. "And we can talk about this again tomorrow, can't we?"

"Absolutely."

"You know what it is?" she said. "Part of me is just pissed off with him that he's called me up and dumped everything at my door. Like I really needed those details about the attack before I went to bed last night. I barely slept."

"It's pretty selfish when you think about it," Daniel agreed.

"Exactly," Michaela said, putting their glasses in the sink. "I feel bad for saying it, but you're right. I haven't seen him for years, he didn't contact me when he moved back to London, and only now does he ring me up with all of this… this stuff."

"And we're busy people. Neither you nor I needed this right now."

"Exactly," she said again.

"Did you tell him about your job with the Mirror Group? I mean, could he find out your work address? If he wanted to?"

"Yes, but it's not as if he's a criminal, Dan."

"No. But he is traumatised. Which could make him potentially unstable."

"That's true. He could blow everything to pieces, couldn't he? We don't even know what he wants, for Christ's sake. I'm going to tell him to leave us alone. I did the wrong thing by speaking to him for so long, didn't I?"

"Not at all." He held her in his arms in front of the kitchen sink. "You were in a difficult position."

"We left it that I'd call him after a couple of days, to see how he's doing. We didn't make any firm arrangements. But I said I'd call him."

"Maybe you just need to have a quick conversation, telling him how sorry you were to hear his news. You can say I was sorry too, because that much is true. But you need to tell him you're not in a position to help."

"You're right," Michaela said. "That's what I'll do."

"And you could change your number in the Tufnell Park flat. While you're still there. As a precaution."

"Maybe," she said. "It seems a bit over the top." And then, with a smile, "And aren't you conflicted from giving me advice? You're not independent, I mean. You have an interest in the outcome of what happens too, don't you?"

"Touché," Daniel laughed and switched off the kitchen light.

Chapter Thirty

FRIDAY 3 MARCH 1995

They'd been invited for a meal at Michaela's parents, Bob and Briony. Daniel drove down to Biggleswade early evening, with Michaela and Anika chatting in the back of the car. Daniel complained that this made him feel like a taxi driver. It seemed strange to him that Anika would have been included in the evening's arrangements. He'd only met her once before and, on that occasion, he felt as if she was judging him the whole time. When he'd asked Michaela about Anika coming along to Biggleswade, she'd explained that they'd all known her so long, she was practically one of the family.

The house where the Simpsons lived was hidden away, accessed via a long private shingled driveway. It wasn't where she'd grown up, Michaela had told Daniel when he first met her parents back in September. They had bought the place a few years ago, so Michaela and her siblings would be able to visit with their children and stay in the annex. Not that any of them actually had children yet, she had laughed.

"I'm starving," Daniel said, as he retrieved their small case from the boot.

"Me too," Anika said.

They rang the doorbell and Bob and Briony answered together, smiling as they welcomed them inside. Briony was very homely with her long grey hair and bright-green blouse. Bob stood in a cardigan with his arm around his wife as he told Daniel how nice it was to see him again. Behind them was Rose, still gaunt after her illness. Bob explained that Michaela's brother and his wife were not able to join them.

Dinner was a stodgy but still appetising affair, roast beef and Yorkshire puddings, with potatoes, sprouts, carrots and peas. As with their previous visits, Michaela's family were keen to hear all about Daniel's life as a criminal barrister.

"I know it's a terrible thing to say, but we were rather excited to hear that you've landed that case – you know, the floating head thing," Briony said.

Michaela said that it was okay to be excited about it, they both were too.

"The floating head thing!" Rose said, as though her mother might have chosen her words more carefully.

"Isn't that what they're calling it in the papers?" Briony said. "It's difficult to know how else to describe it."

"Have you met your client?" Rose asked.

"I have, but I'm not really able to discuss it," Daniel said. "I hope that doesn't sound too awful."

"Of course not," Bob said. "We wouldn't expect you to."

"It's frustrating," Michaela said, "because he won't say anything to me either. You'd think I'd be entitled to one or two titbits of information."

"You're entitled to nothing of the sort," Daniel smiled. And then, attempting to change the subject, "I will say this though, Mrs Simpson. This is absolutely delicious – thank you so much for going to such trouble."

Briony beamed at him. He had judged his remark perfectly.

"I'll tell you who I feel sorry for," Anika said. "That Greek bloke they arrested. I think they questioned him for a couple of days and then, BAM! – you suddenly get all these stories in the papers about his gay lovers in Greece." She turned to look at Michaela.

"They were nothing to do with me," Michaela said.

"Apparently he had to move out of his flat, he had so much abuse," Anika continued.

"Okay," Daniel said, "I do have a view on this. As I understand it, he was initially questioned out of custody, but at some point he was arrested and then released on bail. And that's when the newspapers got hold of the story. Now I'm prepared to accept that arresting Kalogeropoulos was an integral step in the inquiry, but once he was released from bail the police should have made clear to the public that he was innocent."

"Do they normally do that?" Bob asked.

"They don't," Daniel said. "But given the press coverage of his arrest, and the lurid speculation about his sexual proclivities, they should have considered doing so."

"So if you're saying that he's innocent," Anika said, "doesn't that mean you're admitting your client is guilty?"

"I'm doing nothing of the sort, and you won't trick me into talking about him either," he said with a knowing smile. "But yes, in all likelihood,

Kalogeropoulos had nothing to do with the murder. He was in the wrong place at the wrong time."

"And the police should have made that clear," Bob said.

"Yes," Daniel said.

"It would have been the right thing to do," said Briony.

"It would," Bob said, "but that doesn't mean anyone's going to do it. There's all sorts of shenanigans going on that would never have happened in my day."

"Daddy retired from his banking job five years ago," Michaela explained. Daniel thought it was sweet that she still called him this.

"And in that time, it feels like the whole country's gone down the tubes. Whatever happened to Major's Back to Basics campaign? I thought that was rather a good idea."

"I think you'll find it was undermined by a string of sex scandals involving Tory MPs," Anika said.

"All of which have been reported in great detail by Michaela's newspaper," Rose said.

"I don't own *The Sunday Mirror*," Michaela said.

"It looks like Britain can't cope without you in the workforce." Rose smiled at her father.

"Are you still staying the night?" Briony asked Michaela. "It would be lovely if you could."

"Yes, we've brought our things."

"You'll have to excuse me, though. We'll need to make a fairly swift exit in the morning," Daniel said.

"Dan's got a lot on his plate," Michaela said.

"Well let's make sure we all have breakfast together," Briony suggested.

Daniel and Michaela slept in the annex while Anika was given a spare bedroom in the main house. Michaela was all for making love, but Daniel didn't feel comfortable doing so, even though the annex was completely separate.

"It somehow doesn't feel respectful. And in any case, I haven't come prepared."

The following morning they all gathered again for breakfast. A good spread of jams and cheeses had been laid out, along with toast and breakfast cereals, to which everybody helped themselves.

"I wanted to ask," Briony began, as soon as they were all settled, "did your old friend Thomas get in touch, Michaela? He sounded in a bad way when he called."

There was silence as Michaela and Daniel searched each other's faces across the table.

"Yes," Michaela said. "He's been phoning me at work too."

"Even though Michaela's told him there's nothing we can do for him," Daniel said.

"Can't you just give him some support, invite him round for dinner or something?" Briony asked.

"Not really," Michaela said.

"We think he might be unstable," Daniel said.

"It's not your fault, Mum, but you've landed us with a difficult problem. He even turned up once at my work and waited for me. The receptionists didn't know what to do with him."

"I did wonder whether you should have given him the telephone number," Bob said in a low voice to Briony.

Daniel and Michaela exchanged another glance.

"Daniel's too polite to say, but he thinks exactly the same," Michaela said.

"I didn't say that," Daniel said.

"I think you did. You told me that they know we're engaged, and we should both have been consulted. Before the number was handed over."

"The problem is," Daniel said, after an awkward pause, "we don't know what Thomas is capable of. We don't want him knowing where we live, that's for sure."

"Yes, please don't tell him that," Michaela said.

"Oh no, we wouldn't do that," Briony said.

"The point is," Daniel said, "we can always go to the police, if the worst comes to the worst."

"I'm terribly sorry," Briony said. "I thought I was doing the right thing. He just sounded so miserable. And he always seemed perfectly nice when I met him."

———

"I thought you were a bit hard on my mother at breakfast," Michaela said to Daniel in the car soon after they'd left. She and Anika were in the back, Michaela leaning forwards while Anika looked out of the window. "All that stuff about us being able to go to the police – well she hardly needed to hear that."

"Are you actually joking?" Daniel said. "You were the one who gave her a hard time."

"I could see my mother was quite upset, that's all. She's actually rather vulnerable despite that bosom-of-the-family 'Marmee' aura she gives off."

"Anika, you're my witness. Was it Michaela or myself that gave Mrs Simpson a hard time this morning?"

Anika turned her head away from the window. "I've no idea."

"But you were there for the discussion. Who was leading the charge?"

"I'm sorry, Daniel, but I'm not getting involved in

your domestics. Bitter experience at home has taught me not to do that."

"I just think it's pretty rich," Daniel said, looking back at Michaela. "Especially when you broke a confidence and told her what I'd said about us being engaged."

"I'll admit that one," Michaela said. "But you did say it."

"Of course I said it. But it was a private remark to you. It's hardly private anymore."

"I've just seen a slightly different side to you today, that's all," Michaela said. "But that's not necessarily a bad thing. Barristers have to be ruthless, I guess."

Chapter Thirty-One

That morning, Daniel and Michaela had found time to eat breakfast together, something that was already happening less frequently in their relationship. They'd chatted about what each would be doing that day. Daniel mentioned Wormwood Scrubs, his second conference in the floating head trial, explaining that his solicitor, Stan, and his junior barrister in the case, Gillian Palmer, had by now met the client several times. As the QC, he came into the process later, similar to a surgeon meeting the patient in the immediate run-up to an operation. But at the point where he became involved, he became heavily involved.

"I suppose I'm saying it's going to be a busy few months," Daniel concluded. "I'm asking for your indulgence, I guess."

Sitting in the prison meeting room, Daniel pictured Michaela's solemn face when he'd said that; something almost fearful in her expression. She had been quite emotional in the last week, which she put down to her period being delayed. She often talked about her menstrual cycle, dropping it naturally into conversation with all sorts of people; he found this endearing.

The conference had just begun and Daniel, sitting slightly apart from the others, reprimanded himself for allowing his concentration to slip.

"Stan never has pens," Gillian was saying. "He's a solicitor and yet he doesn't seem to own a pen."

"I didn't bring a pen because I knew you were coming," Stan said.

"And I brought several because I knew you wouldn't have any."

To demonstrate that he was alive to the joke, Daniel smiled too. Gillian had been instructed a couple of months before him, and she and Stan knew each other well. Looking at them now, he was slightly jealous of their easy relationship.

"I'm not even trusted to carry my own pens," Rod said, from the other side of the table.

This caused a reflective pause and a nervous cough from Gillian, before Daniel seized the moment to move things forward.

"I wonder whether now would be a good time to go through your instructions?"

"Good idea," Stan boomed, and Rod nodded in a way which confirmed his agreement to the blindingly obvious. Even sitting down, Rod's height made him a dominating presence in the room. But there was more to it than that. Daniel was aware that his client had a presence, a charisma, commanding attention without saying much or even anything at all. He only had to rub the back of his neck and it looked impressive. And disconcertingly, Daniel had no idea what Rod thought about having him as his barrister. He was used to being treated with deference by his clients, but to Rod he was clearly just another person in the room.

"So a quick reminder," Daniel continued, "these instructions were taken by Stan back in September. I understand you're happy with them, Rod."

Rod nodded again. Daniel was studying the first couple of pages of his file, although he was completely familiar with the contents.

"So, you went no comment at the police station on July the fourth, when you were first arrested, and the same again on the seventh of July. And you also made no comment in your defence statement."

"That's right," Rod said.

"And your attendance at the school reunion on the twenty-third of November 1993 isn't something you're contesting. Nor is the fact that you sent Liddell a handwritten card which he received on the thirtieth."

"That's right," Rod said again.

"And what was the reason for sending that card?"

Rod looked at the others, then at Daniel, and then smiled, as if the question was beyond idiotic. "What do you think it was?"

There was the squeaking of a chair from his left – Gillian's probably – but Daniel remained calm. "No, I'm asking you. Because I'm keen to hear things in your own words."

"I sent him the card because I wanted to fuck him," Rod said.

"Okay. And was this something that you'd desired for some time?"

"No, it was recent. I hadn't seen James for ages. It was good to see him at the reunion."

"Okay, thanks. And this may be obvious too, but you

said in the note, 'You're such a cunt'. Could you explain what you meant by that?"

"We used to say that to each other at school. It was a term of endearment if you like."

"And we have all the documents disclosed to us by the prosecution, some of which contain descriptions of what happened between you and James Liddell at that reunion. We can come on to those later. For the moment, let's continue with your instructions."

"Sure," Rod said. Both Stan and Gillian nodded too.

"Can we move to the fourth of December? The last day Liddell was seen alive, and generally assumed to be the day that he died. You spoke to the lady who lived in the flat below yours that afternoon, it says here about four o'clock?"

Rod nodded.

"And sometime between seven and seven forty-five you had a conversation with a colleague from your work. That was on Upper Street."

"Jenny," Rod said.

"Yes, Jenny."

"Could I ask what happened between your speaking to your neighbour and meeting Jenny?" Gillian asked. She was a precise-looking woman about Daniel's age, and her fountain pen hovered over her notebook as she waited. There was a pause. "I understand that we can't recall everything that happens to us," she continued. "And that you may not remember that particular afternoon well."

"I can't," Rod said.

"You can't what – sorry?" Gillian looked slightly perplexed.

"I can't remember what happened," Rod said, as if it were the least important thing in the world to him.

"What I'm really interested in," Daniel said, turning back to his papers, "is how the evening unfolded after you met Liddell at Islington Green. The instructions aren't very detailed from here," he resisted the temptation to glance at Stan, "but I can see you met Liddell around eight thirty. And that you arrived at your flat half an hour later. How did you travel back there?"

"We caught a bus. James liked travelling on buses, which surprised me. He was a bit of a wanker to be honest."

"So to speak," Stan added.

"And you started drinking when you got back?" Daniel continued.

"For a while. But I wasn't feeling well. I started getting my flashing lights."

"Ah, a migraine," Stan said. "My wife suffers from those too."

Daniel and Gillian both turned to look at Stan, who shrugged, acknowledging that his intervention was perhaps not the most relevant.

Daniel looked at the file closely. "So these instructions don't talk about flashing lights. Did you mention this when you spoke to Stan?"

"I'm sure I would have done, as it turned into a full-blown migraine. That's why James ended up leaving early."

"And it says here that he left by bus."

"Yes, I walked him to the bus stop. He said he'd be heading to a pub or a club in Soho."

Daniel stopped, having noticed the use of those two words together "be heading". Was this a Freudian slip? "And nothing physical happened between you at all?" he said, after a pause.

"No, nothing at all."

"All right, I'm sorry to home in on this point, but it's the elephant in the room, isn't it? If you bring somebody back to your flat and – I'm sure we've all had experience of this – if there is already an expectation of sexual activity, we would expect some mention to be made of that, wouldn't we? From the card you sent him, he was anticipating being tied up and – in your words – having his cock sucked, wasn't he?"

Rod suddenly laughed, and quite loudly at that. "Yes, you're right! He did expect that, and we talked about it too. He said something along the lines of: 'If I'm not going to get any action here, I'll have to find it in Soho'."

"Okay, so that explains the pub or club you mentioned."

"I got the impression he was pretty disappointed. And I told him I was sorry. We'd do it another time. 'It's not my fault, if I'm getting a migraine, is it?' I said."

Daniel was suddenly encouraged by how things were going. His client was answering his questions, prepared to talk about anything it seemed, and was more relaxed too. He was not being quite so precious.

"Okay, just going back a second, you both had a drink at your home but neither of you were drunk?"

"No. I was as sober as I am now."

"What were you drinking?"

"I had some cans of Budweiser in the fridge. James told me he'd been drinking lager earlier, so that's what he wanted."

"And you had some too, even though you were getting flashing lights?"

"That's why I stopped. They came on suddenly and I knew I had an hour at most before I was incapacitated."

"Ah, I see. So you told him he'd have to leave."

"That's right. But he wasn't the kind of guy to stick around nursing a migraine patient in any case."

"I understand that. So he left promptly?"

"Pretty much."

"And what time would that have been?"

"I'd say ten o'clock – perhaps slightly earlier."

"And you've just mentioned walking him to the bus stop."

"On Graham Road, yes."

"Even though you were getting a migraine?"

"I thought the fresh air might do me some good."

"And that was the last time you saw or spoke to him?"

"Yes, the last time."

"Right, I'm going to gloss over the next day when you are off work which I now know is because you had a migraine–"

"Okay…"

"And pick up the story on the seventh of December. So on this day you received a message on your answerphone?"

"Yes, I'd been in work that day, and the machine was blinking when I got back home. I didn't recognise the voice, but he said there was a carrier bag on the north side of Tower Bridge. He described exactly where. And he said I was to go there that night and throw the contents of the bag into the river."

"Did he say what the contents were?"

"No."

"And what about the consequences of not following his instructions?"

"He said if I didn't do exactly as instructed, I would be shot in the temple within two days." Rod pointed two fingers towards the side of his own head. "I took that to mean here rather than in a place of worship," he added, with a perfectly straight face.

"But how did you know this message was really for you? It might have been left on your answerphone accidentally."

"He said my name. He called me Rod at the beginning of the call. And at the end, I believe."

"You believe?"

"I deleted the message. I found it freaky."

"And how would you describe the voice of the person who left the message?"

"Male, as I say. No particular accent, but it wasn't a good recording – there was hiss. I had to listen to the message twice."

"And quite understandably you found the message 'freaky'. And you deleted it."

"Yes. I appreciate now it would have been useful to have kept it."

"And clearly you believed the threat against you to be genuine."

"Wouldn't you have done?"

"I may well have done too, yes."

Rod had taken his glasses off and breathed on both lenses before polishing them with a cloth. "I mean you are on my side here, aren't you, Daniel? It's important for me to know that."

Just when things were going so well, Daniel felt the sands slipping away from beneath his feet. He'd heard of barristers being sacked in their first conference – all because of a misunderstanding, or a petulant client thinking he knew best. Surely this couldn't be happening to him now. How would he tell Michaela? What would he say to Bill?

"Of course," Daniel said. "I'm absolutely on your

side. But I need to understand the precise nature of your instructions. If I can't do that, I won't be able to represent you to the best of my ability. Because that's what I'm intending to do."

Rod nodded, prepared to accept the logic of this explanation. Daniel felt pleased with himself. The danger had hopefully passed but he needed to remain vigilant. He was dealing with a client at least as intelligent as himself. And that fact had to be respected.

"Okay," Rod said. "Where did we get to?"

"We got to the message on the answerphone," Gillian offered.

"Yes," Daniel said. "And your instructions say that you left your home that evening. What time would that have been?"

"Perhaps around ten o'clock."

"Okay. And you walked to the bridge. What made you decide to walk?"

"I always walk around London if I can. Plus the fact I needed some time to think."

"And it took you how long to walk to the bridge?"

"Just over an hour."

"So you would have arrived significantly earlier than the timings given by the prosecution witness. Perhaps an hour and a half earlier."

Rod nodded.

"We can come back to that," Daniel said. "So, Tower Bridge is the closest River Thames bridge to your flat, isn't it?"

"I expect so."

"And when you got to the bridge, did you find the bag straight away?"

"Yes. It was concealed. But the message said exactly where."

"And where was it concealed?"

"As you get to the north tower on the side, there's this bit that juts out, a semicircle. The bag was hidden round there, wedged up against the tower, held in place by a big stone. It was a Sainsbury's bag."

"And did you look in the bag straight away?"

"Of course."

"And, in your own words, what did you find?"

Rod stopped again, and then, shaking his head very slightly, said, "It was just a flowerpot. A terracotta flowerpot, the size of a small football, I'd say."

What Daniel wanted to ask was whether this all struck him as a bit of a coincidence. That he'd been led to a bridge, the closest bridge over the Thames, by an anonymous message on his answerphone. And that there he'd found this flowerpot in a Sainsbury's bag. And when he'd thrown the flowerpot into the river, this was seen by a homeless woman who had then reported seeing a man throwing a severed head into the river. And later, an actual head happened to be discovered in the Thames. And this head coincidentally belonged to the man Rod had invited back to his flat in Hackney for sex two nights before he threw the pot into the Thames. He wanted to ask Rod whether he expected any of his legal team to believe the story, let alone twelve members of a jury.

"I know exactly what you're thinking," Rod said. "But I've been set-up here. Don't you understand that?"

"I'm not sure I do understand," Daniel said. "Set-up, by whom?"

"By the man who killed Liddell. He made that woman say what she saw – he gave her money no doubt. I'm prepared to believe she was on the bridge, and that I didn't see her, but I don't believe she was on the bridge that night by chance. It was all a set-up. She was paid to be there."

"All right, I understand that much," Daniel said. "But how would the person doing the setting up have known to go to you?"

"The person who killed James Liddell must have forced him to set out in detail how he'd spent his entire evening before he went to the club in Soho. Because that must be where he met his murderer. And of course Liddell's evening included going to my flat in Hackney for sex, which then didn't happen. I was actually a very easy person to frame."

"This has been very helpful, Rod, thank you," Daniel said. "I think we should call it a day here though."

Stan looked at his watch. "Okay. Let's schedule another conference in the next couple of days."

The three lawyers immediately looked at their diaries. There was no obvious time slot.

"I'll sort it out with your clerks," Stan said.

"I can probably fall in with your arrangements," Rod said.

Daniel acknowledged the humour with a nod of his head. "It would be useful next time to have a chat about how we approach this trial. We don't have to decide this now, but my inclination at this stage is not to call you, Rod."

"You mean not call me as a witness?"

"Yes, exactly that."

"Whyever not?"

"Because it may work better for us if we don't put forward a positive case. It doesn't mean that I don't believe what you've told me. In fact the whole story about the bridge is very plausible. But it may still be better for us to simply test the quality of the evidence against you. As I say, this is just what I'm thinking at the moment. We can leave this open, even until the trial is in progress."

They were all standing now. Rod was pressing his lips together in a perfect straight line. It was impossible to tell what he was thinking. Daniel reached over the table and shook his client's hand.

"We'll see you very soon."

Chapter Thirty-Two

The sofa where they'd sat so awkwardly on their first date was now where they were most comfortable. Whole evenings were spent there, eating, talking, relaxing, drinking, making love. Daniel would lie with his legs and feet escaping the edge, his head resting on her lap, while she watched television, absent-mindedly stroking his hair. In this position it seemed too much effort for him to turn towards the screen, so he'd stare at the ceiling listening to whatever was on, supplemented by her commentary.

He'd told her of course that there was little reason for her to watch the news. He would say to her that she read all the papers, she was part of the huge machine creating these stories, so why did she religiously tune in? It would have been a fair point if he didn't himself watch all those silly legal dramas.

"Oh, not him!" Michaela said. Then for Daniel's benefit, "That self-righteous prig, Jonathan Aitken."

"He's not that bad, is he?"

She didn't answer, as she was intrigued by what

Aitken was about to say. He had approached a podium where he stood staring slightly manically at his audience.

"If it now falls to me to start a fight to cut out the cancer of bent and twisted journalism in our country with a simple sword of truth and the trusty shield of British fair play, so be it. I am ready for the fight. The fight is against falsehood and all who peddle it. My fight begins today. Thank you and good afternoon."

Something about his words disturbed Michaela. She watched Aitken as he walked arm-in-arm with his wife and daughter after the press conference. Directly below her head, Daniel was cackling.

"He was talking to you, wasn't he?"

"That's not funny." She actually felt quite annoyed with him.

"But he was. He was talking about going into battle against you, darling."

"Oh stop being daft, Daniel."

"You know, I rather like that phrase. 'A simple sword of truth'. I might use it in a closing speech. I could see it playing well with a jury."

It was hard to believe that Aitken would lie so brazenly in public and be prepared to have his lies tested in a court of law. But she also knew she'd trust *The Guardian's* word over Aitken's any day of the week.

"What's happening to us all, Daniel? Does the truth mean nothing at all these days?"

Daniel was saved from answering by the telephone. He sat up and held an index finger in front of him. "To be continued."

She watched as he walked through to the hallway where the telephone was located.

"Oh hi, Sally – yes, good thanks."

He was always perfectly friendly with his ex-wife. In

itself this was something of a lie considering the things he said about her.

"You want me to have them when?" Daniel said, placing a doubting emphasis on the final word. "I don't think that's going to work. Yes, any weekend may be good for you, but not for me. I'm about to go flat out on a trial. I thought I'd told you? Well, you can read about it in the papers. It's going to be all-consuming. Yes, understood. I won't expect any favours from you. Goodbye."

He returned to the reception room looking pleased with himself. "That was Sally."

"I gathered."

"She was trying to get me to take the kids for a weekend."

"I heard the whole conversation, Daniel."

"Can we get back to the news now?"

She suddenly felt sad, and it must have been because of how Daniel had spoken to his ex-wife.

Chapter Thirty-Three

Thomas was standing a few yards from the entrance when Michaela came out of work alone. His hands were thrust into the pockets of a dark-brown Afghan jacket he must have picked up in a vintage shop. A canvas bag was thrown over his shoulder.

"Hello, Thomas," she said.

He smiled as she caught his eye. "Hi."

He looked better than expected somehow, his beard was neatly clipped, and his skin looked clear and glowing. She'd imagined that he'd look more jaded, a little haunted even.

"I was surprised when you called," he said.

"It was a bit out of the blue, I know."

"We haven't spoken since January. So what changed?"

"I just wanted to speak to you. I thought we needed to do that."

He nodded. "That's what I was thinking too."

"Shall we go for a quick drink? I actually need a drink tonight."

"Sure."

There was a drinking culture at the Mirror Group, colleagues often going for a pint after work. So she'd told Daniel that she was having a drink with colleagues. She knew he wouldn't approve of her meeting Thomas, even if it was to draw a line under the whole business. She figured that it would be kinder not to tell him when he was preparing so hard for his trial.

"I know a place that's not far," Michaela said.

"I do too. It's historic, about a ten-minute walk. I think you'll like it."

So typical of Thomas to suggest somewhere better.

"That sounds good," she said.

They started walking, Michaela following his lead.

"I've been trying to sort myself out," he said. "This hasn't been a good time. I didn't feel good about just turning up at your work that day."

"I know it hasn't been easy for you. Because what happened was..." she couldn't help but pause, "absolutely terrible."

"And I was reaching out to all kinds of people. Not just you. I couldn't stay in Phoenix, even one week longer. I had to come back here. Then I wasn't able to work. So guess what, I had too much time on my hands. But I was glad you called, because I wanted to say I'm sorry. I'm going back to work after Easter. So we'll have our drink then go our different ways, okay?"

They had reached the river, in fact had been walking alongside it for a couple of minutes. The same river that James Liddell's severed head had been pulled from by the police a year earlier.

"This is all great, Thomas, but where are we heading? What's the name of this pub?"

"It's called The Grapes. It's not too far from here now."

"How do you even know about this pub?"

"I've been there, it's famous."

They had turned away from the river and were walking on a street past an open area of green with a few trees. And then, just as he'd said, The Grapes, a tiny pub nestling under what looked like an old townhouse.

They went inside. It wasn't exactly quiet, but it wasn't busy either. A few people in suits, bright ties, just out of work. Thomas went to get the beers and she sat there feeling slightly exhausted. It was nearly the end of the week and she knew Daniel would be working all weekend, what with his trial starting on Tuesday. She would be left to her own devices, but that was fine, she could finish the novel she was reading, maybe arrange to see a friend.

"Yes, so this pub is described in the first chapter of *Our Mutual Friend*," Thomas said, as he returned with the drinks. "Charles Dickens?"

"I know who wrote it, thanks."

He happened to have a copy in his bag, perhaps he was still reading it, and he showed her the passage he was talking about.

"I'm sorry I couldn't help you when you needed it," she said, after she'd glanced at it.

He replaced the novel in his bag. "No, I understand. I completely get the fact that not everyone is in the right place to offer help."

"Thank you, Thomas." They sipped their beers.

How normal he seemed, sitting opposite her now. She wondered whether Daniel's and her response to him making contact had been a complete overreaction. Certainly she'd given Thomas nothing by way of support which didn't make her feel great. And that long discussion with Daniel. He'd been so convincing in his arguments. But really, what was all the fuss about?

"Tell me something about Daniel," Thomas said. "I don't know anything about him, other than that he's a barrister."

"Well, he's very busy at the moment because he's about to start a trial at the Old Bailey."

"Well, that's amazing. I went there. You can just go in and watch any case."

"It's the same in the States too, no?"

"Sure, but the Old Bailey! Is he defending?"

"Yes, the guy in that murder case, you know, the head in the Thames?"

"What a case to be working on. How did he get that?"

"Well, who understands how the legal world works? I don't. And Daniel doesn't tell me. They have their own clerks, they're like hustlers – or managers. And Daniel's a QC, so they tend to do the big cases. But he's pleased to be working on this."

"I'll bet."

How ridiculous it was that Daniel had talked about involving the police. He might have liked Thomas had he given him half a chance. But instead he was just intent on seeing the possible problems.

"And what about you?" Thomas asked. "What have you been up to?"

She talked about her job, how she was happy to be working under a female editor who she got on well with. "But I'm not sure why I'm working in crime really. I often think it's not my bag."

"It's not really mine either."

She realised her insensitivity immediately, after what he'd been through just months earlier.

"I'm so sorry. Do you want to talk about it by the way?" she asked.

"No, it's fine. I've talked about it plenty enough with a counsellor. My parents paid. They're good for something occasionally."

She smiled and looked at her watch. They'd been in the pub for an hour.

"I won't keep you," he said.

"I just thought we should have a conversation."

"Sure. And we've done that now, and it's been great."

He stood up, so she did too. And they made their way out of the pub. He checked that she'd be all right getting home. Of course, she told him. She did it every day.

"Okay," he said. "I promise I won't be bothering you again."

She put her arms around him and they hugged briefly, like two old friends. And now she felt sad. This would be the last time she'd be seeing him, as he was making clear, and she felt sad at what she was losing. But what was she losing? She no longer had any relationship with this man, as Daniel had been so keen to point out.

"You take care," Thomas said. And there it was. Thomas brought kindness with him to any situation, to any conversation, that's how he'd always been. And yes, it was true that he'd once been decisive in cutting off their relationship, but in a way that was kindness too; he honestly thought they had no future together, so why string her along?

She remembered the conversation between Daniel and his ex-wife, a conversation so lacking in kindness. It had affected Michaela in a disproportionate way perhaps.

"Look, Thomas," she found herself saying. "We don't have to say we'll never see each other again. It's fine for us to meet up once in a while. In fact, I'd like that. I know that's not the message I was giving out before. But now I've seen you again, I don't want this to be the last time."

Chapter Thirty-Four

S ometime after midnight, two miles west of the pub where Michaela and Thomas had been drinking, Daniel made his way towards Tower Bridge. A chill wind blew a collapsed cardboard box into the road, and Daniel shivered despite his woollen coat.

He approached the bridge from the north side. He tried to make a habit of visiting the locations of key events within his trials. And as close as possible to the time when they would have happened. It could be invaluable preparation.

As expected, there was no one around at this time. He went under the outer arch, and he could still see nobody at all. He had a memory of his parents taking him near here when he and his sisters were still very young, sitting on a bench somewhere and watching as the bridge was raised. His father had described it as a wonderful feat of technology. Tonight it was cold, and slightly creepy if he were honest. He would take a few minutes to find where his client had said the carrier bag was hidden, and make his best guess as to where the witness was situated when she saw the object being tossed into the water.

It was a two-minute walk to even get to the first of the main towers, and here was the recess just as Rod described. Daniel made a quick walk around it, imagining Rod's surprise as he removed a terracotta flowerpot from the carrier bag. He had been thinking about this aspect of Rod's account, and strange as it had first appeared, he was now very much inclined to believe that, just like Nikolaos Kalogeropoulos, his client was an innocent man who'd strayed into the quicksand of unfortunate circumstances. Perhaps the whole plot had been masterminded by another of James Liddell's school contemporaries.

Daniel himself was holding his own Sainsbury's carrier bag. It contained a small football which he used for kickabouts with Max in the park. It was nowhere near as heavy as a terracotta flowerpot would be, but it would serve his purposes for tonight.

He was now standing in approximately the position where Rod would have been that night, and he couldn't resist the temptation to lift the bag above his head and mime throwing it once or twice. The things he found himself doing as a barrister. He couldn't imagine George Carman going to such lengths to prepare for a trial and certainly not at this time. Daniel wasn't going to let go of the bag of course, that would be a waste of a perfectly decent football, but he liked to keep his re-enactment somewhat realistic. There was a sudden flash of light and the sound of laughter, male and disorderly. It felt like a cold wet hand had grabbed Daniel's innards.

"I know exactly what you're doing – you sly devil you."

Daniel spun round to see where the voice was

coming from. He could see nothing. What kind of dangerous madman was he dealing with? Then, on the other side of the road, he saw someone rising from the ground. A man. He must have been lying down. The man stooped to pick up a shoulder bag and then brushed his coat down. And then, waving congenially to Daniel as if he knew him, he called, "I'm coming over."

He looked perfectly respectable as he crossed the road. He was smiling broadly, shaking his head to himself as if something was terribly amusing.

"Daniel O'Neil, I presume. Fergus Richardson, Treasury Counsel."

The penny dropped. The prosecutor in the case, no doubt doing similar preparation as him. Daniel laughed and took the outstretched hand.

"You gave me a start," he said.

"Sorry about that," Fergus laughed. "You looked like you thought you'd done something terribly wrong. As though I'd caught you red-handed at the scene of a crime."

"Which in a sense, you had." Daniel was keen at least to be seen to play along with the joke. He was beginning to recover his equilibrium.

Fergus pulled a photo from his camera. "I love these things, don't you?"

By reputation, Treasury Counsel barristers retained by the Old Bailey were a class apart – highly intelligent individuals often destined to be high court judges. They were known within legal circles for being both extremely posh and dangerously chummy. Always appearing most concerned for both their opponent and their client's welfare, they would simultaneously be looking for an opportunity to stitch them up.

Fergus was still studying the photo. "Can't really see

it properly in this light of course. Oh bugger, it doesn't look like it's come out properly. Do you mind if I try and take this again? Just do exactly what you were doing before."

He was about to cross the road again, but Daniel cut him short. "I'm sorry? You want me to pose for a photo to help with your trial preparation. That doesn't sound quite right. I'm not sure what the Bar Council would have to say about that."

"Fuck the Bar Council, old boy. I'd do the same for you. In fact I'll take two. You can have your very own copy tonight."

"That's kind," Daniel said. "But I think it's better if we leave it."

"I know your client is very tall of course. But even seeing you here a moment ago was giving me a pretty good idea."

"Well I'm not exactly short," Daniel said.

"That's not what I was saying, old chap." Fergus patted Daniel hard between the shoulder blades. "I'm just pointing out that it would make our lives a lot easier to have a photo. Isn't that what we both came here for?"

"I understand. It's just there's a rule against it, isn't there? You know about adducing evidence."

"I'm not adducing evidence! These photos are to help me with my preparation."

"There's something else then."

"You're probably thinking about coaching witnesses."

"No," Daniel protested loudly. "That's completely different."

"Anyway, I can't believe we're standing on Tower Bridge at one in the morning arguing about the code of conduct. That's hilarious. I can't wait to tell my wife. She thinks I'm bonkers enough anyway."

"I sometimes think we're all a bit bonkers," Daniel said. "Otherwise we wouldn't be doing this job in the first place."

"Well said. Anyway, understood if you're not comfortable about the photo. 'If it doesn't smell right don't touch it'. That's what my old pupil master used to say. Do you want me to stand here so you can take a look from the other side of the road? From the witness's viewpoint?"

"It's fine honestly. I've pretty much seen all I wanted to."

"But you've only just got here. If all your trial preparation is this sketchy, I'll be home and dry," Fergus laughed. "Listen, I've got some coffee in my car if you fancy a cup?"

"That sounds good," Daniel said. "I'm absolutely freezing if the truth be told."

"As long as you're happy that there's no rule about sharing caffeine with the other side. We should probably check the Written Standards for the Conduct of Professional Work before I get out my thermos."

Chapter Thirty-Five

L ike an endless historic loop on repeat, refreshed only by having new faces calling out the same words, the jury members were taking their oaths in Court Number One at the Old Bailey.

Two minutes earlier, Rod Bannister had listened impassively to the court usher reading a list of the jurors' names. He had made no objections.

Yesterday, the legal arguments before the opening of the case had been heard. Daniel had won a small victory on behalf of his client. The evidence pertaining to several gay pornographic videos found in Rod's flat was ruled inadmissible. This had been a promising start to the trial.

Although Daniel had appeared in several other courts at the Old Bailey, up until yesterday he'd never set foot in Court Number One. With its oak panelling, ceiling of white arches and circular skylight, the courtroom embodied traditionalism, majesty, formality. The impression was that nothing inside it had changed in the last hundred years.

The dock placed directly in the centre was just three or four yards to Daniel's left, raised above the floor like a tiny castle on a hillock. Stark and imposing, it reminded all who entered the courtroom exactly what purpose this small theatre of justice served.

Rod sat inside the dock wearing a navy suit. The sense of chilled anticipation when he finished climbing the staircase and emerged directly into the dock had almost been tangible. It must have been dark below as he'd blinked once or twice, seemingly taking a moment to orientate himself. Daniel had given his client a slight nod of his head. He felt for him, caught in what must feel increasingly like a Kafkaesque nightmare. Rod had raised his eyebrows in return.

To Daniel's right, Judge Dollimore was enthroned in a high-back chair. He was one of around a dozen judges trying cases at the Central London Criminal Court. Daniel had not encountered him before, but he had a reputation for being fair if not slightly pedantic. Yesterday, the judge had been attentive, courteous, perhaps in a hurry to start the proceedings proper. Right now he was studying papers on his desk as the swearing in of the jury continued.

Daniel watched intermittently as each jury member promised to consider the issues faithfully, according to the evidence. They were directly in front of him and his opposing counsel, Fergus Richardson, who sat at the other end of his row on the right. The front bench of barristers was separated from the jury only by a long table and chairs which would be used for placing items of evidence. Establishing trust with the jury, and in time a rapport, would be crucial. These twelve citizens were the most important people in the court. Obviously Judge Dollimore mattered, and the performance of Fergus

Richardson would matter, and whether the witnesses would be credible would matter a great deal too. But at the end of the day, these twelve were the ones Daniel would have to win over.

He did a quick head count. Seven were women, two of whom he'd have called "grandma types", elderly, with grey hair and glasses. It may have been prejudice, but Daniel assumed these older women would be more likely to convict. Much more likely, say, than the earnest young lady in her early twenties or the power-dressed businesswoman in her fifties. Generally, the men were more casual. Two or three wore pullovers. One, with tousled ginger hair, looked distinctly antsy. A bald man in a suit sat rigid and formal, his whole demeanour separating him from the other jurors.

Now that the jury had been sworn in, the judge addressed them, thanking them for their time and saying that, as far as he was concerned, they were now engaged in the single most important job in the country.

"And I say that, Members of the Jury, because you will decide whether the defendant walks away from the court as a free man, or whether he is sent to prison." One or two jury members could not resist turning to look at Rod Bannister. "Yes, the liberty of this individual will rest entirely in your hands. Because it will be up to you to decide which witnesses you believe. And it will be your decision alone as to what the precise sequence of events was. And if, when you are asked to consider your verdict, you are not sure, then you must acquit the defendant. Remember, it is the prosecution that brings the case. And it is the prosecution that must prove that case by the time the trial finishes."

"Hear-hear," a voice behind Daniel murmured.

Daniel knew that this was Stan Lever, his solicitor, seated directly behind him.

The judge polished his glasses as he continued speaking. "I would ask you not to get involved in any conversations regarding the case. Should anyone ask about it, you must tell them that I have directed you not to talk about it. Equally, you must avoid reading newspaper reports about what happens in this courtroom."

Daniel felt a tap on his shoulder, and he turned around. Stan solemnly passed him a plain white postcard. Yesterday he'd done the same and when Daniel turned it over, *I'VE HEARD FERGUS RICHARDSON IS A SHEEP-SHAGGER* was written in blue ballpoint pen. Keeping the card close to his body, so that even Gillian, his junior counsel seated next to him could not see it, Daniel flipped the card. *HIS HONOUR IS A CROSS-DRESSER* was today's message. Daniel attempted to block a mental image of Judge Dollimore in a miniskirt by instead focusing on his words.

"I know of course that there has been much salacious media coverage and you must put any knowledge you have to the back of your mind..." he smiled, "...or further away if you can manage it. Also, you must not visit any location that features in this trial. There will be some which you'll be taken to, and you will hear about those shortly."

There was another tap on Daniel's shoulder. Stan was holding yet another white postcard. Daniel took it from him.

"I would ask you also to assess how people give evidence as well as what they say in that evidence," the judge continued. "Simply listening to the words of the witnesses is not enough. We've all had experience of not believing things that are told to us, and you must use the skills you have learned in life to make these judgement calls."

Daniel turned the latest card over and read, *RIGHT NOW HE'S WEARING HIS WIFE'S UNDERWEAR.* He folded both cards and slid them into his jacket pocket.

"We all have a duty to ensure that the trial is conducted fairly," Judge Dollimore continued. "And on that point, I would say only this. If something is bothering you, please let me know via a written note. I have already seen the defence solicitor passing small cards to his QC, and you must follow his example and do exactly the same, raising any concerns or questions with me through the court usher. You must not wait until the trial is over. And finally, let me make one thing clear. All of the things I've just asked you to do are not polite requests. They are my directions. I will now ask Mr Richardson to open the case."

And so, in the courtroom where Dr Crippen, Lord Haw-Haw, the Kray Twins, John Christie, Ruth Ellis and Dennis Nilsen had all stood trial and been found guilty, and where his head of chambers George Carman had successfully defended Jeremy Thorpe in "The trial of the century", the most important case of Daniel's own career was about to begin.

Fergus Richardson stood up to his right. He began by introducing himself and the other barristers by name.

"Now that the introductions are over, Members of the Jury, I am going to ask that a bundle of documents is handed to you. It is not too extensive. The arrangement is for you to share one between two. Could these now be handed by an usher to the jury? We will look at this bundle in detail in due course, but by way of example, you will see at the very beginning the indictment. That is the formal document that sets out the charges that you have heard. The bundle, which is helpfully divided, has various documents, maps and photographs, all of which I will explain as I set out the prosecution's case.

"The defendant's full name is Roderick Clive Bannister. He is a housing benefits officer. The prosecution allege that he murdered a man by the name of James Liddell. We will say, almost certainly, that he did so by strangulation. And that he then separated the head of his victim from the rest of the body using some sort of serrated instrument. We will also say that the night that followed that of the murder, Mr Bannister buried Mr Liddell's body without the head in a remote field in Derbyshire. Yet he waited another two nights before he threw Mr Liddell's head into the Thames from a bridge. So why did Mr Bannister not bury the head with the rest of the body in Derbyshire?

"We will argue that the defendant killed Mr Liddell as an act of revenge for behaviour that occurred many years before when both men were pupils at St Columba's school. We will suggest that the different treatment of Mr Liddell's head was a deliberate part of that revenge plan. We have evidence to show this, and we will place considerable reliance on the testimonies of other men who attended the same school as Mr Bannister and Mr Liddell, and in particular those who went to a school reunion in November 1993.

"So let me take you through a short chronology of this case. On Saturday the twelfth of March 1994, partygoers on a pleasure boat on the River Thames spotted a severed head floating near to their boat. You can imagine their shock as an innocent birthday party turned into what must have felt like a scene from a horror movie. It took a few weeks for the victim to be formally identified as James Liddell. The last time Mr Liddell was seen alive was on the night of the fourth of December 1993.

"We will say that Mr Liddell and Mr Bannister arrived in the defendant's flat in Hackney around nine that evening. What happened later in the flat that night we cannot tell you in great detail. But suffice it to say that there were no more sightings of Mr Liddell alive after he entered Mr Bannister's flat. We will argue that Mr Bannister killed Mr Liddell in his bathtub, and we will argue that it was here that Mr Bannister also cut off Mr Liddell's head."

And so Fergus Richardson continued to take the jury through the prosecution's case, step by step. From the personal assistant of Mr Liddell who opened the abusive card written by Mr Bannister, and who also heard Mr Liddell making an arrangement with somebody on the telephone that same day. To the meeting in an Islington bar that Mr Liddell was seen having with a young man called Nikolaos Kalogeropoulos, who would be referred to throughout the trial as Nikos. The evidence that Mr Liddell and Nikos separated around eight fifteen pm and the CCTV camera on Upper Street which showed Mr Liddell and Mr Bannister walking together near Islington Green minutes later. The testimony of a bus driver who remembered both men boarding the No. 56 bus which was heading towards Hackney. The witness who reported seeing a man throwing a head from Tower Bridge into the water below. And the fact that this same witness later picked out Rod Bannister in an identity parade. The significant conversation that Rod Bannister had with his sister the day after Mr Liddell was murdered. And finally, the field in Derbyshire where the body was left, which Fergus Richardson said was significant. The fact that Mr Liddell's killer drove to this remote area before leaving the torso in this ideal hiding place, shows that he was thinking very clearly.

"In terms of what you might expect in the next few days, Members of the Jury, tomorrow morning we will take you to Tower Bridge where we say that the head of Mr Liddell was thrown from the bridge by Mr Bannister. We will also that same day be visiting Mr Bannister's flat where we will see the bedroom and also his bathroom where we say that Mr Bannister cut up Mr Liddell's body. And on Friday we will be visiting the site in Derbyshire where the torso was found. Assuming that we are on track and running to time, we will start to hear from witnesses in this trial beginning on Monday morning."

Chapter Thirty-Six

Guided by Fergus Richardson of the Treasury Counsel, the jury of five men and seven women trying the alleged killer of James Liddell were first taken to Tower Bridge. Accompanying them were a group comprising the defence team – Daniel, Stan and Gillian – various court officials including Judge Dollimore, several police officers and half a dozen members of the media. Richardson had said to the jury, and it almost sounded like a joke, that for the next couple of days they would be on a tourist bus, being shown the key sites in the murder case.

On the bridge, Richardson pointed out the spot where the witness said she was prostrate in her sleeping bag when she saw the actions that would form the basis of her evidence. The jury were encouraged to spend time on both sides of the road, and to wander across it as freely as they liked. All traffic had been diverted to allow this to happen.

Further down the street, Daniel saw Gillian chatting with a policewoman who she seemed to know well.

Daniel himself had been left in the company of Stan who was not in the best frame of mind. He was complaining about having had a massive argument with his wife the evening before.

"And so – this has only ever happened once before by the way – I ended up on the sofa, with just a blanket. It was bloody cold last night too."

"Sorry to hear that," Daniel responded.

"These things happen. How's the path of true love, anyway?"

Daniel glanced at him with momentary incomprehension.

"You and the fiancée!" Stan spat out.

"I've barely seen Michaela this past week. She's still renting her own place for the time being. Because I've been working until the small hours in chambers, she thinks there's little point in her coming over."

"Ships that pass in the night, eh?"

"Not even that."

"Uh-oh," Stan said, looking up.

Daniel looked up too and crossing the road purposefully was the trial judge's clerk, a man in his late twenties whose hair was entirely grey. Yesterday, Daniel had decided the premature ageing process rather suited him. In court he wore full morning dress complete with stripy trousers. Today it was light-brown corduroy trousers and a blue blazer with silver buttons.

Without so much as a good morning, the clerk began speaking in a low, unctuous tone. "We were wondering if we have something right." By this he meant the judge had a question for them. It was convention that all communications between judge and defence team would go through the judge's clerk.

"Only too happy to help," Daniel said. He felt

himself studying the clerk as if he were an exhibit in a museum.

"We were wondering if we've surmised correctly that you are not going to give evidence?"

"We haven't decided," Stan said, too gruffly in Daniel's opinion.

"It's quite likely that we won't give evidence," Daniel said. "But we're not completely certain. I hope that's not too unhelpful."

"We haven't decided," Stan repeated.

The clerk looked from one to the other for a moment, as if they were saying totally different things and he wasn't sure who to believe. He managed a smile in which both corners of his mouth were still turned down. "Thank you, that is most helpful." He disappeared back over the road to join the judge.

"Prick," Stan said.

"It's important we maintain good relations," Daniel pointed out.

"This grandmother doesn't like being taught to suck eggs."

Travelling in their specially requisitioned coach, the group continued next to Upper Street in Islington where they were shown the pub that James Liddell was seen drinking with Nikos on the evening he was presumed to have died. And the spot where the prosecution said he met the defendant before it was alleged that they caught a bus together. They were even shown the bus stop where the bus driver believed they'd boarded. The coach then followed the same route as the bus, down Essex Road, making a right turn into Hackney.

The group finished their tour of the day at the defendant's maisonette, where the prosecution alleged the murder had taken place. The front door, which was at the rear of the property, opened directly onto a narrow, carpeted staircase, and it took some time for the whole entourage to troop up to the landing in single file. From there they were first taken to the living room. They were also shown the two bedrooms, one of which was used simply for storage, and the other which contained a double bed. The prosecutor explained to the jury that while it was believed that the men had used the bedroom, there was evidence that the cutting up of the body had taken place in the bathroom. The bathroom, which was opposite to the top of the stairs, was tiny. Fergus Richardson suggested they go inside in groups of two or three. Daniel poked his head round the door with Stan who muttered something about fluff in the extractor fan.

On the coach returning to Central London, Daniel thought about what the next day would hold. They would be taken to Derbyshire to see the field in which James Liddell's torso had been buried. He wondered what kind of person goes on a car journey with a body in their boot, then digs a hole in a remote field with only owls and bats for company. It was a calculated and dispassionate attempt to conceal evidence that potentially placed the murderer, whoever he was, in the same league as Fred West. He remembered the field in Much Marcle which had featured on the news the night he telephoned Michaela. He decided that he would take a night off from preparing for the case, and would contact her as soon as he got home. Hopefully she would come over and spend the night with him.

Chapter Thirty-Seven

T he first witness entered through the door at the back of the court. Walking slowly, he navigated the narrow passage between the journalists, past the dock without looking at the defendant, and after a brief glance at the barristers on his right, took his place in the stand. In low gruff tones, he swore to tell the truth, the whole truth, and nothing but the truth.

Daniel studied him. He was a proud-looking man in his seventies, but judging by his bloodshot eyes, he hadn't slept properly in weeks. Life, it seemed, had dealt him a series of blows, but he gave the appearance of a man still ready for a fight.

Fergus Richardson stood up and smiled at the witness, who was only a few feet in front of him.

"Is your full name Cecil Arthur Bannister?"

"It is."

"Mr Bannister, what is your occupation please?"

"I'm a retired town planning officer."

"And you live in Sherrardspark Road in Welwyn Garden City?"

"I do."

"A very well-planned town, Welwyn Garden City, I believe."

The witness smiled for the first time. "I agree."

"Mr Bannister, can you confirm how you are related to the defendant?"

"I'm his father."

"You're going to have to speak up, Mr Bannister, so that the whole court can hear you."

"I'm sorry. I am the defendant's father."

"I believe your wife is deceased."

"Yes, she died in 1963."

"And one other thing, Mr Bannister. Please do feel free to turn towards the jury when you speak. You don't always need to direct your answers towards me."

The witness nodded but remained looking directly at the barrister.

"Do you have any other children?"

"A daughter. Gail. She's five years younger than the defendant."

"Now, in your own words, Mr Bannister, could you describe your relationship with your son?"

"Not good."

"In what way, not good?"

"We haven't spoken for a long time."

"How long is it since you last spoke to the defendant?"

"It's been years, really. It was about 1982. Or 1983."

"Is there a particular reason why you and the defendant don't speak with each other?"

"He was always a disappointment. We were never close. Not for as long as I can remember. The final straw was when he stole my money."

"Would you like to tell the court what happened, Mr Bannister?"

"Well, I'm not a wealthy man, but he said he needed fifty thousand to help him buy a flat."

"Fifty thousand pounds?"

"Yes, I had to borrow more on my house to help him. It's caused me a good deal of financial hardship. But he said he'd pay me back."

"And did he pay you back?"

"Not a penny. He as good as ran off with my money."

"Now this might seem a slightly odd question, Mr Bannister. Did your son's behaviour surprise you?"

The witness paused before answering, looking up to the public gallery as if he'd promised to say certain things to somebody up there. "No. Not at all."

"Why did it not surprise you?"

"I always knew he was untrustworthy. I hoped it would be different with that loan. But his promise was just another one of his lies."

After Fergus Richardson had finished with the witness, Daniel rose.

"Mr Bannister, it's right that yours was never an easy relationship with your son, isn't it?"

"I just said that, didn't I?"

"Indeed, Mr Bannister, you did. And your son is a homosexual, isn't he?"

"Yes, I believe he is."

"You believe he is." Daniel repeated the sentence deliberately, letting it hang in the air for a moment. "You don't like homosexuals do you, Mr Bannister?"

"I wouldn't say that."

"But you did throw your son out of your house when he came out about his sexuality, did you not?"

"That's not how it happened. That's his word against mine."

"The same could be said about the loan, couldn't it?"

"No, that's the truth."

"Just going back to your son's sexuality, you're happy to confirm that you have nothing against gay people?"

"Yes, I am happy. To confirm it."

Daniel stood absolutely still, coolly appraising Mr Bannister.

"What do you want me to do, swear on the Bible again?" the witness continued.

"That won't be necessary, Mr Bannister. I would like to ask you about a letter which was printed in the *Welwyn Hatfield Times*." Daniel turned for a moment towards the judge on his right-hand side. "We do have copies for you my Lord and my learned friends, and indeed for the jury which could be put in their bundle. Can I apologise, we've just realised they have not been punched with holes?"

Fergus Richardson intervened at this point. "Could we suggest a separate folder for documents produced by the defence? We can provide this tomorrow."

"Very well," the judge said. "I don't want a lot of loose paper floating round the court."

"The folders will be here first thing tomorrow," Fergus Richardson confirmed.

The judge nodded. "Members of the Jury, don't put them into your bundle. You will be provided a separate folder tomorrow. Yes, Mr O'Neil."

"Thank you, my Lord," Daniel said. "As I was saying, this letter appeared in the *Welwyn Hatfield Times* in June 1988. It's not a long letter, so for everybody's convenience I will read it out loud. And just to add a little historic context, if I may, the letter refers to the introduction of what was widely known as Clause 28, a series of laws which prohibited the 'promotion of homosexuality' by local councils. The new laws led to many protests, which are also referred to in the letter. 'Dear Sirs, it's all very well lesbians chaining themselves to BBC news desks, and actors like Sheila Hancock and Stephen Fry protesting their little socks off in Piccadilly, but in my view the new rules don't go far enough. Of course we shouldn't be promoting homosexuals and their despicable activities in schools. We should actually be chemically castrating them, so they can't indulge in these practices at all. I know I speak for many people when I say this. Yours, Cecil Bannister, Sherrardspark Road, Welwyn Garden City'." Daniel paused and raised his eyebrows at the defendant. "Rather a nice phrase that, 'protesting their little socks off in Piccadilly'. Do you recognise this letter, Mr Bannister?"

There was silence.

"Mr Bannister, do you recognise this letter?"

The witness bowed his head slightly. "Yes."

"Were you the author of this letter, Mr Bannister?"

Another pause. "Yes."

"So you wrote the part about chemically castrating homosexuals to stop them carrying on their despicable practices."

"Yes!"

"I have no further questions for the witness," Daniel said, and sat down.

The next witness was the defendant's younger sister. Daniel had decided that after his success with Cecil Bannister, he would not ask Gail Morley any questions. In any event, she was not in the witness box for long. She told the court how she had telephoned her brother on the fifth of December 1993. This was the following day after it was believed James Liddell had died. She called several times as she had needed her brother to help her out by picking up a prescription for her, but it was not until around three in the afternoon that he'd finally answered the phone. The witness said that she had found her brother unusually distracted, hardly willing to have a conversation at all. When she had mentioned the prescription, he said he had too much on. He suggested she ask somebody else. He told her that he had a headache, but her overriding impression was that he had something pressing heavily on his mind, something that he was keeping hidden from her.

The third and final witness in court that day was Jackie Levine, who made quite an entrance wearing a lime-green woollen skirt suit with a leather buckle. As she approached the witness stand, it looked to Daniel as if the outfit had been made by a designer. He knew that the witness was being put up in a bed-and-breakfast for the duration of the trial, at the prosecution's expense. Surely her expenses didn't go as far as a hefty clothing budget.

There was a pause before the witness could start, as she had dropped something. It sounded like marbles rolling around on the wooden floor in the witness box, but after she had bent down to pick up a few, she informed the judge what they actually were.

"They're my aniseed balls, my Lord. I'm sorry, the bag split."

"Please take your time, Ms Levine," the judge said.

"They're medicinal. For my throat, see."

"Do pick up your aniseed balls, Ms Levine."

The witness disappeared from view again, and after she'd collected all the sweets she could find, she made her vows with great expression, like an overly earnest actor.

She was then taken through her evidence by Fergus
Richardson, first describing how on what she now
believed was the seventh of December she had been
settling down to sleep for the night when it all happened.

"What time would this have been, Ms Levine?" the
barrister asked.

"Late."

"How late?"

"After midnight."

"Where were you?"

"I was in my sleeping bag."

"You were in your sleeping bag, yes, but where were
you located?"

"Oh," she smiled nervously, "on the bridge. On
Tower Bridge."

"On Tower Bridge at that time, was it quiet?"

"Yes. There was no one. Until the man came along."

"What did this man look like?"

"He was tall. Very tall."

"And the man came along. How did he come along?"

"He was walking."

"He was walking where?"

"On the other side of the road."

"On the other side of the road in which direction?"

"Towards me. From the north side."

"How well could you see the other side of the road?"

"Very well. There are lights. Or lamp-posts. Lights I
think."

"How much of the man could you see from where
you were lying in your sleeping bag?"

"All of him."

"And while in your sleeping bag, did you look at
him?"

"Yes, all the time, cos he was suspicious."

There was a moment's pause while Fergus Richardson thought about what she'd said, as she was still pronouncing the word suspicious to rhyme with fishes. "Ah, how was the man suspicious?" He accentuated the final word, restoring its proper pronunciation.

"He had this bag, this Sainsbury's bag. And he looked a bit guilty. Like he was about to do something."

"And did he do something?"

"Yes. He took a head out of the bag, and he threw it. Into the water."

When it was Daniel's opportunity to ask the witness questions, he pressed her further on these moments.

"Miss Levine, you said that the man you saw looked suspicious?"

"Yes."

"He looked suspicious because he was carrying a Sainsbury's bag, that's what you said?"

"Yes."

"People carry Sainsbury's bags all the time, don't they?"

"Well, yes."

"The man was on the other side of the road, wasn't he?"

"Yes."

"And he threw the object off the bridge into the river, yes?"

"Yes."

"He had his back to you when he threw the object. That's right, isn't it?"

"Yes."

"And he had his back to you when he took the object out of the bag, didn't he?"

"He did, but I saw what it was. It was a head."

"It was dark wasn't it, Miss Levine?"

"There were lights."

"There are no lamp-posts on Tower Bridge. I've checked."

"There are lights. I don't know where. But you can see."

"And you were tired, I expect, as it was the middle of the night."

"I was about to go to sleep."

"And you said the man had his back to you when he took the object out of the bag?"

"Yes, but I saw it."

"The object was in front of him, and he had his back to you, was that not the case?"

"I saw it was a head. That's why I went to the police station."

"I suggest your identification of the object was mistaken, but you would disagree with me, wouldn't you, Miss Levine?"

"Yes."

"Finally, if I may, Miss Levine, you gave your address earlier as Fairfax Road in Swiss Cottage. That's correct, isn't it?"

"Yes."

"I believe that is a bed-and-breakfast, isn't it?"

"Yes," the witness admitted.

"How long have you lived there?"

"About twelve days."

"Oh. So you would have moved in about a week before this trial?"

"Yes, about that."

"Where do you normally live, Miss Levine?"

"No fixed abode."

"So some might say that you've done pretty well from

this trial in terms of being given a nice bed-and-breakfast to live in. But I expect that again you'd disagree with me, wouldn't you, Miss Levine?"

"I don't know what you're saying," the witness said.

"Thank you, I have no further questions."

Buoyed by what he considered to be his successes that day, Daniel visited his client in the cell beneath the court after the judge had called time.

"I hope you're not going to tell me how well that went," Rod said, as soon as Daniel was admitted into the small room.

"Well, it's early days of course," Daniel said. "But I thought it was a good day for us, yes."

"She was the one I trusted," Rod responded. "The only one I could be open with."

"Who are we talking about?" Daniel was momentarily disorientated.

"Gail. My sister. She's always been my closest friend. And today she betrayed me."

"I'm not sure the phone call she described was as significant as the prosecution would have us believe."

"It was significant to me."

"I didn't think your father acquitted himself well today," said Daniel, trying to change the subject.

"Well, you did trip him up, didn't you?"

"Yes, it's all part of what we do," Daniel said.

"He's a right shit, isn't he?" Rod said.

"Mine was too," Daniel said. "Went off with some young Australian woman when I was ten years old. I never saw him again."

Rod nodded. It was hard to tell if it was a nod of sympathy, or a simple acknowledgement of the disclosure.

"Couldn't you do something about it?" Rod asked.

"About what? Sorry, I'm not sure I understand."

"Couldn't you do something about all that stuff Gail was saying?"

"Do something about it?" Daniel repeated.

"I mean couldn't you stop her?"

Daniel suddenly felt unequipped for this conversation, like he was riding into a deep river on a bicycle.

"It's procedural, Rod. Your sister was the prosecution's witness. They call their witnesses and they give their evidence. And then I'm allowed to ask questions if I want to."

"So you couldn't stop her saying any of those things." Rod seemed genuinely perplexed, but he wasn't the only one.

"No, I couldn't."

"Why, though?"

"Because I'm your barrister, not your magician," Daniel said.

Rod gave a small chuckle, then there was silence. "I understand," he finally said. "But I still think you could have done better." He was looking at the floor when he said it, but Daniel could see that he was sticking his bottom lip out like a small boy. He glanced up and the two men met each other's eyes. Then after a couple of seconds, Rod gave him a slight wink.

"You're very easy to take the piss out of, Daniel O'Neil."

"You bastard," Daniel said. "You absolute bastard."

There was a moment before both men laughed. Quite suddenly, Daniel felt a terrific sense of relief.

Chapter Thirty-Eight

The witnesses on the second day of evidence were all men who were in the same year at St Columba's school as Rod Bannister and James Liddell. They came in, one after another, middle-aged men seemingly eager to talk about their school days, some in ties that looked like the type they might have worn all those years ago. Several of the men were balding, one had a limp, many were overweight, a couple looked like they'd recently had serious health problems to contend with. But together they built a consistent picture of a relationship between the two boys that had begun as healthy competition but turned into something more insidious and unpleasant. One of the men, Matthew Sullivan, had his own theory about why James Liddell was particularly cruel when Rod's mother developed the cancer that she would succumb to in her son's final year at school.

"Some of us knew that James grew up in care, even though he didn't like to talk about it. It was one of the things that probably made him so competitive, trying to prove that he was as good as everyone else. But he also resented the kids that had been brought up in a normal family home and enjoyed any sign of that home falling apart. He seemed to relish the fact that Rod's mum had cancer. He saw her and Rod after school in St Albans one evening and spent some time the next day imitating how terrible she looked, and how she had walked in a stooped way, much to the amusement of a whole group of us. I felt bad laughing about something so awful, but James was such a strong character, I didn't feel I had any choice."

Matthew had also attended the school reunion on the twenty-third of November 1993. Fergus Richardson asked him whether he could remember any conversations between Rod and James that evening.

"There was some quite good-humoured chat about how at one time they'd both wanted to be the head boy at the school. It was pretty obvious to us that the headmaster would pick one or the other, and James was sort of rubbing it in, in a friendly way, that he'd been chosen over Rod all those years ago."

"How did Rod react to being teased about that?"

"He was fine about that. But I could see he was getting upset later on in the evening."

"What caused him to get upset?"

"It was when James found out that Rod was working as a housing benefits officer. He was literally howling with laughter. There was a big crowd and I could see Rod was trying to keep his cool, but James was going on about how Rod always said he'd be a producer working in Hollywood. And now, here he was processing housing benefit claims in Hackney."

"What else did Mr Liddell say about that?"

"Well, he mentioned the sort of people Rod must be

working with and took great delight in imitating an old woman dribbling as they filled out her form together. It took me back to the imitations he used to do of Rod's mother when she was ill, but this time it was a woman with lice jumping from her hair onto the application form."

"How did Rod react to this?"

"He said that they don't fill in the forms together, they arrive at the office already completed. It's only with a complicated claim that they meet the person. Still, James told him, it wasn't quite as glamorous as working with film stars. And then he started boasting about how he himself was living the life, had his own luxury yacht, and was running a company that turned over millions every year."

Daniel chose not to question most of the witnesses that day. Instead, he sat mainly in silence, occasionally whispering something to Gillian, his junior. When he did question the odd witness, he picked only on small details of what they'd said and kept his cross-examinations very short.

Chapter Thirty-Nine

They'd awoken early and Michaela had quickly cottoned on to the fact that he was hard. She had been feeling particularly horny herself in recent days and without even bothering to take off the T-shirt she'd slept in, she straddled him and they humped noisily for a couple of minutes before he came.

"Is that what they call a zipless fuck?" Daniel asked.

"No! Why would that be a zipless fuck?"

"It didn't involve zips, for one thing."

"A zipless fuck is a fuck with no emotional commitment. Just a fuck, with no other motivation. I think the couple aren't even meant to know each other."

"Where does it come from that phrase?"

"Erica Jong. *Fear of Flying*. Have you heard of it?"

"Yes, but I've certainly never read it."

She resisted the temptation to point out that he probably hadn't read any female writers. Instead she said, "I've got a copy somewhere. It's bright yellow and has this quote saying it's the most erotic novel ever written by a woman. You can borrow it if you like?"

"When I've got more time."

"It's probably at my parents' house, if they haven't slung it out. My mother's pretty good at getting rid of my books she doesn't approve of."

"Listen," he said. "I wanted to say I'm sorry if I haven't been myself lately."

Michaela thought immediately of the conversation with his ex-wife which she'd been trying to tell herself was out of character for him. "That's sweet, Dan. Was there anything in particular?"

"No. Just aware that I've been a bit of a crotchet-bag recently." He leaned over and kissed her on the nose.

"Well, I've hardly seen you since the Jonathan Aitken evening. The night you spoke to Sally." She waited to see if he'd pick up on this.

"I've been preparing for the trial of course. But now that it's started–"

"And I understand that. How's it going by the way?"

"Have you not seen the coverage in the papers?"

"I don't think so." She'd actually read two reports in *The Guardian* but didn't want to appear overly eager in following his career.

"You haven't?" He sounded disappointed.

"I suppose you can't tell me how you think it's going?" It was annoying that his professional ethics were again stopping them from having a normal conversation.

"I did have a notable success with the defendant's father. That was in several reports."

"I get it. If it's in the public domain, you can mention it."

Daniel smiled sadly, like he'd been caught out. "Today will be interesting. We've got Liddell's PA in the witness stand. She opened a card that was sent by my client."

"At last. Some inside information. Hallelujah."

"That's all for now though. I'm going to grab a shower." Standing naked he turned to look at her lying partially uncovered on the bed. "If I had a piece of paper, I'd sketch you right now."

"I can find you some."

"I haven't got a pencil either."

"I can find you a pencil too," she laughed. "I've never seen you draw anything. It might be fun."

"I actually don't have the time." He wrinkled his nose.

"It wouldn't look anything like me anyway."

"I don't know, I'm pretty good at sketching."

"Yeah, but it's hard to capture beauty like this."

"True."

He disappeared, leaving her with her thoughts. Their conversations first thing in the morning had a different quality. Dan was less guarded, before the shutters came down more fully. Having said that, the sex wasn't the best ever; it was all over too quickly for her liking, leaving her feeling unfulfilled. While he was in the shower, she took the opportunity to lazily touch herself under the duvet.

Chapter Forty

J enny Montague was a resolute-looking woman in her fifties, her hair an unnatural ash blonde. Daniel imagined that she'd once had the kind of looks that made men point out her existence to each other, speak crudely about her in low tones. Now, she'd developed into what his youngest sister might call "a battle-axe".

"You've told the court that you thought the conversation with Mr Bannister that day was an unusual one. That's a fair summary, isn't it?" Daniel asked.

"Yes."

"For example, you said that it was odd that he didn't know what film he was going to see."

"Rod is a big fan of cinema. He considers himself to be a bit of a film buff. But it was his attitude more than anything. He was in a very weird mood."

"I'm just trying to focus on what you told my learned friend. You specifically said that he mentioned going to the cinema but didn't know what was playing. I'm right that you said that, aren't I?"

"Yes, I did say that."

"People often go to the cinema without planning it beforehand, don't they?"

"I don't know. You tell me."

There was a titter from one of the jurors and Daniel felt his hackles rising. He wiggled his toes in his shoes to distract himself from his irritation. "Mrs Montague," he made sure he was smiling, "if it's okay with you, I'll ask the questions and you answer them."

She nodded.

"Isn't it the case that people often see films in an impromptu way, that they arrive at the cinema and then find out what's playing?" Daniel continued.

"I don't think I'm qualified to comment on the nation's cinema-going habits."

This time there was an outright cackle from the jury. Daniel turned to stare at the man with ginger hair, who flushed with embarrassment.

"I am reminding the court that we are engaged in a deadly serious process," Judge Dollimore said, testily. "I would be grateful if we could remember this at all times."

The judge's intervention had given Daniel a moment to regather his thoughts. Jenny Montague was a difficult customer in every respect, able to think on her feet and with a natural wit that made him question his decision to cross-examine her.

"If we could turn to something else that Mr Bannister said, which you also found unusual. That people keep on making the same mistakes, that this happens throughout their lives. That's what you told the court he said, isn't it?"

"Yes, he did say that."

"Isn't that the sort of general observation we all come up with from time to time?"

The witness looked steadfastly at Daniel before replying. "I suppose so. But I keep telling you that it wasn't so much what he said, it was how he came across."

"Mrs Montague, I would put it to you that everything you've said in court this morning doesn't amount to a hill of beans. In other words, you have told us nothing of significance. I do understand of course how after Mr Bannister was arrested and became public enemy number one, you felt that you should do your bit to help out. Is that fair?"

"That's not the case at all," the witness said.

"One final question if I may. Your story recently appeared in the *Daily Mail*, did it not?"

"Yes, it did."

"For those of us in court who don't read that particular tabloid newspaper, it was all about how the witness worked with my client in Islington. The headline was I MANAGED THE FLOATING HEAD MURDERER. Would you mind telling us how much you were paid for that story?"

"Five thousand pounds."

"Five thousand pounds. Thank you, Mrs Montague, you've been very helpful."

Later that day, Daniel cross-examined Tricia Armitage, Liddell's PA, about the day she had steamed open the envelope marked private and confidential that was addressed for her boss. The card it contained, with its explicit sexual proposition, was an exhibit in the courtroom. Daniel pressed the witness on whether this was the first time she had surreptitiously opened his private correspondence and she admitted that she had done it several times before. He probed her on why it had taken so long for her to bring the card to the attention of the police, and she explained that it was because she had separated from her boyfriend and the card got lost in his flat.

"Please help me with one thing then. What was the card doing in his home in the first place?"

"I thought it would amuse him – that's why I took it there."

Daniel then pressed her on the conversation she heard. "This was a telephone conversation. So, at best, you were only able to hear one half of it. That's right, isn't it?"

"Yes, that's right."

"And you were listening to this conversation through a closed door, were you not?"

"Yes, I was."

"Do you often listen to people's private conversations through closed doors, Miss Armitage?"

"Sometimes. I'm no saint, I'll admit that." She turned to look at the jury and smiled.

"At the risk of asking you something very obvious, do you know why people close doors when they have private conversations?"

"Because they don't want people listening to them."

"That's right, but can you think of another reason why they close the door?"

"To tell people not to listen to their conversation."

"Perhaps. But I'm thinking more about the doors themselves. Why do people actually close them?"

"Because it makes it harder for anyone outside to hear." Tricia sounded pleased to have thought of this answer.

"Thank you, because it makes it harder for someone outside to hear. Do you know what kind of door James Liddell had in his office?"

"A wooden door?"

"It was, but do you know what kind of wooden door?"

"I don't know."

"The answer is that it was an oak fire door, and it was fifty-four millimetres thick. Unusual to have a fire door for the boss's room, but that's what it was. We have some photographs of the oak fire door, my Lord, which we will now make available to the court."

After the ushers had distributed the photographs showing the door's thickness, Daniel continued with his cross-examination.

"Miss Armitage, you told the court that you listened to Mr Liddell's telephone conversation through this closed door."

"Yes."

"And you told my learned friend that you could hear the conversation clearly."

"Yes, I did."

"How did Mr Liddell introduce himself when he made the call?"

"I'm sorry, I don't understand."

"Normally, when we make a call, we say who it is that is calling. Did Mr Liddell introduce himself to the person who answered?"

"No."

"Is that no, meaning he didn't introduce himself, or no, meaning you didn't hear him introduce himself?"

"I didn't hear him introduce himself."

"And you are quite certain that you could hear him throughout the conversation?"

"I heard what I heard."

"Thank you for that. Can you remind us of the first thing you heard Mr Liddell say in that conversation?"

"He called the other person an arsehole."

"So the first words you heard him say were 'You arsehole'?"

"I think so."

"And what did you hear after that?"

"He said, 'I got your stupid card'."

"So he said: 'You arsehole. I got your stupid card'. And then what did he say?"

"He said, 'Okay then, so what shall we do about it?'."

"I'm right in saying that after that, you didn't hear anything else."

"That's right."

"So you are telling me that the entire conversation you heard was, 'You arsehole. I got your stupid card. Okay then, so what shall we do about it?'?"

"Yes, that's what I heard."

"You made all that up, didn't you?"

"No, it's what I heard."

After this, Daniel went on to question the witness about the traffic noises that might also have distracted her from hearing the conversation clearly. It would have been rush hour, and the side of the office on which both Tricia and Liddell were located was the same side as a busy road. The witness said that she'd never noticed any traffic noises in all the time she had worked there. And that in any case, the windows would have been shut in the winter. Daniel immediately felt that the good work he'd done earlier might have been undermined by this moment. He looked over at Rod. He was staring blankly towards the gallery of spectators. Daniel felt the need to talk to him after the day's proceedings.

Chapter Forty-One

R od was reading when Daniel came down into his cell. Gillian had left quickly after the day had finished, so it was just the two of them. Rod looked up and nodded at Daniel. Daniel had been feeling more relaxed with his client since that joke they'd shared together on Monday, but even so, he could rarely remember his client actually smiling at him.

"What are you reading today?" Daniel asked, sitting down a few feet from his client.

Rod held up his book. It was by Raymond Chandler.

"Do you like him?" Daniel tried again.

Rod shrugged.

"I've not read Chandler myself. Would you recommend doing so?"

"I probably wouldn't be reading it if I didn't like it," Rod said flatly.

"Fair enough," Daniel said. He was feeling irked that, like trench warfare, a tiny amount of hard-won progress could rapidly disappear two days later.

"How do you think it went today?"

"How do you think it went?" Rod asked.

"I thought it went well. I would say I was effective in the cross-examination of both witnesses. Particularly so with Tricia Armitage."

"Fair enough," Rod said.

"Are you happy with my advocacy on your behalf?" Daniel asked. He immediately wondered why he'd done so. He couldn't ever remember asking a client this.

"Yes," Rod said. "I'm happy."

"It's just you don't ever say anything. It would be nice if you actually made a comment to me from time to time. I mean, I'm busting a gut out there for you, Rod."

Rod was resting his hand on his chin as he looked at Daniel. As if he was seeing something about him for the first time. "And what should I be saying exactly?"

"Just 'Well done', or maybe 'You were good today'. Or even 'That part of the cross-examination didn't go so well, but you're doing great work overall'. Something along those lines perhaps?"

"I'm sorry, Daniel. I didn't know it was my job to give you positive affirmations. I kind of thought that the money you earn would be reward enough."

"That's a fair point, I suppose," Daniel conceded.

"And I'm still a bit pissed off that you're not calling me as a witness," Rod said. "It's like you don't believe my story if you don't want to put it before the court."

"It's not that I don't believe your story, because I absolutely do," Daniel said. "Although actually, it's immaterial whether I believe it or not. But the important point is whether I think it will play well in front of a jury."

"And you don't think it will?"

"Well, let me ask you this. Why did you go no comment in your first two police interviews?"

"That was the advice from my duty solicitor. He thought it best to wait until we hear what they had against me."

"Right. But you'd told him your story, yes? About the answerphone message, and the flowerpot?"

"Of course I had."

"So he must have at least suspected the same as me."

"Which is?"

"That your story is a little complicated."

"Right…"

"But on the other hand, the prosecution's case isn't watertight. So the most effective thing may be to simply pull their case apart."

"I suppose," Rod said. "Thanks for explaining that to me."

Chapter Forty-Two

"Interesting fact about the Viaduct Tavern," Thomas said, as they sat down with their pints. "Many people believe this place was built on the site of Newgate Prison. In fact, look over there." He pointed diagonally across the road. "You see the trees? Just beyond, there's a small fountain."

"I see it," Nikos said.

"Okay. So that's the exact spot where the prison would hold its executions."

"For murderers, like Rod Bannister."

"Not just murderers. And don't forget, he's not been found guilty. Not yet, anyway."

"True, but I think he will be," Nikos said.

"Perhaps." Thomas smiled.

In the weeks leading up to the trial, Nikos had been nervous about giving evidence. But now he'd played his part and faithfully reported what happened the night he'd met Liddell. After leaving the court, he'd lit a cigarette, standing for a moment with his back to the historic building as he inhaled deeply. At that moment, he was approached by this man with a beard, his hair tied up in a way that showed his neck and ears. The man had kind eyes, dreamy even.

The man told him he'd been in the spectators' gallery. He'd taken a day off work as he thought he'd drop in to see how the big trial was going. There had been quite a queue to get in that morning. It was popular, Nikos agreed. The stranger introduced himself as Thomas and told Nikos he'd done well in the witness stand. They'd decided to go for a drink.

"You know in days gone by, the courtrooms were the real entertainment in London," Thomas said, sipping his pint. "Where the scandal happened, and the gossip started. These days it's rare for cases to get this much attention."

Nikos nodded. "It's been in all the newspapers."

"I'm a little disappointed I didn't get to eyeball the defendant though. Do you know why he wasn't in court?"

"Yes, the usher said he is not well today," Nikos said.

"Oh well, that aside it was great."

Nikos told Thomas that when he was having the conversation which formed the basis of his evidence, he was sure he'd only be in England for a year. But his tutor on his business studies course had recommended him for a job in a company providing specialist holidays to Greece. Nikos' knowledge of the country and islands along with his business skills made him the ideal candidate.

"So even though I'm Greek, I feel like a proper Londoner now. I have no plans to leave."

"Me neither. I'm an American in London and I love it."

There was a pause for a moment. Thomas looked at

the small group sitting on the next table to theirs, as if he was trying to tune into their conversation.

"So you think I was okay giving evidence?" Nikos asked. "I was very nervous."

Thomas looked back at him and smiled. "I thought you did very well. Calm under pressure. Not ruffled by the questions."

"Thank you. What other witnesses did you see today?"

"A woman who used to go walking with the defendant in Derbyshire."

"Why did they need to hear from her?"

"Their walks were very close to where the body of the victim was found. And then there was the person who overheard your conversation in the pub. The barwoman."

"Oh, yes. Davina."

"Do you know her?" Thomas asked.

"A little. I used to go into that pub a lot. She once suggested we meet up when she wasn't working."

"Like that was it? And did you meet up?"

"No, never. It was Davina who went to the police. I hadn't realised the man I had a drink with was the person who was killed."

"It's kind of weird how these things happen."

"I was angry with her because the police thought I killed him. For a while. And there were news stories, about my private life."

"That's hard, man."

"They even found photographs of old boyfriends in Greece."

Thomas nodded gravely. Nikos was impressed that he didn't immediately ask for more information. And slightly disappointed too.

"So what brought you to London?" Nikos asked.

"Academia. There was a lecturing job I was recommended for."

"What do you teach?"

"American literature. Specialising in Herman Melville."

"I see," Nikos said vaguely.

"He wrote *Moby Dick*? About the whale?"

"Oh, yes – of course. I don't read too many books if I'm honest," Nikos said.

"Who needs books when real life is all around you, eh?"

Nikos laughed.

"Hey," Thomas said. "I'm going to have to go now."

"Okay, but perhaps we can go for another drink sometime?"

"Sure," Thomas said. "As two outsiders in London, we should definitely stick together."

Chapter Forty-Three

The witness made her way slowly across the court. Daniel noticed her careful steps; how spindly her legs were. Did this attenuation happen to all women at a certain age? He recalled his own grandmother talking about being unsteady on her pins.

Standing in the witness box, she placed her right hand on the Bible. Everything about her spoke to her integrity and honesty – her modest outfit, her solicitous manner, the earnest way she took her oath.

Fergus Richardson stood up and began speaking.

"Is your full name Miss Grace Alice Ovett?"

"Yes, that's correct."

"What is your occupation please, Miss Ovett?"

"I was a secretary. I've been retired for twelve years now."

"And you live in Navarino Grove in Hackney?"

"I do."

"Can you confirm how you know the defendant?"

"He lives above me. There are only four flats in our block. We all know each other."

"How long have you known the defendant?"

"Well, it would be 1983. That's when he bought his flat. There were several years when he wasn't living in his property. But he'd send me postcards from wherever he was."

"So, on and off, for about twelve years?"

"Is it as long as that? Yes, I suppose it must be."

"How would you describe your relationship with the defendant?"

"Very good. I never had a son – but I think of Rod much like I would my own son. That's why this whole thing has been so upsetting for me."

"I understand, Miss Ovett. Please do take your time."

"Could the witness be given some water?" the judge requested.

The witness was passed a glass of water and took a sip before returning it to the usher.

"So, would it be fair to say that you have the kind of relationship where you might drop by each other's flats on a regular basis?" Fergus Richardson continued.

"Yes, for a chat, or to help each other out. Rod has been tremendously helpful to me over the years. Whenever I needed to buy anything heavy, I'd get Rod to do that for me. And he always helped me put up my Christmas cards – I get so many I have to use the top shelves in my living room which I can't reach. He never complained, although he did tease me rather a lot."

Daniel looked at the witness and then at the jury members, noticing particularly the two elderly women. They were listening intently to every word. Perhaps they were imagining being in the same position, living above a friendly middle-aged man, someone they held in their affections like a son, then being thrust into a murder trial at the Old Bailey to give evidence against him. From the disclosed documents, Daniel knew the ground that Grace Ovett would be covering. But seeing her standing here now, he realised for the first time how damaging her testimony might prove to be.

"I want to take you back to the morning of Monday the sixth of December 1993, Miss Ovett. You hadn't been well, had you?"

"No, I'd had a heavy cold which had been going on for over a week."

"Had you seen Mr Bannister over the weekend at all?"

"I hadn't seen him. But I'd heard him moving about in his flat. And I'd been round as I wanted him to buy me some eggs."

"What day would this have been, Miss Ovett?"

"The Sunday. I rang his bell around two o'clock in the afternoon. I was pretty sure he was inside, but he didn't answer the door, which was unusual for Rod. I thought perhaps he wasn't well either. Or maybe just very busy."

"So you went around on the Sunday and received no answer. And when did you next try to speak to him?"

"That was first thing on the Monday. I wanted to make myself a boiled egg for my breakfast, so I was hoping to catch him early."

"What time would this have been?"

"About eight o'clock. I rang the bell again, but then I noticed the door was actually open. So I went inside and called his name as I climbed the stairs."

"Did you notice anything different about his flat at this point?"

"Yes, I immediately noticed the strong smell of lemon cleaning liquid. It was rather overpowering. I've been inside Rod's home many times and I've never smelt anything like that before. He rarely cleaned it at all. It was one of the things we'd joke about."

"Did you find Mr Bannister that morning?"

"Yes. He was in his bathroom at the top of the stairs. I popped my head round the door."

"What did you see?"

The witness glanced to her right at Rod Bannister in the dock before turning back to Fergus Richardson. "He was standing on top of the bath. He was washing the walls of his bathroom with a sponge."

"When you say on top of the bath, which bit of the bath do you mean?"

"I mean, the edge. The rim. I thought it was a most peculiar thing to be doing at eight in the morning. And the bathroom window was wide open."

"Did you notice anything about the defendant's appearance?"

"It was absolutely shocking. He looked stricken."

"What do you mean by stricken?"

"He was very pale. And he looked like he hadn't slept all night. He looked very cold too. All over. In fact, I reached up and touched his hand when I said hello to him. It was ice cold to the touch. And the thought struck me that he had perhaps already been in his bathroom, cleaning, for some time. Several hours maybe."

"Did you have a conversation with the defendant?"

"Yes. I asked him if he was all right. And he said he was. I asked him if he had any eggs. And something else rather odd happened. He jumped down from the bath and ran over to his kitchen and he came back with two eggs. I thought that was very strange. Rod and I don't stand on ceremony with each other you see. Normally, he'd tell me to look in the fridge myself. He'd make a joke of it, say something like, 'You know where the fridge is, Grace. You've taken enough things from it in the past'."

"But he didn't say anything like that."

"No. He ran off to get the eggs himself. It was as if he was hiding something or didn't want me looking around his flat."

"Thank you, Miss Ovett. I have no further questions. Would you remain where you are, please?"

Daniel had to admit that his opponent had made an excellent job of examining the witness. To establish her as someone close to his client who thought of him like her own son made what followed particularly devastating. He had arranged with his junior that she would cross-examine this witness. He hoped that she would be able to rescue something from the situation.

Gillian Palmer stood up.

"Miss Ovett, you've told the court that on the Sunday when you rang on the defendant's doorbell, you were pretty sure that he was at home. That's what you said, isn't it?"

"Yes, that's right."

"Can you remind the court where Mr Bannister's front door is in the property?"

"It's at the back."

"At the back. And can you see Mr Bannister leaving his flat, when he goes through his door?"

"No, I can't."

"Would you say that you always hear him closing his door when he goes out?"

"No, not always."

"So it's perfectly possible that he might have left his flat on the Sunday without your being aware of it?"

"I suppose now you put it like that, it is possible."

"So do you have anything further to say about your statement that you were pretty sure he was at home when you rang the bell on the Sunday?"

"Yes, I don't think I can be sure. I'm not sure why I said that."

"Moving now to the following morning when you found Mr Bannister cleaning his bathroom. You described to the court how he looked, stricken. Pale. Like he hadn't slept, didn't you?"

"Yes."

"Miss Ovett, do you mind telling the court how tall you are?"

"I'm five feet two inches."

"Did you know that Mr Bannister is six feet four inches?"

"Well, I know he's tall, but not the exact height."

"So that makes Mr Bannister some fourteen inches taller than you, doesn't it?"

"Yes."

"And when you saw him that morning, he was standing on the rim of the bath. Do you have any idea how high the rim of the bath is from the floor?"

"Maybe eighteen inches?"

"Slightly more, actually. The rim of the bath is twenty-one and a half inches from the floor. So that means that Mr Bannister's head would have been about thirty-five and a half inches above your head when you saw him and had the brief conversation. That's right, isn't it?"

"Yes, I suppose so."

"So that is almost three feet difference between the

heights of your heads, just half an inch less. Do you recall any other conversations with Mr Bannister when you were standing at such different heights?"

"Not offhand, no," the witness admitted.

"And would you say that when you look up at someone who is almost three feet higher than yourself, your perspective is quite a different one to say sitting down having a cup of tea with that person?"

"Yes, I would agree with that."

"They look quite different, don't they?"

"Yes."

"When you described him as looking stricken, pale, and like he hadn't slept all night, you were making this assessment of him when he was this much higher up than you?"

"Yes, I was."

"And as you have said, you don't have any memories of having similar conversations with Mr Bannister in these positions, so you have nothing to compare it to when you say he looked stricken, pale, and like he hadn't slept, is that fair?"

"Yes, I would say that is fair."

"Let's move on to cleaning products, Miss Ovett. If you were going to clean your own bathroom, what products might you use?"

"Jif. Sometimes bleach."

"They both have strong smells, don't they?"

"Yes, they do."

"Do you open your own bathroom window when you use these products?"

"I do, yes."

"And this being quite early in the morning in December, it would have been quite a cold morning would it not?"

"Yes, I'm sure it was."

"So when you describe his hand as being ice cold to the touch, that's probably not altogether surprising is it?"

"No."

"Because you told the court that you had the impression that he might have been in his bathroom cleaning for several hours. He would have had a hand that was cold to the touch without being inside his bathroom for anywhere near that length of time, isn't that fair to say?"

"Yes, that is fair."

"Thank you, no further questions, my Lord."

"Nothing further from me," Fergus Richardson said.

"Thank you, Miss Ovett. You are free to go," Judge Dollimore said.

Grace Ovett stepped down from the witness box and threaded her way out of the court. As she passed the defendant, she looked towards him, but he was blowing on his glasses and polishing them with a cloth. He did not look back at her.

Fergus Richardson stood up. "The next witness is to be read and that is the statement of John Trice to be found at page eleven."

The judge momentarily intervened. "Members of the Jury, as has been mentioned, the evidence in this case will take a number of forms, including from time to time the evidence of a witness being read from the statement. The reason it is done in that form is because that particular piece of evidence is not disputed. It is however, and I must emphasise this to you, part of the evidence, and very important therefore that you listen carefully to it. Yes, Mr Richardson."

"Thank you, my Lord. The statement of John Trice. 'I am a housing benefits officer and colleague of Mr Rod

Bannister. On Tuesday the seventh of December, Rod came into his work. He'd been off sick on the Monday. I noticed how quiet he was that day. I made a comment to my manager Jenny Montague, and she agreed that he wasn't his normal bright and breezy self. The next day, Wednesday eighth of December, Rod was again very quiet – he didn't join in any of the banter. Later I heard loud noises from inside a cubicle in the gents' toilet. It was Rod vomiting. I asked him if he was all right and he said he had a lot on his plate'. The statement ends there."

The final witness of the day was Vasim Syed, the car mechanic from Clapton. When the prosecution had taken him through his evidence, it was again Gillian who cross-examined him.

"Mr Syed, do you work full time in the tyre shop?"

"Yes, I do, five days most weeks, but sometimes I'll work an extra half day to help out."

"How many customers might you change tyres for every day?"

"Ten maybe. On a busy day, it might be more."

"So you could end up seeing fifty or sixty customers a week, especially if you've worked that extra half day."

"That sounds about right, yes."

"So, I'm making a conservative estimate here, you've perhaps seen over three thousand customers since Mr Bannister came in that morning in December 1993?"

"Yes, I'd say so."

"You told us earlier that you are absolutely certain that Mr Bannister's tyres were in surprisingly good condition. Do you have contemporaneous notes that confirm this?"

"No, I don't keep those kind of notes."

"And you also told us that you are certain that Mr

Bannister asked you questions about recording his registration number, didn't you?"

"I did say that, yes."

"I don't suppose you took any notes about that either, did you, Mr Syed?"

"No, I didn't."

"Thank you. I have no further questions."

Chapter Forty-Four

The irritating thing for Michaela, was not that Daniel was working that evening, but that he had specifically asked her to come over to his flat to see him. They had talked about it on Wednesday morning at the end of a hurried breakfast. He'd recently given her a set of his keys, and when she let herself in around seven, she'd been expecting him to join her fairly soon.

In readiness for his arrival she'd started cooking, although Daniel's kitchen was not well-stocked. He could be forgiven for this, his trial was taking precedence over everything, including shopping. She managed to make a basic tomato sauce to which she added chilli powder and tinned mushrooms. Who in their right mind bought tinned mushrooms?

He still hadn't arrived by eight thirty, so she cooked the pasta and ate alone with Radio 4 in the background. It was probably wrong to expect any kind of normal relationship with a criminal barrister, particularly when he was mid-trial. Could she even expect him to be anything close to normal, when he spent so long in the company of murderers, rapists and paedophiles? And yet she had agreed to marry this man, knowing that it would be far from plain sailing. Was she cut out to be the wife of a barrister? Their wedding was, she suddenly realised, now less than a month away.

She telephoned her mother, who immediately asked whether they could possibly – and she knew these things weren't easy – invite Ronnie and Emma. Maybe they could squeeze them in somehow.

"Mum," Michaela said, "it's not that kind of event. Because it's his second marriage, Dan just wants very close family and a couple of friends each. So please explain that to Ronnie and Emma."

"All right," Briony said. "Ronnie will be disappointed though. You've always been such a favourite of his."

"Yes and I'm very fond of Ronnie too, but Dan and I have talked this over and it's what we both want."

"It doesn't sound like you had much of a say."

"What are you talking about?" Michaela protested. "I just said we both made the decision."

"Look, I don't want to argue with you. I'll pass the message to Ronnie and Emma. Now, you said there was something else, didn't you?"

"Yes, the cake. You were going to ask Denise whether she could make one for us."

"And I did ask her. She wanted me to check whether you definitely just want lemon sponge."

"Yes, that's what we said, isn't it?"

"That's fine," Briony said shortly.

"What's wrong with lemon sponge?"

"Nothing's wrong with lemon sponge. I'm just checking, because that's what Denise asked me to do."

"What does Denise think is wrong with lemon sponge then?"

"Nothing, I expect."

"So why did she want you to check we definitely want it?"

"I don't know, why don't you ask her? Maybe she doesn't think it's very celebratory."

"Is that what she said?"

"No, of course not."

"So that must be what you think."

"Oh for goodness' sake, Michaela."

"If you must know it's Daniel's favourite type of cake." There was silence at the other end of the phone. "What's the pregnant pause all about?"

"I don't think I'm going to be able to say anything without upsetting you tonight," her mother said. She surely wasn't about to become tearful.

"Look, Mum. I'm very stressed out. Daniel's in the middle of this fucking trial. I'm hardly seeing him. And I've been pretty much left to organise this whole shebang, even though my work is also pretty full-on right now."

"It's all right, darling. You don't have to explain yourself to me. A mother knows."

Daniel still wasn't back when the call finished, so Michaela phoned a few university friends she'd been meaning to contact. She needed to explain about the wedding and why they weren't invited before they heard about it from other sources. Frustratingly, she found herself going through much the same ground as she'd just discussed with her mother. She also spoke to Anika who quickly took offence that Michaela hadn't ordered her a vegetarian meal for the wedding.

"I didn't think you were so worried about it these days," Michaela said. "But I'll order one for you, of course."

"What do you mean, not so worried about it?"

"I mean every time we go out together, you eat meat."

"No, I don't." Anika sounded incredulous.

"Well, you ate burger and chips that night we went bowling. And you had roast beef when we went to my parents. That hardly makes you the world's most assiduous vegetarian."

"Maybe so, but when I go to a wedding my parents become terribly interested in what I've eaten. And I want to be able to tell them the truth."

"That's quite a complicated set of rules you're following there."

"Fuck you, Michaela. What's wrong with you tonight?"

The final person Michaela spoke to, although he knew about her wedding, was not someone she needed to explain his lack of invitation to.

"Thomas," she said, when he picked up. "I've been meaning to call you ever since we had that drink. I really enjoyed seeing you again."

"Me too," Thomas agreed.

"What have you been up to?"

"Oh nothing terribly interesting. How about you?"

"Just making a few calls about my wedding. And in the process, upsetting absolutely everybody I speak to. Is there a word for when you manage to do that?"

"In my case, it would be déjà vu," Thomas said.

Michaela shrieked with laughter just as she heard a key in the lock. "I've actually got to go," she said. "I'll call you again soon."

She looked up as Daniel came in.

"Oh, you're here," Daniel said. "That's a nice surprise."

"It shouldn't be. We arranged it," Michaela said.

"We did?" He came over to her and rested both hands on her shoulders.

"Yes, Dan, on Wednesday morning. Remember?"

"Oh God, I'm so sorry. I completely forgot, there's so much going on."

They put their arms around each other and hugged in the hallway.

"I understand, honestly." She broke away from him and went into the kitchen. "I made some food if you're hungry?"

"I've actually eaten."

"Who with?"

"Gillian. We were working late so we grabbed a quick bite." She tried not to look crestfallen. "Look it's been very intense this week. I'm so sorry I forgot about our arrangement, I'm an idiot."

"I understand, honestly."

"Let's go to Ronnie Scott's."

"What, now?"

"Yes, we can catch a late show there. I'll drive."

"Don't feel you have to, Dan."

"No, I want to. I can be ready in ten minutes."

She was touched. "That would be amazing. The evening's finally starting to look up."

Chapter Forty-Five

On the day that the prosecution was due to wind up its case, the first witness was Dr Katherine White. From his seat, Daniel noticed Dr White's striking looks as she entered the courtroom. She was about his age, with brown wavy hair down to her shoulders. She was wearing a pleated red blouse with a small collar and smart grey trousers, and carried herself with the elegance of Catherine Deneuve. When he'd last spoken to his client, Rod had asked why she was being called as a witness, and Daniel had explained that Dr White's evidence was important in establishing the identity of the victim.

Fergus Richardson stood up and smiled at the witness.

"Is your full name Dr Katherine Marie White?"

"Yes."

"What is your occupation please, Dr White?"

"I'm an oral biologist."

"And you live in Princes Gardens in Ealing?"

"I do, yes."

"Dr White, can you explain to the court what your job involves?"

"Yes, my working life is basically divided into three parts: teaching, research, and forensic science. I'm based at the UCL Medical School where I lecture three days a week. I also undertake my own research at UCL. And from time to time I am called upon to help identify human remains."

"Would that aspect of your work be the forensic science part?"

"It would, yes."

"Beginning with teeth, Dr White, how useful would you say they are in establishing the identity of a deceased person?"

"They're invaluable. The teeth and surrounding structures contain more information about the lifestyle of an individual than any other part of the body."

"Perhaps you could explain to the court why that would be?"

"Teeth do not renew themselves like human bones do. So everything that happens to the body during life leaves its traces in the teeth."

"Thank you, Dr White – that's fascinating. Now, of course the job of positively identifying Mr Liddell from his head would have been much easier had we been able to find his dentist. Would you agree with that statement?"

"Yes, absolutely."

"However, as we did not discover his dentist – if indeed he had one – could you explain the information you obtained from his teeth which helped to match the head to Mr Liddell?"

"Yes, so as I was saying, because of the information stored in the teeth we can make plenty of deductions.

The gender of the victim is recorded in chromosomes that are preserved in tooth pulp. Straight away I could confirm therefore that the victim was male. I was also able to tell that the victim was forty-nine years old."

"I'm sure the whole court is as impressed as I am with that," Fergus Richardson said. "Can you explain in layman's language how you were able to ascertain that?"

"Well, it does become rather complicated," the witness said, smiling. "But in short, the precise age of the victim at death can be calculated by extracting amino acids from the teeth, and then working out the ratio of molecules. These change in a standard way as the body ages."

"Okay, thank you, Dr White – that's probably as much detail as we need on that point. What else were you able to say about the victim?"

"Sometimes we are able to discover the illnesses that the victim suffered, even as children, as prescribed drugs can also leave traces in the teeth. However, as we could not find anything in this case, I concluded that he had not had any such illnesses which were treated."

"So, all of this information was used to narrow the field of candidates that the police stored for missing people, is that correct?"

"Yes, that's right. We had built up a dossier of information on this individual, and the police were able to narrow the field down to about half a dozen people of the right age and sex."

"Thank you. Can you tell us how you confirmed a positive identification with James Liddell?"

"Yes, of course. So we must remember that the head was quite badly decomposed and damaged as you will see in a moment from the photograph. We made our checks against the narrowed field of missing persons and for this purpose we asked the police to produce as many photographs as possible, and as close to the time of death as possible for each person. This was so we could carry out the process of facial superimposition."

"Could you tell us a little bit more about that, Dr White?"

"We analysed the photographs we were given and, in each case, worked out the focal length of the cameras which had been used. We have to remember that photography distorts the image, depending on the focal length of the lens. Once we had been able to work out the type of lens for each picture, we used an electronic camera programmed with the same degree of distortion to photograph the head."

"I believe that you can now demonstrate the results for us."

"Yes, but before I do, can I just add one thing?"

"Of course, please go ahead."

"An important part of this process was fixing the head to a goniometer, which is a versatile stand with calibrations that means we could position the head at any angle. This was key as the head had to be photographed in exactly the same position as the pictures of the victims in real life that we'd been provided. If somebody's head was slightly in profile, in a photograph, or angled forwards, we would do the same with the head on the goniometer. When the angle was exactly right, we took the photograph with the electronic camera."

"Right, my Lord, we will now undertake the demonstration for the court. Could the witness be allowed to leave the box so she can operate the projector?"

"Of course," the judge said. "I'm not volunteering to do it myself."

Fergus Richardson turned to the judge and, when he realised it was a joke, laughed obligingly. "Could the lights in the courtroom be turned off please?"

Dr White climbed down from the witness box and there was a hushed sense of expectation as the courtroom became darker. There were some creaking sounds from behind Daniel, presumably the occupants of the spectators' gallery leaning forwards in their seats for a better view. A photograph of a smiling James Liddell was projected onto a screen. The shot was of his shoulders and head, but in the background there was what looked like the edge of a boat, and behind that the sea.

"This photograph was taken in August 1993 by an unknown person," Fergus Richardson informed the court.

The snapshot was replaced by a photograph of the severed head that had been pulled from the water. It was held in place at the same angle as the 1993 image by the goniometer. There were audible murmurs from the gallery.

Dr White then overlaid the photograph of the head onto the head-and-shoulder picture of Liddell on the boat. The effect of the two photographs matching each other so closely was almost eerie.

"If we can leave that picture on the screen for a moment, my Lord, while the witness returns to the stand?"

"By all means, yes."

"Dr White, could you talk us through what these two photographs together show?"

"Well, they show, beyond doubt that the head found

in the River Thames was that of James Liddell who is pictured in the photograph. I would point out the exact fit of the eye sockets and the jaw-line, and how the shape of the heads match perfectly. Also, please note the position of the mouth – and the exact match of the teeth."

Next in the witness box was the home office pathologist, who talked through what he described as the limited conclusions that he could make from the post-mortem. The first of these conclusions was that the head had been in the water for a period of between three and four months. The court were told that the post-mortem was conducted on the sixteenth of March 1994, four days after the head was found floating in the river. The date of death, as put forward by the prosecution, was the fourth of December 1993, with the head being thrown into the river three days later. This confirmed the pathologist's estimate at the post-mortem. His next conclusion was that the head had been severed, probably shortly after death, with a serrated tool or implement such as a saw. He did not believe that the separation of head and torso had occurred in the water, which was confirmed by the later discovery of the body in Derbyshire.

Following on from the pathologist was the Crime Scene Manager, Derek Buckman. Having taken his oath, he apologised to the court for his heavy cold, which he said he tended to get at around this time every year. As if to reinforce the point, he blew his nose loudly, the sound echoing around the courtroom like the trumpeting of an elephant. Judge Dollimore sat back in his chair, looking distinctly unimpressed.

The evidence from Derek Buckman encapsulated a range of discoveries made by members of his team,

JAMES WOOLF

including the scenes of crime officers. He went into great detail about the prevalence of cleaning products which had been used recently in the defendant's bathroom. He talked at some length about a hair found in the bedroom of the defendant which had been identified as belonging to the victim. There was a discussion about a burnt mound of materials found in a corner of the garden that the defendant owned along with his flat. Although tests had been inconclusive as to what exactly had been burned, some of it was printed material, making it at least likely that one of the items was a book. This provided support to the theory that the defendant had burned the paperback which Mr Liddell had been given by his lodger and which he had been carrying on the day he met the defendant.

After Derek Buckman left the stand, the lights in the courtroom were again switched off to enable various pieces of CCTV footage to be played to the court. There was a technical hiccup which delayed proceedings for a while. Eventually this was sorted out and the often grainy shots were played to the court. These included the defendant and the victim walking together on Upper Street in Islington. The jury were also shown the video of Jackie Levine picking out the defendant in the identity parade.

"The next item today will be the formal evidence of attendance at the post-mortem and of the arrest," Fergus Richardson told the court.

"Very well," the judge said.

The prosecutor proceeded to read the statement of DCI Ruth Hobart.

"'On sixteenth March 1994 I was in attendance at the post-mortem at the office of Her Majesty's coroner. On Wednesday the sixth of July 1994, I was in attendance at the identity parade at which Roderick Clive Bannister was picked out by Jackie Levine. On Thursday the seventh of July 1994, I was on duty at Bishopsgate police station when I spoke to Mr Bannister. I told him that I was formally arresting him on suspicion of murder and that he did not have to say anything but that it may harm his defence if he did not mention when questioned something which he may later rely on in court. I also told him that anything he did say may be given in evidence. Mr Bannister told me he understood. The following day on Friday the eighth of July 1994 at ten am, I charged Roderick Clive Bannister with murder. After charging him with murder I formally cautioned him to which he made the following reply: 'Not guilty'."

Chapter Forty-Six

"DC Luke Crossley please."

The young detective was sitting with his notes right outside the court. As soon as he heard his name, he got up and walked into the courtroom. It was smaller than he'd imagined but every last space seemed to be crammed with people. Walking past the journalists, he was pleased to be wearing his uniform. At least it made him look the part even though he was feeling as nervous as hell. He took the witness stand and concentrated on keeping his voice evenly modulated as he was sworn in.

Fergus Richardson stood up and made eye contact with him.

"Is your full name Luke David Crossley?"

"Yes, Your Honour."

"Oh, please don't call me that, I'm sure I don't deserve it," Fergus said breezily. "What is your rank please?"

"I am a detective constable with the Metropolitan Police."

"And where are you stationed, Mr Crossley?"

238

"I am based at Bishopsgate police station."

"Thank you, and can you tell us what area of work you were engaged in between the fifteenth of June 1994 and the twenty-fourth of June 1994?"

"Yes, I was working with a team of detectives. We were tracing and interviewing men who had attended the same school as James Liddell."

"What in particular were you speaking to these men about?"

"We were interested in a school reunion which had taken place in a pub on the night of Tuesday twenty-third of November 1993."

"Which pub was that?"

"It was one in Central London. I don't have the name here in my notes."

"Both James Liddell and the defendant were at that school reunion, is that correct?"

"That's correct, yes."

"Can you confirm who you interviewed on the twenty-fourth of June?"

"I interviewed the defendant, Roderick Bannister."

"Did you interview him alone?"

"No, I was accompanied by DC Terry Harris."

"And would that interview have been about events at the school reunion?"

"Yes, but also about Mr Bannister's relationship with Mr Liddell at school."

"Where did this interview take place?"

"At the defendant's flat in Hackney."

"What time did the interview take place?"

"It was about seven pm."

"Can you tell us what happened when you visited the defendant in his flat?"

"Yes, we rang on the doorbell, and when he opened the door, he seemed surprised to see us."

"In what way did he seem surprised?"

"I believe he pulled his head back slightly."

"What happened next?"

"I explained that we were carrying out an investigation into the death of James Liddell. 'You may have read about it in the newspaper', I told him. He said that he had indeed heard about it and that it was very shocking."

"Were those his exact words? 'Very shocking'?"

"Yes."

"What happened next?"

"He invited us into his flat and we went into his living room."

"Is that where the remainder of the interview took place?"

"It was, yes."

"Was there anything that happened during the remainder of the interview which you found unusual?"

"There was one thing. As soon as we arrived in his living room, he asked if this meant he was a suspect."

"Do you remember the exact words he used?"

"It was just what I said. 'Does this mean that I'm a suspect?'."

"Had either of you up to that point given any indication that Mr Bannister might be a suspect?"

"No, not at all."

"How did you reply to Mr Bannister?"

"I told him that we were carrying out routine enquiries, and that we were trying to trace as many of the men who had attended the reunion as we could."

"Thank you very much. If you would wait there, there may be more questions."

Daniel stood up. "I have no questions for the witness, my Lord."

"Very well," the judge said.

"In that case, my Lord, that completes the case for the prosecution."

"You are free to go, Mr Crossley," the judge said.

Luke Crossley quite suddenly felt elated by the fact that he was not going to be cross-examined by the defence barrister. He had been worried that the lawyer's clever wordplay would dissect him piece by piece in front of the jury. He almost skipped out of the court. It was as if he himself had got away with something.

Not putting forward a positive case on behalf of his client, Daniel was operating with one hand tied behind his back when it came to calling witnesses for the defence. He chose three witnesses who broadly testified to Rod's good character, two of whom had also been to the same school, and one who was a colleague Rod worked with in 1979. It appeared that Rod had had few if any close friends in recent years; if he chose to socialise, he would do so with people at work.

The fourth and final witness Daniel called was Lloyd Lipsey. Daniel liked to think of him as his star turn. Lloyd was a well-known television actor. Daniel had assumed Lloyd Lipsey was his stage name, and that he would give his evidence under his real name which would be much more prosaic, but this turned out not to be the case.

Lloyd and Rod had had a relationship with each other when they were in their late twenties and his evidence was useful in making Rod appear more normal, and perhaps more glamorous, in the jury's eyes. More normal in that it showed he had participated in a loving relationship between two consenting men. Significantly, Lloyd was able to confirm that Rod was not into any unusual or violent sexual practices. Although it was not the prosecution's case, there had been speculation in one of the tabloids that Liddell's death had been a result of a kinky sexual practice that had gone horribly wrong. Daniel saw no harm in covering all bases and demonstrating, at least by implication, that this would not have happened.

The other main point he was keen to establish was that at the time that Rod and Lloyd had had their relationship in the early 1970s, the events that had occurred between the defendant and James Liddell at school were not preying on Rod's mind. Lipsey confirmed that he could not remember Liddell being mentioned by name and certainly never in the context of someone Rod harboured a grudge against or was the target of future revenge. Daniel was hoping that the actor's evidence might be picked up by the newspapers. Even though the jury had been told not to read press coverage of the trial, Daniel was sure that some would, and it could only be a positive thing if a more appealing image of his client were to surface: the loving and perfectly normal ex-partner of a popular television star, rather than the crazed local government worker, as he'd so far been portrayed.

Fergus Richardson treated Daniel's witnesses with contempt by not bothering to ask questions of any of them. It was as if he was saying that their appearance in the trial was a distraction. He was perhaps confirming his eagerness to press on with the next task in hand, the important milestone of delivering his closing speech.

Chapter Forty-Seven

THURSDAY 4 MAY 1995

M uch had been written and spoken about the tactics of barristers in court. The importance of case preparation, for example. The skills that could be learned and deployed when questioning a witness. There was a theory that sometimes found its way into advocacy training courses, that closing speeches should be written before the trial began. That is, that the barrister should decide, based on the indictment and the evidence available, what information would be needed in their speech in order to win the case. The trial would then become a process of eliciting the right answers from each witness, in order for those answers to then be used in the closing speech. Daniel himself was not a subscriber to this theory. He worked on his closing speech throughout the trial, sometimes even making tweaks and changes after he'd heard the closing speech of the prosecution.

Fergus Richardson's closing speech began at ten fifteen in the morning and finished some two and three-quarter hours later. He began by saying that this was a premeditated murder, one that had – quite manifestly –

been carefully planned. The prosecution submitted that by luring the victim into a trap with the promise of specific sexual favours, it was beyond doubt that the defendant knew of Liddell's sexual preferences, which included being tied up and made helpless. He had clearly played up to these sexual proclivities when he sent him the card. This was no spur-of-the-moment crime. Instead, it was calculated and carried out with the utmost calm and the deadliest precision.

And it was the accumulation of evidence which had been presented to the court that the jury now needed to focus on. They needed to let the evidence build a picture in their minds. Because, Richardson said, the case was very much like a jigsaw puzzle. Any individual piece on its own may not tell the jury that much. But when everything was pieced together and viewed with consideration, the picture was a most compelling one.

There was the background information provided by the defendant's father, who described a relationship in which all trust between father and son had broken down, after Cecil Bannister claimed that his son had, to all intents and purposes, stolen fifty thousand pounds from him.

And there was the defendant's behaviour in the run-up to the evening on which he met James Liddell. They had heard from Jenny Montague who had bumped into the defendant by chance soon before he would meet Liddell. She had told the court that in all the time she'd known Roderick Bannister, she couldn't remember him ever being in such a strange mood.

And then there was the defendant's conduct in the immediate aftermath of the murder. The distracted phone call with his sister the day after Liddell almost certainly met his death. Gail Morley had formed the strong impression that her brother was keeping something hidden from her. The recollections of the defendant's colleagues at work, who noticed that Roderick Bannister was far from himself in the days after Liddell's death. One had heard him vomiting in the toilet. The evidence too of the defendant's neighbour who found him washing down the walls of his bathroom at eight o'clock on the Monday morning after the murder. The barrister reminded the court what Grace Ovett had said, that Mr Bannister almost never cleaned his flat, and certainly not at this time on a weekday morning. The lack of cleaning he undertook had in fact been something they had joked about together. And then there was the strange fact that Mr Bannister had leapt from the rim of the bath to fetch eggs for Miss Ovett from his fridge, when she would have normally expected to fetch them herself.

From the chronology, Richardson said, they knew that Mr Liddell's head had not yet been disposed of. Could it be that Mr Bannister was worried that his neighbour might discover the head? Perhaps he was even storing it in the fridge. They couldn't, however, be sure when the defendant had disposed of Mr Liddell's body. But it was perfectly possible that it was also lying in the flat even as he and Miss Ovett spoke, and that the defendant was equally worried she might find that too.

Richardson also reminded the jury that the defendant changed all four tyres of his car. This was on the Tuesday morning, the day after he had been seen cleaning the bathroom. Why this sudden flurry of activity? And why had the defendant asked the mechanic whether a record would be kept of his registration number? The mechanic also recalled the car's tyres being in extremely good condition when the defendant had driven into the garage. What then was the purpose of changing all four tyres? Most likely, the prosecution submitted, that Mr Bannister was worried that he might be identified by a tyre print found at the remote rural setting in Derbyshire where he had buried the body.

Then there was the evidence that placed the defendant in all the right places at all relevant times. The conversation with Jenny Montague on Upper Street soon before he would meet Mr Liddell. The CCTV evidence showing him walking towards the bus stop with the victim. The evidence of the bus driver who may have been one of the last people to see James Liddell alive.

Critically, Fergus Richardson said, they had also heard from Jackie Levine, who had told the court in some detail how she'd seen the defendant throwing the severed head from Tower Bridge late one night. But not just any night, Richardson told the jury. This was the same day that had begun with the defendant rising early and making a trip to the garage to change his tyres. Notice again the concentration of activity around that period. And not only that, this same witness, Jackie Levine, had picked the defendant out in an identity parade almost eight months later. The jury had been shown the video of this identity parade. If they wished, they could make a request to view it again.

The court too had heard from an old friend of the defendant who used to walk with him in Derbyshire and testified to his extraordinary knowledge of that particular area. Their routes had taken them within yards of where the victim's torso would many years later be found by the police, following a tip-off from a farmer that earth had been disturbed on his land.

There was also the forensic evidence, Richardson told the jury. The traces of cleaning materials in the bathroom found months after the defendant's death – a far greater quantity of cleaning materials than might be expected to be found in a domestic setting – all of this corroborating the evidence of neighbour Grace Ovett. And why, Richardson wondered aloud, would the defendant have gone to such lengths to clean his bathroom? It was the prosecution's case that he did so because the bathroom was where he severed Mr Liddell's head, using a serrated implement. This would have been a very messy business, Richardson said, as the jury could well imagine. And it was the prosecution's contention that some blood ended up on the walls of the bathroom, blood that the defendant needed to clean off.

Then of course there was the forensic evidence matching the victim's head to photographs, and the single hair belonging to the victim that had been found in the defendant's bedroom.

The last thing examined by Fergus Richardson was the motivation for the crime itself. It was very clear, he said, that this was not a sexual encounter that had gone badly wrong, as certain sections of the press seemed inclined to conclude. This was a crime of revenge – no more and no less than that. When Bannister and Liddell had been at school together, they had had the kind of competitive, difficult and complex relationship that would be remembered by their peers many years later. Friends recalled Liddell mocking Bannister when his mother had terminal cancer. He had done so in front of other boys who were too afraid at that time to do anything other than join Liddell in his cruel laughter. Then, of course, there was the immediate trigger for the murder, the school reunion in November 1993, when Liddell had again publicly ridiculed the defendant, this time for what Liddell saw as Bannister's menial occupation as a housing benefits officer. The jury would recall the witness's description of Liddell literally howling with laughter when he remembered how Rod had always said he was going to be a big producer working in Hollywood.

It was a compelling case, Fergus Richardson said, when the pieces were put together, and the picture was viewed as a whole. The Crown's submission was not that James Liddell was a person without fault, or even the kind of individual that you would want to have as your friend. More than this, the jury must remember that the crime of murder was absolute. It did not depend on the victim being likeable. It could not be excused because the victim had been unkind about the defendant's occupation. No, the prosecution's case was simply this. That James Liddell had, over the years, provoked the defendant to such an extent that he planned and executed Liddell's murder. And that he took sufficient pleasure in doing so, that he had made a point of severing the head of his former adversary – the head of his nemesis who had also been *head* boy at their school, a title the defendant coveted – and had thrown that head into the River Thames, where it was, at some point, bound to be discovered. And that he had thrown the head fully two days after disposing of the rest of the body. He certainly wanted to make a point.

Fergus Richardson finished his speech by saying that there was no doubt that the person who had been murdered was James Liddell. This much had been demonstrated so ably by Dr Katherine White through her forensic science work. But crucially, the prosecution was also saying that on the evidence they had heard, the jury could be certain that James Liddell had been murdered by the defendant. They could surely reach no sensible verdict other than a verdict of guilty.

Fergus Richardson thanked the jury for their careful attention and sat down, nodding with satisfaction as one of his underlings, sitting behind him, leaned forwards and tapped his shoulder, no doubt murmuring something complimentary.

Daniel too had to admit that his opponent had made a thorough and wholly professional job in his concluding speech.

After lunch it would be his turn.

Chapter Forty-Eight

"Members of the jury, my learned friend earlier used the analogy of a jigsaw puzzle, when it comes to looking at the evidence in this case. He said that when viewed as a whole, it makes for a very compelling picture. Well, I'm not quite sure what kind of jigsaw puzzles my learned friend used to do as a child, but when I was a boy, the jigsaw puzzles that I completed offered up a much clearer picture than this. Perhaps he grew up in a house where the jigsaw puzzles all had missing pieces, and he became accustomed to being satisfied by a picture that was literally full of holes. Because it does seem to me that there are far too many holes in the story that the prosecution has presented for you, members of the jury, to be certain of anything. Too many things that we just don't know. Too much evidence that is simply not available.

"The jury might accept that the victim went back to the defendant's flat on the evening of the fourth of December, as there is reasonable evidence to suggest that. I'm thinking now of the recollection of the bus driver or the single hair of Liddell's found in the bedroom. But where is the evidence that Mr Liddell actually died in my client's flat? The traces of blood, his DNA perhaps, the bloodstained clothing, the possessions and clothes that my client would have needed to dispose of? Where are the recollections from neighbours of suspicious noises in the night, bangs, gasps, shouts or screams? Where are the sightings of the defendant lugging suspicious-looking packages into his car, or setting out on late-night journeys – either in the car to Derbyshire, or by foot to Tower Bridge? Where is the forensic evidence linking my client to the body? Where is James Liddell's distinctive attaché case or the novel we know he was carrying?

"My learned friend speculated that the burnt printed material found in the defendant's garden could have been this novel, to which I can only say, 'Where's the evidence for that?' I'm sure we've all had the odd bonfire in our garden, to get rid of all kinds of rubbish. In criminal cases, the onus is on the prosecution to prove its case beyond reasonable doubt. Have they done so, or is there, as the defence would argue, an insufficiency of evidence?

"Just thinking about the picture presented by the prosecution again and the jigsaw analogy. Without wishing to focus too much on my learned friend's favourite childhood hobby, I might even suggest that he grew up in a house where the jigsaw puzzles were all stored in the same box with the result that the pieces got mixed up together. No doubt you'll remember instances of this happening from your own childhoods, members of the jury. Because, again, I would suggest with the greatest of respect to my learned friend, that the evidence from some of the witnesses hardly seems to belong in this story at all. And I'm thinking particularly of the evidence of Jenny Montague.

"She was, as you will recall, shopping for ingredients for a special meal for her husband when she encountered the defendant. The prosecution has tried to cast this conversation as being deeply suspicious and meaningful, when it was actually perfectly innocuous and trivial. The interaction between my client and Jenny Montague tells us nothing. So what if the defendant did not know what was playing at the cinema that night. So what if he was not forthcoming about his plans for that evening. We must also remember that Jenny Montague was one of the witnesses who came forward after my client had been arrested and after his name had appeared in every mainstream newspaper in the land in connection with the crime. No doubt she was keen to play her part in the hunt for justice. She is an upstanding member of the community after all. You can imagine the witness poring over the conversation that she'd had with my client in her mind, straining every sinew to find meaning in what my client had said when actually there was none. Remember too that this same witness went on to sell her story for five thousand pounds to a tabloid newspaper. You might conclude that it was in her interest to make her account appear as engaging and relevant to the case as possible.

"Then when we turn to another witness, we find that their sworn testimony also fails to shine a light on what happened. I am referring now to the evidence of the defendant's father, Cecil Bannister, which merely contributes to the fuzzy picture we have in front of us. Mr Bannister, it turns out, was so prejudiced against homosexuals that he wrote to his local newspaper, calling for them all to be chemically castrated. How then can we expect anything like impartiality from him when it comes to assessing the character of his son who is, as we know, a homosexual?

"Then there was the evidence of Jackie Levine, who late at night, on a bridge with no lighting, saw a tall man withdraw something from a Sainsbury's bag. The witness says it was a head. But he had his back to her. His body was between her and whatever he was holding. The witness says that she saw this man clearly. But it was dark. The witness says that she was close enough to see everything clearly. But the man was on the other side of the road. We might also remember that this witness is usually homeless. She has been staying in a rather nice bed-and-breakfast for the duration of this trial in Swiss Cottage no less. You might conclude that she would have wanted to be as helpful to the prosecution as possible.

"'But', you might say, 'this witness picked out the defendant in the identity parade'. Yes, she did indeed pick my client out in an identity parade. But mistakes can be made in identity parades. And if this was a mistake, it was perhaps an understandable one. You will recall that the one thing that Jackie Levine seemed to be sure about was that the man on the other side of the bridge was tall. 'He was tall. Very tall', were her exact words. So when she was asked to help out in an identity parade, it is not altogether surprising what happened. She picked out the tallest man she could see. Could I ask my client to stand up? You will see how tall he is. Six feet four inches in fact. He was by far the tallest of the ten men who lined up that day – I don't think I need a tape measure to make that assessment. I'm not right about everything, members of the jury – you can ask my ex-wife – but I'm pretty confident that my client was by far the tallest of the men lining up.

"Moving on now to Tricia Armitage, who steamed open her boss's private mail, read it, then later fished the same piece of mail out of the bin for the entertainment value of her boyfriend. Don't get me wrong, I'm sure that this witness is also an upstanding member of the community. But you will also remember, this was the witness who listened to a private conversation through a fire door and then asked us to believe that the conversation went as follows: 'You arsehole, I got your stupid card. Okay then, so what shall we do about it?' I don't know about you, members of the jury, but that's not the sort of conversation I'm used to hearing. It doesn't have the ring of truth about it, does it? It sounds more like a piece of dialogue from a very bad film, the sort of film you quickly switch off if you happen to stumble across it on television. You might conclude that the conversation reported by the witness was misheard. Or misremembered. Or bearing in mind the witness's propensity for deceit, simply made up.

"Now we move on to the evidence of Grace Ovett, a much more trustworthy witness, we will all agree about that. But the problem with her evidence was that she was doing her best to describe the appearance of somebody who is not only much taller than she is, but who was also standing on the rim of his bath when they spoke. Can you really accurately describe someone as looking 'stricken', 'very pale', and 'like he hadn't slept all night' when they are three feet higher than you at the time? The witness was also surprised at the coldness of the defendant's hand and concluded that he had probably been in his bathroom all night. But it was a December morning as we know. The window was wide open and because of my client's raised position at the time, freezing air was no doubt blowing directly onto his hand.

Hardly surprising therefore if my client's hand felt cold to the touch. And when I put all of these points to the witness, you will recall how graciously she admitted that, on consideration, they were all perfectly valid points.

"And let us talk finally about the evidence of the mechanic Vasim Syed who seemed to remember very specific details about the tyres on the car my client was driving, and the conversation they had that morning. But then, as you will also recall, my learned friend calculated that since he saw my client the witness would have come into contact with some three thousand other customers. Mr Syed admitted that he doesn't take notes of the condition of the tyres he changes, or of his conversations with customers. So how can we be sure that he has not confused some of the details he told us about with those of other customers? It would be perfectly understandable and natural if he had done so.

"And finally, members of the jury, let me turn to what you might believe to be the elephant in the room, the fact that my client has not himself appeared in the witness stand. I should probably remind you that this is his absolute right in this courtroom. There are many perfectly valid reasons why a defendant may choose not to take the stand, and you should not hold it against him if he does. You can only hold it against him if you feel that the prosecution's case is so strong that it absolutely deserves an answer. Well, I would put it to you that the evidence presented to you by the prosecution is at best opaque – probably more like 'as clear as mud'. If we look at all the witnesses they lined up in this case, you don't need to be Hercule Poirot to work out that they were very much struggling to land the killer blow. In fact, I would put it to you, that the prosecution has not proved anything beyond reasonable doubt at all. And this is the test that must be satisfied for you to reach a guilty verdict.

"You may, members of the jury, think that I have been trying to bamboozle you in this closing speech. But if you think I have been beguiling you this afternoon, which I don't think I have, and if you reject every word I say, you still have to ask yourself, 'What is the prosecution's evidence? What does it amount to?' Because forgive me for repeating this, you have to be sure. If you think he did it, he's not guilty. If you're pretty sure he did it, he's not guilty. You have to be sure that this fifty-year-old man of previous good character, has committed the crime we have been hearing so much about. And I would say that the upshot of all of this, members of the jury, is how can you be sure? How can you be sure when, forgive me for saying this, the prosecution don't even seem sure themselves?

"I hope by the submissions I've made to you that I have helped you analyse the case. I hope that I have helped you realise that when you retire to consider your verdict, the only reasonable verdict you can return is one of not guilty."

Chapter Forty-Nine

"I was watching, Daniel. I got time off and I was in court the whole day."

Daniel laughed out loud. "You're a sly beggar, Michaela Simpson."

"I didn't want to say I was going. I thought it might put you off."

"It would have done, almost certainly. So? What did you think?"

"You were fucking amazing, Dan. *Fucking* amazing. I just wish I could have seen your face. Or seen you making the speech on TV. It would have made great television."

Daniel looked around the small room in the Old Bailey. Just a table and chair. And the telephone he was using. But his heart was positively brimming. "Thank you. Honestly, that means so much to me."

"I'm not sure it should. I make my living writing, but I could never have written anything like that."

"It's something you learn. Like skiing. Or cooking poached eggs."

"Poached eggs, what the hell are you talking about?" Michaela laughed.

"God knows, I'm just so happy to have got that over with, I can't tell you."

"I'm not surprised. And not just the writing. Your delivery was so good. Your comic timing. I wanted to laugh so much but didn't feel I could. I was straining my stomach muscles, holding it back, it was painful."

"It wasn't meant to be that funny."

"I know, I was nervous. I was shitting myself before you started. On your behalf of course."

"Listen, the reason I'm calling is that Stan's taking us out for dinner tonight. I thought he might, but he just confirmed it. I wanted to give you proper notice this time."

"Thank you. Is Stan your solicitor?"

"Yes. He can't spare any more time on this case, but he wanted to thank us."

"Is that with Gillian?"

"Yes, the three of us. Kind of a debrief. Of course we've got the judge's summing up to go, so we're not out of the woods yet."

"Where's he taking you?"

"The Groucho Club. He's a member."

"Very fancy, very swish. Not the usual haunt of lawyers though, is it?"

"This is fancy, Stan," Daniel said, taking in the airy yet modern dining area. "Very – what's the word… swish."

"Cheers," Stan said.

"Cheers," Daniel and Gillian repeated. They drank from the French red which Stan had chosen.

"This will open out nicely," Stan said.

"But not the kind of place where you'd expect to find lawyers," Daniel said.

"It was your head of chambers that introduced me to the Groucho, if you must know," Stan said grumpily.

"That will explain it then," Daniel said.

"I think he uses it to find future clients."

"George is rather partial to mixing with the rich and famous. Last week he was telling us about how he picked up the glove of some famous actor in the theatre, I can't even remember who she was. I can see why he'd like it here."

"Okay," Stan said, unnecessarily tapping his knife on the table. "While we're waiting for our food, and before I get too drunk, let me do the speech. Firstly, you guys have done a terrific job. Regardless of the verdict, you both did brilliantly."

"We make a great team, don't we?" Daniel turned to Gillian.

"You really do," Stan confirmed.

"Thank you. Both of you." Gillian seemed genuinely touched.

"I was a bit worried when we started," Daniel said. "That you had too many cases on the go. But I have to say, Gillian, you've been with me every inch of this journey."

"I appreciate that."

"I had my doubts too," Stan said. "But they were about you, Daniel. I needed a lot of persuading to give you this brief."

"Well, that's always good to hear," Daniel said. They all laughed.

"Your speech though, I have to say," Stan continued.

"You took an axe to everything Richardson had just said and demolished it."

"The jigsaw stuff was priceless," Gillian agreed.

"Well, the jigsaw was an open invitation," Daniel said. "I rewrote a fair amount in the lunch-break."

"It was worth it," Stan said. "How do you think the jury received it?"

"Good, I think. But you probably have as much an idea on that as I do."

"They seemed to be lapping it up," Gillian said.

"I agree," Stan said.

"I tried to make eye contact with all of them at some point," Daniel said. "The bald guy in the suit's a lost cause, but I managed all the others. I don't want to tempt fate, but I might even have won over those terrifying grannies."

"Oh my God, not them," Stan said.

The food arrived. Spaghetti Bolognese for Daniel, fish for Stan and Gillian.

"How do you think Rod's bearing up?" Gillian asked.

"Hard to say. What do you think?" Stan turned to Daniel.

"At the end of today, he gave me a little smile. I asked him if he wanted a chat and he said he was fine. He said he was reading a really good book. Make of that what you will."

"You didn't answer my question," Stan said. "Instead you told a story. Which is typical of a barrister."

"Sorry. I think he's fine. I'm sure it's been an ordeal for him, of course it has, but he's been remarkably relaxed, considering, hasn't he?"

Stan widened his eyes. "I suppose so."

"I find him a difficult person to read," Gillian said.

"I've chatted to him a couple of times during the

trial," Stan said. "He had one or two procedural questions. But he seemed satisfied. He doesn't give much away, I agree."

"We've been down to see him a fair bit, haven't we, Gillian?"

Gillian nodded. "Probably every other day. But I get the impression that you're the one he's opened up to."

"It's probably a men thing," Daniel said. "But it's really important," he suddenly realised he was talking way too loudly, "it's really important," he lowered his voice, "to me at least, that Rod feels we've done a good job. And I say that not because I think he's innocent and I'd hate to see him go down. I also really want his approval – if that doesn't sound too weird?"

Gillian was looking at Daniel closely and he felt the need to continue.

"There was one evening I went down to see him. And I'm sure I was just asking for a sign of his approval. It was pathetic really, like a little boy seeking his father's affirmation."

Gillian nodded, but Daniel was far from sure that she really understood what he'd been saying.

"I don't care what he thinks of me," Stan said. "Just as long as he doesn't put in a formal complaint."

"Not much chance of that, is there?" Gillian said.

"Ah, Gillian – you're so naive," said Stan.

"It probably depends a lot on the verdict," Daniel said.

"It depends a hell of a lot on the verdict," said Stan.

Chapter Fifty

MONDAY 8 MAY 1995

"Members of the jury," Judge Dollimore said, "on Friday, after you had been deliberating for some three hours, I gave you appropriate directions to enable you to separate and go home for the weekend and hopefully find some time to relax and put the case out of your minds. I hope you all did have a pleasant weekend and I hope you have all come back refreshed and ready to resume your deliberations.

"Let me once more reassure you, if you need any reassurance, that you must not feel under any pressure of time, or any other form of pressure at all. I shall now ask you to listen while the jury bailiffs are sworn in your presence, and after that I will invite you to go with the jury bailiffs once more and return to your jury room where you will resume your deliberations."

The following day, just after three pm, the jury returned to the courtroom where they were addressed by the clerk of the court.

"Would the jury foreman please stand?"

The man in the suit rose to his feet.

"Would you please answer my next question yes or no. Members of the jury, have you reached a verdict on the single count of this indictment upon which you are all agreed?"

"Yes."

"Members of the jury, on this single count, do you find this defendant guilty or not guilty of murder?"

"Not guilty."

"Members of the jury, on this single count, you find this defendant not guilty of murder, and that is the verdict of you all?"

"It is."

"Thank you. Would you sit down please."

The judge addressed the defendant. "Roderick Clive Bannister, please stand up. You have been found not guilty of this crime of murder by the verdict of this jury. I make no comment on whether or not this is a true verdict. It only remains for me to say that you are now free to leave the court and to resume your life as best you can. Please accompany the defendant from the dock."

Rod smiled briefly at Daniel and was led past the journalists and out of the court.

"I am spared from addressing remarks to the loved ones of the deceased due to the simple fact that he had, as we understand, no surviving members of his family. I will therefore move on to DCI Ruth Hobart, who I believe is present today. There is no doubt that this investigation was a difficult and complex one, the circumstances of the case being what they were. As far as

I'm aware, there are few cases each year which attract the level of media attention as this one. Whatever the verdict might have been, it was always clear that your team was working under immense pressure, and that you operated with skill, care and sensitivity.

"Mr Ferguson and Mr O'Neil, this difficult trial has imposed great demands on all who have had the responsibility for its preparation and conduct. In my view the trial has been conducted faultlessly throughout, and in a manner consistent with the very best traditions of the Bar of England and Wales. Those of us who have been fortunate enough to see you and your legal teams at work cannot fail to have been impressed by the high quality of the services which you provided to your respective clients.

"Ladies and gentlemen of the jury, I have reserved my final remarks in this case for you. The jury system in this country has evolved over the last eight hundred years. It is the process whereby we try to ensure that any person who faces a serious criminal charge receives a fair trial. Trial by jury is the very foundation of our criminal justice system. And it has been clear to me that throughout this trial each of you has discharged your duty as a juror with great distinction. Each one of you has entirely fulfilled the oath that you took at the beginning of this trial and I am grateful to each and every one of you."

Stan tapped Daniel's shoulder and then shook his hand so hard that it was painful.

"I hope you'll join us for a celebratory drink in chambers," Daniel said.

"Of course," Stan said. "Are you coming, Gillian?"

"Wouldn't miss it," Gillian said.

"I'm going to invite Rod too," Daniel said. "But first I just need to make a quick call."

Just outside the courtroom Daniel passed DCI Ruth Hobart, the woman who'd headed up the police investigation. As she caught sight of him, she seemed to regard him with such venom that a chill travelled down his neck. He could understand how she felt. But it was all very well looking aggrieved. Perhaps she could now turn her attention to catching the true perpetrator of the crime.

In the small room he used for telephone calls, he tried to reach Michaela at work, but she was not around. Next, he called Sally's house and was pleased that his younger daughter picked up the phone.

"Audrey, it's Daddy. I just wanted to tell you that I won the big case I was working on."

"That's brilliant, Daddy, I'm so proud of you."

"Thank you, sweetheart. Are Imogen or Max around?"

"No, they're both at friends and I'm stuck doing boring homework."

"Ah – sorry to hear that. Tell the others I said hello, won't you? And don't forget to pass on my news."

When the taxi dropped Daniel, Stan, Gillian and Rod off at chambers, Bill shook them all by the hand and told them that a bottle of something very fizzy was already in the fridge.

"George insisted you use his room too. He's in there waiting."

"Daniel, congratulations!" George said as he opened the door. "Come inside. I'll bet you're glad you didn't get me for this case," he added to Stan.

"I'm sure Rod is," Stan boomed.

"You guys definitely did me proud," Rod said, looking around the famous barrister's room.

Bill came in with the champagne and filled a glass for each of them.

"To a great victory," Stan said.

"I'll drink to that," Gillian said.

They clinked glasses and there were murmurs of appreciation as they sipped the sparkling liquid.

Daniel said, "And thanks so much, Stan, and you too, Gillian – this has been great teamwork. I couldn't have done this without you."

They drank their champagne and then the lawyers all congratulated each other again.

"I wasn't sure which way it was going to go," Stan ventured.

"Me neither," Gillian said.

Then Daniel turned to Rod who was standing slightly apart.

"This was all about you, Rod. I always believed in you."

"Thanks, Daniel," Rod said. "The trial felt like a rollercoaster at times, but we got the result we wanted, eh?"

"We certainly did. And you can trust me when I say that justice isn't always dished up in our system. But it certainly has been today."

They all agreed with that. And then Bill was sent to find another bottle of bubbly.

Chapter Fifty-One

A voiding the theatre-goers thronging on the pavement, Michaela turned off Charing Cross Road and headed down Old Compton Street.

She hadn't mentioned to Daniel that she was meeting Thomas that evening. Deliberately. She wasn't comfortable about keeping it from him, but at the same time she couldn't face all the explaining that would be needed to make him understand that everything was fine. She'd first have had to tell him about the evening she'd met Thomas after work. He wouldn't have been impressed that they'd gone for a drink by the river. And then he'd have needed convincing that, despite their fears, Thomas was actually fine and posed no threat to their relationship at all. And finally, because she hadn't told him about the harmless drink in the pub a month ago, it was now doubly impossible to tell him about this evening's arrangement.

When she'd called Thomas, Michaela had been very clear that they'd just be meeting as friends, nothing more. Thomas was fine with this. He said it would be

267

lovely to see her. True to form, when Michaela suggested an Italian restaurant, he had a better idea. He would prefer Mildreds, a vegetarian bistro in Soho. She didn't complain. Thomas was a vegetarian after all. And she didn't have the energy for a discussion about it following her bruising encounter with Anika. She also remembered that he got frustrated when he ate out and found the only things he could choose from the menu were pasta, or worse still, quiche.

Daniel was attending a guest speaker event, a legendary lawyer she'd never heard of. His absence had provided her with the perfect opportunity to make this arrangement.

"I think you'll be pleasantly surprised," Thomas said, when they took their seats.

They talked about his lecturing job for a while. The restaurant was small and pretty crowded, so it didn't feel like they had much privacy, but the food when it came was rewarding and plentiful. Thomas seemed to know their waitress sufficiently well to have a conversation with her. He admitted he'd been to Mildreds several times before.

"So, what's new with you?" Thomas asked, as they tucked into their main course.

"Oh, not so much," Michaela said. "I'm getting married of course. In eleven days' time."

"To Daniel, the fabulous barrister."

"Yes, he's been on cloud nine since that case finished."

"I'll bet. It was a great result for him."

"But we're way behind with our wedding preparations, as you can imagine."

"How do you feel about it? Getting married?"

"What do you mean?"

"It's a big step, isn't it? I've never been married. Not sure I'd want to."

"Of course it's a big step. And how do you think I feel about it? I'm very happy. I'm very much in love."

"That's great. It must be so interesting hearing about his work every day."

"Oh, there is some other news actually. Did I mention that I'm writing short stories these days?"

"Writing short stories?" He sounded intrigued.

"Trying to, anyway."

"No. You very definitely didn't mention that."

"Well, I am."

"Cool," he said, stretching out the word. "How long have you been doing that?"

"Oh, not long. A few months. It started out me just trying to manage my stress. I'd write notes about the awful things I'd heard that I couldn't put in my articles. A way of getting them out my head. Then I found I was turning one into a story."

"That's fascinating."

"Well, wait till you read it."

"You want me to?"

"Don't you teach a course on short stories?"

"The American short story, yeah. Thomas Thurber, Dorothy Parker, Poe, Cheever, Raymond Carver – a whole load in fact."

Michaela winced. "Maybe it's not such a good idea to read mine after all."

"Oh, come on. I know you're just starting out. I won't be brutal. What does Daniel think of them?"

"He hasn't read any."

"I guess he's busy."

"It's not that. I haven't told him about them." Michaela giggled.

"Oh. Ouch. Okay."

"Not ouch. He's just not much of a reader. He might pick up the odd legal thriller."

"John Grisham?" Thomas chuckled.

"Exactly," Michaela said, rolling her eyes. "He bought me one of those but I never read it."

"Well, I'd love to read one or two of yours. Do you have any on you?"

"Of course not. Do you think I walk round with my short stories in my handbag? Am I that much of a narcissist?"

An hour and a half and two bottles of wine later, they were sitting on the top deck of the bus heading towards Michaela's flat.

"I'm just so curious what you'll make of them. There's one in particular I think you'll like. I'm going to start with that one."

"Will you read it out loud?" he asked.

"If you want."

"Of course. I love it when writers read out their work."

"But just to be clear, this is an invitation to hear one or two of my stories and nothing more. I just want your reaction to them, that's all. We're just friends, yes?"

"Of course. You're getting married. I totally understand that."

"As long as you know. Because if you try any funny business, you'll be in a taxi faster than you can say F. Scott Fitzgerald."

"I get it, Michaela. I mean, what kind of depravity do you expect from me? It will be lovely to come back and discuss your stories. And nothing more."

She smiled and they were silent for a while. She remembered her first date with Daniel. Over a year ago now and so much had happened. He'd wanted to kiss her on the bus, and she'd told him not to be in such a rush – funny to think of that now. She found herself turning to look at Thomas, a wisp of his hair that had escaped from his ponytail, his lips. Could she even remember what it felt like to kiss him?

She found it perfectly natural to be leaning against Thomas now. The bus had picked up speed, taking the corners faster than it ought to have done. They weren't the only passengers having to lean this way and that. But he was now facing away from her, looking through the window. And she wanted his attention.

"Thomas?" she said.

"What is it?" He turned towards her. A slightly quizzical smile on his face.

She found herself getting lost in his eyes.

"Yes?" he asked again.

"It's just – oh, I don't know."

She leaned into him and planted a kiss squarely on his mouth. He looked incredibly surprised. "Okay. That was nice," he said.

They pressed closer together and kissed for a long time, like teenagers. They used to kiss all the time when they first became a couple.

"I thought we were just friends," Thomas said.

"Yes. We are. Kissing friends."

They didn't speak after that, and when their stop arrived, she led him in silence by the hand to her flat. It turned out that there wasn't time for her to read any of her short stories to him that night after all.

Chapter Fifty-Two

FRIDAY 19 MAY 1995

I t was about midday, a slow day, and Daniel and Chris were sitting at their desks, opposite each other, in their room.

"I'm not feeling it today," Daniel said.

"How do you mean?" Chris asked.

"I don't know, this aggravated burglary. It's not doing it for me. Do you ever get days when you wonder why you bother?"

"Occasionally. You're probably distracted though by your wedding. At least, I imagine you are."

Daniel looked up from his desk in surprise. This was breaking their unwritten rule, wasn't it? That he and Chris never discussed anything from their personal lives. "Maybe," he said. "That's probably what it is."

As he said it, he became aware of the door-handle moving up and down on his left-hand side – creaking as it did so. The mechanism often caught slightly, but after a moment whoever was on the other side must have pushed forcefully as the door flew open.

Daniel and Chris both turned to see who it was. Rod Bannister walked into the room.

"Rod," Daniel said. "This is a surprise."

"Sorry to burst in on you like this, chaps," Rod said, looking around him. He was holding a carrier bag and Daniel thought back to the trial. "I came to say thank you, Daniel, properly – you know."

"Oh, that's kind. Chris, I'd like you to meet Rod Bannister. My recent client."

"Hi," Chris said, waving stiffly from his desk.

"I hope I'm not disturbing you," Rod said.

"Not at all," Daniel said, rising from his chair and going over to Rod. "So this is my room. Not so amazing. Not like George's. Rod saw George's room last week," he explained to Chris.

"It's just a room, isn't it?" Rod sounded bemused that it had become a subject of conversation. "Anyway, I wanted to say thank you. It was all a bit of a blur after the trial. And I've got you a present too."

He handed the bag to Daniel who withdrew a small box, an old box, with tattered blue velvet covering it. "Oh, you shouldn't have," he murmured.

"They're antique," Rod said.

Daniel opened the box and found a set of cufflinks, gold, each with two gems.

"Are these…"

"Diamonds and rubies, yes. And this is gold."

"Of course."

"Rather lovely, eh? They were my grandfather's."

"But they must be worth a small fortune," Daniel said.

"I don't know." Rod sounded surprised. "Probably a bit, but I'd noticed you wearing cufflinks. And I was thinking a lot about it during the trial. About what I could give you if we won the case. So I settled on these."

Daniel was aware that Chris was listening in on every word of the conversation.

"It's very kind of you, but I'm not sure that I can accept them."

"What?" Rod clearly wasn't expecting this.

"We're not allowed to accept gifts. Not when they might be worth several thousand pounds."

"But I don't wear cufflinks," Rod said. "I don't have any use for them."

"It's the rules, I'm afraid," Daniel said. "Chris will back me up on this."

Chris nodded. "If they're worth several thousand pounds, he probably..." He winced, as if he couldn't bear to finish the sentence.

"Can't you just take them, regardless of the rules?" Rod asked.

"I feel bad, but I really can't. They're just too valuable."

"All right," Rod said, sounding disappointed. He took the box back from Daniel, closed it and replaced it in the bag. "But if you can't accept my present, I'll buy you lunch."

"I'm going to have to turn that down too. I've already bought sandwiches. I do that on my way into work sometimes, it saves time."

"You're a barrel of laughs," Rod said, without a trace of humour.

Then Daniel had another idea. They ended up sitting outside at the Inn. Rod bought his own sandwich on Fleet Street and they ate lunch on a bench in Middle Temple Gardens.

"Sorry about the present," Daniel said.

"Don't be silly, I completely understand. Sorry I put you in an awkward position."

"It's fine, no need to apologise."

"This is glorious," Rod said. "Lovely to have this on your doorstep."

"I know. Centuries of history."

"Lovely weather too."

"Gorgeous," Daniel agreed.

"I mean, don't get me wrong, I like popping down to London Fields, for a walk, or a picnic sometimes. But it's not like this, is it?"

They ate their sandwiches and chatted about nothing much in particular. Rod said he'd seen his sister and they were friends once again. Daniel mentioned that he would be married in eight days' time and Rod congratulated him. Every so often Daniel remembered that he was eating lunch with a man he'd just represented in a murder trial.

"For me, the hardest part was the three days when the jury were out," Rod said, changing the subject. "Do you know if they had any questions for the judge?"

"I don't," Daniel told him. "I was in the dark, just like you were, at that point."

"I see." There was a pause before Rod continued. "It meant a lot to me, you know, what you said after the trial."

"When I said what, exactly?" Daniel asked.

"About always having believed in me. That I was innocent."

"Well that was true."

Rod smiled and brushed his hands together, causing a few crumbs to fall to the ground. "Thank you," he said. "I'm glad."

Chapter Fifty-Three

D aniel and Michaela were in a fancy restaurant on Upper Street. She'd told him they needed an evening to go through a few last-ditch things before the big day.

"Something strange happened yesterday," Daniel said.

"Go on," she replied.

He told her how his former client had come into chambers. "You know – Rod?"

"*Rod* Rod," Michaela said excitedly, popping a fried white bait into her mouth with her fingers.

"Rod Bannister, yes."

"What did he want?"

"To thank me, for a start. Which isn't unusual."

"Well, you did just get him off a life sentence for murder."

"That's true." Daniel lowered his head to sip his pea soup. "My God, this is hot. Like molten lava."

"Did you burn your tongue?"

"Probably. Anyway, we were working at our desks,

midday. And Rod just walked in. Into our room. Like he was walking into his kitchen or something."

"Okay…"

"I mean, normally if we have a visitor, they'll be told to wait in reception. And we'll come down to meet them. Have our conference in a spare room. I'm not sure he even spoke to the receptionist."

"That is strange. Is your room easy to find?"

"Not especially. It's on the second floor."

"But he just wanted to say thank you? So nothing alarming," she said.

"No, nothing alarming."

"These fish are absolutely delicious."

"Oh, good."

"How's yours?"

"A bit like pea soup."

"All right, just asking."

"I can taste the bacon, which is good," Daniel said.

"Yes, that is good."

Daniel explained how Rod had brought a present along which he couldn't accept, but how they ended up eating lunch together in Middle Temple Gardens.

"It was all pretty relaxed. And strangely enough, it's starting to feel more like he's a friend."

They looked at each other. Daniel finished his soup, wiped his top lip with a napkin and smiled, pleased with himself.

"But hold on, Daniel. Isn't it against your code of conduct to suddenly become friends with an ex-client?"

"Not strictly a breach, no. Because I'm not representing him anymore. But it could be frowned upon, I suppose. Well, it would be if it's a guy and a female client. And they end up, you know, having an affair. There was this time, apparently, when this silk married an ex-client and his position just became untenable in chambers. He stopped being a barrister, if I recall. But this is quite different of course."

"It's a very fine line, Dan."

"How do you mean?"

"I mean, your bloody code of conduct. It's like a religion to you. You quote it like the frigging Bible. So to become friendly with an ex-client, who most newspapers still think is the murderer. How on earth do you square that one?"

"It was probably a one-off. I feel like I got to know him during the trial, but strictly speaking, we're not actually friends of course. And the newspapers are wrong. He's an innocent man. He was framed by someone else, the real killer probably. That part wasn't explored in the trial."

"I see."

"So, really. You can look at it as just a thank you from a grateful client."

"I suppose. It all feels a bit weird though."

"It's unlikely to happen again. Anyway, aren't we meant to be talking about our wedding?"

"We are. But can we just finish this?"

Daniel paused, looking slightly baffled. "I thought we had finished." He could see that she was struggling with a thought. "What is it, Michaela? It's not such a big deal, honestly."

"It's just you always present yourself as such a moral person. You've got your rules and your boundaries. So I'm just surprised that you casually have lunch with a possible murderer."

"He's not a murderer."

"I said a possible murderer."

"Will you lower your voice, please?"

"I'm sorry. I'm just surprised. That's it. No more."

"Okay."

They sat in silence.

"So?" he asked. "Are we going to talk about the things we need to do before our wedding?"

"I can't be bothered now."

"Me neither."

"We'll do it tomorrow."

"Sure."

Chapter Fifty-Four

Nikos told Thomas he'd been introduced to The Coffee Cup by his tutor. They'd met there when the tutor was keen to recommend Nikos for the job he was now doing.

"He wanted to take his time with our conversation. He did not want to rush over the details on the telephone."

"It sounds more like he might have had an ulterior motive," Thomas said.

Nikos thought for a moment. "I don't think it was like that." He smiled.

"Anyway, I'm glad he did introduce you to this place," Thomas said. "The raisin toast is…" He pressed his thumb and forefinger together, making the sign of perfection.

They drank simultaneously from their cups.

"It's nice to see you," Nikos said, looking at the last dregs of coffee granules in his cup.

Thomas nodded in agreement. "I'm glad you called actually. I've been feeling a little low."

"Oh. I'm sorry to hear that."

"Ah, it's nothing really. I kind of got myself into a stupid situation."

"It is easy to do," Nikos said vaguely.

"And this wasn't totally my fault. More hers, I'd say."

"Hers?"

"Bit of a complicated story. But I've got involved with a woman I used to see years ago. When I was last living in England."

Nikos cleared his throat.

"It's a fucked-up situation," Thomas continued. "Cos she's getting married. Today actually. It may be right now. Three o'clock is a fine time for a wedding, isn't it? She's probably saying 'I do' right this second. This woman I fucked three times in the last ten days."

"Wow."

"Yeah, I know. She feels bad about it. She knows it's not the right thing to have been doing. Told me she just needs to get me out of her system. That's what she actually said. Like, I'm something impure in her petrol tank that's making her engine judder and do strange things."

"Who is she marrying?"

"You know the court case? The one you appeared in. The barrister who was defending Rod Bannister. That's the man she's marrying."

"The man who cross-examined me?"

"Sure, him," Thomas said, as though it was no big deal.

"Isn't that a rather big coincidence?"

"No. I went to watch him in court. Deliberately. Checking out the competition, I guess."

"You didn't mention that when we met."

"I know. Sneaky, eh?"

"So… are you in love with her?"

"Fuck. Good question. Yes, I think I am." It was as if he was realising it for the first time.

There was a long silence. Nikos looked out of the window. A couple were walking hand in hand. A mother laughed at something her teenage son just said. All were enjoying their Saturday afternoon in Hampstead.

"Shit, you're right!" Thomas suddenly said. "I've gone and fallen in love with her. Now that I know I can't have her forever."

"It's all a mess," Nikos said.

"Too right. But you know what, Nikos. I don't want to shy away from the pain. It's only when you're in touch with your pain that you are reaching for something deeper within yourself."

Nikos nodded. "Is she very beautiful?"

"Michaela? Yes, although her ears are too big. But that's what I love about her most. They're not gigantic. Just a little too big. And she's aware of that. She covers them up with her hair. But I uncover them. After we make love, I tuck her hair behind her ears. Generally, I despise people with too many perfect qualities. How about you?"

"I haven't thought about it too much," Nikos said.

"It's when I'm seeing her upset or angry about something, when I see her fractures and scars, that I feel closest to her. Trust me to go and fall in love with her now. And realise it on her wedding day."

Chapter Fifty-Five

Paul Summerfield QC held up his hand, acknowledging the laughter, then allowed it to die down.

"But much as Daniel is obsessed by our Bible, the great legal textbook, Archbold, and impressive as it is that he quotes from it verbatim, like some people might quote Wordsworth, there is, of course, another side to Daniel; a little-known side, you might say. Ladies and gentlemen, you might think the most important thing in Daniel's life is his work, but if you do believe that, you need to think again.

"Because there are three young people sitting here tonight, and you will all have noticed them. Their exquisite presentation. Their exemplary behaviour (barring one fit of the giggles during the service, which I will gloss over). I'm talking, of course, about Daniel's delightful three children. Now, where are they?"

He very obviously cast his eyes around the room, as though – despite the loud laughter from Max and Audrey – he was finding it difficult to pick out the table where they sat with their cousins. And then pointing dramatically with a teaspoon, he shouted, "There they are!" before addressing them directly.

"Imogen, Audrey and Max, I probably don't need to tell you how much your father loves you. But I might need to tell everyone else what a doting father he is, and how he's always thinking about you, his children, even during the periods when you are apart. I believe that the very first person that Daniel spoke to after the Roderick Bannister trial finished was you, Audrey? Isn't that right?"

Audrey could just be seen nodding proudly.

"And that phone call, I believe, says so much. It speaks volumes. And yes, until today, I might have said that these three special people are the most significant others in Daniel's life. But now we must, I believe, acknowledge that there is a new somebody else, who is as significant to Daniel as his children.

"I'm sure that for some of you, today is the first time you've met Michaela. But even from that brief introduction, you will know that Daniel has chosen the most beautiful and spirited woman as his life partner. Her intelligence and wit, but also her integrity and dignity, shine through in everything that she does. And because of this, I know that Daniel and Michaela will have many beautiful and loving years together.

"And so, ladies and gentlemen, before I lurch too far into sentimentality, I would like to finish with a toast. To the bride and groom. To Daniel and Michaela."

The thirty or so friends and family dutifully raised their glasses.

"To Daniel and Michaela," they repeated.

"Thank God that's over." Daniel laughed as the taxi pulled away from the venue.

"I know," Michaela said. "That best man speech, honestly. I thought it would never end."

"He did his best."

"I suppose so. I don't know about you, but I'm exhausted."

"Me too," Daniel said. "But I've felt like this for weeks. Ever since the trial finished actually."

"That's understandable. It was mentally and emotionally draining for you."

"Yes, including the whole lead-up to it."

"You were under pressure, weren't you, to perform?"

"Exactly," he said. "Enormous pressure."

After a pause, Michaela said, "And I've been busy too."

"I know," Daniel said. "To be honest, when we get there, I'll be quite happy not doing anything much at all. Just flopping on beaches, sampling the local food and drinking far too much alcohol."

"That sounds good to me," she smiled.

"It's kind of why I suggested the Greek islands. But I know the cultural side of things is important to you too."

"Yes, but we'll take it easy for the first couple of days. And then we'll go somewhere like that castle," Michaela said.

"Neratzia Castle?"

"That's the one."

"We could do. But from the guidebook it doesn't look so amazing. Not compared to what we have at home."

"Well, it doesn't have to be that castle. But I'll want to do something. Otherwise I'll just get itchy feet."

"So, why don't you jot down a few things you'd like to do? And we'll make sure we tick them all off."

Michaela nodded and withdrew a novel from her bag.

"What's that about?" he asked. He didn't want Michaela to get lost in her book for the whole taxi ride. And then, quite possibly, the flight too. He wanted to engage with her, have a conversation.

"Daisy Flett," Michaela said with a slight giggle. "It's her diary really. It's good."

"How did you come across it?"

"Anika bought three books for me to take away. She told me she'd sort out my honeymoon reading for me."

"That was kind. Slightly controlling maybe," he added.

"There's one sentence you'll like." She started leafing through the book, her face a study in concentration. Daniel leaned across and kissed a frown that had appeared on her forehead. "Here we are. 'The real troubles in this world tend to settle on the misalignment between men and women'." She smiled. "There. Discuss."

"Misalignment? That's a niggly kind of word."

"It's really just the story of a very ordinary woman," Michaela said. "She gets into ordinary relationships, lives in all sorts of different places, things don't work out usually."

There was music playing in the taxi, so quietly he hadn't noticed it before. They hadn't said as much as a word to the driver since they got in the car. He wondered why he didn't turn the music up to keep himself entertained.

"Talking about living in different places," Daniel said, "it's slightly crazy that we're now married, and you're still renting your flat."

"I agree. But we'd like to stay in Islington, wouldn't we?"

"Yes. We'll do some serious house-hunting when we get back."

"And the reason I'm still renting my flat is because yours is too small for us to share."

"I know. I didn't buy it with a future wife in mind. I bought it because I had a few hours to make a purchase."

"I understand, Daniel. And I'm obviously keen to start looking. But we agreed we'd do that when we got back. I'm not imagining that, am I?"

"Of course not. We had a conversation about it."

She read her book for a couple of minutes, while he looked out of the window. They had now escaped the traffic and picked up speed. The cars on the other side of the road were flying past in dazzling bursts of blurry light.

"I'm looking forward to moving," Daniel said. "We had that slightly difficult period when Thomas got in touch with you. But now, I feel we can move seamlessly into the rest of our lives."

"I think you overplayed that difficulty, Daniel. Exaggerated the threat from Thomas somewhat."

"Almost certainly," he agreed. "But either way, it's all in the past now."

"Yes." She didn't sound convinced.

"It *is* in the past, isn't it? The last time we spoke about it you hadn't heard from him for weeks."

"Well… we have been in touch. A bit."

"What do you mean, 'You have been in touch a bit'?"

"We've spoken a couple of times. He's actually fine, Daniel. He's not dangerous or anything. He knows there's not much I can do to help him, not that he needs help. He has his own friends. His own life. I've been careful not to give the wrong impression."

Daniel had been looking at her very curiously as she spoke. Not only listening to what she said but trying to work out if there was something he was missing.

"I thought this had all finished, Michaela. Did he turn up at your work again?"

"No. He only did that once."

"But you said you've spoken a couple of times."

"Yes, on the phone."

"You changed your number. You changed your telephone number so he couldn't contact you."

"I phoned him."

Daniel rubbed the palms of his hands over both eyes and turned to look through the window. "You phoned him?"

"Yes, I phoned him."

"Why did you phone him?" He was speaking slowly now, in a voice so quiet she could barely hear.

"Because I wanted to see how he was."

"Why though?" He turned back towards her, anger flickering in his eyes.

"Because I wanted to. Now will you stop questioning me like I'm in the fucking witness stand?"

"For Christ's sake, Michaela. You say you don't want him to get the wrong impression. Yet you telephone him because you want to know how he is. What's going on?"

"Look, I won't do it again. Okay?"

"You haven't seen him, have you?"

"No."

"You're quite sure about that, aren't you?"

"I'm very sure about what I have and haven't done, thank you."

Daniel was narrowing his eyes.

"I haven't seen him," Michaela repeated.

"Well, thank God for that anyway. But right now it sounds like us getting our own house would be the very best thing we could do."

"I agree."

She started to read her book again and this time he didn't try to stop her.

Chapter Fifty-Six

It was five o'clock. Daniel was considering reading through his new instructions on the multi-handed armed robbery case for an hour, when Bill called.

"I've got Rod Bannister here. Will you come down?"

"Sure," Daniel said. "I'll be two minutes."

Daniel came into reception and, with his head, Bill indicated the start of the corridor where Rod was looking at an abstract painting. He was wearing a dark-blue cotton jacket. Daniel was once again struck by how distinguished his ex-client was, how utterly unperturbed he always seemed by anything that life had to throw at him.

"Rod," he said. "What can I do for you?"

"Do you have a minute?"

"Use George's room," Bill said. "He won't be back in today."

"Thanks," Daniel said and opened the door for Rod.

Rod explained that on Monday Islington Council had confirmed they would be making him redundant. He suspected they'd been working out how to do this ever since the trial finished. They'd settled on a reorganisation of the department, which led to two housing benefits officers being redeployed, and one losing his job. Rod was the one they said couldn't be accommodated elsewhere.

"I'm sorry to hear that," Daniel said. "And you think it's connected with the trial."

"I'm certain of it. There was an article about me going back to my job in the local paper, and that led to some angry letters."

"But you were found not guilty. You are not guilty. This is outrageous."

"I just wondered if you could give me some advice," Rod said. "Legal advice."

"There's a problem with that. What I know about employment law could be written in capital letters on a pair of Y-fronts."

"I see."

"But we have employment people. I could get you somebody good."

"Would it be expensive?"

"I can't get you advice for nothing. But I'll see what I can do."

Rod looked thoughtful. "They've offered quite a generous redundancy package. So I need to factor that in too."

"It sounds like they really do want to get rid of you."

"Very much so." Rod suddenly looked sombre.

"I'm sorry you're going through this. And immediately after the trial. It must feel like it's come at a bad time."

"It does rather," Rod admitted.

"Look, I've pretty much finished work for the day. If

you wait in reception, I'll get my things and we'll go for a pint. What d'you say? All on me."

"Sounds great," Rod said.

"And listen, if the worst comes to the worst, you can always sell those antique cufflinks."

Rod suddenly chuckled. "Very funny."

"Pretty lucky I didn't take them off your hands, all things considered."

"Fuck you," Rod said.

Both men were soon laughing loudly.

Chapter Fifty-Seven

The conference on the armed robbery case finished at five thirty. There was bright sunshine when Daniel left the solicitors' firm in Hackney. It was going to be a beautiful evening. He reckoned that he might just be able to find his way to where Rod lived. He wasn't in a rush to get back home, Michaela was seeing a friend, so why not test his sense of direction?

He wouldn't have had a clue which way to head if he hadn't once had a school friend who lived in this area. He was pretty sure he used to visit him on Graham Road, near Hackney Central station. Now that Daniel thought about it, he vaguely recollected saying something to his friend about the battle of Navarino. Surely that was in connection to Navarino Road, which was therefore likely to be near Graham Road.

As he walked, he complimented himself on his powers of deduction. He liked the fact that he was able to recall specific details from a conversation many years ago, and then piece something together from the information. Fifteen minutes later he found himself in

Navarino Grove, which was off Navarino Road, looking up at the small block where Rod lived. Mission accomplished. The window of Rod's kitchen suddenly opened, and Rod called out to him.

"What are you doing here?"

"I was in the area," Daniel called back.

"You want to come in?"

"Could do. Unless you fancy a drink?"

"All right." The window closed and Rod disappeared from view.

Daniel stood alone in the road. He wondered how Grace Ovett was, the kindly neighbour who'd appeared in the witness stand. Had she and Rod re-established anything like their old friendship in the weeks following the trial?

After a couple of minutes, Rod came down the passage at the side of his block. "There's a rather nice Victorian pub on the corner of Queensbridge Road and Richmond Road," he said.

"Is it nearby?"

"Five minutes, if that."

"And you must tell me how you got on with Emma Carr, my employment friend."

"Well, she was very helpful. But to cut a long story short, I'm taking the money."

"I thought you might," Daniel said, and Rod turned towards him and smiled.

Chapter Fifty-Eight

It was a sunny day and they'd been standing on his balcony for about fifteen minutes, with Daniel pointing out the landmarks of London. It was cramped, all five of them out there, but he always liked to include some educational element whenever he saw them.

"I could stay out here forever," Audrey said.

"I'm sure we all could," Daniel said, "but perhaps we should make some tea."

They went back into the flat, and Daniel and Rod headed into the kitchen to sort out the sandwiches and soft drinks.

"They're great," Rod said, indicating the children in the other room.

"They have their moments. But you're right, on the whole they're fantastic."

"It's a shame Michaela's away. It would have been nice to meet her too."

"She's very nice," Imogen said, having appeared suddenly in the doorway.

"I'll bet," Rod said.

"How do you know my daddy?"

"Imogen, could you help us bring everything through to the living room?" Daniel asked.

Imogen sighed, picked up a lemonade bottle and plonked it on the table. Daniel and Rod followed along, bringing everything else.

"Grub's up," Daniel said.

Audrey and Max started piling sandwiches and biscuits onto their plates.

"Are you a barrister in Daddy's chambers?" Imogen asked Rod.

Rod laughed. "No, I'm not a barrister. In fact, I'm not working at all right now."

"He's having a well-earned break," Daniel said.

"So what is your job?" Imogen persisted.

"Most recently I was working for Islington Council."

"So how do you know Daddy? You haven't said."

"Rod was my client," Daniel said. "You know, in that recent case I did."

"The murder case?" Audrey shouted excitedly.

"Yes, but he was found not guilty. Which was right, because he wasn't guilty."

"So you're not a murderer?" Max sounded disappointed.

"I'm afraid not," Rod said.

"He's just a normal person, like you and me," Daniel said.

"At least that's what I like your daddy to think," Rod said.

Daniel rolled his eyes. "Okay, who'd like a slice of this cake? It's shop bought, but it looks surprisingly good."

Chapter Fifty-Nine

"It means such a lot to me, seeing you on my birthday," Thomas said, reaching across the wooden table in the café to touch her wrist. Michaela sipped her coffee. "I really appreciate it."

"It's not as if Daniel would have seen that film with me."

"You mean talking pigs who double up as sheepdogs aren't his thing?"

"Not so much," Michaela laughed. "He's more into action movies."

"I like a good action movie myself, don't get me wrong. But this was very sweet."

Michaela opened her bag and withdrew some moisturiser. She squeezed a small bead onto her finger and began applying it to her palms.

"My hands are so dry tonight."

He nodded.

"Thomas, you know I said that I couldn't come back with you tonight?"

"Of course, and that's fine. That's why I booked the cinema in Holloway, so you could get home quickly."

"Anyway, I told Daniel that I'm staying with my parents. So now I can come over."

"Are you sure?"

"Yes, perfectly sure. Don't you want me to?"

"Of course I do. It's not that at all. I just don't want you taking unnecessary risks."

"I'm not," she said.

"Well, that's fantastic news. I'm very happy."

She was looking into his eyes intensely. "Can we go soon? I'm feeling really horny. I hope you're up to performing."

"Always," he said.

They paid their bill and left the café.

"Can I be absolutely honest?" Michaela said as they made their way towards her car. "I've been building up to telling you that we can't carry on seeing each other. That we need to finish. Then a few nights ago, I realised I just couldn't do it."

"I see. I'm not surprised you were feeling that way."

"I just wish you'd contacted me when you first came back to London."

"Me too. And I feel terrible that you're now in this position. Having to make up stories in order to see me."

"You get used to it, that's the frightening part."

"But you must do whatever you must do. I'll totally understand either way."

They reached the car and she unlocked it.

"That's the problem, Thomas. And almost certainly why I can't put an end to this. You're too bloody nice."

Chapter Sixty

"I'm worried Michaela's having an affair," Daniel said, as soon as they'd settled into their seats with their pints.

"What makes you say that?" Rod asked.

"It's all adding up."

They'd been drinking regularly in the Duke of Richmond ever since that evening in June when Daniel found his way to Rod's flat. Conferences in the run-up to Daniel's next trial were happening fairly frequently. On other evenings, Daniel was happy to stroll from Newington Green, where he and Michaela had moved, down the road to Hackney.

"And I'm pretty sure I know who with," Daniel continued.

"Thomas," Rod said.

"Well remembered. I really don't know what to do."

"It's a bloody difficult one. I'm sorry for you, mate."

"Thanks." Daniel pressed his lips together, winced slightly.

"What makes you think she is having an affair?"

"Not one thing really. A load of small signs, I suppose."

"Such as?" Rod was totally focused on their conversation. Daniel liked that.

"She never seems completely honest about Thomas. I have to extract the information from her. I told you how he just came into our lives out of the blue, didn't I? And that we spent months trying to get rid of him."

"I remember."

"Well, after we got married, she told me that she'd spoken to Thomas a few times, which was news to me. But when I pressed her on that, she admitted that it had been her who'd called him."

Rod nodded, weighing this up. "What else?"

"A few weeks ago she told me she'd seen Thomas. Just as friends. But why didn't she mention it at the time?"

"Anything else?"

"Her social life is suddenly much busier. Or she's been working late, or away. And the other night she stayed over at her parents. It was arranged very quickly. Things aren't usually arranged quickly with them. And she didn't want to talk on the phone that night. She said she needed the time to talk to her mother, who suffers from depression."

Rod said something about there not being a single smoking gun. Daniel agreed.

"The other thing," Daniel said, "is that I'm not always the best judge of people. I sometimes put my trust in someone when I shouldn't. I'm worried that might have happened again."

They decided to get some food and after that they drank a couple more pints. Pretty soon they were both a little worse for wear and the bell was ringing for last orders.

"Listen," Daniel said. "I might have been wrong about Michaela. I know I can be a little paranoid sometimes."

"I may be able to help you out," Rod said.

"How do you mean?"

"Well, I could follow her if you like. Very subtly. If it would be helpful."

"I'm not so sure," Daniel said. "It seems a bit over the top."

"Yeah, you're probably right. On the other hand, I haven't got anything else to do. I'm obviously not working at the moment."

"It sounds like the kind of thing a criminal would offer to do, Rod."

"I'm offering to do it because you're my friend."

"Okay, I appreciate that. Thanks."

"I thought it might be helpful. But it's no big deal, honestly."

"She does have regular work trips," Daniel said at length. "She recently went to Exeter. Some story she was doing. And Rose West's trial is coming up."

"Where does she stay when she's on a work trip?"

"A cheap hotel, usually."

"Well, it's not beyond the wit of man. That's all I'm saying," Rod said.

"You're rather distinctive-looking. Michaela came to the trial. When I made my closing speech."

"I can make myself look very different when I need to. And it's all about context too."

"It's a thought," Daniel said.

"Sure."

They finished their pints.

"I suppose, if she is having an affair, a work trip would be the perfect excuse to spend the night with him, wouldn't it?"

"Without a doubt."

"Let me think about it, Rod. I appreciate the offer."

"No worries. I'm easy either way."

Chapter Sixty-One

FRIDAY 6 OCTOBER 1995

I t was the stuff of nightmares. A packed Winchester Crown Court had been subjected to a catalogue of shocking details on the first day of Rose West's trial. They'd heard how Fred and Rose had kidnapped young vulnerable women, many of them runaways, and tortured them in the cellar of their home at 25 Cromwell Street, often for several days, before murdering them. Their naked dismembered bodies had been buried beneath the house. It was clear that the victims had been trussed up and gagged so that they could not scream for help. But not only this, the Wests had also killed their eldest daughter, Heather, and Fred West's stepdaughter, Charmaine.

The Crown prosecutor, Brian Leveson QC, had explained that the Wests were obsessed by violent sex, and shared a knowledge about each other that bound them together. It was inconceivable for Fred West, who had hanged himself on New Year's Day, to have acted alone.

Michaela had listened to the litany of horror as she

sat with the other journalists. She had tried not to imagine what it would have been like to have been tied up and brutally attacked and raped, knowing the whole time that, in all likelihood, it was only going to end one way.

As she left the court, she tried freeing her mind from the details she'd heard. The reality was that she would be attending this trial for at least the next couple of weeks. Perhaps she would be made to cover the whole thing. She needed to have some kind of break from it over the weekend. On Saturday she would be writing and filing her story, so she would have to do something completely different on the Sunday.

Thank goodness Thomas would be joining her at the hotel later that evening. He'd been a rock recently, the calming influence in her life. Sometimes it seemed that he was the only sane person she knew.

The Wykeham Arms pub and hotel was half a mile from the court building; she was more than happy to walk. Making her way towards the nearest road, she was joined by another journalist. He was small, almost bald, with a moustache and immaculate beard on his round face. She'd met him once or twice before, covering other trials, and had always found him slightly too flirtatious.

"That was fun, I don't think," he said.

"Not so much fun," Michaela said.

"I'm Neville, by the way. I'm not sure we've ever been introduced."

"Michaela." She had a feeling he was about to ask her out.

"So, are you staying in Winchester over the weekend, or heading back home?" he asked.

"Staying here," she said, deliberately not asking about his plans.

"Me too."

"I'm feeling exhausted after all that."

"It was pretty relentless wasn't it?"

She made a left turn and it seemed that he was heading in that direction too.

"Where are you staying?" Neville asked.

"Oh, just in a pub." He was looking at her quizzically, so she added, "The Wykeham Arms."

"Nice! I'm further out of town."

She nodded.

"Are you busy later on?" he asked.

"Look, Neville – I honestly am tired. And there's probably something else you should know about me." She stopped walking and held out the hand with her wedding ring.

"I'm not asking you on a date." He sounded irritated. "I just wondered whether you'd like to grab a bite to eat. It's company, isn't it?"

"I have other plans tonight."

"Well, you might have said earlier."

"Sorry for wasting your precious time," she said. She couldn't believe how ridiculous he was being.

"It's fine," he said. "I'm going to get a taxi from this rank. I guess I'll see you on Monday."

She had only been waiting a short while in the bar before Thomas arrived. He smiled and kissed her on the lips. She told him that another reporter had already tried to take his place that evening.

"Within one minute of us coming out of court, he was practically asking to spend the night with me. He's called Neville. As if I'd spend the night with anyone called Neville."

"It's not the best name, is it?"

"How was your journey?"

"Not too bad. Did you get here last night?"

"Yeah, just in time to check in and hit the sack."

"Do we have a nice room?"

"We have a very nice room."

"I can't wait to see it," Thomas smiled.

"By the way," Michaela said, "what are we doing on Sunday? I want to get away from everything."

"I've been thinking about that. And I've done a little research."

"I thought you might have."

"We're not far from Southampton. And from there, we can get a ferry to the Isle of Wight."

"Brilliant idea."

So the Isle of Wight was where Michaela and Thomas ended up going, catching a mid-morning ferry on Sunday from East Cowes. They didn't realise that they had been followed onto the ferry by Rod Bannister, who had also walked through the dining room when they were having their meal on the Friday evening. And it was on the Isle of Wight that Rod took the intimate photos of Thomas and Michaela, strolling hand in hand on the coastal path. He even managed a long-distance shot of them enjoying a passionate kiss.

Chapter Sixty-Two

Daniel had been stewing on the matter for two weeks. Rod had given him the photographs, explaining that he'd waited the whole of Saturday outside The Wykeham Arms, and that Michaela and Thomas hadn't come out. But on the Sunday, they'd emerged for their trip, and he'd followed them at a distance all day.

The morning after receiving the photos, Daniel had taken them to his chambers and locked them in his desk drawer. Since then, not a working day had gone by when he hadn't unlocked it and studied the pictures. Michaela and Thomas looked so comfortable in each other's company. It was misty on the Isle of Wight and the pictures had a dreamy quality. The grainy image of the kiss on the coastal path was particularly painful. The wind was making Michaela's hair blow behind her, almost at a right angle, but that didn't seem to put her off what she was doing.

Daniel thought it best not to say anything to Michaela while he was in mid-trial. In any event, she was in Winchester and he didn't want to tackle things over the phone. But now the armed robbery case was over, and Michaela was back for the weekend.

The lapse in time since he'd received the photos had at least given him a chance to prepare what he was going to say. He obviously couldn't admit that he'd asked Rod to follow her.

They were in the kitchen, their favourite room so far in their new house. It was large and spacious, and they'd talked about having dinner parties in there when they were both less busy. Michaela had cooked home-made pizza which they'd eaten with a bottle of wine. The meal had finished, and they were still sitting at the table. Daniel decided this was his moment.

"You know when you've been staying at this hotel, has it just been you or have you had company?"

"It's just been me. It's been so boring." She wrinkled her nose in that way she sometimes did.

Daniel drained the last dregs of wine from his glass. "It's just I telephoned one night. When you were eating your supper."

He thought he saw her shudder slightly, but she was looking directly into his eyes when she responded. "I always call back when I get your messages."

"Yes, I know that. I didn't leave a message this time."

"Okay, so why are you telling me this?"

"It was the first weekend you were staying there," Daniel continued. "I think it was the Friday night that I called. The first time I'd rung the hotel, in fact."

"Go on," Michaela said.

"I asked to speak to Michaela Simpson, and the lady obviously knew who you were. And she said, 'I think she's in the dining room having dinner with her husband'. And very calmly, I said, 'In that case, don't disturb them. I'm her brother and I was going to tell her some nice family news. But I'll wait till I see her in person. Probably best not to mention that I called in case you worry her'."

Michaela had been staring at him throughout the speech. He smiled at her when he finished, as if to say that it was now her turn.

"Actually, I did have dinner with somebody that evening," Michaela said. "It was this idiot reporter called Neville, who insisted we keep each other company that night. I'd forgotten all about it, but you've reminded me. He started chatting as we left court that day. It was really nothing. The lady must have got the wrong end of the stick."

"Maybe. What's Neville look like?"

"Short and practically bald," Michaela laughed. "Not good-looking at all."

"No, Michaela, that isn't going to work. Because I also asked the lady, 'What do you think of her husband's ponytail? We've been trying to persuade him to cut it off for years'. And she said that she rather liked the ponytail. She thought it suited him. So I think you must be mistaken, Michaela. It couldn't have been Neville."

"Oh, Christ," Michaela said. "Jesus fucking Christ."

"I don't think it was him either."

"It was Thomas. You know it was Thomas. I've been fucking Thomas. I don't know what came over me."

"How long's this been going on?"

"A while. Quite a while."

"So how long is that?"

"Since before the wedding if you must know. A week or two before. I don't know why, Dan, I really don't. I must have felt lonely. But it's terrible what I've done. And I'm so, so sorry."

Chapter Sixty-Three

FRIDAY 3 NOVEMBER 1995

He telephoned her from chambers late afternoon, then set off for Winchester immediately. There was an accident which caused some delay, but he still arrived within ninety minutes. Because of the bad associations they had with the hotel, they opted instead for a local Chinese restaurant Michaela had discovered. She assured him that she hadn't been there with Thomas. The previous weekend Daniel had also driven up, this time on the Saturday, and they'd spent the day together. His intention was to check in with her every weekend.

"I know what you're doing, Daniel," Michaela said, as they sat in the restaurant. And then in a quieter voice repeated, "I know exactly what you're doing."

"What do you mean?"

She sighed, her whole body tense and weary. "I've noticed, Daniel. When you make these weekend arrangements, you give me as little notice as possible. And you did the same when you drove up last Wednesday evening. And the phone calls, at weird times.

I mean one night you called the hotel at midnight. Midnight, for God's sake. I was asleep, I thought someone had died. So, I'm just saying. I know exactly what you're doing."

Daniel dabbed at the corner of his mouth with his white napkin and inspected the small blemish that this had created. "Maybe you're right," he said. "But if I'm still suspicious, is that surprising?"

"You're going to have to trust me when I tell you that it's all over with Thomas."

"It went on for five months, Michaela. You were cheating on me with that man for five months."

"I know that. And I've told you how desperately sorry I am. I spent practically the whole night in tears – my face looked like a frigging pumpkin the next morning, and I begged you for forgiveness. And then I ended things with him straight away, as you know. I mean, what do you want from me, Daniel? What the fuck do you want from me?"

Daniel glanced around him. "Would you mind keeping your voice down?"

"You *always* say that. And we're the only ones in the restaurant."

"Even so. There are staff."

"Fuck the staff, I don't care."

"It might take me a little while," Daniel said. "You have to understand that. I'm not the one who strayed here."

"If you're never going to trust me again, then this isn't a marriage. It certainly doesn't feel like one. It feels more like some sort of system of managerial checks."

"Have you spoken to Thomas since you told him it was over? I'm just curious."

"No," she said. "No I haven't."

"How did he take it, by the way?"

"He was quite relieved if you must know. He's a very moral person. I think you'd like that about him."

"Are you trying to be funny?"

"No, I'm not. The point is, he hasn't tried to contact me since. And I haven't contacted him. So you'll have to trust me again, or this won't work."

"I'm trying. Believe me."

"It isn't fun anymore, Daniel. When we were first together it was fun. And you were nice to me."

"Don't tell me, Thomas was so much nicer to you."

"Yes! – if you must know. He was gentle and caring. And I didn't feel like I was on trial."

For a moment, Daniel's conscience faltered, and shockingly, he glimpsed himself as she saw him. And he pitied her. "Oh, God. How did we ever get into this mess?"

"I don't know, I really don't."

"Do you want this marriage to work still, Michaela? Do you really want this to work?"

"Yes, of course. Otherwise, I wouldn't be here. We wouldn't be having this conversation."

"I mean, the way you talk, it's like I'm some kind of monster, or prison guard or something. Is that how you think of me?"

"It's just I want you to trust me. I mean, you trust Rod. He was on trial for murder and you trust him. You trusted him enough to invite him to meet your children."

"Yes, but Rod was innocent. He didn't actually do anything wrong."

"There was plenty of evidence against him from what I read."

"Look, I'm not going to start reiterating arguments

312

from the trial. He was found not guilty. And since then he's become a friend."

"You know my views about that. That's your lookout and I won't make a big deal out of it. The only reason I mentioned him was to say, if you're willing to trust him, could you please, please, start trusting me?"

Daniel nodded and smiled sadly. He reached across the table and took her hand in his. "You make a very fair point."

Chapter Sixty-Four

They were driving to Michaela's parents for dinner when the conversation happened.

"You know, Dan, I've been meaning to ask you something for ages." Michaela was trying to paint her nails as she spoke. "I just want to clear something up in my own mind, if that's okay?"

"Sure, why not?"

"So you know that woman you spoke to on the phone?"

"What woman?"

"From the hotel. You rang that Friday evening and she told you I was having dinner with my husband, and that she liked his ponytail."

"Oh, that. That seems so long ago now. What about it?"

"She's called Penny," Michaela said. "She runs the place with her husband."

"Yeah, I know who she is," Daniel said. "She always answered whenever I rang. And I met her too, of course."

"So you're sure it was Penny you spoke to that evening?"

"As sure as I can be, I suppose."

"I haven't told you that I became quite close to Penny. I was obviously very upset about everything for a while, and one night she and I went out and got a bit drunk. I told her everything. I mean she'd noticed anyway that I'd managed to share my room with two different men but had been too polite to say anything. Anyway, the point is, she never had that conversation with you. She swore on her mother's life. And there's no one else it could have been – the waitresses don't answer the phone there. And there are no other women."

"What are you saying?" Daniel asked, stopping the car quite suddenly at a red traffic light.

"I think what I'm saying is that you haven't been totally honest with me either."

Daniel was silent for the whole time they sat at the red light. He was looking ahead, concentrating, as if he was trying to read the number plate of the car in front.

"Aren't you going to say anything?"

He released the handbrake and continued driving. "It was Rod," he said eventually.

"What do you mean, it was Rod?"

"He followed you that weekend. He saw you in the hotel. He went to the Isle of Wight on the same ferry as you did. He took photos of you."

"You paid Rod to follow me?"

"He did it as a favour actually. I reimbursed his expenses, of course."

Michaela was silent for a minute. And then Daniel thought he heard a sob. She was trying to stifle the noise as best she could, at the same time pressing her hands over her eyes.

Daniel carried on driving, unsure what to say. Eventually he suggested that they didn't have to go to her parents that evening.

She shook her head and a tear dripped off her face and onto the shiny black bag on her lap.

"We could make an excuse," Daniel said. "If you prefer, we'll just turn back. I don't mind calling your parents. I can stop and make the call from a phone box; I'll tell them you've got stomach cramps. I'll think of something. What do you say?"

Michaela didn't answer. But she had stopped crying. And she was using the overhead mirror to reapply her make-up, which Daniel understood to be her way of telling him that she wished to continue with the evening's arrangement. He carried on driving towards Biggleswade.

———

It was a full house at the Simpsons that evening. Michaela's younger sister Rose, now looking so much better, was introducing her new partner Brad to the family. And Michaela's older brother and his wife were also invited.

Bob, in another comfortable cardigan, was at his convivial best, serving everyone gin and tonics before dinner. Michaela downed hers immediately and requested another.

This time Briony had made shepherd's pie, which was served with parsnips, carrots and fresh peas. Brad had very kindly shelled all the peas for her, she told everyone.

They had placed Bob and Daniel at each end of the table. Michaela was on Daniel's right.

"Well, we've all had quite a year, I'm sure," Briony said. "What with Rose's recovery from her illness, and Daniel and Michaela's lovely wedding." There was murmured agreement around the table.

"And then there was Daniel's case which kept the nation entertained for weeks," Rose said.

"I'm not sure it was meant to be entertaining," Daniel said.

"And I wasn't quite sure about the verdict, if I'm honest," Rose came back.

"The wedding was very lovely though," Briony said, trying to steer the conversation back on to safer ground. "I know more relatives would have liked to have been invited, but it was still a very happy occasion."

"We were all invited, that's the main thing," Bob said.

"Except Brad," Rose pointed out.

"I don't think Brad was on the scene then," Briony said.

"He was actually. We just hadn't told you about it. Had we, Brad?"

Brad smiled nervously and shook his head.

"Then it's hardly our fault he wasn't invited," Michaela said. It was her first comment since she'd sat down, and Daniel noticed her parents exchanging looks.

"It was all very lovely, anyway," Briony said, for what must have been the third time. "And I'm sure we will all welcome any new additions to the family whenever they come."

"What's that supposed to mean?" Rose asked. Brad whispered something into her ear.

"You know, if and when Daniel and Michaela are ready to do so," Briony explained, "we will be delighted to welcome any little ones into the family."

"I think that's rather up to Daniel and Michaela," Rose said. "If that's going to happen it's really their lookout."

"Absolutely," Briony said.

"We have talked about it actually," Daniel said. "We're not in any great rush."

"I'm sure you have," Briony said, "because that's what sensible couples do. I'm just saying that a woman can't leave these things indefinitely."

"Michaela's only thirty-one. She has absolutely loads of time." Rose sounded indignant on her sister's behalf.

"Yes, people do leave it later these days, Bri," Bob pointed out.

"All I'm saying is that it will be very nice when it happens," Briony said.

"I love how we're all sitting around the table discussing my fertility," Michaela said.

"That's not really what we're doing, darling," Briony tried again. "I was simply making the point that I'm happy to wait for grandchildren, whenever they arrive."

"Well you might have to wait a fucking long time. Because I'm leaving Daniel first thing tomorrow morning." And with that Michaela got up from her seat and hurried out of the room, leaving her plate half full of food.

The remaining four members of the family turned simultaneously to look at Daniel, whose mouth was very slightly open.

"We've just been having… there's a slight thing… I think what I'm trying to say, is that this will all blow over. Please excuse me." Daniel also rose from the table and went off in search of Michaela.

Chapter Sixty-Five

It was seven fifteen when Bill parked in his allotted spot and got out of his car. It was a crisp and beautiful morning. On New Year's Day, Bill had managed to sneak in a few hours of birdwatching and he was feeling all the better for having had a chance to relax. He unlocked the door of chambers. His intention was to make an early start, get a few things done before the other clerks joined him. The first working day of the year was usually quiet, which Bill liked, a chance to ease himself back into his work. Many of his tenants would have been away and would not return to chambers until Monday, or even the week after that. And those that did make it in today might well leave it till lunchtime before making an appearance.

He stepped inside and noticed immediately that the light in reception was on. This was odd, as Bill distinctly remembered doing a check before he locked up on the Friday night. Perhaps somebody had needed to pop in and get a file or check a reference. Thorough as they were in their work, you could never underestimate the sloppiness of barristers when it came to leaving lights on in chambers or windows open. They sometimes even managed to leave the main door unlocked.

Bill went into the kitchen and filled the kettle. A feeling of uneasiness came over him, something he couldn't quite put his finger on. The sense perhaps that he was not alone in the building. It was a slightly crazy thought, but he would make his tea and do a quick check to put his mind at rest.

The first few rooms were empty, and Bill started to feel a bit of a chump that he was wasting his time with this rather than getting on with the paperwork that needed his attention. Then he suddenly thought about the awful story that had been doing the rounds at the end of last year, the silk who'd hanged himself in his room. He had been found first thing by the senior clerk, but what had alerted the clerk, apparently, was the yapping of a tiny dog who was stuck in the room and was jumping up and down trying to reach the barrister above him. Bill had heard that the silk had recently bought this puppy and that he used to take it with him into his meetings. The puppy would sit dutifully on his lap while whatever case or business matter was being discussed. It was strangely touching that the barrister wanted his dog with him at the end.

Bill had virtually completed his check when he heard something from one of the remaining rooms on the second floor. Was it from Daniel and Chris's room? It sounded like a murmur, or a groan. Bill sincerely hoped that he wasn't going to discover something inappropriate going on. It wouldn't have been the first time if he did. Members of the bar could be surprisingly disinhibited – what was it about legal discussions that proved such an aphrodisiac?

Bill opened the door cautiously. The lights were off, and it took him a moment to spot Daniel in his chair. The chair was away from the desk and he was leaning right back with both arms outstretched towards the ceiling. In his hands was a piece of paper, or a photograph perhaps. He was staring at it, engrossed apparently. And he was mumbling to himself.

"Daniel?" Bill said, approaching and noticing the distinctive smell of spirits on the barrister's breath. "What on earth…?"

"The Isle of Wight. This was taken on the Isle of Wight," Daniel slurred. He swivelled his chair so Bill could see the photo, a couple kissing with a grey sea in the background.

"Very nice, very romantic," Bill said. "Now will you please sit up for me?"

"I like the fact that she's taller than most women. But not so tall that she ever looks awkward or gawky."

"Daniel, what's going on?"

"Nothing much. Is it too late to wish you happy New Year or have I missed all that malarkey?"

It occurred to Bill that Daniel might have been in his room for some two or three days. The stench of sweat, and something equally unpleasant, was mingling with the alcohol. And now that his eyes had adjusted to the gloom, Bill could see the state of his youngest QC. He'd definitely been in his clothes for some time and his hair was matted and had marmalade in it, if Bill wasn't mistaken.

"Okay, sit up. And put that bloody photograph down. I'm going to make you a cup of coffee. A black coffee. I'm also opening a window. It doesn't smell too clever in here."

"All right. No need to fret. No need to get on your high horse."

Bill wandered over to the window and opened it with some relief. He then went back into the corridor. A few minutes later he returned to Daniel's room with the coffee.

"Now get that down you."

As Daniel took a hesitant sip, Bill picked up an almost empty bottle of Jim Beam from the floor, and several empty bottles of beer that were on a flower table. He placed them just outside the door.

"It's strong, this coffee," Daniel said.

"It needs to be."

"She's left me. Michaela's gone."

"Yes, I'd gathered that."

He remained with Daniel while he drank his coffee, pulling up Chris's chair so he didn't have to stand the whole time. When Daniel had finished his drink, Bill told him what was going to happen.

"In five minutes' time, I'm going to call you a cab. And it's going to take you home. I don't want anyone in chambers seeing you like this. And when you're back home, you are going to sober up for a couple of days and then you will be seeking help. Professional help. All right? You might want to check in somewhere. There's this place we know, a cross between Champneys and The Priory: we've used it before and can help out with the bill. And I'm going to clear your diary for the next three months. The story will be that you are unwell and need time to recover. We won't charge you rent for the time you're away. And you will sort yourself out, I promise you that, Daniel. I'll telephone you in a day or two to check you're getting back on track. Have you got any questions?"

"Just one if I may, Bill?"

"Yes?"

"What's happening in the five minutes before you call the cab?"

Bill couldn't help but smile. Even in this sorry state, Daniel's attention to detail hadn't deserted him. "I'm going to find you a fresh shirt to change into and we'll put that one in the bin. In fact, I'll probably burn it because it stinks. I think you must have thrown up on it."

"Yes," Daniel nodded gravely. "Now you come to mention it, I think I did."

Chapter Sixty-Six

"I'm going to this kind of health farm in Buckinghamshire," Daniel said. "My clerk's arranged it. It's a chance to get back on the straight and narrow. But I might be gone for a few weeks, I don't know yet." He stood at the window watching the rain falling onto the street below while he waited for a reply.

"Well, that all sounds good," Rod said, at the other end of the phone.

"Yes, they're even paying for me."

"I wish someone would pay for me to stay on a health farm."

"Mad, isn't it? Anyway, I'm hoping it'll have a swimming pool. And plenty of other things to do inside. Because the weather's lousy."

"Lots of jigsaw puzzles," Rod said.

"Hmmm. Maybe not."

"Particularly not if they have missing pieces, eh?"

Daniel laughed, finally getting the reference.

"Are you busy in the next few weeks?" Daniel asked.

"Not especially. I'm going to do a bit of walking, but nothing else is planned. Was there anything you needed?"

"There is one thing, actually. There's literally no one else I could ask to do this."

"Go on, I'm intrigued."

"It's not very exciting."

"I'm not after excitement, just tell me what you want me to do."

"Can you keep an eye on Michaela? Would that be all right? I'll give you her address. She's living with Thomas, as you know. But I'd like to find out a little more."

"I can watch them from a distance. See what they're getting up to. Is that what you meant?"

"Yes, exactly that."

"Okay, so that would be fine."

"I'll pay your expenses. And a little more besides."

"I'm happy to help out, you know that."

"She is still my wife, after all. And I do still love her."

"Of course you do, mate."

"I ask a lot from you, I know," Daniel said. "But this is sensitive. I'm still hoping to get back together with Michaela. Is that a daft idea?"

"Not so daft," Rod said. "People can be unpredictable."

"I told you my father ran away from the family when we were kids, didn't I? I worry that I'm doomed to have a succession of failed marriages as a result. And that I'll grow apart from my children, like he did. I've certainly made a promising start in that direction."

"You're just a little raw. And that's how any normal person in your situation would be feeling right now."

"Thanks."

"But listen, enjoy your relaxing break. And I'll keep an eye on Michaela while you're away and report back. How does that sound?"

Chapter Sixty-Seven

To celebrate Daniel's reintegration into London society, Rod cooked him a curry at his flat. He told him he'd sourced all the ingredients from his local Turkish supermarket.

"You should see that place; they pile the aubergines up like purple castles. It's the most beautiful thing."

"And this curry is to die for, Rod. It's also one of the spiciest dishes I've ever had the pleasure of getting third-degree burns from."

"I hope it's not too much for you." Rod suddenly seemed concerned.

"It's fine, really. Amazing in fact."

"I've been in competition with myself," Rod said. "Like personal training to eat the hottest curries ever."

"I'm well versed in that art too," Daniel said.

"I've finally found a partner in crime, then?"

"Curry crime, yes."

"So how was the health farm? You were there four weeks, weren't you?"

"Just over."

"That's quite a long time. You have my sympathy."

"Yes, and I've become an expert in differentiating the various flavours of Shloer. Because not a drop of alcohol passed my lips while I was there. They are not big fans of booze in that place. It's so good to have a beer tonight, but I am going to leave it at one."

"Sure, no problem."

"Anyway, I've also become rather good at yoga. And meditation too."

"A changed man."

"I had to do something to pass the time, Jesus Christ. And I promise you, it's not like I'll never allow myself to get drunk again."

"Thank heavens for that."

"When the right occasion occurs, my friend, I will be there for it."

"Good to hear. You may be surprised that I too have had the odd spell of abstinence."

"You have?"

"I once spent an entire summer on an ashram. And I have to say, I liked it."

"Well, if we ever go on holiday together…" Daniel smiled.

"It will certainly not be to an ashram," Rod laughed.

True to his word, Rod reported back on what he'd discovered about Michaela and her domestic situation.

"Okay, mate. It's not all good news, I'm afraid. From what I could see, Michaela and Thomas are close. I don't want to say they're in love, but they're tactile when they're out and about, supermarkets or whatever."

"I thought you might say something like that," Daniel said. "I rang her a couple of times when I was away, and she couldn't get off the phone fast enough, to be honest."

"The only possible ray of light was when she went out for a night with her friend Anika. Not sure if you know her?"

"Yes, I know Anika."

"Unfortunately, I didn't manage to follow them to wherever they went that evening, but I did stick around, and I heard a very drunken conversation outside Thomas's flat late at night. And I'm pretty sure Michaela said she felt bad about you."

"Really?"

"Yes, like how quickly everything fell apart. It was a drunken conversation, and it didn't last long. But it was something."

"Hmm," Daniel said. "Yes, I guess it was something."

Chapter Sixty-Eight

THURSDAY 4 APRIL 1996

E ven at five fifteen in the morning, the Gatwick Express was practically full. As the train pulled out of Victoria, the young guys on the other side of the aisle cracked open their cans of lager. Four clicks in quick succession.

Rod leaned towards Daniel and motioned with his eyes.

"Oh to be young and carefree, eh?" Daniel said in a low voice.

"Indeed."

"But we're relatively young. And very much carefree, aren't we?"

"Job-free, maybe," Rod said.

"Speak for yourself. This is my last hurrah."

"Yes, I know you're going back after the bank holiday."

"I could have done so much earlier, but Bill insisted I take my time."

"That was good of him."

"Yes. Anyway, he's started to populate my diary."

"And I've been impressed how restrained you've been on the drinks front." Rod looked across the table.

"I'm sorry if I've been boring."

"It's fine."

"But I'm definitely letting my hair down this weekend, don't worry about that."

"There's a time and place for everything."

"Exactly. And this might just be the time…"

"To get shit-faced?" Rod suggested.

"Something like that."

Rod nodded, as if together they'd established an undeniable philosophical truth. "Well, I appreciate the break anyway."

Daniel stood up to take his jacket off, folded it, then nestled it into the overhead compartment. He sat down again.

"I wouldn't be having a holiday otherwise," Rod continued.

"How do you mean?"

"Well, I don't imagine I'll be working for some time."

"You'll find something," Daniel said.

"Maybe. Keep your eyes open for me."

"I'm not suggesting you should be looking in the legal world."

"Nor me. But if you hear of anything going that I might be suitable for. Anything at all. Money's a bit of an issue right now."

"Getting through the settlement?"

"Very much so." Rod narrowed his lips. "As they used to say, it's coffee and cake time."

"That doesn't sound so bad."

"How are you affording this by the way? It's not like you've earned anything for a while."

"That's for me to know and you to guess."

"Just curious, that's all."

"Well," Daniel said, "I'm expecting a little windfall. I haven't got it yet. But Sally's had our house on the market for a while, and it's now under offer."

"So half of that will be yours?"

"More, actually."

"Nice. Anyway, I appreciate it. It's been a few years since I was in Barcelona."

Chapter Sixty-Nine

SUNDAY 7 APRIL 1996

They'd started that day in La Rambla, the narrow snaking avenue running south from Plaça de Catalunya to the harbour, where street performers and flower sellers mixed with the tourists, and where you could buy anything from newspapers to birds in cages. Rod said it was easy to distinguish the natives from the travellers; they looked so much cooler and moved at a third of the pace.

They stopped off in the food market, buying pastries for later in a store fronted with a striking mosaic.

"Careful not to look too closely at the butchers' stands," Rod cautioned.

"Why's that?"

"They may have sheep's testicles hanging like bunches of grapes."

"I see."

"I'm told they're quite delicious when sliced up and fried. Full of protein too."

"It sounds like you might have tried them."

"Maybe I have," Rod laughed.

They synchronised to the local time by brunching mid-morning and then waiting until three before eating their lunch on the waterfront. Rod chose grilled prawns while Daniel ate an exotic-sounding fish. They washed it down with a bottle of Cava and afterwards an industrial strength Orujo.

The drinking continued later in a bar they found tucked inside what looked like an ancient gatehouse close to the main boulevard. It had a glass floor and, oddly, a round snooker table. They'd moved on by now to local beers, and several hours later they drifted out of the bar close to midnight and realised they hadn't eaten supper.

"Let's eat in the hotel," Rod said. "Get something sent to our room."

"I agree, but not sheep's testicles."

"I doubt they'd serve them. It's more of a locals' thing."

They ordered tapas and ate it sitting on the balcony. Daniel was ready to turn in when Rod produced a bottle of Brandy de Jerez.

"Bloody hell. When did you pick that up?" Daniel asked.

"You were taking an absolute age in that leather shop, haggling for a few measly belts for God's sake. So I nipped out. Found a small purveyor of Spanish spirits."

"You're a dark horse," Daniel laughed.

"And you've only just noticed?" Rod said, unscrewing the lid and pouring two generous measures.

They sipped it and looked at each other.

"It's like a sweet sherry," Daniel said.

"A pretty good one, though." Rod drank the rest of his glass in one swift movement.

Daniel followed suit and they stood for a while

looking over the balcony at the flickering lights of night-time Barcelona. Then Rod refilled their glasses.

"To absent friends," Daniel said.

"And enemies."

"Is it just me, or is the balcony starting to rotate?"

"I would say that's just you. But now you come to mention it…"

"I love the fact," Daniel said, "that every tiny light out there, is somebody's living room, or balcony, or lit-up swimming pool. I'm not expressing this well, but you know what I mean."

"They're all people. People we don't know. But connected."

"Something like that."

"Top-up?" Rod asked.

"If I must."

Rod poured more Brandy de Jerez.

"Chin-chin, old chap."

"Chin-chin," Daniel said. "By the way, I'm not sure we need to drink to our enemies, do we?"

"What are you talking about?"

"You know, what you said earlier. The last toast. Or was it the one before?"

"When was that?"

"About two minutes ago." Daniel laughed.

"That long? No wonder I can't remember. Anyway, whatever you prefer, my friend. You're in charge."

"Some people would just be better out of the way completely," Daniel said.

"Like James Liddell, you mean?"

"I didn't actually mean him. But you must tell me some time who you think did that."

"A conversation for another time maybe?"

"Sure."

"I know who you were talking about though – people best out of the way."

"I imagine you would. You spent enough time following him around."

Rod was poking both of his forefingers behind his glasses, rubbing his eyes. Daniel wondered why he just didn't take his glasses off.

"But you know," Rod said carefully, "anything can be arranged at a price."

"So they tell me. This balcony is definitely spinning."

"It's the whole hotel, isn't it?"

"It's not too unpleasant."

"I always liked roundabouts when I was a kid," Rod said.

They drank more.

"I really should be stopping," Daniel said. "I'm going to regret this in the morning."

"Daniel, chill out. We're on holiday."

"Just out of interest, what is the going rate for something like that?"

"A bottle of Brandy de Jerez?"

"No, the other thing we were talking about."

"Oh," Rod said vaguely. "I don't know. Fifteen grand maybe. That's what I'd do it for."

"It's almost worth it. It really is."

"Not a lot for someone about to sell a house in Barnsbury, say."

Daniel chuckled. Looked reflectively into his glass.

"Is that a yes?" Rod asked. "I could do with the money. And I've got plenty of time on my hands."

"You'd need cash, I'm guessing."

"Of course I'd need cash. Are you crazy?"

"You always know when you're paying someone dodgy, because they invariably want cash."

"Dodgy? I object to that. I'm a true professional."

"My apologies!"

"So? Do we have a deal?"

"We have a deal," Daniel laughed. "In fact, I might even be able to get chambers to stump up the money. They paid for the health farm after all."

Chapter Seventy

SATURDAY 25 MAY 1996

The telephone rang around eleven pm. Daniel picked up and was pleased to hear Rod's voice. In the six weeks or so since the holiday, Daniel had been busy. True to his word, Bill had lined up plenty of work and he'd needed to hit the ground running. As a result he found himself usually staying late in chambers and had only spoken to Rod a couple of times. On one occasion, Daniel was asking for advice about what car he should buy. Not that Rod was an expert on cars, but Daniel found it reassuring to talk things through with his friend. The only thing they never discussed was his ongoing cases. He'd been tempted to do that too – he was sure Rod was capable of finding the odd killer argument – but so far, he'd resisted.

"What's up?" Daniel asked.

"Apropos of our discussion in Barcelona, I've got a possible plan."

"What discussion?"

"The balcony discussion."

Daniel felt a shot of adrenaline coursing through his

veins. "Rod, I was shit-faced. I barely remember what we said. But whatever we did say, it was meaningless."

"I know, I know," Rod said reassuringly.

"Seriously, I don't want you getting any crazy ideas, do you understand?"

"I'm not getting any crazy ideas, don't worry. I know it's all entirely theoretical. But I'm seriously short of money. That's why I've been thinking it through a little, I suppose."

"There is nothing to think through, mate. Absolutely nothing."

"All right. I just said it's entirely theoretical, didn't I?"

"You did. And that means there's nothing to discuss."

"I agree. But I still think you'll find my plan interesting. You want to hear it or not?"

"Not particularly."

"It's just, if you did want him out the way, and I hear what you're saying, but if you did, I have a very neat way of getting into his flat. That's all."

"That's very interesting, Rod. Now can we please talk about something else?"

"Okay. Fine. What would you like to talk about?"

Chapter Seventy-One

"Liz is very pleased how the documentary's turned out. She's excited," Michaela told Thomas.

"Oh, okay." Thomas was resting his head on the arm of the sofa and stretching out his legs. "That's nice."

Michaela patted his knees which were on her lap. "She said the part with you has become the centrepiece. The bit that gives it all meaning."

"She said that?"

"Yes. You come across really well."

"I thought I might have been a little over the top. You know, talking about my feelings. And forgiveness. It's not very English to talk about forgiveness, is it?"

"Liz liked it. She said you were the most mature out of all the people she interviewed."

"I find that hard to believe," Thomas said.

As he said this, the telephone rang.

"I'll go," Michaela said. "You're too comfortable to move."

She slipped off the sofa and he watched her cross the room, pick up the phone.

"Hello? Oh, hi."

She caught Thomas's eye and mouthed 'My mum'. He gave her a thumbs up from the sofa.

"What is it?" Michaela was saying. Her whole demeanour had changed. "Mum? What's wrong?"

Thomas swung his legs off the chair and sat up.

"For fuck's sake," Michaela said. "Why?" She nodded slowly. "Christ. Poor thing. Yes, I will. Of course, I will. I can go tomorrow. I'll do that, yes. Oh my God, I just don't believe it. They seemed so happy together."

Thomas had joined her on the other side of the room and was gently touching her shoulder with his fingertips. She turned towards him and winced.

"Okay, Mum," Michaela said. "Tomorrow. Absolutely. And I'll speak to you when I get there."

She put the phone down and shook her head.

"What is it?"

"It's Rose's boyfriend. He killed himself."

Thomas screwed up his eyes. "Brad?"

"Yeah, carbon monoxide poisoning."

"Shit! That's awful."

"He did it in his parents' garage too."

"That's terrible. For everyone."

"I know. I'm going to see Rose tomorrow."

Chapter Seventy-Two

SUNDAY 23 JUNE 1996

"There were three of them. And it happened around midday. It was Christmas Day. And I was alone."

Rod was watching television as he ate his kebab. He remembered trailing Michaela and Thomas around Allied Carpets, and Michaela telling him that a friend was making a BBC documentary on the victims of crime. She was gauging his interest in taking part. And now here he was, Thomas talking to the nation like a religious or political leader.

"I was working in my parents' home the day it happened, reading student coursework. There were three of them. All men. In their twenties. I didn't even hear them come in. It's still unclear how they got in, but that's not important now."

"Were they armed?" the voice of an unseen interviewer asked.

"Yes, they were. Two had guns, and one a club or baseball bat. And it was a pretty vicious attack." Thomas stopped. Composed himself.

"That must have been very traumatic."

"It was. I think I was in shock for several months afterwards. I was beaten up. Robbed. Humiliated in a sexual way."

"Can you tell us a little more about that humiliation?" the interviewer asked.

Rod registered the intrusiveness of the question. A few years ago, they would never have asked that. These days everybody wanted the gruesome details.

"They pulled my trousers down and stuck a gun up my butt, if you really want to know," Thomas said. "I honestly thought they were going to fire it."

Rod stared impassively at the screen.

"They didn't though," Thomas said. "They killed our pet spaniel Jojo instead. For no reason. I guess they found it amusing. It was just a terrible day for me."

The camera panned away from Thomas to the interviewer, a young woman with round glasses. She had tears in her eyes. "And how did you manage to move on, Thomas, after this experience?"

"Okay, it helped a little that the guys were caught straight away. One of them turned himself in, and so they got all three. And they received prison sentences, but not long ones."

"How long were the prison sentences?"

"Sixteen months each, I think. And they served half of that."

"That's very short," the interviewer said.

"And there was no publicity. It was never reported as far as I know."

"So nobody knows who they are. You must have been left with all sorts of angry feelings about that too. How did you deal with it all, Thomas?"

"Honestly, I had to make a decision. I could carry the

trauma around with me for the rest of my life. Which I knew would be like a festering wound inside me. Or I could try – somehow – to forgive the guys that did this."

"But how did you do that, Thomas? Because I think our viewers will want to know this."

"Literally by saying out loud that I forgave them. I would name each of them as I said it too. Each day I would spend fifteen or twenty minutes saying it out loud."

"So what would that sound like, Thomas? Can you recreate it for our viewers?"

Thomas composed himself and looked at the camera, as if he were speaking to the men directly. "I forgive you, Rory Hewitt. I forgive you, Dwight Shaw. I forgive you, Drew Sanders. I forgive each of you for what you've done." He gave a half smile. "At first the words didn't reflect what I felt. They were just sounds. But as the days went by, and as I kept repeating these same words, I started to believe what I was saying. And it was the strangest thing, as if I was becoming the words themselves. As if the forgiveness was me. It changed my thinking about myself and the world."

"But, Thomas, I have to ask you. These men hardly received proper prison sentences."

"That's right. But I forgave them – I totally forgave them. It was the only way. I could never have moved on otherwise."

"So with no proper justice, you've found it in your heart to forgive these three men. Many of our viewers are going to watch this and find it quite incredible."

"Well, it came from within," Thomas nodded as he spoke. "That's all I can say."

The documentary moved on to the next case study. Another victim of a different crime, this time a financial fraud. Rod switched the television off with his remote control. He thought about Thomas forgiving the perpetrators of the crime, naming them when they'd managed so far to remain anonymous. And unexpectedly he found himself laughing.

Chapter Seventy-Three

TUESDAY 25 JUNE 1996

I t was early evening and Michaela and Daniel were walking in Hampstead Heath, somewhere they used to love to visit together in the good old days. She had called him the night before, saying that they needed to meet. There was something she wanted to discuss. He had spent today listening to a bank manager being questioned by his opposing counsel in an attempted murder case but had found it hard to concentrate. His mind kept straying to the arrangement he'd made with Michaela. On the telephone she'd been friendly, breezy almost, and he'd dared to hope that she was missing him and was placing the first block down towards rebuilding their relationship. It would be a long process, he knew this. But they were still married, and he was willing to apologise for any behaviour that she'd found too much to bear. With the benefit of hindsight, no woman would want to be trailed to a hotel in Winchester. He understood that now. The extreme situation he'd found himself in had caused him to react in certain ways. But now might be the time for everything to return to a more normal state. As he'd driven towards Hampstead, he'd thought he might even use these words: *It's time for us to return.*

"You remember how we once spent pretty much a whole Sunday morning looking for the women's bathing pond?" he asked her as they walked.

"Oh yes," Michaela said. "And I was getting so frustrated. Because I kept hearing about these women who swim in the pond, there are even some that claim to have a dip every day of the year, and I really wanted to try it out."

"I think we did find it in the end, but by that time we were both starving and ate our picnic instead."

"That's right," Michaela laughed. "Your memory is better than mine."

"It's better than most people's. But that isn't necessarily a great thing. There are some memories I'd rather forget. Things I've done that I'd rather I hadn't, you know."

She took her sunglasses off and placed them in a case inside her bag. The same bag with the bold harlequin design that she'd been carrying the day they first met. Was she sending him a message by using it today? If she was, it was subtle, but nonetheless. It might even have been an unconscious action.

"Can we talk about what I wanted to talk about?" Michaela asked. She was suddenly more businesslike, the change in tone alarmed him slightly.

"I'm here to talk about whatever you want to."

"Which is the future," she said.

"And I'm always happy to talk about our future."

She turned to look at him with her searching brown eyes. "Not our future so much as my future with Thomas," she corrected him.

Just as she said this Daniel almost tripped up on something half hidden in the undergrowth. "Fucking thing." He turned to look at a discarded umbrella. "Who leaves an umbrella just lying around?"

He stooped to pick it up, all of his rage transferred to the tatty object in his hand.

"There's a bin over there," she said, pointing.

He looked again at the collapsed and busted frame, no use to anyone, and walked slowly towards the bin, relieved at least to have a moment's respite to gather his thoughts. He dropped the umbrella with the other rubbish and brushed his hands together several times in an exaggerated motion.

She was sitting on a bench now and he sat next to her.

"Last night," she said, "when I spoke with Thomas, he made... I wouldn't call it a proposal exactly, but he wanted to sound me out, I guess."

"Sound you out about what?"

"About us getting married."

"But you're married to me."

"I realise that, Daniel," she laughed. "That's rather why I'm here."

"I see. So you love him, do you? You love Thomas?"

"Yes. More than I've ever loved anyone."

He let this new fact sink in for a moment. "This is unexpected," he managed.

"Would we need a lawyer?" she asked. "Or can these things be done more simply?"

"I don't think we need a lawyer."

They talked for a few more minutes and then she said that perhaps they should be making tracks. As they walked back towards their cars which were parked on Hampstead Lane, he felt an incredible weight in his stomach, something expanding within him that was almost preventing him from breathing.

"Thanks for being so reasonable," Michaela was saying, though he hardly registered her words. He got into his car, closed the door and smiled perfunctorily as she stood outside, looking in at him through the window. She appeared slightly concerned. He started his engine.

He was going to drive straight home but changed his mind almost immediately. It was practically the same route anyway, down Highgate Hill, then picking up the Archway Road. He would just carry on to Hackney when he got to Highbury and Islington.

Rod answered the door and told Daniel that he was eating. Another of his famous curries. He apologised that there was only a small portion left and Daniel told him that he wasn't hungry.

Daniel followed Rod up the stairs, and they stood in his living room. Rod looked down at him and narrowed his eyes.

"You don't look good, Daniel. What's going on?"

"It's finished. It really is finished. It's the first time I've realised. But it's been brought home to me. I know it now. Michaela wants to divorce me."

Daniel was suddenly breathing very deeply, his body shuddering, and he attempted to block the path of a tear that escaped from his eye.

"Come on, man, it's okay," Rod said. He put his arms around his friend and held him as Daniel wept for the collapse of his second marriage. "It's okay, mate, you can let it all go now."

"And the worst thing is I saw that complete idiot on the television at the weekend. It's like I can't get away from his smug fucking face."

"I saw that too. Very forgiving, isn't he?"

"I just want everything to be over, Rod. This whole thing with Thomas. I want it all over. Thomas. Everything over with. Everything."

"I understand," Rod said, patting him gently on the back.

Chapter Seventy-Four

I t was eight in the evening and Thomas telephoned Michaela as they'd arranged.

"How's it all going?" he asked. "How's Rose doing? I just can't imagine."

There was a pause. "Well… she's amazingly strong, really. Just kind of getting on with things."

"What kind of things?"

"You know, helping his family with the arrangements. Writing a eulogy for the funeral. She's got a whole list of tasks and she's just getting on with them. I'm not sure what's going on underneath."

"It's her way of coping."

"That's right. I just don't think I'm being much use, because she's not talking about it. She's not actually talking about what he did. Or why he did it."

"Maybe she's not ready to talk," Thomas said. "Maybe she has to get the practical things over with first. And then when she's run out of those, she'll be left with her feelings."

"That's a good way of putting it, Thomas."

"And the funeral will help her to grieve. Because that's what funerals are for, isn't it?"

"I guess so," Michaela said.

"Why do you think he did it?"

"I've no idea. Rose told me he'd suffered from depression as a teenager. But he'd been treated for that. And had been okay since."

"So it seemed."

"Exactly."

"What time did he do it?"

"In the evening."

"What, this sort of time?"

"Later. Because he was staying with his parents. They'd spent the evening together, a normal evening, they'd watched the news and stuff. Then his parents went to bed. And he stayed up. And later he went outside and into the garage. He used their car. That's how he did it. They found him in the morning. That's as much as I know."

"What must it be like to do that? To know that you're about to end your life. To know that you're going to die that night. You're just going to watch some TV with your parents, say goodnight to them, let them go to bed. And then…"

"Don't, Thomas. Please."

"It's just so weird. I can't quite get my head round it."

"Me neither. So, what are you up to tonight?"

"Nothing much. I might read a book or something."

"That sounds good."

"By the way, did you think any more about what we were discussing?"

"Yes. And I even went to the trouble of meeting up with Daniel."

"You did? You met up with him?"

"On Tuesday, yes. And everything's going to be fine. I'm tired now. But we can talk more about it tomorrow. Yes?"

"Sure. Same time?"

"Same time. I love you, Thomas."

"I love you too."

"It's going to be all right. We're going to do this."

"You bet we are."

He hung up and picked a novel from his shelf, a John Updike that he'd read before. He'd barely sat down when the buzzer went.

"Hello?" he said through the intercom.

"Pizza for you," a voice said.

"I didn't order pizza, I'm guessing you have the wrong flat."

"I don't think so. You are Thomas Mason, right?"

"Yeah."

"It's a gift. From someone called Michaela."

"Oh. That's so sweet."

He buzzed the man in and opened his flat door.

"Thanks so much," Thomas said. "The problem is, I've already eaten."

The man was looking at him curiously. "Didn't I see you on television the other night?"

"Yeah, you very likely did."

"That was such a terrible story. There are some very sick people in this world."

Thomas nodded and the man handed him the pizza box.

"I have to say though," the man continued, "I really admire the way you dealt with that. Amazing."

"Thanks," Thomas said, and looked inside the box.

"It's veggie," the man said. "One of my favourites."

"Do they always put pineapple on the vegetarian pizzas here?"

"Not always."

"Let me get you a tip," Thomas said. "I always like to do that."

"Are you sure? We're not really meant to, but the pay isn't great for this kind of work, as you can imagine."

"Of course," Thomas said. "Come in a moment – no reason to wait in the hallway."

The man followed Thomas into his flat. Thomas started rifling through a kitchen drawer.

"I aways keep some coins in here for moments like this. The problem is, I have so much junk. Bills, pens, playing cards, plastic cutlery. I mean, who keeps plastic cutlery? Ah, here we go…"

He was so engaged in what he was doing that he didn't realise that the man had come right up behind him. Thomas had collected a few coins and as he stood up straight the man put an arm around his face and sliced Thomas's throat with a knife. Thomas tottered on his kitchen tiles like a clumsy dancer just as the man plunged the same knife into his chest. Thomas fell to the ground. A gurgling noise was the only sound he made.

His assailant picked up a tea towel and wrapped it several times around the knife before carefully putting it in an inside pocket. Then he picked up the pizza box that Thomas had placed on a work surface, and three coins which had fallen to the floor and rolled away. He placed them in his pocket too, looked briefly around him and quickly left the flat.

Chapter Seventy-Five

SATURDAY 29 JUNE 1996

They met in the usual pub in Hackney. Rod had called and said he had something important to discuss. Daniel was preparing for the next stages of the attempted murder trial but agreed to meet for an hour at nine.

"So you heard what happened?" Rod asked, after they'd sat down.

"I don't think so. What do you mean?"

"It's been on the news – at least the BBC has reported it."

"I'm not sure what you're talking about, Rod. Could you make it easy and tell me?"

"Thomas has been found dead in his flat."

"Thomas? *The* Thomas?"

"Yes. His throat had been cut. And he'd been stabbed."

Daniel's mind was racing. But Rod was perfectly calm as usual. He had taken off his glasses and was polishing them with a turquoise cloth.

"Fucking hell, Rod. What are you saying to me?"

Rod put his glasses back on, leaned forward over the tiny table and spoke in a low voice.

"I did what you wanted."

"No! – No you fucking well didn't."

"On Tuesday you told me that you couldn't get away from his smug fucking face. And that you wanted everything to be over. Everything. You wanted his life to be over."

It felt like a frozen rope was being dragged through Daniel's stomach. "I never… I never said that." He was aware of the whiney, pleading tone in his voice – as if it could be all reversed if he could only find the right way of asking.

"You certainly did say that, Daniel. Because I heard you. So you might now want to thank me." Rod smiled his most charming smile. "For services rendered."

"For fuck's sake. Are you completely and utterly mad? What services?"

"Come on, Daniel. This isn't complicated."

Daniel looked over his shoulder. There was nobody behind them, but he couldn't continue this conversation here. Rod was starting to say something else, but Daniel cut him off.

"No – Rod, no – just shut up. Not here. Let's go for a walk."

Rod looked down at their unfinished pints.

"It doesn't matter about those." Daniel stood up and without even waiting for Rod to do the same, left the pub. His mind was filled with a thousand unwelcome thoughts – like maggots attacking his brain. An image surfaced, of Thomas lying dead, his ponytail an island in a pool of blood, his throat gaping.

Daniel refused to speak again until he was sure they wouldn't be heard.

"Okay, Rod," he said as they entered London Fields, "please tell me this is all a joke – that it's your black humour getting the better of you."

"I wouldn't joke about this."

Another realisation ploughed into Daniel with brutal force. "So you killed James Liddell. That's what this means too."

"Of course I killed James Liddell. I assumed you knew that."

"No – because I kept telling you that I believed in you. That I believed in your innocence."

"Isn't that what all barristers tell their clients?"

"Jesus Christ, Rod. What did you do to that poor man?"

"Thomas. Or James?"

"Thomas."

"Like I just said. I killed him. I delivered a pizza, which he didn't have time to eat. Because it was all very quick. I killed him, Daniel. Just like we agreed I would."

"Like – we – agreed?" Daniel spat out the words, accentuating every syllable.

"Please don't pretend that's not what you were asking me to do on Tuesday. And you also seem to be forgetting our long chat in Barcelona. When we agreed terms."

"But I told you. That all meant nothing. Nothing. We were paralytic, for God's sake. We were barely making sense. I can't remember most of what we said that night."

"Let me remind you then. You said, 'Some people would just be better out of the way completely'. And I told you that anything could be arranged at a price."

"I don't remember anything like that."

"Well, I remember it all." Rod sounded indignant.

"And in any case, I told you, it was drunken nonsense."

"You can call it that. But we agreed terms."

"What the fuck do you mean, we agreed terms? What terms do you think we could possibly have agreed?"

"I told you I'd take care of the situation for fifteen thousand." Daniel had stopped walking on the path and was staring at him. "Yes, fifteen thousand," Rod said.

"For crying out loud. How can you just go round to someone's home and…" He couldn't bring himself to finish the sentence.

"It was very quick, as I've said."

They'd reached the children's play area and Rod wandered over to a swing and sat down.

"He died happy," he called over to Daniel. "He thought Michaela had just bought him a pizza. Sweet."

Daniel went closer and stood to one side of the swing. "You're a complete lunatic. And I should go straight to the police," he said.

"I'm not sure I'd do that if I were you," Rod said quietly. "Particularly as you were the one who commissioned me to do this job."

Daniel found himself rubbing his forehead repeatedly with his palm as his ex-client launched the swing into motion with his feet.

"Anyway," Rod said, "what I'm also saying – in the nicest possible way, my friend – is that it's time for you to pay up."

Daniel watched in disbelief as Rod oscillated higher and higher, using his strength and agility to propel himself towards the night sky.

Chapter Seventy-Six

The next night, Rod called at eleven.

"When am I going to see the money?" he asked Daniel.

They went back and forth about whether they'd even had an agreement, exactly as they'd done in the park.

"I just want the money, Daniel," Rod said. "That's the bottom line here."

"I thought we were friends."

"I did too. And that's why I bent over backwards to do your every bidding and call. The three trips to Winchester. The long days spent tracking Michaela and Thomas while you were doing your meditations and yoga, whilst enjoying a glass of Shloer!"

"And I appreciated those things."

"But this assignment was always different."

"It was not an assignment."

"Agreement then."

"It wasn't even close to an agreement."

"You knew this could never just be a favour, Daniel. You knew it full well."

"I had no idea what you were about to do. No idea at all. I was back at work trying to get on with my life."

"Do you know how bad this would look for you, Daniel, if this got out?"

"Of course I do. And you'd be spending the rest of your life in prison. Is that what you want?"

"I just want the money, Daniel. Why don't you have a good think about that? And call me tomorrow with a plan."

Chapter Seventy-Seven

"You know my door's always open," Bill said. "Whatever's troubling you, let's talk it through."

"Thanks," Daniel said. He had caught Bill at the end of a long day but doubted the senior clerk would be able to help much. But equally, he had no one else to turn to.

Bill sat down in his chair and Daniel sat next to him. Bill swivelled to face him and smiled. "Well?"

"It's a bit of a long story to be honest, Bill."

"Okay." Bill looked at his watch. "Give me the condensed version then."

"I don't quite know where to start, to be honest."

"The beginning maybe?"

"All right, so the week after the floating head trial finished, Rod Bannister came into chambers with a present for me. It was a set of antique cufflinks. Diamonds, rubies, gold."

"Okay. I hope you didn't take them."

"Of course I didn't take them."

"Thank God for that," Bill smiled. "You can get into all sorts of trouble accepting gifts from dodgy clients."

"Yeah, I know that, Bill. But what happened that day was I went for lunch with him. We sat in Middle Temple Gardens."

Bill sucked air through his teeth. "I don't like the sound of that very much."

"This is just the start of it, Bill. Rod Bannister became a good friend of mine."

"You're joking, aren't you? You got him off a murder and you became friends?"

"I went on holiday with him. For four days. To Barcelona."

"Oh, Christ – you didn't, did you?"

"Yes, I did."

"You idiot, Daniel." Bill was now shaking his head and tutting. Daniel was already doubting the wisdom of approaching him in the first place. "What got into you? Why didn't you come to me and say you were thinking about it?"

"I don't know, Bill."

"All right, damage limitation exercise. This doesn't have to get out. Who else have you told?"

"Nobody."

"Good. Keep it that way. Can you imagine if the papers got hold of a photo of you in the Costa Brava with Rod Bannister? The headlines. It doesn't bear thinking about."

Daniel nodded.

"I know you've been on a downer since Michaela left. But that's no excuse for going on holiday with the defendant in a murder trial. I'm seriously disappointed in you."

"There's more, Bill."

"Don't tell me. He told you on the holiday he was guilty."

"Well, that did come out–"

"All right, that's one for the Bar Council. I think you're probably okay on that front, to be honest. But Mark Stobbs is excellent. I'd speak to him. Adrian Turner's ever so good too."

"Thanks," Daniel said. "I might do that."

"Phew," Bill said. "Well that's sorted anyway."

"There's more, Bill."

"For God's sake, what now?"

"When I went to the health farm, I got Rod to keep an eye on Michaela."

"You mean follow her?"

"Kind of, yes."

"You asked Rod to follow your wife? You complete cretin."

"I know, it's bad."

"Not bad, Daniel – that is bloody terrible. Whatever possessed you?"

"I don't know."

"Have you told Michaela?"

Daniel hesitated briefly. "No."

"Just don't. Because that would be a serious complaint. Disciplinary tribunal. Expensive defence team – the full works. Just don't tell her. You hear me? Draw a line under the whole thing. All right?"

"Yes, understood."

"That's it, isn't it?"

Daniel paused. "Yeah, that's it. Everything."

"Christ, Daniel. You have been a stupid boy. I know you've had a bad year, but – oh, Jesus. Anyway, these things happen, I know. Now's the time to keep schtum and let it all blow over."

"Thanks, Bill, that's good advice."

"It's all right. I'm glad you told me anyway. It's

always good to have a heads-up on these things. By the way, you're looking tired. I'd go home and get some rest if I were you. Switch off."

Daniel got into his car and glanced at himself in the mirror. An ashen face peered back. More than tired, he had the look of the damned. As if he could just go home and switch off. He could barely face spending another evening alone in his house right now. Would there be another late-night phone call with Rod, like the one last night, the conversation going back and forth like a deadly game of badminton? It was an intractable problem and Daniel had never felt such a crushing sense of loneliness. There was literally no one else he could talk to about this. He had tried with Bill and the results were almost laughable. At least he'd had the sense to stop the disclosures when he did.

He was barely aware that he was driving at all until he registered the trembling of his right hand. He glanced in disbelief at the little dance his fingers were doing on the steering wheel, then tried gripping it more tightly. But this just displaced the trembling further up his arm, to his elbow and beyond. He now felt a tightness in his chest, his breathing becoming shallow as if the world didn't contain enough oxygen for him. He hastily wound down the window, the car veered to the right, a horn blared, and the irate face of a taxi driver flashed past on the other side of the road. Daniel quickly pulled in to his left and stopped the car before he caused an accident. His mouth was dry, and the trembling was affecting both of his limbs now. Was he having a heart attack outside Sadler's Wells Theatre? To his left, people were gathering for a performance, idly chatting on the pavement. One or two looked towards him and he felt self-conscious and ashamed. He leaned forward, placing his elbows on his knees, and supporting his forehead on his upturned palms. But his head was like a salad spinner and he thought that he might throw up. He told himself to keep calm, that if he just stayed in this position, even for a minute longer, he would start to feel better.

There was a sharp knocking on the door and Daniel sat back up. A policewoman was peering in through the open window at him. She must have been standing in the road.

"Is everything okay, sir?"

"Yes, fine thank you, officer," Daniel said.

"It's just, you can't park here. It's a bus stop, sir. It's not allowed, I'm afraid."

"I'm not feeling very well, I'm sorry."

"Are you all right, sir?" She suddenly sounded concerned.

"I think I'll be okay. I had to pull over. I'm just under a lot of pressure at the moment."

"Work pressure?" she asked.

"Yes. I'm a barrister."

"I thought that was rather a nice suit you were wearing."

Daniel looked down at his jacket – dark grey with a pink pinstripe. "Thank you. I bought it in Stanley Ley in Fleet Street."

"Very nice, sir – I do like a bit of pink on a man. Is it a case, sir, that you're worrying about?"

"A case? Yes, that's right. But I'm starting to feel a bit better now."

"You need to talk to somebody, sir. That always helps. I talk to my husband – far too much, he'd say. Can you not talk to your wife about it?"

"I'm on my own at the moment."

JAMES WOOLF

"I see. Someone else then? A problem shared is a problem halved, I always say."

"Thank you, officer. You've been most kind. I'll be all right now."

"And a hot bath works wonders too. You should try that."

"Thank you, I will."

"All right sir, you take care of yourself, won't you?"

"I'll try," Daniel said and restarted his engine.

Chapter Seventy-Eight

The stalemate with Rod had continued for four days. Whatever Daniel said, Rod always came back to the same thing. He wanted his money for the services he had rendered. He didn't necessarily need it in one lump sum, but he was expecting to receive the first payment some time very soon.

It was just after ten that night when the phone rang again. Daniel's first thought was that it would be Rod. He answered warily.

"Daniel?"

"Hello, Michaela. How are you doing?"

They hadn't spoken since Thomas's death.

"You heard about Thomas, didn't you?"

Daniel paused. "I read about it, yes. It's awful, I don't know what to say."

"I wasn't ringing for sympathy."

"I am sympathetic, though. Deeply sympathetic. It's a terrible thing. Whatever went on between us, I feel devastated for you."

"Listen, I really want to talk. Can I come over?"

"Now?"

"I'm in an awful bind here. I just don't feel safe."

"Can't we speak now, on the phone?"

"Please, Daniel. I want to see you."

"Well, I'm not sure how much help I can be."

"Believe me, you can be a lot of help."

She was at his house within twenty minutes, looking gaunt, her hair unwashed for some time, it appeared. She had a packet of Silk Cut that she fiddled with, taking out individual cigarettes, then replacing them in the box.

"I'm not going to smoke one," she said. "It makes me feel calmer doing this."

"It's okay," Daniel said. "Can I get you a drink?"

"Yes, a tea." She sat at the kitchen table without waiting to be asked.

He made a pot and put out a plate of dark chocolate biscuits.

"I've had the most terrible few days, Daniel. It's literally been like living through a nightmare. I can't believe Thomas is gone. That he's been taken from me."

"It's dreadful. I don't know what to say."

"He was a good person. Why is it always the best people that get taken?"

"I wish I had an answer for you."

"I know you do." She grabbed a chocolate biscuit and bit into it. "You never used to have chocolate biscuits in the house, Dan."

"Small comforts and all that."

"I can't speak to anyone else about this," Michaela launched in. "My family's in a state of meltdown. My sister's partner died just before Thomas. And they were all pissed off with me before that anyway. For leaving you. Anika's been seconded abroad since the start of the year. So I'm pretty much sailing this ship alone. And it's all one big fucked-up situation. But I'm sure the police are going down the wrong track."

"The wrong track?" Daniel crammed a whole biscuit into his mouth and started munching.

"Yes. They're crawling all over the university where he worked. Interviewing students, fellow lecturers, anybody who might have known him there. They're likely to make an arrest soon, they told me. But I don't know, I think it's probably got something to do with that documentary. The one with Thomas in."

"Ah…" Daniel hoped the relief in his voice wasn't too evident.

"He named the men who'd attacked him."

"That's right. And he said there'd been no reporting on the case at the time."

"I don't know – it maybe had nothing to do with that. I'm just worried about myself now." She reached out and put her hand on his arm.

"Why?" He stroked her hand briefly and then took another biscuit.

"Because I lived with him. I wasn't there the night he died. Maybe whoever did it is going to come back and finish the job." She stood up and started pacing around the kitchen.

"No, Michaela. That's not going to happen. I've worked with enough criminals to know that's not the sort of thing they do."

"You don't think so?"

"Yes, one thing's got nothing to do with the other. Whoever did it would never risk going back to the scene of the crime like that. And you're the innocent party here, surely."

"Yeah, I guess. It doesn't always feel that way though.

I was the one who persuaded him to do the documentary. And now I've got that on my conscience for the rest of time."

Daniel nodded slowly. He knew exactly what she meant.

Chapter Seventy-Nine

Daniel was saying goodnight to the receptionist when he was stopped by George Carman in reception.

"Ah, Daniel. How's everything going?"

"Very good thanks, George. I was on my way home actually."

"I've been meaning to catch up with you for a while. Shall we spend a few moments in my room?"

"That would be very nice," Daniel said.

They went through to George's room and he reached up to a shelf and withdrew a bottle of whisky. He opened it and poured two large measures, handing one to Daniel.

"Here, to your good health."

"Thanks very much, George. And yours."

They sipped their drinks.

"I know you've had something of a rough ride this year," George said. "I'm thinking about your marriage here."

"Yes, that was unfortunate," Daniel said. He

wondered if Bill had said anything to George about their conversation on Monday.

"In my experience, men rarely choose their second wives carefully enough. Have a seat by the way."

The room had a table and chairs which were used for meetings. But in the corner, there was a leather sofa and a comfortable armchair. Daniel opted for the sofa and George sat opposite him.

"Yes, Bill's been keeping me up to date, of course."

"I thought he might have been," Daniel said.

"How was that health farm recuperation place we sent you to? I nearly said 'funny farm'. Was it helpful?"

"Yes, very helpful." Daniel felt himself prickling slightly.

"I don't really go in for that kind of stuff myself. And I couldn't believe it when Bill told me how much it was costing us."

Daniel swilled some whisky around his mouth. He suddenly had an idea where this might be heading.

"I mean it's right that we did pick up the tab," George continued. "I'm not sure Bill should have made that call himself though. And I have told him that."

"I'm more than happy to return the money," Daniel said.

"Oh, don't be ridiculous," George laughed. "That's not what I'm suggesting at all. Not at all. You're a highly valued member of chambers. I mean, some of us have to bring in the big bucks round here, don't we? And your share price definitely went up after that River Thames head-case thing. And it seems to be going up again. So don't worry about the funny farm, don't worry about that at all."

"That's very kind of you. To be honest, it all happened rather fast. And if I remember rightly, it was

Bill who made the call to them and settled it all. But as I say, I'm very happy to…" He allowed his sentence to tail off, thinking that would be the end of the matter.

George was manoeuvring his tongue in the crevice below his lower lip, while scrutinising Daniel from behind his glasses. "Well of course, if you absolutely insist, Daniel, that would be very good of you. I'll get Bill to provide the details of what we paid them."

"That's no problem at all," Daniel said, kicking himself for his last speech. The health farm was in the region of twenty thousand pounds if he remembered rightly. How on earth was he meant to come up with a sum like that? He'd just heard from Sally that she'd temporarily taken their house off the market, so his potential windfall would not be materialising any time soon. "I'm only too happy to help," he repeated to George.

"You know what I've been thinking, Daniel. You and I aren't too dissimilar. Very good on our feet. Partial to a drink. Something of a rogue occasionally. Might even be the kind of chaps that live a bit of a double life from time to time, eh?"

Daniel smiled glassily. "I don't know what you might be inferring, George," he laughed, "I really don't."

George reciprocated with a satisfied chuckle of his own. "Anyway, what I really wanted to say was how happy I was to hear that your troubles are at an end. It's good to put all that unpleasant stuff behind you, isn't it? Clear water and all that."

"Absolutely," Daniel said. Then drained the last drop of whisky from his glass.

Chapter Eighty

That evening, Rod phoned again and without so much as a hello, said, "When are we going to meet for me to get my money?"

"Can I be completely candid?" Daniel said. "Even if I were considering paying you the money, which I'm not, it's now completely impossible. Sally's not going to be selling our house any time soon, and I've also got to repay chambers a small fortune for my bill from the health clinic."

"Those aren't my problems. I'm living hand-to-mouth here."

"I can help you find a job. I've been thinking, I do have some good contacts in business. I can put in a word."

"The problem is, I can't believe a word you're saying anymore."

"I'll help you, I will."

"To be honest, I'm tiring of this conversation," Rod said. "If you don't pay up what you owe me, I can no longer be held accountable for my actions. That's the simple truth."

"Is that some kind of threat?"

"You could call it that," Rod said casually. "I obviously know where you live. I'm also aware of the house on Barnsbury Road where I can find your children. And clearly, I know where Michaela lives. I was there only too recently as you'll recall."

"Look, Rod – please don't do anything rash. I'm going to do whatever I can. Just give me a little time to sort things out. Do you hear me?"

"I'm waiting, Daniel. But I'm rapidly running out of patience."

It was after midnight and Rod's words were still reverberating in Daniel's head. He put on a jacket and for some reason a tie. He found himself tidying papers on his living-room table, sorting them into neat piles. He had never quite understood what people meant when they said that everything was closing in. But now he understood only too well. The very space he'd been allotted to live and breathe in was becoming more constricted by the hour.

He took a bottle of whisky from his drinks cabinet. It was a fifteen-year-old single malt given to him by a grateful client. He'd been saving it for a special occasion – what was the point of that? He opened the bottle now and poured the golden liquid into a metal hip flask until it spilled over the top and onto the carpet.

Putting the hip flask into his jacket pocket, he went out of his house and started walking. He wanted to go to the place where it had all started. The River. He craved the relief of the breeze over the Thames. It was about three and a half miles from his house and, as he now knew, Rod had made a similar journey on foot before throwing James Liddell's head from the bridge. Turning away from the Green and onto Mildmay Park, he could see the attraction of a late-night walk if you had seething thoughts you needed to still.

Just over an hour later, he finished the last of the whisky and walked onto Tower Bridge. That night when he'd run into Fergus Richardson here, just before they started the trial together. What would he give now to turn back the clock to then? He remembered their conversation, sharing Fergus's coffee in his car. How Fergus had joked that they should check the Written Standards before they did so. It had all been so easy, so affable. Everything in Daniel's life had been on the ascendancy. Not only was he about to start the biggest case of his career, but his wedding to Michaela was also fast approaching. Now, in a little over a year, the contents of his life had been unceremoniously turned upside down like a tin of spaghetti upended into a saucepan. And it was all because of one man. His former client, Rod Bannister.

The wind blew his scarf as he leaned over the bridge. If he jumped into the river now, how long would it take for his body to be found and identified? What sort of conversations would take place in chambers when the news broke? What would George say to Bill? How would Sally tell Imogen, Audrey and Max?

Daniel scolded himself for being so maudlin. He was better than this surely. Stronger. That kind police officer was right. His problems were worse because he'd been bottling them up, keeping everything to himself. And he couldn't do that anymore. As he stared into the dark water below him, the answer was obvious. He would have to share his burden, properly this time. He would tell Michaela everything.

Chapter Eighty-One

I t was eight pm when Michaela arrived at their house in Newington Green. She told him that her bags were in the car, which was a surprise. Daniel helped carry the three battered cases from the boot. She made it clear after he'd done so that this was not a reunion in the full sense of the word. She was moving back in with him as a friend and not his partner. She wanted to use the spare bedroom, for the time being at least.

"I'm moving back into this house, because it's safer for me here than being in the flat on my own."

From Daniel's perspective, the words "safer for me here" might just as well have been spoken through a megaphone. But this was why he'd called, why he'd telephoned her first thing that day. He was going to make a clean breast of everything. And that included Rod's threats to him, to his family, and to Michaela herself.

"I'm not proud of what I'm about to tell you. Quite the opposite, and that's why it's taken me so long to muster the courage to begin this conversation."

They were sitting in the kitchen by now. Michaela

had said she was hungry and was working her way through a pile of crackers and marmite. She stopped chewing long enough to say, "Just tell me, Daniel. And tell me quickly."

He started with the things she knew. Rod going to Winchester, following her and Thomas to the Isle of Wight. By beginning here, it seemed easier to move on to the rest.

"Think of this as a continuation of the slide that started last year," he said.

He explained as best he could why he'd repeated exactly the same mistake when he asked Rod to keep an eye on Michaela and Thomas back in January.

"You'd only just left me, and I couldn't accept that our relationship was over. I needed some thread of hope to hang on to, no matter how thin."

Michaela sat staring at him, shaking her head silently. So he ploughed on with his story. He told her about the evening Rod had invited him for dinner, how he'd talked about following Michaela and Thomas around supermarkets, and about the conversation he'd overheard her having with Anika, a detail which had given Daniel a modicum of hope.

He tried to paint the picture of the day's heavy drinking in Barcelona that culminated in the bizarre conversation on the balcony, a conversation which even now he was hazy on the details.

"And then six weeks later Rod called me, as if he was continuing a discussion of something we'd already agreed. But it wasn't like that, Michaela. There had been no agreement. I really can't stress that enough."

Michaela was crying now; tears were cascading down her cheeks which he took to be a good thing. She must know which way this story was heading, and that made it easier for him to continue. He told her how in that same telephone conversation, Rod had mentioned a possible way of getting into Thomas's flat. But Daniel had been at pains to tell Rod that he was barking up the wrong tree. The drunken conversation in Spain had never amounted to any plan or agreement.

"It was just the sad ramblings of two middle-aged men, both of whom had had too much to drink."

He half expected her to comment at that point, to agree, or to tell him to finish the story, but she remained silent, so he continued. He told her about what he now realised was the trigger for Thomas's murder, when he'd broken down in tears at Rod's flat the same evening that Michaela had talked to him about divorce.

"And he held me, almost like a father holding his son. And he reassured me that everything would be okay. Even then I had no inkling of what would happen."

And then he told her of his total shock when Rod had confessed to him what he'd just done.

"Even until that day, I'd believed he had nothing to do with James Liddell's murder. And stupidly, as I now realise, I thought all that talk about Thomas was just macho posturing."

Michaela had stopped crying a while ago. She'd been sitting perfectly still, scrutinising him with increasing intensity, a disconcerting absence of emotion had replaced the tears.

Daniel finished his account, explaining the rapid deterioration of his friendship with Rod, Rod's demands for money, his threats, including to Michaela herself. Even this last telling detail elicited no emotion from her. Daniel sat puzzled, waiting for a response. And then, made uncomfortable by the silence, he stood up and took her plate to the sink where a pile of crockery was demanding his attention.

"That's it," he said as he squirted washing-up liquid into the sink. "That's basically everything."

"So it was you," she finally said from behind him. "It was you all along."

"No," he said, turning around. "It wasn't me all along. That's the whole point, Michaela. You have to understand that this man is not normal."

"You killed Thomas." Within that short sentence her voice had risen to the pitch of a perfect scream. And in an instant, she was upon him, a windmill of arms and elbows, scything, digging, slapping, punching him. And all the while she was screaming, "You killed Thomas – you killed the love of my life, you fucking bastard!"

He did his best to defend himself without fighting back, raising his hands in defence, trying to catch hold of her wrists which was impossible, repeating her name loudly but steadily, telling her to stop – to calm herself, to try to be still for a moment.

She had reached for a metal pan from the stand and he ducked as it twisted ominously towards his head, ricocheting off a cupboard behind him and glancing his shoulder.

"Michaela – for Christ's sake, Michaela." He'd gone right up to her now, trapping her in the corner of the room, encircling her with his arms, going so close that, starved of space, her slaps and punches became limp and pitiful.

Then he felt a surge of pain, pain searing in his groin, electric pain – she must have kneed him in the testicles – and he sunk to the floor like a burst paper bag.

"God damn you, Daniel!" she screamed and a black Dr Marten shoe hurtled towards his face. He rolled slightly to the left and the kick connected only with his shoulder, but that was painful too. "God damn you," she said in a quieter voice.

The attack had stopped as suddenly as it had begun. Her footsteps receded on the kitchen floor. He was coiled on the floor in agony, cupping his hands between his legs, pulling tightly in the hope that some pressure there might diminish the pain.

She had locked herself in the spare room and for the next two hours did not respond to his calls or entreaties to come out. Around eleven pm he approached her once again.

"Michaela, we need to talk," he called through the door. "We must decide what to do."

"Why don't you kill yourself," she suggested.

It was after midnight when, lying motionless on the sofa and staring at the ceiling, he heard her come into the living room.

She sat on an armchair. He sat up on the sofa. Neither of them spoke for a few minutes.

"It's got late," he finally said.

"I know."

"Are you working tomorrow?"

"Meant to be," she said.

"Listen. It was a mistake to allow myself to become his friend, a huge mistake, I totally accept that. But he is unhinged. And I never sanctioned what he did. The opposite, in fact. I fought against it. You have to understand that."

"I've heard all that. It's a problem, isn't it?"

"That's right." He suddenly felt relieved that the

burden was no longer just his own. That there were now two of them, each with an equal need to do something.

"Anyway, it's simple enough," she said. "I'm going to the police. You can come with me, if you like."

"No, that's the one thing we can't do. It would be the end of everything for me. I would never work as a barrister again."

Michaela laughed. "I don't actually give a fuck whether you work as a barrister again or not. I'm more concerned that this psychopath is going to chop my head off and roll it down the M1."

"But I might face criminal charges for arranging a contract killing. I didn't do that, of course. But you can imagine how this might look. And Rod can be very persuasive."

"That's your problem. I'm going to telephone them right now."

"Can you just stop, for a second? Stop to think about me, for one second?"

"Why should I think about you?"

"There's other things we can do. Can we just take some time to think this through? Please!"

"That man killed Thomas. In cold blood. And now he's threatening me."

"I can give him the money."

"No, I'm phoning the police."

"Please, Michaela – don't do this to me."

"I want him brought to justice."

"You may not get justice. He may just get off again. And if he does, you can bet your bottom dollar that he will come after you. He never forgets, Michaela. He killed James Liddell thirty years after they left school. He was storing up the grievance for that long."

"So what are you saying? That you should pay him the money?"

"Yes. That's all he wants after all. I'll get a loan. That could take a couple of days, but I'll get one. And that will be that. He'll be happy, he'll be off our cases."

"And you think that's safer for us?"

"Yes, because you never know what could happen in court. It might not even get to trial."

"So what do we do next?" she asked.

"I'll telephone him tomorrow morning, explain that the money is on the way."

"If you really think that will work, then do it. But make sure you pay him everything. Everything he's asking for. Give him a tip for all I care. I can't walk about knowing that at any moment I might get bundled into a waiting car."

Chapter Eighty-Two

TUESDAY 9 JULY 1996

F irst thing in the morning, Daniel telephoned Rod as agreed. He kept the conversation short, saying that the money was coming. If Rod could just sit tight for a few days, everything would be sorted.

Later, Daniel rang him again. He'd spoken to his bank and bureaucracy being what it was, it would be a week before he had the money. He apologised for the delay, but assured Rod that everything was on course. He would hand over the full amount in cash on the sixteenth.

That evening the telephone rang again and Daniel leapt on it as if it might explode if he didn't pick up immediately.

"Hello? Oh, hi. How are you?"

He mouthed 'Sally' to Michaela who was standing next to him in the living room.

"Yes, not too bad thanks," Daniel said in a level voice. "What's the news? My news, do you mean? Well..." He looked around him. "My news is that

384

Michaela's moved back in with me. Yes, lovely, eh? Just yesterday actually. So, that's great, isn't it? And you?"

He nodded a couple of times and made a wheel turning gesture with his right hand. Michaela gave him a half smile.

"So he just booked a holiday? That's nice, I guess. Romantic. You want me to have them for a week? All three, yeah? I'm not being hesitant. It's actually a good idea for me to spend some time with the children right now. When do you want to drop them off? Saturday? Oh, the twentieth. Yes, that's fine. We'll look after them, no problem."

He put the phone down and Michaela said, "I can't believe you just agreed to that."

"I didn't have any choice. And in any case, everything will be sorted by the time they arrive. We're coming out of this nightmare, remember?"

Chapter Eighty-Three

MONDAY 15 JULY 1996

They spoke on the phone at lunchtime. Daniel didn't want to go to Rod's flat, so suggested meeting in London Fields at ten the following morning. That would give him time to collect the money from the bank first.

"It will hopefully be quiet at that time," Daniel said.

"It will be deserted," Rod laughed. "No one living in Hackney gets up before three in the afternoon."

Daniel dared to laugh too. For a moment he was reminded of the times they'd joked so easily with each other.

The next day he arrived at the meeting point ten minutes early. He stood in the play area, shivering slightly, wishing he'd at least brought a jacket. He was in exactly the spot where he'd watched Rod on the swing, the night he'd heard about Thomas. It seemed appropriate to meet here to finish this dreadful business between them once and for all.

He saw Rod walking towards him. In no particular

hurry it seemed. He was sensible enough to be wearing a duffel coat. He looked completely calm, as stylish as ever.

As he stopped in front of him, Rod looked at Daniel and nodded. Suddenly, Daniel didn't have a great feeling about how it was going to go.

"It's chilly," Daniel said, and Rod nodded again. "Shall we sit on that bench?"

"Wherever you like."

They both sat down, and Daniel withdrew the folded envelope from his trouser pocket. He counted the money out. He counted fifteen thousand pounds, right in front of Rod. The money was in twenty-pound notes, and he did it one note at a time. The counting seemed to go on forever. There were seven hundred and fifty notes after all.

"So you agree, that's fifteen thousand pounds?" Daniel said.

"Yes. That's fifteen thousand."

Daniel put the money back in the envelope and gave it to him. Rod placed it in the inside pocket of his duffel coat.

"So that's it," Daniel said.

Rod remained silent. Daniel held out his hand for Rod to shake, to finish the deal. But Rod didn't take it, and Daniel became very aware that he was sitting there, offering his hand like some kind of idiot. But it was okay, Rod didn't have to shake his hand. So instead Daniel said, "We're finished now, Rod. We're all settled up."

Rod frowned slightly. "Not quite. There's just the small matter of the interest now."

"What do you mean? I don't understand."

"I want another five thousand pounds," Rod said evenly. "Because nineteen days have gone by since the job has been completed. Nineteen days in which I didn't know if I was going to get paid." He'd removed his glasses and was rubbing them with a cloth. "Nineteen days of the worst type of stress," he continued. "So it's only right and proper that you should pay me some interest."

"You can't do this to me. I've paid you exactly what you said I owed."

"After nineteen days you have finally paid what we first agreed. But now I want interest."

"For fuck's sake. Have you been stringing me along, playing me for more money the whole time?"

"Not at all. But until you pay me the interest, nothing has changed."

Daniel looked at his former friend for some twenty seconds, but Rod was looking into the distance and didn't meet his eye.

Michaela was waiting for Daniel when he returned.

"I heard your car pull up in the driveway," she said.

It was now almost eleven and he didn't know what to say. He'd thought that he would be returning home jubilant, like somebody just released from a private hell. But if anything, it was the opposite.

He slumped into a kitchen chair and she sat across the table from him.

"It's not over, is it?" Michaela said.

Daniel put his hands over his eyes. "He wants another five thousand pounds. Interest. That's what he said."

"Can't we just find the money somehow and pay it?"

"No, because he'll just want more. He'll never be happy. This is never going to end."

Daniel was sobbing now, still shielding his face with his hands.

"So now you have no choice," she said. "You know exactly what you have to do next."

Chapter Eighty-Four

"That's quite a story, Mr O'Neil," DCI Ruth Hobart said. "I don't believe I've ever heard anything like it in my life."

"Well, it's all true," Daniel said.

Hobart was heading up the investigation into Thomas's murder and Daniel had gone straight to the top. They were in an interview room and he'd explained everything, beginning with the end of Rod's trial, the day that he and Hobart had encountered each other outside Court Number One when she'd looked at him so venomously.

Hobart lit a cigarette. She leaned back in her chair and blew smoke towards the ceiling. "It's frighteningly easy, isn't it, to end up on the wrong side of the law?"

"I'm not sure I follow," Daniel said.

"I mean, you're a barrister, a pillar of society. And look what you've ended up doing."

"I haven't broken any law."

"Really?" She sounded far from convinced.

"I may have crossed the odd professional boundary.

390

But the person you should be arresting is Rod Bannister."

"But you did pay him fifteen thousand pounds to kill your former wife's new partner."

"I paid him after he'd done it. And that was to protect my family who he was threatening to harm. It wasn't a payment for the killing."

"That's rather a moot point, isn't it?"

"I don't consider it to be a moot point at all."

"It sounds like you should have come to us earlier, Mr O'Neil. Much earlier." She seemed to be enjoying putting him through the wringer.

"Perhaps. But I'm here now, aren't I?"

"I agree that we need to arrest Mr Bannister. It's what we should do about you that I'm less certain of."

"I can assure you, you wouldn't have a cat's chance in hell of making anything stick in court. No prospect of a conviction at all. I deal with this type of thing most days of the week. It's my bread and butter."

"Well it's kind of you to offer free legal advice. But I tend to take my lead from the CPS as to whether to press charges."

"They'll tell you exactly the same as me."

"Perhaps they will. You're free to go, Mr O'Neil."

Chapter Eighty-Five

FRIDAY 19 JULY 1996

There were some forty journalists at the press conference. DCI Hobart was hopeful that it would lead to widespread coverage, but these things were never predictable.

"On the nineteenth of April 1995," she began, "a murder trial started at the Old Bailey which was to last just under three weeks. The defendant, Roderick Bannister, was found not guilty by the jury on the eighth of May. This case was widely reported by the press, as I'm sure you will remember.

"The reason we're here today does not relate to that particular crime, but to another murder. Thomas Mason was killed in his own home on Thursday the twenty-seventh of June 1996. This crime has also been covered extensively in the press.

"For my own part, I simply want to say the following. We have good reason to believe that Mr Bannister was responsible for Mr Mason's death that evening. And for the avoidance of doubt, by responsible I mean that Mr Bannister personally visited Mr Mason in his flat with the intention of killing him, which he proceeded to do. I'm not going to go into detail about how we came by this information. There are legal reasons why I'm unable to do so.

"You will notice that we have made available recent photographs of Mr Bannister. Please print them along with any articles you publish, in order that your readers may become familiar with his appearance. Mr Bannister is an extremely dangerous criminal and he is at large right now. He should not be approached under any circumstances. Should anybody have information about Mr Bannister's whereabouts, a dedicated telephone number has been set up. For operational reasons, I will not be taking questions about the current state of this investigation."

Chapter Eighty-Six

The doorbell rang early in the morning.

"They're here," Michaela called.

Daniel emerged from the bathroom with wet hair. "Okay," he said. "Here goes."

He went to let them in and found Sally and Stuart on the doorstep, as well as the children.

"Lovely to see you all," he said. "We won't bring their bags in just yet. I have a little surprise."

"Look at you three," Michaela said, as the children came in. "So grown up."

Sally smiled brightly at Daniel, as if to say she was glad he and Michaela were back together once again.

"We're on our summer holidays," Max said proudly.

"They're so excited about that," Stuart said.

"Of course they are," Daniel said.

"Who'd like a fresh coffee?" Michaela asked. "I've just boiled the kettle."

Sally looked at Stuart who nodded enthusiastically.

"That would be great," Sally said.

"So you must be Michaela?" Stuart seemed intrigued to meet the woman who'd replaced Sally in Daniel's life.

"Guilty as charged," she laughed.

"The children have been looking forward to seeing you again," Sally said.

"Your wedding was such fun," Max added.

"Yes, Max – but you have seen Michaela since then," Daniel pointed out. "Several times."

"How are things, Daniel?" Stuart asked.

"Good thanks. Busy as ever. And you?"

"I'm an electrician," Stuart chuckled. "You don't want to hear about that, surely?"

"I don't know. It makes a change from boring old law."

"Sally and I saw that story about your client on the news." Stuart clearly didn't want to talk about his job.

"I saw that too," Imogen added.

"Oh yes, all rather unpleasant, isn't it?" Daniel said. "So you guys are off to Venice. I've got that right, haven't I?"

"Yes, we can't wait," Sally smiled.

"We thought we'd push the boat out," Stuart added.

"Quite literally," Daniel said. "I'm sure you'll have a fabulous time. But what I was going to say earlier is you aren't the only ones having a break. I've booked somewhere at short notice for us too."

"You did?" Sally said.

"Yes, we'll be heading off very soon in fact. I just need to put their bags in the car."

"Where are we going?" Audrey asked.

"Yes, tell us!" Max joined in.

"We are going to a lovely holiday cottage in Wales," Daniel said.

"Not exactly Venice," Imogen said.

"I'll tell you what, I'll sort out the bags now."

Daniel went out to the drive and opened the boot of his car, looking around him as he did so. He hauled the three bags from the front step and loaded them into the boot, fitting them alongside the cases he'd already packed. Instead of going back inside, he walked along the pavement for a minute in either direction of the house, carefully inspecting the cars that were parked on the street.

"I want to know more about that man we met at your flat," Imogen said from the back seat, soon after they started driving. "You helped him, didn't you?"

"I represented him in court, if that's what you mean."

"It's because of you that he was found innocent of the murder, isn't it?"

"Well, the jury concluded he was not guilty. That was for them to decide. That's how our legal system works, you see."

"And now he's done another murder."

"It would seem so, yes," Daniel said.

"So he is a murderer," Max shouted. "I knew it!"

"That's your fault then, isn't it, Daddy?" Imogen said.

"In what way, my fault?" Daniel was running his left hand through his hair while steering with his right.

"Because you helped get him off the last murder. If it hadn't been for you, he'd be in jail."

"But that's your daddy's job," Michaela chipped in. "That's what barristers do."

"Yes, I know," Imogen said. "But you must feel funny

about it now. Considering what happened to that other man."

"What you say is logical," Daniel admitted. "And my former client is a dangerous man. I didn't know that when he came round for tea, of course. But he needs to be caught. And the police are hunting for him now, so there's nothing to worry about."

"Will they find him?" Audrey asked.

"Oh yes," Daniel said.

"It's just a matter of time," Michaela agreed.

When they stopped for a break at a motorway service station, Daniel returned to the car before the others and drank his coffee alone in the car park. He again made a point of scrutinising as many of the cars that were parked around his own as he could.

"All clear?" Michaela asked, approaching him.

"I think so. I've been keeping an eye out on the roads too."

"This is fucking nerve-wracking, Dan."

"It will be okay when we get there. Where are they anyway?" Daniel had just noticed that the children weren't with her.

"They all wanted to go to the toilet again. Imogen said she could find the car."

"I said not to leave them on their own." Daniel was already moving quickly across the car park.

"It's okay, Daniel, they'll be back in a minute," Michaela called after him.

"It's not okay," Daniel continued walking, "I want to find them now."

"All right, I'm coming too."

Daniel was now running towards the building, almost clattering into an elderly couple carrying hot drinks.

"Careful, mate," the man barked over his shoulder.

"Which toilet did they go into?" Daniel asked Michaela.

"The same ones as before."

"You look in the ladies, I'll do the gents."

There were plenty of small boys standing at the urinals, but Max was not one of them. "Max?" Daniel called. "Are you in here?" He did a full circuit of the toilet again and then called out, "Max, it's Daddy, will you please stop mucking about?"

He came back out of the gents. Michaela was shaking her head.

"They're not in there," she said.

"For fuck's sake," Daniel said.

"We probably just missed them. I expect they'll be back at the car by now."

"No, we'd have seen them," Daniel said. He started calling out their names, then began running erratically around the thoroughfare of shops, cafés and arcades. "Max – Audrey – Imogen!" He was aware of people looking at him in a strange way, as if they might be witnessing something that could later appear on the national news.

"Stop, Daniel – stop a moment." Michaela had caught up with him and was pulling him by the arm towards the exit.

"What is it? What are you doing?"

"Let's just go back to the car," Michaela said. "I'm sure they'll be there."

"And what if they're not?"

"If they're not, we'll get somebody to make an announcement. You need to calm down, Daniel. You're panicking."

Daniel nodded his agreement and they set off at a good pace towards the car park. As soon as they were within sight of the car, they saw the children. Imogen was sitting on the bonnet and the other two were laughing and joking with her.

"You took your time," Imogen said.

"Where did you go?" Audrey asked.

"Look, please, just stay with us at all times," Daniel said. "It's so easy to get lost in these sorts of places."

It was still several more hours before they would reach the holiday cottage. They broke their journey another two times, both without incident. On their final stop they ate an early supper in a family-run restaurant in Abergavenny. Daniel allowed himself the indulgence of a glass of wine. After that, the children all fell asleep for the last leg of the journey.

They arrived at their location, an isolated cottage at the bottom of a gravel track. Daniel found the two sets of keys in a birdhouse in the front garden. They let themselves in. The children were impressed by the size of the place, the little rugs by the bed in each bedroom, and the fact that there was a games room with a table tennis table.

"This is amazing," Max cried out.

"I love it," Audrey added.

"Where are we near to here?" Imogen asked.

"The nearest town is Brecon," Daniel said. "But I don't think you'll find that terribly exciting. There's loads to do in this house anyway, that's the good news. That's one of the reasons I chose it."

"Are we near the sea?" Max asked.

"No, we're not near the sea," Daniel said.

"You're joking, aren't you?" Audrey said. "We've driven all day and we're not even near the sea."

"We must be near the Brecon Beacons," Imogen said.

"Yes, we are. But I don't think we'll be wanting to climb those. They're really for serious walkers. It can be dangerous if you're not very careful."

"We've got to do something," Imogen said. "Unless you're planning to keep us all prisoner here."

"Of course not," Daniel laughed. "We'll find plenty to do, I'm sure."

"We could try the Brecon Beacons," Michaela suggested.

"Yes, possibly." Daniel flashed her a meaningful look.

"As long as we're careful," Michaela said.

"Yes," Daniel said. "If we're very careful."

That night Michaela and Daniel slept in the same bed for the first time since she'd moved back in with him. He didn't try to initiate anything, and she soon fell asleep with her arms wrapped tightly round his chest. Daniel had to free himself from her clutches half an hour later in order to get to sleep himself.

Chapter Eighty-Seven

D aniel awoke in the sun-drenched room at five thirty. Lying next to Michaela, he felt anxious and irritable. He silently cursed the owner of the property for using such thin curtains and no blackout. The man probably got his wife to run up a job-lot for next to nothing. After an hour or so, he gave up on sleep, rose to his feet, and went through to the kitchen. He was leafing through a folder of information about the property when he was joined by Michaela.

"Coffee?" Daniel asked.

She nodded.

"It's cheap crap but just about the only thing they've left for us." He began filling the kettle. "According to this, the village shop opens seven days a week. And early too. I'll go there soon. Stock up."

"Where do you think Rod is hiding out?" Michaela asked.

"That's what the police asked me. I don't have any information."

"But you know him well. Better than anyone

probably. Would he be staying with his family do you think?"

"He's far too clever for that. In any case, he's fallen out with his family."

"Does he own property?"

"He owns nothing. He's flat broke and bollock-busted, that's the problem."

"Apart from the fifteen thousand pounds you gave him."

"He's probably spent that already."

"And you don't think he's going to just turn up here?" Michaela asked.

"Of course not. He wasn't following us. We checked."

"I just think you should be applying your mind to this, Daniel. It's really important you do. Is there nothing he ever said to you about places he likes; places he hangs out?"

"I can't think of anything. I've told you."

"I'm just worried, that's all."

He put his arms around her. "It's all right, Michaela. We're safe here."

She allowed him to hold her for a moment and then, breaking away, walked to the window. He stood next to her. Rain was slanting in sheets across the patio, empty except for a stack of white plastic chairs and a table with an ashtray on it.

"I was hoping we could all go for a walk later," Michaela said. "But look at this."

"It's Wales, isn't it?" he laughed. "Anyway, it's a good excuse to keep everyone inside."

"But why would you want to do that, if we're so safe here?"

"We can't be too careful, I suppose."

"Daniel, you're contradicting yourself."

"I know, I'm sorry."

He continued to look out of the window. Beyond the garden and path, there were hills and mountains. All within walking distance, presumably.

"This is the type of place where Rod would go walking. It's his biggest passion in life, walking."

"Apart from killing people. Anyway, do we have to keep talking about him? It's making me anxious."

Soon afterwards, Daniel put on his raincoat and left the house. The coolness of the breeze and the rain on his forehead felt good. It was only a five- or ten-minute walk and he didn't want to take the car. Instead, he had his metal-framed rucksack on his back, the same rucksack he'd used for school hiking trips in the sixth form.

He couldn't resist peering into his car as he went past. He walked to the end of the path, turned right, and then took the track which he'd read was a handy cut-through to the village. It climbed sharply, and by the time he reached the top he already had a view of the cottage in which they were staying. The cottage in which his children were asleep in their beds, unaware of the real purpose of this trip. It all looked so calm, so picturesque, like a scene from a sleepy drama. Surely nothing bad could happen to anyone in a place like this.

He walked past a couple of houses and a small pub. The bell jingled as he entered the village store.

"Good morning," the woman behind the counter said brightly.

"Good morning," Daniel said. "We're staying locally. Just stocking up."

"Very good idea," she laughed. "I'm sorry the weather is so miserable."

It was one of those stores in which every last space

was crammed with odd items. It doubled up as a post office, and it appeared that it sold everything, from scented candles to hot-water bottles, insect repellent, needle and thread, camping gear, an abundance of waterproof clothing, kitchen equipment, crockery and cutlery, local maps and guidebooks, even a small selection of paperbacks. Daniel was only interested in the food and drink at the rear of the shop.

He wheeled his basket around the floor, placing any items he took a fancy to inside. Slightly salted butter, cherry jam, rolls, croissants, a fruit cake, some decent fresh coffee, teabags, peppermint tea for Michaela, *The Sunday Times* for himself, Weetabix and Frosties, fresh vegetables and salad, sun-dried tomatoes, green olives filled with pimento, and three plastic bottles of milk. In less than five minutes, he had filled up his basket.

"Just here for a few days?" the woman asked as she rang up the items.

"That's right. A week actually."

"From London, are you?"

"How did you know?"

"I can tell."

"Is it my accent?" Daniel was genuinely curious.

"It's the things you've put in your basket. Very London choices."

"Blimey," Daniel laughed, "you ought to be running your own private detective agency, never mind a shop."

The woman laughed too, pleased by the compliment.

The children were up when he returned home and watching cartoons in the lounge with Michaela. They were eager to eat breakfast. They did so sitting around the kitchen table.

"So what are we going to do today?" Imogen asked.

"I was thinking we might have a table tennis tournament," Daniel said.

"Are we not going out?" Imogen said.

"You can see what the weather's like."

"It is pretty shocking," Michaela agreed.

"Maybe we can go out later?" Audrey said.

"Yes, for a drive," Max said.

"I think we did rather a lot of driving yesterday," Daniel pointed out.

"So if we did go out later," Imogen said, "where would we go?"

"I'm not sure we will be going out later," Daniel said. He became aware that Imogen was looking at him closely. "But of course if everyone wants to, then we'll try to do something. But let's play some games first. What do people think of the table tennis tournament idea?"

Chapter Eighty-Eight

MONDAY 22 JULY 1996

D aniel ate breakfast alone early. He told Michaela that he was going for a walk to clear his head. As he went up the gravel path away from the cottage, he had a sensation that he was being watched. He stopped a couple of times, exaggeratedly turning around to see if anyone was behind him, or in the scrubland either side of the path. There was no one. He put the sensation down to anxiety and his situation.

The holiday cottage didn't have a telephone, so Daniel made the call from the single public phone booth in the village. He was gratified when he was immediately put through to DCI Hobart.

"Is there any more news about tracing Rod?" Daniel asked.

"Not a lot, I'm afraid," she responded.

"Can you tell me what you have, as I'm feeling a bit anxious here?"

"Anxious about what?"

He was surprised he had to spell it out to her.

"What I'm saying is, are you sure we're safe here in

Wales? Given that Rod made direct threats to myself and my family."

"Just sit tight where you are, Mr O'Neil, that's my advice. And in any case, we don't believe he's still in the UK. Bannister has contacts in Spain, and we have good reason to think that he's already slipped the net and left the country."

"I see," Daniel said.

"I do have one piece of good news for you."

"What's that?"

"It doesn't look like we'll be pressing charges against you."

"Right."

"I had a quick chat with our CPS guy, and he didn't think it would be in the public interest. It's not official, but I'd be very surprised if they decide anything different. And while I may not agree, I have to accept what they say. So you can relax and enjoy the rest of your holiday."

Daniel thanked her and ended the call. He began the walk back to the cottage feeling deflated. Why did Hobart dislike him so much? That was surely sarcastic about enjoying his holiday. He was also far from convinced that they were exploring every avenue available in their hunt for Rod. That's what was worrying him. Whether or not he'd face charges was inconsequential in comparison.

As he descended the hill, Daniel looked again at the cottage with his red Golf GTI parked outside. From this angle, it looked like the door was open on the driver's side, but that couldn't possibly be the case. He never left the door open, and it wasn't as if Michaela would have done so either. Unless she'd needed to fetch something from the car in a hurry, but he couldn't think what that might have been. He quickened his pace slightly, soon losing his vantage point. It had surely been an illusion. The vehicle was blurred from that distance anyway and he had the car key in his pocket.

But there it was, as he approached the cottage from the road, the door was wide open. It definitely hadn't been when he'd left a few minutes earlier to make the phone calls.

He approached the car gingerly. Perhaps he'd stopped some opportunist thief. There wasn't anybody inside, and, as far as he could see, there wasn't anyone hanging around the drive area either. On the front seat however, the driver's seat, there was a small package.

Gift-wrapped.

He grabbed it with a feeling of dread and ran to the cottage, locking the door again as soon as he was inside.

"Hello?" he called.

From the games room he heard the clipped sounds of table tennis. He poked his head round the door. They were all inside.

"We're having a lovely game of doubles here," Michaela said, a slight edge to her voice.

"Yeah, are we going for our walk yet?" Audrey asked.

"Soon," Daniel said, and shut the door again.

Back in the kitchen, he tore open the wrapping paper. Inside was the box that Rod had tried to give him in chambers. The cufflinks. And a note written on a card. The same card type he'd used in his message to Liddell.

Daniel
Are you sure I can't tempt you to take these?
I really have no use for them anymore.
R

Daniel's brain was fogging, overloaded with thoughts, too much new information to piece together. He returned to the games room.

"Michaela – can I have a word? Now, if you don't mind."

She came out immediately.

"What is it?"

"Can we speak in our room?"

She followed him up the stairs.

"He's tracked us down. He left this in my car."

She took the box from him.

"The cufflinks. Oh fuck."

"He's found us. I don't know how. We were so careful. So fucking careful." He could hear the panic mounting in his voice.

"I know we were."

"What do we do, Michaela? I don't know what to do next."

"We need to speak to the fucking police, Daniel. That's what we have to do. Get them over here. We need a squad-load of the fuckers."

"I realise that, but Rod's outside somewhere. He might be waiting for me."

"We can't just sit here and do nothing."

"Shall we both go to the phone booth?" he suggested.

"And leave the children on their own?"

"No, bad idea. I'll go. I'll go now."

"I can do it," she suggested.

"No, I'm not letting you go. I'd never forgive myself if something happened."

"Staying here with the children is not so appealing either right now."

"Look, it's up to you. As you say, there are no great options."

"I'll go," she said.

They went downstairs and she grabbed a kitchen knife, putting it in her handbag. He saw her to the front door. They looked out together. Everything seemed quiet.

"I would leave the keys here," he said.

She nodded and he leaned over, kissing the side of her forehead.

"I'd better go," she said.

He returned to the table tennis room and suggested they play doubles.

"Not more table tennis," Imogen said. "I'm sick of table tennis."

"Come on, just one game. I've hardly played."

"I thought we were going to go out," Imogen said.

"We can't just yet. Michaela's gone to make a phone call."

"Oh my God, you two and your phone calls. Isn't this meant to be a holiday?"

"She'll be back in a few minutes, Imogen."

"And we'll go when she gets back, yes?"

"I don't know, I really don't know. I'm a little bit stressed by something at the moment, so I'd appreciate it if you could just stop asking me questions." His voice had risen to a high peak.

"Let's play table tennis," Imogen said, shaking her head as if her father was crazy.

They had been playing for less than two minutes when there was a loud thudding noise.

"Who's that?" Audrey asked.

"It's just someone at the front door," Daniel said.

"The bell probably doesn't work," Imogen sighed.

The banging continued.

"Who is it?" Audrey repeated.

"Could you all stay in here for a moment?" Daniel said.

Michaela couldn't be back already, that would be physically impossible. Daniel tried looking out of the living room to see if he had an angle on the entranceway, but no matter how he positioned himself, he couldn't see anything. The knocking continued.

"Who is it?" Daniel called.

"I saw your car out here," a man with a Welsh accent said. "So I thought I'd introduce myself."

"Who are you?"

"It's Evan. The property owner."

Daniel thought immediately of Rod pretending to be a pizza man when he killed Thomas.

"Are you not going to open the door?" the voice said.

There was no sense in delaying. Michaela would be in mortal danger when she returned if he didn't open it. He unlocked the door and looked out with extreme wariness. A small ginger-haired man beamed at him.

"I can always tell when my guests are from London. They're ever so cautious – you know, very crime-conscious. But it's perfectly safe round here. I hardly lock my own front door, to be honest. Anyway, is everything okay?"

"Thank you, yes, it's fine."

"I just came round to say hello, check you have everything you need."

"We have, thank you, yes."

The man nodded. He was clearly expecting an invitation to come in.

"Look," Daniel said, "if you don't mind, I'm very busy today. But I do appreciate your visit."

"No problem, no problem at all."

They said their goodbyes and Daniel returned to the table tennis room. But he could barely concentrate on the game. He was worrying about Michaela. How long had she been now? If she wasn't back in a few minutes, he would have to go out himself and look for her. Then he realised that he could have asked the property owner for help. He could have explained that they had an urgent situation and got him to phone the police. Why didn't he think of that at the time?

There was more knocking on the door and Daniel dropped his bat on the table with a clatter and ran out.

"It's me," Michaela said.

Once inside she told him her news.

"It's not working. The telephone box."

"It was earlier."

"Well it's not now. It was completely dead – silence. No matter how many times I rattled the hook, I couldn't get a dialling tone."

Chapter Eighty-Nine

"Did you try the village store?" Daniel asked.

Michaela shook her head. "I didn't think of that."

"Surely they've got a phone. I'll go this time."

He set off immediately, heading out of the cottage at pace.

He had barely been on the gravel track for more than a minute when a low voice from behind said, "Don't turn round. Just keep walking."

It was Rod's voice. Of course it was.

"I have a gun by the way," Rod said.

"How did you find me?" Daniel asked. His chest was thudding, and he felt a shortness of breath.

"I was following practically the whole way from London but lost you in the last few miles. Luckily this is a small place and I knew you'd visit the shop."

"And where are we going now?" It seemed important to retain a semblance of normality in their conversation.

"Just for a walk. I fancy a stroll up that hill, if that's all right?"

413

Daniel didn't reply. This was his ultimate nightmare. Being marched up a remote hill to his certain death.

"You and I need to spend some quality time together," Rod said from behind him.

"I don't suppose I have any choice."

They continued walking, Daniel occasionally feeling the sharp prod of the gun to the left of his lower spine. As instructed, he hadn't yet turned to look at Rod. It took him a few minutes to realise that he was shaking. Involuntary shivers beginning somewhere in his back and running up to his shoulders.

"Are you cold?" Rod asked.

"I'm not cold," Daniel said. "You won't do anything to my children, will you?"

"Daniel, please – all in good time."

"I'm such an idiot. I should never have trusted you. This whole thing is my fault."

"Don't be too hard on yourself."

"I just feel terribly guilty," Daniel murmured.

"Hmmm," Rod said.

Neither spoke for a few minutes. They reached a gate and Rod instructed Daniel to go through.

"Okay, you can turn around now."

Daniel did so. Rod was completely bald, though still wearing his glasses.

"You shaved your hair."

"Yes, what do you think?"

"I wouldn't have recognised you."

Rod laughed, seemingly delighted. "I quite like the severity, although I have to be careful. About sunburn."

"It suits you," Daniel said. He was trying to match Rod's friendliness, although he suspected that wouldn't last long. He suddenly noticed Rod's left hand inside his jacket sleeve. The tip of the gun protruding.

"Come on, let's get to the top," Rod said. "It won't take long."

They walked without speaking, Rod still slightly behind, still holding the gun beneath his sleeve, a large bag on his back.

Perhaps it wasn't all over yet though. When they reached the top of the hill, he might still be able to appeal to Rod's better judgement.

"Nearly there," Rod said.

Daniel nodded, wondering what was inside Rod's bag.

They reached the top and Rod told him to sit down. Daniel looked at him questioningly.

"Just sit, Daniel. I'm going to sit next to you. I want to talk."

Daniel did as he was told. The wind was gently ruffling his hair. He could hear sheep in the distance. But other than that, there was silence.

"Lovely, eh?" Rod said.

Daniel surveyed the view. Hills, farmland, odd cottages and outhouses dotted around, all built with pale stone, harmonising with the landscape. Thin roads snaked discreetly around the hills. There was not a single person in sight.

"It's beautiful," Daniel said, doubting he'd ever see such a view again.

"Look, Daniel," Rod said, "I'm sorry. I'm sorry about lots of things. I realise I haven't always been a great friend to you. And I'm not proud about what's going to happen."

"What is going to happen?" Daniel asked grimly.

"I hope you'll find it in yourself to forgive me."

"Forgive you for what?" Daniel thought he might as well know the worst.

"The easiest thing about killing Thomas, was that I was sure he'd forgive me. That documentary came at the right time. I knew that if he ever had the opportunity, that's what he'd do. And that was reassuring. Quite different too from Liddell and the others."

"Others?"

"There were another two. It's a long story. No time for it now."

They were silent for another minute before Daniel spoke.

"There are things you might want to consider, Rod. And sitting here, we have a moment to do that, perhaps."

"What other things should I be considering?"

"I know how easy it is, once you've set off down a certain road, to think that's the only road. That there's no turning back. But that doesn't have to be the case, Rod. You're in charge of your own destiny. You know that, don't you?"

"It doesn't always feel that way."

"But it's true. I've seen it myself. You control so much of your life – you do what you want to do. More than most people, I'd say."

"Maybe."

"And because you have that control, you can decide to be a better person. It's never too late to be a better person."

"Why would I want to be a better person?" Rod had taken his glasses off and was sucking the end of one of the arms contemplatively.

"Because everything you do has a consequence. Think about Thomas's family in America. He has a big family from what Michaela told me. Both parents alive, brothers, sisters, cousins, uncles, aunts – the list goes on.

And all of them right now are struggling to come to terms with what happened. Every one of your actions has consequences, Rod. Just because you've killed before, it doesn't mean that it's right to do so again."

"I know that, Daniel. And I am thinking everything through right now, I promise. I'll be going to prison for the rest of my life either way."

"The courts do respond to small acts of humanity. They take that into account. It's well-known."

"They'll give me an upgrade on my cell maybe. A pine toilet seat instead of a plastic one."

"And you talked about forgiveness earlier. I can tell you one thing. If you do anything to hurt my children, or Michaela, I promise you, Rod, I will never forgive you. Not for as long as I live. Or for as long as I'm dead, or whatever else I happen to be. I would never forgive you; do you hear?"

"I hear you, Daniel."

Chapter Ninety

They returned to the cottage together in bright sunshine. Everything was quiet except for the lone tweeting of a bird. Daniel thought about screaming out, perhaps there were houses near enough for someone to be alerted, but it was way too risky. Rod would surely just shoot him on the spot and then head into the cottage to finish the job.

"Sit on the front of your car a second," Rod instructed him. Daniel did so and Rod withdrew a silk scarf from his bag. As he wound it around Daniel's mouth, Daniel saw the source of the tweeting – a robin standing on the birdhouse to his left. It wasn't the sort of thing he'd usually notice, but today he registered all of the details – the eyes too far apart, the beak comically high in its face – almost in its forehead – the way the robin opened it so widely as it urgently proclaimed its message to the world. Daniel couldn't help but conclude that his arguments on the hill earlier had all failed. In which case the robin was pronouncing his death sentence, just like judges used to do in court.

"Open your mouth," Rod said.

Daniel did so, and Rod pulled the scarf tight, gagging him.

"Now give me your keys. Okay. Let's go."

Rod silently unlocked the front door and prodded Daniel with the gun to step inside. There were no sounds at all. The table tennis game must have finished long ago. Rod went first into the living room, then motioned Daniel to follow him. The room was empty. From there they went through to the kitchen, where Rod pulled rope from his bag and started to bind Daniel to a wooden chair. Having done this, he secured the chair to the heavy wooden table.

Daniel tried to speak but the gag was right inside his mouth.

"Shut up," Rod whispered to him. "If you make any sound, or try to alert them, then that is it, I promise you."

There was a gasp and they both looked up to see Imogen standing in the doorway.

"Oh my God," she said.

"No one do anything," Rod said calmly, pointing his gun towards Daniel. "Both stay where you are and keep absolutely quiet."

Daniel wished he could say something to Imogen. Reassure her, or just tell her that he loved her.

"Okay. You're coming with me," Rod said to Imogen.

Leaving Daniel where he was, he put his hand gently on Imogen's shoulder. She looked briefly back at Daniel as Rod escorted her out of sight.

Daniel struggled with his binding, but it wasn't giving so much as a millimetre. He couldn't rock the chair because it was tied so securely to the table. He tried moving his jaws, pushing with his tongue against the scarf, hoping to loosen it, but that too was useless.

Where were Michaela and the others? Perhaps she had got out the *Tom Sawyer* paperback that she'd found last night. Maybe she was reading it to Audrey and Max, trying to pass a little more time before he returned home, none of them with any idea of what was about to happen.

Rod had been gone at least a minute now, perhaps two. Daniel was feeling light-headed – his brain overloaded or empty – he hardly knew which. What the hell was he doing up there? Daniel strained to hear sounds, but all was quiet. Another minute went by. Daniel thought now he might have heard footsteps above him, the creak of a loose floorboard. But then it was all quiet again.

Another two or three more minutes went by, Daniel was in an agony of suspense. And then he heard it. Slightly muffled, but definitely a gunshot. And a minute later another one. He was listening to his own family being murdered. And he could do nothing. There was another gunshot. And yet another. There had been four shots now – definitely four – one for each of them, and now – nothing.

Daniel was sobbing in his chair when Rod returned to the kitchen. It would be his turn now. And Daniel was ready for it, for sure. Rod was standing right in front of him. He was crying too, tears silently trickling down his face. He looked at his gun and brushed some dust from the handle. He then pointed it at Daniel for a moment, then stopped.

"There's nothing left now," Rod said. "No place for me to go. Nothing worth remaining for."

Slowly rotating his arm, he pointed the gun towards

himself, then slid the barrel end between his lips. There was a moment in which Daniel watched Rod's eyes bulging widely behind his glasses before he pulled the trigger. The bang splattered the white cupboards with continents of red as Rod slumped backwards onto the floor.

Daniel looked down at him. Lying on his side now, the back of his head half blown away. The pool of blood around Rod's head was spreading wider on the checked linoleum floor, like an unstoppable liquid army. Daniel felt nothing now. He considered trying to free himself. But what would be the point?

A door closed somewhere, he heard it, then footsteps on the stairs. His own name was being called. It was Michaela's voice. Daniel felt a surge of joy. Michaela at least had survived. Somehow, she had managed to stay alive.

She was calling his name still as she came into the kitchen.

"Jesus fucking Christ," she said, surveying the carnage in front of her. Then she bent forwards towards her knees, as if trying out a new exercise. Daniel heard noises, retching noises. As if her body wanted to purge but could produce nothing. She turned and looked at him, a blank expression in her face.

"They're alive. The children are alive." She began unwrapping the binding from his face.

"Alive?" It surely couldn't be true. He'd heard what he had heard. She was toying with him. Surely.

"He tied me up, fired into the air," she said. "Did the same with them. His idea of a joke, the sick bastard."

He pulled her towards him, hugging her, smelling something close to vomit on her breath but not caring.

"Where are they?" he asked.

"All in one bedroom. All together now. I managed to get free. I told them to wait."

She continued to work on his bindings, freeing him eventually. Daniel ran up the stairs. He needed to see them. They were in the largest room, sitting in a clump on the bed, their arms entangled around each other. There were crying sounds, Max's shoulders were shaking, perhaps they were all crying, it was hard to tell.

"Daddy," Imogen said when she saw him.

"It's okay," Daniel said. "He's dead. We're all safe now. Rod's dead and everything is going to be all right."

Chapter Ninety-One

SUNDAY 28 JULY 1996

He was sitting in his dressing gown at the kitchen table, drinking tea. She came in, headed straight for the narrow cupboard and began withdrawing its contents, slamming them on the work surface beneath: cider vinegar, sun cream, egg cups, greaseproof paper, an electric coffee grinder given to them for their wedding and still unused, paper cup-cake holders, an Abba *Greatest Hits* cassette, chef's matches, dried herbs, a metal teapot and a thick purple candle.

"Where the bloody hell are they?" Michaela muttered. "Don't worry, no need to help."

She continued pulling out the seemingly random items, before finally finding a small box of aspirin. She filled a glass of water, popped two tablets out in front of her and dropped them one by one into the glass and came over to the table.

Daniel watched as the aspirins fizzed and broke apart like asteroids entering the earth's atmosphere, revolving in the water as they turned to tiny fragments before disappearing completely. Michaela picked up the glass and drank it steadily in one go.

"Headache?" he asked.

"Period pains. How long have you been down here?"

"A while."

"You know it's three o'clock?"

"I couldn't sleep. I made a pot of tea."

"Tea keeps you awake."

"Not if you're awake anyway."

"So why not just drink black coffee?" she asked.

"I don't like black coffee."

She surveyed him sadly across the table with her brown eyes. "It might help if you talked to me. I can't help you if you don't talk."

"What's there to talk about?"

"Anything, Daniel. Just let me into whatever's going on in your head, because I don't have a clue right now."

"There's not much going on in there. And that's the truth. I worry about the children. Will they ever get over it, do you think?"

"Is that what's been keeping you awake?"

"Partly. I mean it was very traumatic for them, wasn't it?"

"It was, yes."

"I'd just rather they hadn't seen the kitchen. With him still on the floor. Why did we let them in there?"

"Everything was confused. At least they got to see that he was really dead."

"No wonder Audrey's having nightmares. Sally says she's been getting them most nights. She isn't happy about it."

"It will take time," she said. "Of course it will. But the children will be fine. Children are resilient."

"I suppose."

"I once found this decomposing corpse in the woods when I was out walking with my best friend. I used to think about it all the time, but I don't much these days. So what I'm saying is I'm sure that they'll get over the experience. Is there anything else?"

"What do you mean?"

"Is there anything else you're worrying about?" She had found a packet of cigarettes in her bag and was doing that thing where she kept removing them one by one, slotting each back into the box.

"I've got my hearing this week," he said. "But that's a foregone conclusion. I'll be suspended pending the outcome of a full tribunal. And then I'll be struck-off. So what's to worry about there?"

"Oh for fuck's sake," Michaela said.

"What is it?"

"You defended a psychopath in court and got him off a murder. And then you befriended him. You somehow made a deal with him to kill the man I was living with. And then you nearly got me and your children murdered too in the process. What do you think about all of that?"

"I'm thinking that you're still angry. And that you'll probably never forgive me."

"Yes, I'm incredibly angry. And I don't know if I'll ever forgive you. I probably won't in fact. I certainly won't if you don't talk to me. If you keep shutting me out."

"And I'm thinking that you miss Thomas," Daniel said.

"I do miss him. I miss the conversations we used to have. The way he looked out for me. Silly things too, like the way he'd get excited if he found a piece of history in the modern-day world. He was a very decent person. He didn't deserve to get caught up in this."

"And you loved him."

"Yes. I did."

"I still feel pretty jealous about that, if I'm honest."

"I want you to be honest."

"I hated it when you called him the love of your life."

"I was trying to kill you at the time, wasn't I? So you shouldn't take it too literally."

"When you came downstairs and found me tied up," Daniel said, "the relief I felt was indescribable. I was elated. I suddenly had a reason to go on living."

"But you haven't said that to me."

"I should have done. I can see that now."

"Thank you."

"We should go back to bed," he said. "You've got work tomorrow."

"Yes, but this isn't me anymore. You think I'm going to spend the rest of my life sitting in court reporting on criminal cases? Are you fucking crazy? After everything we've been through?"

Daniel laughed. "It wasn't what I was suggesting."

"It's not going to happen. I've been thinking about doing something very different."

"What sort of thing?"

"Maybe a professional training. To become an architect. Or a clinical psychologist."

Daniel smiled. "Well, they're *very* similar."

"It would take too long to become an architect. I'd be nearly forty. Anyway, what about you? What are you going to do?"

"Consultancy perhaps. Start a business. Maybe I'll do another professional training."

"We could do one together."

"I was just thinking that."

"We should take our time to think about it."

"For sure. But whatever I do decide on, I can promise you one thing. I will be doing it by the book."

"Of course, Daniel. As if I'd ever expect anything different from you."

THE END

Acknowledgements

I would like to thank everyone who read and made invaluable comments on *Indefensible* during the writing process. In particular, my writing buddy Hannah Persaud (who also suggested the title), Ian Critchley (for one or two knockout editorial ideas), Ben Davies (for a close read and his automobile expertise), my brother Simon (for his knowledge of Hackney), June Wilson for her close reads and support, and for his fine professional input, John Rickards.

The following people provided the benefit of their specialist knowledge. For their help on matters relating to the Bar and in particular New Court Chambers in the 1990s, a massive thank you to Bill Conner and David Goddard (not forgetting also their kind consent to appear as characters in the book). For advice on the state of decapitated heads that have been floating rather too long in the River Thames, and other forensic matters, I am greatly indebted to David Tadd. For his excellent help on trial preparation and defending clients at the Old Bailey, David Etherington KC.

I would also like to thank the Bloodhound Books team, including Betsy Reavley, Shirley Khan, Tara Lyons and Abbie Rutherford.

I would also like to thank my mother who inspired my love of literature, but sadly is no longer around to see this novel published.

And finally, huge love to my family for their unstinting loyalty and support.

A note from the publisher

Thank you for reading this book. If you enjoyed it please do consider leaving a review on Amazon to help others find it too.

We hate typos. All of our books have been rigorously edited and proofread, but sometimes mistakes do slip through. If you have spotted a typo, please do let us know and we can get it amended within hours.

info@bloodhoundbooks.com